Endorsements for
Angelina & the Law of Attraction

"REFRESHING! Many self-help books give you tips and tools on how to build your dreams. **Angelina & the Law of Attraction** immerses you in an experience that shows you —not just tells you— how dreams are built. This novel is a catalyst to the alchemy of creating the life of your dreams. This book is a MUST READ!"

Eva Gregory, author of **The Feel Good Guide to Prosperity** and co-author of **Life Lessons for Mastering the Law of Attraction** with Jack Canfield.

"Maria Mar takes us on an incredible metaphysical ride with her novel **Angelina and the Law of Attraction.** Through the clever use of story, she shows us how we lose our mind to an internal chorus of naysayers and bullies, and how we can remember who we really are and what we love. Thank you, Maria Mar, for entertaining, educating, inspiring and enlightening us. Reading your book is like purchasing a ticket for the Dream Express. I'm climbing aboard!"

Leonard Szymczak, Author of **The Roadmap Home: Your GPS to Inner Peace**.

Maria Mar's shamanic, allegorical story, **Angelina and the Law of Attraction**, is a wild ride into the subconscious realms, where our dreams are either killed by our fears or born as Divine expression. Mystical wisdom cannot be taught. It must be experienced. Through Angelina, Maria imaginatively takes us on a shamanic journey to meet the hidden beliefs that limit the expression of the true self. As a facilitator of mystical experience in the *Sacred Feminine,* I am impressed by how thoroughly she captures our inner voices, including feminine intuition. To attract the life of our dreams, the journey must be made. And **Angelina and the Law of Attraction** reminds us that every woman's journey is a heroine's journey.

Misa Hopkins, author of the best-selling book "**Sacred Feminine Awakening: The Emergence of Compassion.**"

"This novel is a magical, delightful story. In addition, it helped me see how we conjure the obstacles that we face in our lives and how all it takes is an inner shift in our consciousness to dissolve obstacles that seem as gigantic as the Grand Canyon."

Corazon Tierra, author, body esteem expert and creator of the **DanzaSpa**

"If you want to discover a creative way to re-program your beliefs and become the creator of your life, take this fictional story and use it as a roadmap to access your infinite potential."

Natalie Ledwell, the **Inspiration Show**, author of **Never in your Wildest Dreams**

"Our deepest calling is to grow and become our own authentic self and to break from the conditioned images of who we ought to be. **Angelina and the Law of Attraction** helps you to awaken the seed of true self that was planted when you were born. This is an exquisite salute to the *Inner Child* and to Life!"

Julia Andino, LCSW-R, **Emotional Landscaping™**

Angelina & the Law of Attraction

A woman's Ride
from her Pressing Problems
to her Brightest Potential

By Maria Mar

ShamansDance Publishing & Productions, New York

Categories

Fiction: Inspirational/Fantasy/Women's Fiction

Self-improvement: Inspiration/Personal Growth/Law of Attraction

ShamansDance Publishing & Production

This book is a work of fiction. Names, characters, places and incidents are products of the author's imagination or are used fictitiously.

For information about customized printed copies for corporations or bulk purchase, please contact **maria@shamansdance.com**

This book is available for fundraising for non-profits serving women, minorities, artists and people suffering financial disadvantage. Contact **maria@shamansdance.com**

First ShamansDance digital edition February 2008

Library of Congress Catalog No.

ISBN 10: 0-9843670-0-4

ISBN 13: 987-0-9843670-0-9

Cover, design and layout by Maria Mar

Printed in the United States of America

Table of Contents

Part 3: The Dreamscape

Part 4: The Knights' Keys

Part 5: The Outer Ring of Self

Part 6: The Inner Ring of Self

Part 7: Epilogue

About

Appendixes

Acknowledgments

Thanks to my creative and business partner, Corazón Tierra, for her faith, persistence and support in the long gestation of this book.

Thanks to my friend Tanya Torres for her encouragement and constant encouragement to print this novel and her beautiful art and poetry that nurtures my soul.

Thanks to J.M Boswell, owner and founder of Boswell Pipes, for his expert advice on Pop's tobacco. J.M. Boswell is considered to be one of the finest master pipemakers in the world. Pop would have nothing but the best!

Thanks to the many experts and teachers who helped me through their websites, tools and blog writing. In the publishing arena, I thank John Kremer and the zillion resources he constantly pours out for authors, including his great free community for authors. I thank Brian Jud for his excellent newsletter and other self-publishing resources. Thanks to Fern Reiss for our self-publishing bible, *The Publishing Game.*

Thanks to Daniel Soto, whose passion and support for everything related to computers has been a god-sent. Without his constant help in this area, we could not have built the online aspect of our business.

Finally and most importantly, thanks to my Spiritual Guides and my *Circle of Light* for their guidance, illumination and protection. The wisdom and the stories come **through** me, but come **from** them.

I dedicate this novel to:

Corazón Tierra

Thanks for supporting me in my Dream. My life is richer and more meaningful because of your healing presence and companionship in the spiritual path.

My Aunt Fanny

Who inspired me to enjoy life and to be myself and helped me so much when I first arrived in New York, determined to make my dreams come true.

To you

Beautiful Dream Express Rider, to your soul and its Dream. May you listen to your Soul. May you follow its dreams. You will get there.

Editorial Note

Throughout this story, I use words that are also shamanic tools and terms from my personal growth systems. I spell these words with capitals and format them in italics so that you can recognize them. This formatting is done intentionally. It has the psychological effect of slowing down your eyes and mind so that you allow the Medicine embedded in these terms into your psyche. Receive these terms as *Psychic Windows* that expand your perceptual universe.

INTRODUCTION

Your Dream Alchemy

In every myth and legend the hero or heroine goes on a quest. What is the quest for? The goal may vary, but at the core, every quest is to find the heroine's destiny; not in the sense of fate, but of the blossoming of her potential.

Myths and legends are blueprints for the quest that each of us undertakes in our life.

The guide to your quest is your Soul. It guides you through its longing, feelings and desires and through the Personal Dream that ignites your passion.

But your daily life must be fertile for your Soul in order for it to stir you towards your Dream.

When you are living a life that is alien to your Soul and to its Dream, then your Soul is caged and your Dream is, like the *DreamSelf* in this story, fading.

The Soul is a wild creature. It cannot survive in its organic, free nature if it is caged. It will get sick.

When caged, the Soul will dry or fade out. It can become vicious or extremely nervous. It may become so frightened that it will one day kill you of a heart attack.

The Soul can sink so low into your toxic waste that its bile can pollute your life and your relationships.

Its creative power may become destructive power and may be turned against the self, until it becomes arthritis, a tumor, phobias, migraines, depression, anxiety attacks or other maladies.

The cage ensnaring your Soul can be a job you hate, a lack-luster life or a relationship that does not nurture or honor your *Essence.*

It may also be your habit of staying in the background and playing invisible, a success that betrays your Soul or a war between creativity and prosperity that has pushed you into choosing one at the expense of the other.

Any circumstance that thwarts you from blossoming into fullness and expressing your *Unique Essence* is a cage to your Soul.

The Soul is also a resilient creature. Open the door of that cage and it will quickly bounce back, finding its way back home to the wild, luscious nature of her Dream.

I offer this story to you as the incantation that can open the door to the cage that keeps you away from your Dream, from your Soul's Purpose and the life you were born to enjoy.

This magical story is evidently fictional. Yet, there is a lot in Angelina's ride that resonates with my life. When I began to write this story, I had lost everything in a housing environmental crisis. I was left homeless and penniless and found refuge in a friend's guest room.

As I faced my crisis, Angelina got into the N train. As I realized that I was going into a deep journey within to face my relationship with money and my war between creativity and prosperity, Angelina's train got deviated into a mysterious route. Angie (my *Inner Child*) became a scout in my life as well as in Angelina's story.

The *Sacred Child* helps us remember our *Sacred Wounds*, so that we can turn them into our *Personal Power.*

This fantasy is obviously not autobiographical. It is, however, a distillation of more than twenty years of helping women in three different continents to break through limitations and embrace their *True Self.*

Angelina's encounters with her *Shadows* reveal many of the common *Shadows* I have found in my work as a shamanic hunter helping women release self-sabotage. Angelina's *Inner Wars* between creativity and prosperity, between love and power and between self and others are archetypal wars suffered by many women and by creative, spiritual people in general.

Angelina's meeting with the Dragonfly Diva allows me as an author to split myself into two: the apprentice and the shamanic teacher. This allows you, in turn, to enjoy the many teachings with which I have been blessed in my training as a *Woman of Power.*

The tools Dragonfly Diva brings into Angelina's journey are powerful shamanic secrets that can change your life.

My hope is that as Angelina discovers how she has created and how she sustains the obstacles in her way; you too open your eyes to the ways in which you are creating your reality right now. This empowers you to shift that reality and create the life that you desire and deserve.

If this story motivates you ~if it nurtures your faith to keep seeking the Dream of your Soul~ I will be happy. If it uplifts your spirit, strengthens your self-love muscles and clears up your dreaming pathways, I will have done my job.

But this story is written to do more than that. Open your heart and mind and you will find here potent shamanic principles that awaken your ability as an alchemist.

The Alchemist is a *Creative Self* within you who understands and masters the *Universal Laws of Manifestation. The Alchemist* within you can use this story as a blueprint to re-design your life in ways that allow your dream to manifest right now, today —and every day of your life from now on.

True magic is the understanding that perception creates reality. Therefore, doing magic is shifting your perception so that you transform what you are manifesting. Alchemy is the process you use to perform this transformation. Alchemy is ~in essence~ the transmutation of one form of energy into another. Alchemy is what Christ did when he transmuted water into wine. It is also what you do when you transform anger into persistence, love into healing or an obstacle into a stepping stone.

I have created this story as a shamanic journey or quest that allows you to shift your perception of the obstacles now standing on the way to your Dream. You now probably see these obstacles as something happening to you and blocking your path. After this journey, I hope that you will see these obstacles as *Sacred Mirrors* that reveal the hidden places where you feel wounded. Once you see them, you can heal them, making them your personal strengths. This is the alchemy through which Dreams are made.

You can see this book as a primer in the art of shifting your perception to *Shift your World*. It is the basic training that *The Alchemist* within you needs to unleash her power.

Each chapter in this book is an alchemy that you can perform in your life to transmute your limitations into your *Secret Tools for Mastery*. The alchemical principles embedded in the story awaken your subconscious or inner knowing. They touch you emotionally, creatively and intuitively.

These alchemical principles and the *Storytelling Way* are designed to ignite the aspects of your *Female Way of Knowing*. As a priestess of the Goddess, I teach how to tap into the *Sacred Feminine*. Follow Dragonfly Diva and you will be walking this path. The *Sacred Feminine* is the path of creativity, love, intuition, beauty heart and body wisdom and soulful living.

Manifestation begins in the territory of your psyche. Your Soul is the compass that guides you in this territory.

For your Soul, your Dream always is and has always been. It is the substance of its being. Unless you are starving your Soul, its longing has to do less with what it lacks and more with what it needs to *Remember*.

Remembrance is the process by which your Soul remembers the pieces of your Dream that were stolen during your *Domestication* as a child. *Remembering* is also the process by which you gather all the members or fragments of self that have been dispersed, becoming wholesome again.

In this sense, manifesting a Dream is not so much "making it happen" from thin air as it is *Remembering* the Dream that already is in your *Unique Essence*.

Your Spirit is infinite. Your Soul however needs to grow, like your body. Your longing for your Dream is the hunger of your Soul to grow into its true nature. This hunger comes from the fact that you have not yet developed your potential to the degree of your Soul's innate perfection.

In other words, your Soul is the expert on your Dream.

As you will see in this story, Angelina —the protagonist—journeys deep within her psyche to destroy the perceptual fences she has created and to retrieve the powers she has given away. She quests for her *DreamSelf*, the aspect of her Soul that already IS her Dream.

The plot for this story began when I was observing people in the rush hour in New York's hectic subway. They were in such rush that they did not stop to hear the musicians playing. They did not help the mothers with heavy baby carriages up the stairs. Sometimes they did not even wait for the turnstile to finish its previous turn before pushing to get in, and then they got angry because they were stuck.

As I witnessed these phenomena, I wondered how many of these people were truly going "somewhere." I wondered if they were rushing to nowhere or truly and effectively moving towards their Dream. The answer stared back at me in their emotionless, unhappy faces.

"What would happen if there was an express train to one's Dream?" I asked myself.

Instead of rushing to get into a train that took you deeper into your hectic routine, this express would take you into your Dream. At the end of the ride, you would be living the life you longed to live. You would be fulfilled and wholesome. You would joyfully share your *Unique Essence* with the world.

This journey in the Dream Express is the answer to my question. I hope that it is also an answer to yours.

This book is one of our **Books Beyond the Page**, books designed to give you a holistic experience of the knowledge they contain. Their power opens beyond the page, breaking the barrier between fiction and reality. The extended experience of a **Book Beyond the Page** is provided through online and local activities and through a series of resources that work synergistically with the book.

To journey into this story, go to the back pages of this book. In the *Appendixes* you will find information about the **Catch Dream Express** membership and events, as well as **Chapter Resources** and **Institutional Resources.**

These resources empower you to use this story as a map for your own quest to rescue your *DreamSelf.* I encourage you to become the protagonist of this story. Use each chapter in the book as a guide to re-write the chapters of your own life.

If you journey into this story, you will have a chance to stop the crazy train of your activities and change the direction your life is taking. You can ride with Angelina in the Dream Express as *Rites of Passage* to your Dream.

I have created this story to bring you into the realization that —no matter how difficult your conditions— you have the power to change the world and re-create your universe. You can assume your *Personal Power* and become the Dream pulsating in your heart.

Step into the N train. It's about to enter the station. You decide if this N stands for "Never" or for "Now." If you decide that the time for your Dream is now, you will soon find yourself traveling in the Dream Express.

Dare to dream BIG and live it!

Maria Mar
The Dream Alchemist

Part 1

Leaving the Comfort Zone

And the day came when the risk it took to remain tight inside the bud was more painful than the risk it took to blossom."

—Anais Nin

CHAPTER 1

A Trick of the Light

Is it the unfamiliarity of the space? Or is it the mass of strange faces? Why does she feel so small in this New York Subway Station? She's used to feeling unimportant. That's normal. After all, she's no Einstein. But this is worse. She's feeling anonymous, as if she had not face, no name.

"No matter," Angelina snaps, giving herself a mental slap. "Wake up, Angelina. You did not come to New York for greatness. It's a job you wanted and you're lucky you got this one. Stop worrying. Think of the big paycheck at the end of the month."

"After all, an unfamiliar guarantee offers more certainty than habitual risk," she mutters between her teeth as she presses her large leather bag beneath her right armpit.

The mass of strange faces squeezes her tightly on both flanks, pushing her dangerously close to the edge of the platform.

She digs in her heels and pushes backwards. The crowd yields and her left shoulder bumps into a cold steel column. Angelina holds on to it with her left hand, keeping a tight grip of her bag with her right hand.

She wishes she'd had a third hand right now to examine the subway map again.

"Am I waiting in the right place to reach my destination?" Angelina asks herself for the gazillionth time.

"Of course it's the right place, you idiot!" she responds, slapping herself mentally again. "Don't be so spineless. You already know the freaking map inside out. It's just that the place is unfamiliar, so you have a feeling of being lost. It will pass. You'll get used to it in no time."

For a split second that thought scares her.

Angelina tries to distract herself from obsessing by meticulously observing details. She investigates the gray, high ceilings and scans the disgustingly dirty tracks. Finally, she notices the impersonal fonts in the signs.

This city does not invite familiarity. Even the spaciousness of the station is dimmed by the crowding and dinginess.

She's heard somewhere that New York City is safer than many other cities in the country, but she can't believe it. This grimy subway station with its dim, dull lights reminds her of a set from one of Dickens's more gruesome stories.

"There could be a serial murderer standing right behind you, Angelina," the *Scary Script Writer* starts. "He's quietly waiting for the train to enter the station so he can push you into the tracks."

Angelina does not welcome this morbid part of her imagination. Not today. Not in this gloomy setting. Not when she is already scared.

"Not a serial murderer," she counters, "A thief is more likely."

She looks around for the least likely candidate.

"How about that weird old lady?" Angelina plots.

The lady in question is so tall that her head stands above the crowd. She wears an extravagant velvet purple head wrap that makes her stand out even more.

"She could be the head of a pick-pocketing gang," Angelina smiles. The thought is ridiculously funny.

The tactic works, as she knew it would. The *Scary Script Writer* despises humor. She is pissed off and leaves Angelina's imagination alone.

The lights in the station suddenly flash and go off. They go on and off three times, each time stealing not only the light, but all the noises —even the silhouettes of the people around her— as if the entire world was going off.

Huge wings flutter so close that she feels their soft, feathery touch sliding along her spine. Angelina shivers, instinctively wrapping her hands around her body.

A massive shadow flies through the wall at the other side of the track. Two pairs of long, iridescent net-like wings protrude from a human-looking shape, slowly circling the gray stone wall.

"The thief is already inside."

The whisper penetrates each of her pores. She is being submerged into a thick liquid. Kaleidoscopic streams flow in a silvery fluid that slowly engulfs her body.

The city noises have stopped. The world has stopped. Silence wraps around her as the thick flow covers her mouth, then her ears. Angelina hears the rustling of wings again. This time it comes from inside her.

"Not possible. Not happening," Angelina forces her brain to think as she blinks vigorously.

The lights in the station are back to their dim dull stare, which Angelina now finds wonderful. The shadow is gone. Everything is back to normal.

Angelina realizes that her hands are wrapped tight around her bag and she is sweating profusely.

"Relax, Angelina," she tells herself. "You're just a little nervous, with so many changes going on: a new city, a new job. It's a lot to take in. Just relax."

Her left hand lets go off the bag and she relaxes the grip of her right hand.

"That's much better," she observes, trying to tease herself into relaxing. "The way you were holding the bag was almost an invitation to the thief."

"I wish I could write novels as fast as my *Scary Script Writer* comes up with these frightening scenarios," Angelina smiles, still trying to cheer herself up.

"But what use would that be?" She immediately considers, her smile turning into a grimace. "The publishers would reject them just as fast."

She's done it again. Her heart is now heavy. Why can't she let go of her idiotic dreams of being a novelist? She might as well dream of being an astronaut!

"Time to burn the list," a harsh voice dictates in her head.

Angelina makes up an imaginary list and mentally types:

Idiotic Dreams

"You are an idiot, Angelina Semidey," she reproaches herself. "You are an idealist idiot who wastes her time whining about her unpublished novels when no one in the world gives a dam about a single word you've ever written."

Angelina mentally types a new line in the list:

Idealist Idiot

"And that's not all you whine about," the harsh voice in her head badgers. "You pine away for that penniless boyfriend of yours, the one you already left months ago. You are a romantic idiot, but life is not a romantic comedy."

Angelina mentally adds a third line to the list:

Romantic Idiot

"Now burn that Idiocy List and grow up!" the harsh voice barks.

Angelina brings an imaginary match to the imaginary list and sets it on fire.

"Time to give up my idiocy," she snarls inwardly. "Time to live in the real world, get a real job and make real money."

The pieces of paper burn in her mind. Angelina concentrates on making the visualization as vivid as possible.

And without warning the burning papers flow out of her mind and flutter above the subway trails, like fire birds.

She blinks repeatedly.

The lights in the station flash again. One. Two. Three times. Only the sizzling song of the fire birds is heard. She looks around, but the crowd in the station is a silent blur. Is anyone else seeing these papers burning? Has she lost her mind?

"Real is as truth is."

A tiny voice whispers deep inside her. This whisper carries a longing so painful that Angelina drowns it. She presses her lips tightly, locking her jaw and pressing down hard, her will becoming an iron press bearing on her heart.

The winged shadow grows against the wall once more. Its wings flutter violently, extinguishing the fire birds.

Angelina shivers as the massive shadow wraps itself around her body.

She is choking. She is trapped in a dark pit. Everything in this pit is dry and smoldering. Gray tendrils of smoke curl up in the pitch black pit.

A deafening cry rises from the pit, like the screeching of a hatchling. There is no doubt in Angelina's heart. This is the cry of life dying as it is born.

Baby wings flap desperately in her ears and her heart. Where is she? What is happening?

She summons all her will power. A shiny metal ladder glows in the darkness. Angelina climbs up.

Each step brings her back to her mind. Back to her goals. To this city. To her new corporate job. To her fierce decision to make money and grow out of her romantic dreams. Up into her mind. Up towards the blinking fluorescent lights. Out of the pit.

"You see, Angelina?" she admonishes herself. "It's all a trick of the light."

The winged shadow disappears and the noise of the city ~blessed noise!~ now floods her senses again. Angelina takes big gulps of air, looking nervously around, but no one seems to have noticed her agony.

A tiny light blinks far into the dark tunnel and the crowd moves as if on cue, pushing each other towards the yellow strip at the edge of the platform.

"Welcome to New York, land of the skyscrapers," Angelina mutters sadly. "Behold my Promised Land."

She does not see the huge wings descending on the back of the tall old lady. She does not see the golden eyes of the old woman burning bright as she restores the light in the station.

Focused on the incoming train, Angelina misses the shimmering tear running down the lady's wrinkled face.

The strange old woman closes her eyes and gently sips the glowing tear.

A gurgling sound rises from the dry, deep darkness within Angelina. The thirsty creature in her heart is drinking. Angelina sighs with relief.

Busy with her grand plans and realistic goals, Angelina does not notice the tiny tear running down her cheek. She wipes it off mechanically as she moves to the side to let the crowd rush into the RR train, now opening its doors.

"This will not hold her for long," the old lady whispers, moving behind Angelina as the crowd pours into the train.

CHAPTER 2

Suds and Bubbles

She is sweaty and sticky in spite of having showered before leaving for her new job. The proximity of these strangers, the dinginess of the New York subway station, it all sticks to her skin, making her feel dirty.

"Bee and Flowerbrand Rose Soap," says a familiar voice in her memory. Angelina smiles.

The scene rushes into her mind, flooding her senses with the overpowering scent of roses. Omar had wanted to buy her a dozen roses for Valentine, but as always, he was broke.

"But I brought you something better," Omar said, and she couldn't wait to see what could be better than her favorite flowers.

"Bee and Flowerbrand Rose Soap," Omar proudly announced.

Angelina's smile fades away. Oblivious to the push of the boarding crowd, she remembers.

She had been utterly disappointed. Red roses, to her, represented an intense passion that transcended the ordinary and resided in the realm of poetry.... but rose soap!

Angelina remembers her effort to keep the corner of her lips up, and the high pitch voice with which she tried to cover up her disappointment.

"Oh, honey, don't you worry, I love everything that has to do with roses, not just the flowers."

The moment she had begun talking she had recognized this high-pitched adolescent voice. She had used it endless times.

"Oh, mom, don't you worry, I really don't like the fashion sneakers. I prefer a simple birthday. I don't need that dress. I want no fuss!"

She hated that tiny voice that had covered up the constant state of deprivation in which she grew up.

And now this.... rose soap. She had been on the verge of tears.

As the strangers push each other in their rush to get into the RR train, the scent of roses rises from Angelina's pores and strings itself into notes that pour into her memory.

"But the rose would not die, and the soap longed to tell her story," Omar had said as he picked up his guitar. "And here is the *Song of the Rose,* just for you."

She remembers every word of it. It is carved in her memory as no velvet twist of rose has ever, or could ever be.

The soft, gentle notes of the guitar had conjured each rose petal as Omar's soft timbre had sung the first phrases.

I was once a rose as red as lovers' lips.
Until the poorest lover slashed and ripped
my velvet beauty for some savings,
and left me sad and craving.

The guitar had broken into ragged, struggling notes as the melody turned into cacophony and Omar's voice became achingly crude.

Scorn the poor loser of a lover
who strangled the beauty of my petals
who mocked the splendor of my spirals
to give his lady.... suds and bubbles.

The notes had recovered their sadness. Angelina's heart was gripped between these two feelings: sadness and anger. Had he known how she would feel? Had he known her so well?

I was snatched without warning, ripped and broken.
My passion smashed into a slapdash token.
Oh, shame and fury! Oh, disappointment!

I am a bargain ointment.

Angelina had laughed, more at herself than at the ironic twist of Omar's lyrics. He was mirroring all her feelings, including the ridiculously sad feeling of being deprived of her own worth. Was this how he also felt?

The metallic noise of the RR train closing its doors blends with the memory of the passionate, troubled notes in Omar's guitar.

Scorn the poor loser of a lover
who strangled the beauty of my petals
who mocked the splendor of my spirals
to give his lady.... suds and bubbles.

He had shifted, his intense gaze fixed on Angelina, gentle notes streaming once more from the Spanish guitar. She had not expected this.

Ay! I did not know that I had been a slave.
'Till in her hands I rose in tiny waves.
My Essence dove into her pores.
and I outgrew the rose.

The scent of the last, unforgettable notes blurs out the noise, as it had blurred out her disappointment.

Beyond the rose, her touch is ecstasy.
Beyond the rose, intimacy.
Beyond the rose, well worth my sacrifice.
Beyond the rose, her kiss is paradise.

Tears are trickling down Angelina's face. She is cleansed from the dinginess of the subway, bathed in the scent of Omar's love. But her heart is broken once more; once too often, and always by longing of what could be or memories of what has been.

The RR train closes its doors and departs with a long metallic groan, wakening Angelina from her revelries.

"I cannot do this anymore," Angelina mutters.

"I will not let him charm me at a distance," she moans, fighting to step aside. "No more suds and bubbles for me, not even if they come with a song."

Angelina dries the tears angrily with the back of her hand and forces herself to return to her new life. Her chosen life. Without Omar.

The RR rattles its way along the rail, producing a long, grating screech.

Angelina grinds her teeth. She didn't know this city was so noisy.

"I shouldn't complain," Angelina tells herself as she throws her weight back and digs in her heels. Another group of men and women in gray suits is already pushing her towards the yellow line.

"I am out of Arizona, out of the chaotic life of a starving artist, and into a new life," Angelina reminds herself. "A promising new position awaits me at an international firm. Remember what you were promised, Angelina 'The sky's the limit for you.'"

"Falling is a way to race through the sky, but I'll bet that's not a limit you are eager to explore," murmurs a raspy voice inside Angelina as the new crowd pushes her towards the filthy tracks.

Angelina pushes the voice away. This inner voice likes to challenge her best plans, but Angelina is determined not to listen to this capricious enemy inside her. She has labeled this voice the *Architect of Failure*, and has banned it from any hearsay in her new life.

"I am going to make things happen in my life," Angelina promises herself once more. "I have clear goals and measurable objectives, and I am determined to succeed."

Down in the tracks, a rat munches on a roach. Angelina's empty stomach churns. She hasn't eaten breakfast.

"No time," she said to herself this morning. "I want to get to the office early on my first day of work. In fact, I want to make the habit of being 20 minutes early every day. That should signal that I am top management material."

The rat scrams, the roach still kicking in its mouth. The N train approaches with an infernal metallic clank.

A monstrous machine seizes Angelina's memory, and the factory comes to life. Mercedes left her youth and her hearing in that earsplitting dingy hell; in order ~Angelina has often been reminded~ to send her daughter to college.

Ten hours of nerve-rattling noise, sometimes two turns per day, turned Angelina's mother into a nervous wreck who cannot hear her children's soft voices and screams at the top of her lungs in public places, to her own and everyone's embarrassment.

Angelina shakes off those memories. She will succeed. She will prove to her mother that her sacrifice has not been in vain. She will prove to her brother that she can also bring home the bacon. Now, however, she does not want to think about Mercedes' sacrifice. It is too painful for her. So painful, in fact, that she has avoided calling home in months. It is always the same conversation: sacrifices, disease, doctor's bills, debts, wasted faith in a God that will someday reward her, and a stubborn refusal to enjoy life here, now, on this earth.

The doors to the N train open abruptly right in front of Angelina, bringing her back to reality. She quickly steps aside to avoid a mass of people pouring out of the wagon. The standing crowd splits into two, allowing the passengers off. This evokes the image of Moses standing at the Red Sea, the waters splitting into two to allow his people through. Mercedes would have liked that comparison.

The people behind Angelina push her into the train. She is part of a giant centipede with hundreds of legs marching in unison into the wagon, while the human torsos on top fight each other for some breathing space.

The train starts with a sudden jerk and a loud crank. Angelina holds on to the metal tube, trying to ignore the cold, distant faces a few inches from her face. The train rattles as it speeds through the dark tunnel.

A few paces behind Angelina, the old lady with the turban stands in perfect balance, her hands cupped. Golden threads of light trickle between her fingers. The lady looks at a man who sits, examining a subway map.

The man looks at the lady, stands up and leaves his seat to her.

She nods gratefully, glancing at the map.

The man hands over the map to the old lady.

The old lady stretches the map on her lap with one hand and then gently opens the other hand.

A golden bubble falls from her hand into the map, following the route of the N train along the paper. As it does, the lines in the paper move.

The train makes a sharp turn. The passengers scream and swagger as they hold on to the nearest thing at hand.

"Suds and bubbles..." the lady whispers with a luminous smile, "...fragile indeed. Yet they can wash away the beaten path and alter the course of events."

CHAPTER 3

Destiny or Destination

"I must make a good impression," Angelina tells herself, focusing on an inexistent point in front of her nose and blurring out the surrounding faces. The voice speaking inside her sounds like a school teacher drilling in a lesson.

"I am starting at a middle administrative level, but I plan to move up in about six months. There is a lot of room for growth in this company, and I am determined to get a top executive salary two years from now."

She clutches her jaw. The memory of Omar streams into her mind, sipping into her heart like good, strong coffee. Omar and his meditation sessions, his New Age music and his sound wave experiments. Omar and his beautiful paintings that took her deep into places she did not know existed inside her. Omar encouraging her to write her poems and stories. Angelina automatically holds on to her leather bag.

"We can create a company to inspire people with my music and my art and your poems and stories," Omar is saying as he shows her his last painting.

Angelina's gray olive eyes brighten, turning into a hazel green. There's a smile trembling in her parted lips.

The train's racket grows distant as Angelina closes her eyes. She can still see the strange painting. Most of the canvas is dark, like a black-purple night that wraps itself around a woman. The woman stands at the center of the canvas. She looks a lot like Angelina: olive skin, medium built and long, straight honey-auburn hair. The woman has no eyes.

This had scared Angelina, who pulled back and had to be coaxed to look at the painting again.

The train swaggers abruptly and Angelina is pushed first to one side, then to the next. She opens her eyes, looking nervously around. When she sees the expressionless faces around her still unmoved, she closes her eyes again. The painting calls her into its darkness.

The woman stretches her hands towards the darkness. There is a tiny light ahead of her.

When she had looked at the night, Angelina had felt lost and afraid. When she had concentrated on the tiny woman surrounded by darkness, Angelina had felt small and powerless. When she had seen that the woman had no eyes, she was terrified. But when she finally saw the tiny light, Angelina had felt that the woman was guided. The entire mood of the painting had changed. She had not been afraid or sad anymore.

"What is that light?" Angelina asked.

"What do you feel it is," Omar asked, "for you?"

"My faith," Angelina declared.

Yet, the painting had haunted her dreams for months. Ever since she decided to leave Omar and move to New York, the darkness kept growing, getting deeper, and the woman seemed to shrink. Her arms were lower in each dream, and the light was dimmer.

"Yeah, right, Omar in his ragged jeans, in his broken-down jalopy, struggling to pay each month's rent, playing his guitar on the streets for dollars a day, working to buy painting to create art that he cannot sell, often will not sell," Angelina reminds herself. Her eyes turn dark, cold olive and the smile becomes a bitter grimace.

"I will not waste away anymore," Angelina swears inwardly, her sweaty hands holding on fiercely to the metal tube. "Not in dead-end jobs, not in stupid creative dreams, not with a loser who doesn't have his feet on the ground. I won't live like mom. That's no life at all. Always scrambling to pay the bills. I want the house, the car, the health insurance, the whole shebang, and I want to enjoy it while I can."

Her eyes are drawn to a woman hiding behind a book. The woman holds the book tightly, pressing it against the metal tube. This takes away space from the other passengers, who scramble for a hold. The lady, however, is oblivious to anything but the words she is devouring, her head bopping up and down in hypnotic appreciation. Curious, Angelina focuses on the title of the book.

"The Secret"

Angelina is instantly magnetized. She's heard about this book. They say it can change your life. It's about the Law of Attraction. She saw the movie with a friend. Could this be true? Could she attract all that she wants effortlessly?

The minute she leans forward, something hot and terrible rises inside her, physically stopping her and shoving her back with such force that she bumps into the person behind her. Angelina wants to apologize, but she is no longer in control of her own responses.

Red, hot lava instantly rises from her stomach into her neck and face. Angelina feels the molten lava of her anger ready to burst out, and tightens her lips. But a hysterically angry woman inside her screams through Angelina's tightly closed lips.

"How can people swallow that Law of Attraction crap?" this mad woman screams, her pitch becoming one with the loud clank of the train.

Angelina covers her mouth, but soon realizes that no one else can hear.

"What is happening to me? Am I going crazy?" Angelina wonders. But the mad woman is screaming at the top of her lungs and Angelina cannot hear her own thoughts anymore.

"How can anyone believe that all you have to do is wish for something and you just get it? All it takes is a quick glance at the world to know this is horse manure!"

Angelina's hands are sweating. She feels a strange, overwhelming desire to snatch the book from the stupid woman and bang her head with it. Why is she so angry?

"Just look, you moron," the mad woman screams, leaping out of Angelina and standing close to the reader.

"Look around you! Do you think that the people in this train want to be trapped, half-asleep, suffocated and crowded, going to an idiotic job they hate just to make some strangers rich and put bread on their table?" The mad woman interrogates, suddenly turning towards Angelina "Do you?"

"No, I guess no one wants to ride during rush hours," Angelina mutters as the stench of sweat and cigarette breath hits her nostrils.

"No, of course they don't!" the angry woman screams even louder, as if her anger had been fully justified.

The hysterical woman is now pacing frantically from one end of the wagon to the other, pushing everyone to the side. Angelina watches the whole scene in disbelief.

This woman looks so much like Angelina, yet her face is distorted with anger and skepticism. Her hair is a chaotic tangle of curls that sizzle like serpents. The image of Medusa flashes in her mind.

Contrasting with Angelina's pale peach outfit, this woman's dress has layers of flaps in red, orange and crimson. The flaps seem to flare like tongues of fire as she moves among the passengers.

"They may be idiots and cowards," the mad woman raves, "but they don't WANT to live in mediocrity. No one does! Not even you!" the angry woman says, pointing at the reader, and then at Angelina.

"Jajajajaja! Oh, sure we would all love to be billionaires!" the angry woman laughs cynically.

"But it's not going to happen. NOT GOING TO HAPPEN! Get it?" She says, poking the reader's forehead with her finger. The woman scratches her head as she reads.

"Those who are poor will stay poor," the angry woman continues, climbing into a seat, in between two uniformed workers. "They will work their butt off like slaves and they will DIE like slaves, American Dream and all."

Angelina thinks of her mother. Her years of poverty flash by like a wasteland seen from the speeding train. She thinks of Omar, so talented, and yet barely surviving. She is subconsciously nodding now.

"Yes, you know that I'm right," the woman charges, encouraged by her effect on Angelina. "You ALL know that I am right.

"The poor will stay poor and those who have rich daddies will go on to have rich husbands and wives and become the bosses and investors," the angry woman says in a nasal voice as she manhandles the expensive attaché and purse of some well-dressed executives.

Angelina thinks of Billy's wife and a resentful moue wrinkles her face. But then, Billy was poor, and she did marry him, and now Billy is doing well. Angelina may not like her rich sister-in-law, but she did believe in Billy. She supported her brother's progress.

"And don't forget the ham in the sandwich!" The mad woman thunders, pointing a finger here and there, like a preacher exposing the sins of his followers. She turns the drama up a notch, distracting Angelina from the course of her thinking.

"Those who are the ham in the sandwich will be eaten up by the system," the angry woman shouts.

By now, she is screaming like a maniac.

"And anyone, ANYONE who manages to move up a notch, does it through freaking hard work. Hard, long, freaking work! Do you hear?"

"That's the God honest truth," Angelina mutters under her breath, as the mad woman dissolves in a puff of red smoke.

Angelina feels sapped, as if all her blood had been sucked by a vampire. Her enthusiasm for her new job is gone. Her wonder about the Law of Attraction is gone.

"Where the heck did this come from?" Angelina questions.

She seeks motivation by fixing her gaze on a colorful ad above the wagon's windows. It shows happy people at work.

"Don't't' give up!

You can make it!

Get a good paying job!

Build the career of your dreams!"

But the sense of futility that the mad woman left on her wake will not go away.

"Is everything a big lie?" Angelina asks herself. Her heart feels heavy. "Am I fooling myself? Am I riding into a lie?"

The train suddenly swerves and a kind-faced woman in her forties bumps into Angelina.

"Sorry!" she says. Angelina looks at the woman for the first time.

Her long black, silky hair sways softly as the woman moves subtly to some inaudible music. She is not moving noticeably, but Angelina can sense a dance inside her. The woman is the only one smiling in the wagon.

"That's okay!" Angelina softly replies with a smile, as she takes a second look, trying to see what this woman is dancing to. She seems to be listening to some music, though she is not using an Ipod or CD player.

Angelina notices her expensive attaché and her exquisite attire. Her designer purse must be worth a lot of money. She is obviously an affluent woman. Angelina gets excited. That's what she wants. That's exactly why she came to New York.

"Maybe she is a big honcho in a marketing firm," Angelina considers. "Perhaps I should get to know her."

She then notices a pair of dance slippers protruding from a canvas bag in the lady's left hand.

"Another dreamer!" Angelina wheezes under her breath, and averts her eyes.

"Make up your mind, lady. You can't eat the cake and have it too!" A voice barks inside Angelina, who is suddenly angry. Something irritates her about this woman, but she cannot understand what. She seems so kind and happy. Just minutes ago, Angelina was eager to meet her. Why is she so angry now?

But there is no time for platitudes. The train is slowing down.

Angelina clumsily reviews the map she got at the train booth. Her stop is not so far away. Eight stops to Lexington Avenue and 59th Street. Then one single stop, across the East River to Long Island City, and she will reach her new life. She holds the map tightly in her right hand.

"The map to my future," she proudly thinks, as her eyes catch a strange ring.

The ring glows on the finger of a man in front of her. She cannot see his face because it's buried behind the New York Times, but the ring catches her eyes briefly. She realizes that the tiny diamonds spell something out. She looks attentively, not knowing why she is obsessing with this stupid ring instead of paying attention to the station.

W-O-R-D-S

The diamonds spell out.

The train slows to a halt. The letters in the ring grow into a glare, blinding Angelina. As the glare softens, the letters rearrange themselves right before her eyes.

W-O-R-L-D-S

Several things happen at once.

The doors open and waves of people move in and out of the wagon.

The diamond letters in the ring grow, glistening so fiercely that they blur everything around Angelina.

A window opens inside the blinding light.

Fiery eyes stare at Angelina from the other side of the window. They are not human. They have scales. A snake, perhaps?

Angelina cannot tell. The window frame catches fire.

There's another woman looking at her from the other side of the window. She is barely a shadow, but she seems to beckon for help. Is she burning?

Angelina hears a deafening woman's scream.

The vision dissolves as the iron wheels screech into motion.

The train is moving again. The man, the ring and the newspaper are gone. Angelina is surrounded by new blank faces.

"There was no scream, you big drama queen," Angelina tells herself. "It was just the train screeching."

She lets out a sigh. To her surprise, it is charged with anxiety.

"New York is definitely stressful," she thinks, automatically pressing the bag against her body. "No wonder there are so many shrinks here!"

"Cheer up, Angelina," she tells herself, trying to smile. "You're on the rise, girl. Just count the stops to your destiny!"

A pair of golden eyes stares at her among the unfamiliar faces packed in the wagon. Angelina does not see the amused smile on the old woman's peculiar face. Angelina is about to discover that her destiny has nothing to do with her destination.

CHAPTER 4

Change Station

According to the crinkled map in her hands, next stop is Lexington Avenue and 59th Street.

Angelina has counted the stops at least five times. She studied New York's subway system as well as Manhattan's neatly numbered streets even before she got here. She is confident that she can find her way around, even though it's her first time navigating the New York subways.

The train screeches to a halt. The doors open abruptly and the wagon empties in a second. Angelina looks through the open doors at the sign.

Lexington Avenue and 59th Street

How come there's no one left in the wagon, except her and an eccentric old lady? People from all the wagons pour out into the station. A female voice announces something over the train's speakers, but the sound is breaking.

Is the train being evacuated? Is there a detour? A delay? Is Long Island City an odd place no one visits? Angelina gets nervous and decides to leave the wagon.

The eccentric lady steps in front of the doors. She is tall and thin. Her long purple velvet dress shimmers as she moves. Angelina observes that this is due to a thin layer of shimmering purple gauze draped over the attire.

"Is this train going to Long Island City?" Angelina asks.

"You are in the right train for your destination," the lady responds as the door closes.

The woman's voice is delicate, but firm. There is a buoyant, trembling movement under her calm words. Angelina thinks of a dragonfly.

"Might as well enjoy the comfort," Angelina tells herself as she takes ample space in the empty seat. The shimmering lady seats on the opposite side of the train.

The lady lowers her head and it seems to disappear into her dress. She is wearing a purple velvet head wrap with a round white and purple orb at each side. For a moment, Angelina has the crazy impression that a giant insect observes her closely, eyes bulging in blatant disbelief.

The train gains speed, as do Angelina's thoughts.

"Will I get a nice office? I'm sure I won't get a window yet, but will they give me a cubicle?" Angelina wonders as she takes out a lipstick and tries to paint her lips. The subtle peach hue goes with her muted peach blouse and matching beige skirt and blazer.

"Peachy, everything's peachy, dearest!" says a voice inside her head. Angelina recognizes the familiar voice that she has labeled as the *Architect of Failure*. "Peach is so safe, so ladylike, isn't it?"

"Shut up," Angelina mutters.

"Be nice, now. Be peachy pitch nice, you hear?" *The Architect* taunts her.

"Scram," Angelina mumbles as she misses the lip line and has to get a tissue. "Look what you made me do!"

"Oh, look what I made her do!" *The Architect* imitates in a silly high-pitched voice. "Never mind that YOU make us wear this stupid peach when your true color is fuchsia, strong, passionate, fiery fuchsia with a tint of mysterious indigo. That's you!"

"Not anymore," Angelina hisses. "Not in this job. It would not get me where I am going."

"That would suite me fine," *The Architect* hisses back.

"What's so wrong with wanting prosperity?" Angelina silently argues. "Why are you obsessed with keeping me down? Go away!"

"Never!" *The Architect* declares. "You will drive us to our doom."

"Suit yourself," Angelina says, and tries to look at the map again.

The train is speeding frantically. It rattles so loudly that Angelina fears it will derail any minute. The shaking is worse than a class 8 earthquake. Angelina holds tightly to the metal railing at the edge of her seat. Her mind races through newspapers, TV screens and endless gossips. Has she ever heard about a New York train derailed or crashing?

No. Never. She tries to relax, comforted by this fact. But the train does not seem to know the news, and threatens to fly off the rails. The rattling is unbearable and Angelina has a hard time choosing whether to cover her ears or hold on for dear life.

"At least I'm getting off on the first stop," she reminds herself as her body shakes like a possessed woman.

You are leaving the Comfort Zone

The sign passes by at such speed that Angelina is not sure it was there at all. She carefully takes off a hand from the metal railing and tries to look at the map. Clumsily she irons the wrinkled map against the seat and then brings it close to her eyes. There is no mention of Comfort Zone in the map. Was the train detoured? Could she be heading in the wrong direction? But she can hardly read the largest letters. The map itself seems to speed by her sight, all the colors and letters blurring as the train rattles madly.

"What am I doing here?" Angelina clearly thinks.

It's not even a thought. It is a realization in her body. As if she had been in some trance and has suddenly woke up, not knowing where she is or what she is doing here. She feels out of place, in a life foreign to her.

"Oh, I know!" Angelina mumbles, pulling herself out of the odd sensation. "That must have been an ad for a mattress. 'Comfort Zone,' Get it? How silly of me!"

The train slows down. Angelina sees the sign for the approaching station.

Change Station

Angelina feels uncomfortable. Why would the train stop here? This is not the first station in the map. In fact, this station is not in the map at all. She looks at the map once more, then gets up and looks at the map in the wagon.

"This is the wrong station!" she screams at the old lady. "Are you sure that this train goes to Long Island City?"

Angelina is so upset that her eyes jump from place to place, trying to assess a reality that is slipping from her control. She looks at the train. It is the N train. She looks at the map. Queensboro Plaza should be next. She looks through the windows to the upcoming station. **Change Station.**

She does not like surprises, especially if they delay her plans. Angelina is punctual and responsible. She is downright fastidious about time. She hates to waste time. Has this lady given her the wrong information? Is this train defective? She may even be in danger! Her heart is racing.

"This train goes to your destination," the shimmering lady insists, a bit annoyed.

"Are you sure?" Angelina demands as the train slows down. Even as she asks, Angelina is wondering what possessed her to trust anything this eccentric woman could say. For all she knows, the lady is mad.

The train hovers back and forth, as if it could not make up its mind whether to stop or keep going. The slow movement seems to pull Angelina backwards into the past, into some old place that she wants to forget. She also oscillates. She does not want the train to stop. Not here. Yet, it may be good if she gets off, for this train is obviously not going the way it should go. Angelina looks at the station.

In the platform a woman seats on a gray bench. Her whole attire is as gray as the bench, so that woman and bench seem to merge. The woman carries a large, heavy load on her back. It sticks out of her tunic, like a hump. Her body is collapsing from the weight, and she seems to be folding into herself. Strong multi-color lights flash by, tainting the woman in red, blue, orange, green, yellow, red, blue, orange, green, yellow.

It comes out of nowhere —a hazy shadow breaking the color patterns of the light as it slides towards the lady. He grabs the woman's backpack firmly, yanking it brutally and disappearing into thin air. It all happens in less than a minute.

"Thief!" A muted voice cries. There is shock, disbelief and a long drawn-out groan in the muffled voice.

Angelina sees the fear-stricken face of the woman as her loss begins to dawn on her. The woman, still bent forward, flaps her arms desperately. She is unable to reach back, yet she knows that something is wrong. She's lost something. It has been stolen. She feels it. Her possessions. There is no weight. No weight. Suddenly the woman stops struggling. Her face becomes blank. Her entire body seems to float up, as if it had lost gravity.

"Poor thing!" Angelina whimpers, backtracking toward the other side of the train. "She lost everything. So quickly. Out of nowhere. Everything... gone!"

The train still oscillates, but the doors shake, struggling to open. Angelina jumps away, sitting as far away as she can. She folds her body, wrapping her arms around her chest, her large leather bag tightly squeezed against her heart.

"I am certain," the eccentric lady slowly answers in an irrefutable tone, her golden eyes piercing Angelina, who looks at the old woman as if she were mad, until she remembers that she had just asked for confirmation.

The lady's delayed response and the nightmarish mood in the station give Angelina the sensation that time is breaking up, that cause and effect are no longer related.

In the midst of this chaos, Angelina holds on to that word: "certain."

She likes certainty. Certainty is food on the table at breakfast, lunch and dinner. Certainty is a roof over her head. One that doesn't leak. Certainty is a new uniform for each school semester, books and notebooks. Certainty is being able to go to parties and attend extra-curricular activities because she has clothing, transportation, and spare money to hang out with friends. Certainty is more than one pair of shoes. Certainty is her mother's face without a deep wrinkle between her brows. Her mother smiling. Certainty is something she's never had. Something she wants badly. Badly enough to seat on an empty train speeding towards a wrong destination.

"Certainty is being bored to death," a passionate voice says inside her. She knows this voice. *The Rebel* has inspired her previously crazy, aimless life. *The Rebel* loved Omar because he was different. *The Rebel* has chosen for her up to now, and has consistently chosen failure. No more.

As the train picks up speed, Angelina ignores the rebellious voice inside her. She avoids looking at the receding station, her eyes fixed on the map.

"Get off!" *The Rebel* roars, stepping out of Angelina's body.

Angelina tries to ignore the woman in front of her. She tries to ignore that this woman literally stepped out of her. She specially tries to ignore that there are two of her walking around, and that her other self possesses a fitter, younger body.

The Rebel wears red velvet pants and a jaguar print tight jersey that emphasize her strong physicality. She stomps around in military boots and walks as if the entire wagon was her realm.

Angelina takes a perfunctory glance at her dainty peach and beige outfit and high heels and she contracts even more into herself.

"Take a freaking risk for once in your life, you coward!" *The Rebel* screams at her in a hoarse voice that has no traces of social decorum.

"Are you crazy?" Angelina cries nervously as she fixes her hair. "Didn't you see what just happened? This place is dangerous."

"Really?" *The Rebel* asks innocently, and then she begins to laugh outrageously.

Something in *The Rebel's* laughter, makes Angelina look back at **Change Station.** Angelina cannot believe what she sees.

The gray woman at the station takes one soft step forward, rising from the bench. The gray bundle of clothing, her heavy formless carcass, all of it stays behind, melting away on the bench.

As the woman rises gracefully, the color lights in the station swirl and wrap around her, forming a splendid design. Light and agile, she smiles ecstatically. Her eyes sparkle as she opens her arms, moving towards the tracks.

"She's going to jump!" Angelina thinks, running to the back of the wagon and looking through the glass window on the rear door.

The Rebel throws herself on the floor, laughing hysterically.

"No! Please, don't jump!" Angelina screams.

The Rebel is hiccupping and holding her stomach. Her sides and her jaw hurt from laughing.

"Nooooo!" Angelina howls, extending her hand, as if by this she could stop the poor woman from throwing herself into the tracks.

The woman plunges into the tracks as huge red, orange, yellow, green and blue butterfly wings open on her back, catching the wind. She flies after the train.

The *Butterfly Woman* seems to be saying something to Angelina, but the train is rattling as it picks up speed, and Angelina sees the butterfly becoming smaller, until it disappears.

CHAPTER 5

Opportunity Lane

"I want the butterfly," a tiny voice pleads behind her.

Angelina's bones respond to the voice as if it was a deep fall, sensing pain at the end. She is still looking out the wagon's rear window into the dark tunnel. As she shifts her glance, she can see the insides of the wagon reflected on the glass. There is no one in the wagon, except for the old lady, still sleeping.

"I want my butterfly!" the tiny voice demands.

Angelina turns around slowly. She is beginning to fear the strangeness of this journey.

A tiny girl, no more than four years old, stands in the middle of the aisle, holding an old Raggedy Ann doll in her arms and looking at Angelina accusingly.

Where did this girl come from? Angelina's mind seeks an explanation that will fit reality. One that will bring order back into this mad ride. The wagon doors did not open at **Change Station**, of that she is sure. Therefore, this girl could not have come in then. She certainly wasn't in the wagon before, either.

"I am bored," the girl says. "There's no fun anymore."

"Honey, where do you come from?" Angelina asks the girl, sweetening her voice in order not to scare her.

"You don't know?" the girl asks, stunned. Her little face turns pale.

"Why should I know?" Angelina asks. She can hear the defensive tone in her voice. "I don't know you."

The girl begins to cry.

"I wa...want my bu...butterfly," she sobs.

Angelina goes towards her, but the girl runs and crawls under a seat.

"Is your mom the... butterfly?" Angelina asks, remembering the strange woman they left behind. Wasn't the strange butterfly trying to say something?

"My mom? The butterfly?" the girl asks, seemingly surprised.

"Perhaps you came in through another wagon," Angelina lucubrates. "Did you come in through the next wagon? Did the doors close behind you? Was your mom left behind in the station? Is that what the... butterfly tried to tell me?"

The little girl begins to cry again, covering her ears.

"That's all I need now!" Angelina thinks as she sits on the opposite seat. "A lost, frightened little girl. Don't I have enough problems as it is?"

Not knowing what to do, Angelina ignores the girl. She takes out the wrinkled map, irons it flat against the seat, and peruses it once more.

"I had to get off the first stop. Queensboro Plaza. The N train." She reviews, looking at the large N on the sides of the wagon. "I got it! There must be two N trains, one express and one local. I got into the local. That's it. It stops at other stops before getting to Queensboro Plaza. That makes sense."

Having achieved this rational explanation, Angelina feels calm and in control. She relaxes on to the seat, closing her eyes. She takes a deep breath and slowly releases it. She feels someone watching her and opens her eyes.

The little girl is standing in front of her, looking at her intensely. Angelina tries to put on a reassuring smile.

"Are you lost, too?" the girl asks softly.

"Me? Of course not!" Angelina affirms. "I have a map. I am on the right train. My stop will come up any minute now."

"Liar!" the tiny girl shouts in a booming voice, pointing an accusing finger at Angelina, who jumps up.

"Liar! Liar!" the tiny girl screams at the top of her lungs. "You always lie! I am tired of your lies. I don't trust you anymore."

"You should not speak that way to adults," Angelina scolds. "That's very disrespectful."

"Why?" the girl asks.

"You are calling me a liar."

"You ARE a liar."

"You don't know me."

"I do, too."

"You don't know me at all," Angelina says, standing up. She is quite annoyed at this brat.

"You are Angelina. You live in Arizona. You love Omar. He is fun and good and he loves you, but you betrayed him, just like you betrayed me. You left him, just like you left me. You lie all the time. You lie about what you want. You lie about what you feel. You lie about what you do. Liar!"

Angelina is frozen in the middle of the aisle. The girl's words strike her like a curse, freezing her on the spot. Currents of electric energy surge around her, sparkling and popping inside her mind and shocking her nerves, but her body is frozen. Her mind is frozen. It takes her a couple of minutes to be able to think again.

"Who is this girl? How does she know all these things? Who put her up to this? What kind of sick joke is this?

"Joke! That's it!" Angelina grasps, and the ice around her melts as she laughs hysterically, looking at the ceiling, under the seats, searching everywhere.

"Okay, guys, come out. Show yourself. I know that I've been cast in one of those stupid funny shows. I don't know which one, but I'm on to you. It's a matter of seconds now before I find the cameras, so show up."

But there are no cameras. The wagon has grown as silent as a tomb. The old lady looks at Angelina with concern, her eyes searching for the girl, who has hidden out of sight.

"Is she yours?" the lady asks softly.

"Mine? No, no! I can assure you," Angelina explains. "You saw me come in alone. Did you see where she came from? Did she board the train at **Change Station**? Did she walk into this wagon from the next one?"

The lady does not answer. She keeps looking at Angelina with a mixture of pity, concern and accusation. Yes, Angelina senses a veiled judgment in her eyes.

"She must think that I am this kid's mother and I am trying to abandon her," Angelina surmises. "That's all I need! A crazy old woman and a crazy kid, looking at me as if I am the crazy one."

The train speeds up and the rattling starts again. Angelina goes back to her seat. She picks up the map, and a black and white photo slips out of its fold, falling to the floor.

A young brunette woman in her mid twenties smiles happily into the camera. She holds a little girl on her lap. There is something familiar in this photo. Angelina bends down to pick up the photo. Her hands are trembling, and it is not because of the train's speeding race. Her heart is racing faster than the train. She has seen this photo before.

Her fingers lightly touch the photo, but the train gives a yank, and her fingers push the photo a few inches away. She stretches her torso and her arm, trying to reach the photo. The train twitches again and Angelina flies through the aisle, banging her head against the opposite seat. She lands with her legs spread-eagle. Her head hurts. Angelina rubs the crown of her head. The photo is lying on the middle of the aisle. Angelina crawls towards it and picks it up.

Tears swell in her olive eyes as she recognizes the woman in the photo. Angelina caresses the woman's face with the tip of her fingers. So young, so beautiful! She saw this photo once, when her mom was placing a new photo in the family album. She remembers it because it is the only photo where her mother is smiling.

"Is that you, mom?" Angie is asking.

"Ujum," Mercedes responds as she quickly flips the page.

"How old were you there?" Angie wants to know. "Let me see!"

"I was the age of illusions," Mercedes says bitterly. "Full of stupid dreams. But I woke up. There's nothing to see there."

Nothing to see, the only smile she remembers on her mom? That would have been worth a million! How about that little girl, smiling happily in the arms of a happy mother? Why was her mother saying that this was nothing? This was everything! This was HER dream, to see her mother happy. But Mercedes would not flip back the page.

Angelina drinks in every inch of the photo. She sees the little girl, with shoulder-long silky hair and long bangs covering most of her forehead. Such a happy face! Angelina sees the Raggedy Ann doll, new and shiny.

"Do you still deny it?" the tiny voice says.

Angelina raises her eyes and sees the girl in front of her. This is the same girl in the photo! The doll in her hands is the same Raggedy Ann doll, much older and tattered. How can this be? It can't be true. The girl in Mercedes' lap can only be one person. Angelina used to have that doll. She got it for her fourth birthday. The girl in the photo can only be Angelina. But then who is this girl in front of her?

"I don't want to go there," the girl says.

"Where?" Angelina asks, her mind so jumbled that she can't make sense of anything.

"There!" the girl says, pointing in the direction where the train is going.

"Who are you?" Angelina stutters. She is afraid of the response.

"You know," the girl answers.

"What...what's your name?" Angelina asks.

"Angie," the girl says.

"I am dreaming. I banged my head against the wall and I am dreaming," Angelina thinks, as lights bursts out all around her in dizzying patches.

"I don't want to go!" Angie is crying.

"But we must," Mercedes is saying as she packs. "There's no alternative."

"What's that?"

"What's what?"

"The altern-na-tif?"

"An alternative is a solution. A different choice," Mercedes explains as she folds and unfolds a piece of garment, frantically pushing it into the already bursting suitcase on the bed.

"We don't have another choice?" Angie asks.

"No, we don't," Mercedes declares with a finality that strikes her daughter in the heart. But Mercedes doesn't notice, busy as she is choosing and discarding pieces of clothing to pack.

"We need to eat and mommy's got to work. And the only alternative is the job I got," Mercedes says, more to herself than to Angie.

"But, why can't you get another job?" Angie asks.

"I didn't get another job, Angie, I got this one," Mercedes says impatiently.

"But there are many jobs!" Angie protests, picking a section of newspaper that Mercedes had discarded and showing her mom the classified ads. "Look at all these tiny squares. Each one is a job. There are many. There must be one right here, where grandma is, where my friends are."

"There are many jobs," Mercedes says in a harsh, cutting voice. "But I am not qualified for most of them. So I have to take this one."

"But..." Angie begins.

Mercedes stops packing and kneels down, holding her daughter by her shoulders.

"That's why you must grow up, why you must study and have good grades," Mercedes says, anguish written all over her face as she presses her daughter's shoulders desperately. Her fear runs from her hands into her daughter's bones. "That's why you must go to college and get a profession, so that you can get a good job, do you understand?

Angie assents, her face very serious. She stays quiet for a while, thinking hard about what her mom just explained. Her face suddenly lights up. She pulls her mom's skirt.

"Now what?" Mercedes snaps.

"When I grow up I will get a job right here, and then we can come back home," Angie says triumphantly.

"When you grow up, you will find out that things don't always go your way," Mercedes says bitterly as she closes the suitcase.

"I don't understand. Things don't go my way? Where do they go? Do they go away?" Angie asks, her triumphant expression changing into dismay.

"Look, Angie, you can't have your cake and eat it too," Mercedes says, squaring herself in front of her kid, her hands on her hips. She is talking to herself, not really seeing her daughter. She does not see how deeply her words are cutting into the girl's Soul.

"You want to have good things, don't you? You want to eat and have a roof over your head, to have good dresses and all those picture books you like? Yes? Well, then you got to study and get a good paying job, and work hard to keep it. Life is not a party. You can't live from those fairy tales you like. Someday you'll have to grow up and wake up!"

Angie's eyes turn gray and their light is dimming. Thick tears fall down her cheeks into the Raggedy Ann doll in her arms. A terrible sigh shakes her little chest.

Mercedes is in a hurry. She doesn't see her daughter's pain, because her own pain is blinding her. She picks up the suitcase in one hand, and pulls Angie along with the other, and they walk away.

Angelina is crying, holding on to the tiny girl.

"She lied," Angie says.

"What? Who?" Angelina asks.

"She lied. I've thought very hard about it, and I know she lied," Angie declares.

"What...what do you mean?" Angelina sobs in a little voice.

"Those fairy tales I like," Angie says with a mature voice. "Somebody wrote them, right?"

"Ye...yes," Angelina confirms.

"And I bet that the writers who wrote those tales got paid for writing them," Angie declares.

"Ye...yes!" Angelina says, drying her tears.

"Then, why couldn't I be paid for the stories I make up?" Angie says. "They are very good! My friends love them!"

"Oh, baby!" Angelina says in a soothing voice. "I sent my writings to agents and publishers. I have a drawer full of rejection slips. I really tried, but we got to eat. We got to have a normal life."

"I don't want a normal life!" Angie roars.

"You don't?"

"No. I want my stories. I want my butterfly!"

"I know, baby, but you don't want to sleep under a bridge with those dirty, ragged, scary people who rummage in the garbage, do you?"

Angie moves away, her face full of fear.

"You don't want to be hungry and lonely all the time, do you?

"I am hungry! I am lonely!" Angie screams. "You are just like her. You are deaf!"

The girl runs towards the train doors. Slipping through them, she disappears.

The train speeds noisily through the dark tunnel. Angelina gets up clumsily and swaggers across the aisle, still dizzy from the blow to her head. She looks through the glass windows of the doors through which Angie just disappeared.

Light blinds her.

The train is slowing down as it ascends to ground level. A baby blue sky with puffy white clouds greets Angelina's eyes, wiping away her tears. A bright green prairie rolls softly towards the round hills in the horizon. Music and laughter trickle through the train doors, reminding Angelina of a town fair. The train comes to a halt in front of a wrought-iron gate. At the top, a large sign in red letters reads:

Publisher's Fair

Below the main sign, there is another in smaller, blue and golden letters. Angelina reads:

Welcome Writers, Publishers and Agents

Angelina's heart leaps. She runs to her seat, opens her large bag, and searches through it hurriedly.

"Here it is!" She whispers. "I brought it."

Tiny stars dance in Angelina's dark pupils. Her heart is warm with hope and her face is washed in innocence. She suddenly looks surprisingly like the child who just left the train.

She picks up her bag while she holds her manuscript against her chest. It burns in her arms, like Omar's memory. Slowly, she walks towards the doors.

The train doors open. Angelina takes one step forward.

Just then the speakers boom, crackling and hissing as a voice announces.

"This is...op... or... ny Lane. Local stop. The next stop is... eens...boro Plaza."

Angelina takes one step back

Her body want to runs out and join the fair. What if she meets an agent or a publisher? What if...?

"What if! You are dreaming with joining the circus again. Don't you get it?" says a harsh voice inside her. "Only freaks work in that circus of your childhood dreams. Grow up. You are heading to Queensboro Plaza. You are heading for a good job. Don't blow it."

Angelina takes another step back.

She remembers Angie. What if the child is right? There is a fair here where writers can meet agents and publishers. Why not take the chance? Thousands of writers are published every year. Why can't she be one of them? Perhaps this is her chance.

"Want to blow a good job to see if you get that one in a million lotto number? Go ahead," barks the harsh voice. It sounds suspiciously like her mom's.

"What are you going to do if nothing happens?" the voice that Angelina labels the *Reality Check* presses. "Then you would have lost your job, your chance for a steady income. And then what? What are you going to do in New York, without a job? You don't even have enough money to go back home! And are you going to go back to Arizona with empty hands?

"What are you going to tell your folks? 'Oh, I just happen to see a pretty fair on my way to work and decided to play hooky!' Grow up, Angelina. Life is not a party!"

Angelina takes two steps back.

"This is crazy," she whispers, shaking her head. "I'm going to Queensboro Plaza."

The manuscript grows cold in her arms. Angelina's heart feels heavy. A numbing cold creeps into her chest.

"I can always come back here after work," Angelina lies to her aching heart. "It's right before **Change Station**, in the local train coming back, I can be here by six today. Then I'll be safe with the new job and I'll still give it a go."

Her heart doesn't believe a word of it. It knows that she is coping out once more. Her heart grows cold and goes back to its hopeless wait.

"Like Sleeping Beauty," a sad, tiny voice whispers in her heart.

Angelina recognizes this movement of pulling away. She suddenly realizes that she has been doing this for a long time. Every time she is about to leap, she pulls back.

The movement starts in her shoulders. It's as if they'd jump back, away from the threshold. Then the pull goes into her stomach, and it begins to whirl inwards. Then she sinks into a pool of doubts.

A sudden mechanical tremor brings her back to the present.

The doors tremble and close. Their tremor makes her body shudder. Her heart sinks as the train starts with a jerk.

As if someone had switched off a light inside, Angelina's eyes turn a deep, black olive. Thick tears fall down her cheeks into the manuscript in her arms. A terrible sigh shakes her chest.

As the train rolls away, Angelina spots a sign slowly flapping in the breeze, like an abandoned child's swing.

Opportunity Lane

The train shoots once more into darkness.

CHAPTER 6

The Trail of Ghosts

"Where is the child?"

It is barely a whisper, but it pierces each pore in Angelina's soft skin and reverberates on her ears and heart.

Angelina turns around to meet the golden eyes of the eccentric lady. She is standing about twenty feet away, yet her voice still sends shivers through Angelina's skin.

Mouth ajar, all Angelina can do is gaze at the old woman, who seems to float slowly towards her.

"You should have listened to the tiny one," the lady in purple whispers, a sad smile on her face.

Angelina's insides are boiling. What on earth is going on here? Who are these people? Why are they meddling in her plans?

As the lady floats towards her, Angelina's mind cannot come up with any more reasonable explanations and it freezes. Angelina finds a strange comfort in this empty mind. The comfort doesn't last, however.

"Pity!" the old woman says as she slants her head to the left, studying Angelina at an angle. "The tiny one was your most awesome power."

"Power? She was just an angry, lost and scared kid!" Angelina snaps.

"Silence," the old lady whispers. Her voice is as soft as velvet, yet it reverberates in every surface of the wagon.

"How dare you!" Angelina opens her mouth to scream. But the reverberation of the old woman's voice gathers around her in dense ripples.

An invisible gag muffles Angelina's voice. The waves whirl closer and closer to her body, binding her torso, arms and legs as strongly as a rope. The invisible binds spread through every muscle, petrifying her entire body and face.

"You could have gone out at **Change Station**, but you distrust change," the lady softly says as she jumps three feet in one graceful leap and lands on her feet on top of a seat. "Life is change. Therefore you distrust life."

Angelina could swear that the woman's shimmering purple veil opened and flickered rapidly, like wings. But Angelina is certain that this is simply impossible.

"The child carries an endless provision of trust, but you see no power in that, do you?"

Angelina tries to refute, but she cannot talk. The lady does not wait for her response, before adding.

"No, you don't. You want certainty. But what is certainty?"

Angelina struggles in vain to get rid of the invisible bonds holding her. The lady, indifferent to her struggle, continues answering her own questions.

"Certainty is an attachment to the past. Oh, no doubt you have other illusions about stability, safety and no-risk," the lady says, tapping the seat with her shoes and producing a deafening metal ring.

"Regrettably, those **solid** certainties are merely an illusion!" she concludes as the metal seat evaporates and she falls to the floor.

The lady quickly rebounds and continues her monologue.

"What was I saying? Oh, yes... Certainty is an attachment to the past. You are certain about what you know, and you can only know the past, because... well, it has already passed. Hindsight is great sight," the old woman says as she floats towards Angelina. She takes one quick glance behind her and the seat reappears.

"Therefore, certainty is the repetition of the past, mistakes and all. In other words, you are creating in the present more of the same thing you had in the past. Well, that's all very good, if you liked what you had in the past. Did you, Angelina? Did you like what you've had so far?"

Angelina is fascinated, albeit reluctantly, by what the lady is saying.

"No, of course not," the lady answers. "If you were happy, you would not be searching for something else. You see the problem, don't you?"

Angelina moves her eyes sideways, which is about all she can move.

"No? Well, it's obvious. Searching for something new while being attached to the repetition of the old is a recipe for failure. Wouldn't you say?" asks the lady, and again answers herself.

"No, you wouldn't say, because what drives you is fear, and fear tries to avoid failure by avoiding anything new, which often leads to precisely the failure you feared."

Thick tears slop down Angelina's face. Frustration. Anger. Indignation. Angelina wants to convince herself that these feelings, and not a sudden sadness that threatens to engulf her, are the feelings behind her tears.

"You could have gone out at **Opportunity Lane**, but you have lost hope," the lady softly says as she darts to another seat and perches on top of its back. This time Angelina takes a good look at the shimmering purple and blue dragonfly wings that open when she leaps.

"The child carries the gifts of hope and faith, born from the innocence of her pure heart. Yet you see no blessing in that. Therefore, you lost the opportunity. You, young lady, despise the gifts of the heart," concludes the old woman. There is such sadness in her voice that Angelina's tears grow thick and swell, in spite of her resistance.

"There is a war inside you," the old woman says as she floats in front of Angelina. Her golden eyes seem to x-ray Angelina's heart. "And you have already chosen sides. Oh, yes! You have sided with the army you believe to be more powerful. In fact, you have chosen the only side that has power in your eyes."

The train swerves violently to the right. Angelina's petrified body slides to the right in one piece like a pawn on a chessboard. The train swerves again to the left, and Angelina slides to the left.

"There has been a detour. The next stop is now *The Trail of Ghosts*," a voice beams through the speakers.

"I quite agree," the lady declares as she points at Angelina, sliding her entire body towards the center of the wagon in one swift motion.

"By the way, I am Dragonfly Diva, and I am not yet sure if I am pleased to meet you," the strange lady whispers into Angelina's ears as tiny indigo and blue sparkles flash from her stirring wings.

The train stops abruptly. Angelina whirls like a top, but does not fall. When the dizzying whirling stops, Angelina searches for Dragonfly Diva, but the lady has buried her face behind a large book. The title glistens in large letters:

The Secret of the Dream Basket

Angelina feels the rising lava again. The heat wave that precedes the mad woman sizzles against her invisible restrains. Angelina can feel the irate being in her fuming and struggling against the spell that keeps her bound.

"SECREEEETS!" the mad woman screams inside Angelina as she twists and wiggles in a vain effort to leave the restrains.

Angelina recognizes that this self carries her constant anger and frustration. She labels her *Crazy Woman*, because that's how Angelina feels when this self bursts out. She loses it.

"Why do people love these dam secrets so much?" *Crazy Woman* foams. "These idiots fall prey to any charlatan who offers a so-called secret about the Law of Attraction."

"'The Law of Attraction doesn't work for you?' *Crazy Wo*man spits, imitating some imaginary snake oil salesman. 'Do not despair. I have the missing secret you need. Buy MY secret and the Law of Attraction will work like a clock.'"

"Jajajajaja!" *Crazy Woman* laughs cynically while she manages to get her arms out of the bonding out of cheer spite. Angelina watches these phantom arms flapping around her body, while her own arms are still restricted.

"If every stupid secret sold was a key to this ridiculous law, the idiotic law would be worthless anyway. One would need 100 years and a couple of billions to purchase all these dam keys."

"Bullshit! Crap! Horse manure!" that's what all that trickery is," *Crazy Woman* screams, spitting in the direction of Dragonfly Diva.

"What's that Dream Basket crap about? I bet my yet-to-be-earned-salary that it's one more stupid gimmick in this Law of Attraction massive con job!"

Dragonfly Diva looks up at Angelina for a second. *Crazy Woman's* arms and mouth are instantly restrained. She still mumbles incoherent words. Her anger has such an electric charge that Angelina's hair stands on end.

Angelina is quiet impress with the power of this angry self within herself. At the same time, she realizes that *Crazy Woman* is constantly angry, constantly fighting with the world. There's always something wrong that she repels or struggles with. Anything makes her angry. She also has a tiny inkling of something else. While *Crazy Woman* screams, stirring the red hot lava of emotions, there's a frozen core inside her. Angelina is secretly experiencing fear.

For the first time in her life, Angelina considers that this constant irritation is a monumental waste of energy and a cover-up. After all, she is now exhausted, but she is still restrained. In all of *Crazy Woman's* rebellious anger, she has not achieved an inch of freedom.

The fear has not gone away, either. It's simply laden with anger and frustration on top, so that she can't get to it.

A question briefly forms in the back of Angelina's mind.

"What would happen if I could use *Crazy Woman's* power without being trapped in her cynical, negative anger?"

Angelina barely has time to register the question, much less to answer it.

The doors of the train open and a hoard of passengers stampedes into the wagon. The loud noise and violent movement frighten Angelina. Her heart jumps and she shakes inside, but the binding spell keeps her immobile.

The profusion of gray, black and red attires makes the passengers look like an army. They are all somewhat opaque, as if they had lived in the dark for a long time. This gives them a ghostly appearance, though they are solid flesh and bone. In any case, they seem more alive than Angelina, who stands at the center of the wagon, as pale and rigid as a statue.

The doors of the wagon close as suddenly as they opened, and the train speeds again into the dark tunnel.

"Take note," says a tightly-wired woman in her late forties to her secretary, an edgy young woman with twitchy small eyes hidden behind large eyeglasses. Her high, tight bun is sliding like the Tower of Pizza, and she keeps it in place with several pencils used as hair sticks.

"Y...yes, *Ms. Perfecta*," says the nervous woman as she anxiously unfolds a black attaché, extracting a portable computer table from it. As she secures the tiny metal table, her boss taps impatiently with her pointy red high-heel shoes.

Ms. Perfecta is dressed in red business attire. Every inch of her appearance is pressed, neat and perfect. Her short hair is combed back and held with tons of spray and gel, so that not one strand is out of place. Her red, long fingernails are perfectly groomed. Her eyebrows are painted in two perfect semicircles of equal size at exactly the same angle, equidistant from each other. Her lips are drawn into a perfect heart shape and filled with the exact shade of red of the outfit and the nails. The executive attire is elegant and polished. Too polished. It reminds Angelina of those manicured gardens that she hates, where every tree and bush has been shaved into a precise form, until they look like decorations instead of breathing living beings.

"Hurry up, *Ms. Slaveaway*," *Ms. Perfecta* admonishes. "I don't have all day."

Her cell phone rings just then. *Ms. Perfecta* gives it to *Ms. Slaveaway*, who opens it and hands it back to her boss, going back to her assemblage task.

"Hello, *Ms. Controller*," *Ms. Perfecta* greets with a perfectly symmetrical smile. "What am I doing, you ask? Waiting. What else is there to do, with such slow, ineffective employees as we have these days? That's right! Ja-ja-ja! If we were to pay them for the quality of the work, they would not reach minimum wage. Oh, certainly, I agree. Were we to pay them for their speed, then they would have no wage at all."

The laptop is on, and *Ms. Slaveaway* is waiting, her fingers positioned above the tiny keyboard, her pale face barely showing signs of being alive. Her body, however, is slowly crouching on the seat as her boss chats away.

"Yes, I quite agree, *Ms. Controller*. We must keep a tight fist and push. Push hard. That's it. Push, push, push! Time is tide and waits for none. Ja-ja-ja!" says *Ms. Perfecta* with a manicured laughter.

Every time that the boss says, "Push!" the secretary jumps, yet she keeps her fingers ready to type.

Angelina, repulsed by the sight, manages to shift her eyes across the aisle.

A pair of teenagers is rummaging through their shopping bags.

One of the girls, stick-thin and wiry, wears the latest fashion, with several layers of ripped off t-shirts in red, gray and black, lots of bangles and necklaces. She carries a heavy backpack. The other girl, dressed in a gray-lavender simple t-shirt and jeans, is slumping so badly that she looks like a sack instead of a body. She tries to close her eyes, but each time she does, her friend elbows her, and the tired teenager jumps.

Angelina would smile, if she could. These girls remind her of her twin friends, Jackie and Jocelyn, the most opposite twins she has ever seen. Jackie is practical, sporty and pragmatic. Jocelyn is romantic, spiritual and creative. Jackie hates going to the new age activities that Jocelyn loves. She gets bored in art and literary soirees. She wants action! Jocelyn hates going to the sports events that Jackie drags her to. Yet, they love each other and accompany each other to everything.

"Oh-my-god-I-can't-believe-this-is-happening-to-me," screams the first girl, stringing the words so tightly together they all seem one word. She frantically searches in the shopping bag. "You did it again, *Slumber*, you've messed up my shopping."

"What did I do NOW, *Do-Do*?" Slumber asks, opening one eye.

"I-told-you-to-get-a-size-zero. ZERO! And look what you got!" *Do-do* exclaims dramatically. "Now I have to return it. Can't you do anything right? I have to do everything myself, or it never gets done right!"

"But, *Do-do*, I'm so tired! I didn't want to come. I told you I'm exhausted!" *Slumber* complains, as she slides back into sleep. "Besides," she mumbles complacently, "if it's size zero, it does not exist. It is nothing. Why worry about it?"

"You are always tired," *Do-do* says, elbowing her. "You are plain lazy, that's what you are. You-lack-motivation-and-will-power-and-all-you-want-to-do-is-rest. Rest! Rest!" She keeps repeating the word as if the sound of it alone was absurd.

"That's why I always have to do everything. I am the one to plan. The one to think ahead. The one to take charge. The one to do everything and check every single detail. I've got to lead you by the neck!"

Angelina's attempted smile evaporates when she observes what she believed was a punk necklace around *Slumber's* neck.

"Wake up!" *Do-do* snaps, notching a chain in her hand and pulling the dog collar around *Slumber's* neck.

"Pay attention! Do Something!" *Do-do* screams hysterically. "You are driving me mad!"

"And you are driving me dead!" *Slumber* whispers, struggling not to be strangled by the dog collar as her companion yanks it repeatedly.

Angelina averts her eyes. A strong, constricting sensation is climbing up her legs. It is as cold and slimy as a boa slithering its way up her body. She feels dread. These people... these strange passengers.... they are...

"You got a B MINUS!" a mother is saying to Angelina's right. She is waving a report card accusingly at her daughter, who must be around ten years old.

"But, mom, I got all As," the *Disappointing Daughter* protests.

"Not ALL," the *Measuring Mother* corrects. "You got one B...B MINUS. That's almost C."

"But...but...but... I tried..." the *Disappointing Daughter* stutters.

The *Measuring Mother* realizes that Angelina is looking at her and changes her demeanor.

"Of course, I am proud of you," the *Measuring Mother* says delightedly. Angelina gets the impression that she is more proud of acting like a good mother than of her daughter. "Yes, I am very proud of you."

The *Disappointing Daughter* relaxes, a smile emerging on her young face.

"But you could do better," the *Measuring Mother* adds between her teeth. "I just know that you could do so much better."

The *Disappointing Daughter* clenches her jaw and fixes her teary eyes on the floor.

A tear runs down Angelina's frozen face. The feeling of dread is rising. It clutches her stomach. She feels a recognizable panic, the type of shock you get on those dreams where you find yourself walking to school without clothes.

"No, please, no!" a tiny voice pleads.

"I will!" another voice answers sharply.

Angelina seeks the voices, hoping to distance herself from the rising dread.

Three women seat close to each other, fighting over a cell phone. The one trying to dial is a gorgeous blonde who looks like a Hollywood star. She is confident and graceful. The one pleading is obviously related, but could not be more different. She is mousy, and her hair, though blonde, is dry as straw.

"No, *Swan Beauty*, please no!" the mousy woman pleads with her gorgeous relative. "I couldn't bear it!"

"But *Uglyducky," Swan Beauty* tries to reason, "You've done such a good job. We've worked hard. You've worked harder than me, even. How can you say that?"

"She says it because it's the truth," says the third woman, snatching the cellular away from *Swan Beauty*. The woman is so masculine that it is hard to recognize any feminine trait in her, though she has a resemblance with the others. Her body is as square as a block. Her shoulders are tense and puffed up. Her jaw looks harder than cement.

"She is useless, ugly and a fake," *Badger Bully* says.

"Stop it, *Badger Bully*," *Swan Beauty* says. "That's not fair."

"Oh, but it issss," *Badger Bully* hisses with cold pleasure. "She has not done enough. She never does enough. She knows this, and she knows that she does not deserve any reward. None whatsoever."

"You see?" cries *Uglyducky*, shrinking.

"I see that she's bullying you," says *Swan Beauty,* snatching back the cellular. She begins dialing.

"They are not going to give it to me," whines *Uglyducky*. "Perhaps they'll give it to you. You're great. But not to me. I don't want to embarrass you."

"You **are** an embarrassment," barks *Badger Bully*. "You embarrass your family, your friends and your boss. You think you are so knowledgeable, so good at what you do, just 'cause you've done it for a while now? Ja! You're not an expert. You are a fake. And people can spot you a mile away."

"Enough!" *Swan Beauty* roars. "You are good, *Uglyducky*. As good as or better than I, and you work harder than the three of us. Don't listen to *Badger Bully*. She's just jealous, mean and bitter. She takes pleasure on shredding your self-esteem. Don't listen to her. Look at me. Listen to me. We are going to get it, okay?"

There is a moment of silence as *Swan Beauty* dials. At that moment, Angelina realizes that these women are sisters. Identical sisters. I-den-ti-cal. How can this be? She goes from one to the other, from the gorgeous star to the dried-out *Uglyducky* to the bulldog. They couldn't be more different, yet they are physically identical.

"Hello!" *Swan Beauty* begins.

"NO!" *Uglyducky* cries as she snatches the phone and hangs up.

Badger Bully laughs a hard, cold laughter.

Angelina knows these women. She is unable to move, yet her whole body coils inwards as she recognizes where she has seen these strangers.

She knows these feelings well. Being an outcast. Not being enough. Not fitting. Not belonging. Feeling that she never does enough, no matter how hard she works. Doing more and more and still not feeling that she deserves the money or the recognition. Badgering and insulting herself incessantly for her flaws and failures.

These feelings are wrapped around her, like the invisible ropes that bind her now. These feelings are the force that pulls her back when she is at the edge of change, about to leap. The arrow is about to be released, but the bow breaks. It snaps into two.

Angelina hears a cold metallic snap. It's the clipping of her wings.

A woman in an ash-covered apron parades along the aisle. She solicitously fixes the bags and packages that protrude from the passenger's feet. The passengers push her away, holding on to their possessions.

"Don't worry, I'm here for you," she says obsequiously, as she gives the passengers her unrequited assistance.

"We are so good, *Cinder*, so good," says her companion as she takes out a garbage bag, holding it open. "Too good for those ungrateful bastards!"

"Oh, *Victima*, don't say that!" says *Cinder* sweetly as she picks up a package and places it in the garbage bag. "They don't deserve such a filthy train. That's why I'm here; to serve."

The owner of the package takes the package out of the bag, protesting.

"But *Cinder*, it hurts. It just hurts to see them take advantage of us. To think that I could be in Florida right now, enjoying the sun and the beach!" her companion says, while she takes out a duster and hands it to *Cinder*.

"Oh, but you wouldn't feel right, would you?" *Cinder* says as she dusts the seats, the tubes and even the passengers, raising a cloud of dust that makes them sneeze and complain, and bathing herself in dust. "Serving and helping are so much better."

"And God is bound to pay it a thousand fold, right?" *Cinder* says to a woman as she snatches her gold chain. The woman goes after Cindy and takes it back.

"Do you see, *Cinder*?" *Victima* cries dramatically, shaking and grabbing her chest. "Do you SEE, *Cinder*? They do not appreciate what we do for them. We sacrifice our best years, we give them all we have, and for what? They cannot even say thanks, the ungrateful lot!"

"But I won't let them down! Poor you! It must be depressing to travel in such an uncomfortable train," *Cinder* says as *Victima* offers her a cushion that she tries to place beneath a passenger's butt. The woman slaps her hands away.

"Damn inconsiderate of them!" froths *Victima*. "What a hard life we have, such sacrifices, for nothing. Damn you! Damn all of you!"

Victima stands up and attacks the passengers. *Cinder* takes a large syringe and injects her companion, who falls into a comma.

Cinder moves closer to Angelina and starts laughing in tiny bursts `as she dusts her hysterically. Angelina is showered with ashes. The gray cloud of dust spreads like a fog all around her.

Angelina's vision blurs. The people in the wagon seem liquid now. Angelina tries to recover her normal sight, but more ashes fall in her eyelashes, blinding her temporarily.

She struggles to see, but the liquefied passengers seem to float slowly and heavily along the aisle, like a miasma. They are formless, except for some distinguishing features —a face here, an arm there. Their voices are a but a far away echo.

"This can't be right," Angelina manages to think.

But a shower of ashes falls over her body, choking her. She opens her mouth to sneeze. Instead of a sneeze coming out of her mouth, the liquefied passengers are sucked into it, one by one, in slow motion.

CHAPTER 7

The Shadow Bundle

Angelina gasps for air. But another ashy wave drags two liquefied passengers into her mouth.

"Let me out!" cries *Victima*, clutching Angelina's heart as she is sucked into Angelina. "I don't deserve to be treated like this; after all I've done for you!"

A dark wind drags *Victima* through the dry brambles surrounding the ruins of an abandoned fortress.

"Ay! It hurts!" *Victima* cries as the thorns stick to her body.

As Angelina faces the dark gray fortress, she feels something cold and hard climbing up her back. Shivering, she hugs herself, as if gathering her loosely held fragments.

She takes one step away from the fortress. The thing sliding through her back digs in deeper. She takes another step, and then another. But the farther she moves from the fortress, the deeper the heaviness of the dilapidated structure creeps into her bones.

She can feel the fortress' hermetic defenses in her upper back and shoulders. It is as if this fortress in front of her was a place inside her.

A refuge or a prison?

Angelina has no time to examine the bastion.

Victima's wails are growing stronger and closer.

"I don't deserve thiiiiis...."

"After all I've doooone for you..."

"Ay, ay, ay!"

Angelina's eyes search for the source of the unnerving wails and find it in the brambles.

Victima's body is completely pierced by thorns. Thrashing about the brambles desperately, she looks like a porcupine fish dragged by turbulent waters.

A strong gale catches *Victima* and folds her thorn-ridden body into a bundle. The wind blows the bundle towards Angelina.

Dangerous or not, the fortress is the only structure that can shelter Angelina from the lethal weapon *Victima* has become. She runs up the stone stairs.

Just as Angelina crosses the entrance, hoping to close the heavy door behind her, the *Victima* bundle latches on to her back.

The weight is so heavy that Angelina falls to the floor. Her shoulders drop down and forward, bent by the weight. Why is this bundle so heavy? It weights like a whole town!

Angelina struggles with the bundle, trying to take it off, but the thorns cut into her. If feels as if someone had back-stabbed her, cutting a rift right through the middle of her upper back; and the blade was now lodged in the back of her heart.

Angelina gets up with great effort. Crouching with pain, she forces herself to move. There's light coming from an archway and she blindly runs towards it.

"I don't deserve this...."

"After all I've done for you..."

Victima's wails are now on her back. But it's no longer just one voice. The wail is growing louder with the lament of hundreds, perhaps thousands of women.

Angelina runs, maddened by these heart-breaking voices.

She can discern Mercedes' voice. It's familiar enough. Her mother must have said this same phrase a thousand times at least. But there are other voices.

"After all my sacrifices...."

"This is how you pay me..."

Their drone pierces Angelina's heart, like a merciless swarm of killer wasps, as she runs down a corridor.

"To think that I renounced my happiness for you..."

"I could have been great..."

"I gave up my dreams for you..."

The voices creep through her back and out of the ruins.

They are old voices, women's voices. She has never heard these voices before. Yet they are familiar, so familiar that they bleed inside Angelina's bones.

And then, among all the voices, her own.

"I am tired of you pushing me around, big brother. Ever since Pop died, you think you are my boss. Get off your high horse," Angelina is saying.

"You shouldn't disappear like that, Angelina. It breaks mom's heart," Bill insists.

"Yeah, well, she breaks mine every time she opens her mouth, and I am sick and tired of it," Angelina replies. "And who are you to judge me? Have you ever helped me? Where have you been when I needed support? I've been alone since Pop died and I can manage well enough!"

The memory slashes like a knife. Angelina wants to escape. That's not how it happened. That's not true. Bill was blaming her, not the other way around.

She runs through a dusty corridor. She runs as fast as she can. Faster. Faster. But no matter how fast she runs, *Victima's* voice screams in her ear. Clouds of dust curl up, like dust devils, along the sides of the ghostly hall.

"Why me?"

"You did this to me!"

"YOU DID THIS TO MEEE!!"

Cinder is coming up the other end of the hall, a broom in her hand and a to-do list in her lips, like a litany.

She sweeps the dust along with *Victima's* screams and the wails of the women.

"So much to do..."

"Ay! It hurts!"

"There's no time..."

"The work never ends."

"I could have..."

"I'm way behind schedule."

"No time for me..."

"Ay! Ay! Ay!"

"I have no time..."

"For my dreams..."

"I cannot ... should not..."

"How selfish of me..."

Cinder's whispers mingle with *Victima's* screams and the women's wails, bouncing against the walls of the corridor.

"I'm here for you!"

"I can do so much for you!"

"I love you soo much!"

"More than I love myself."

"I'm here to serve you."

"At my expense."

"Ay! Ay! Ay!"

Angelina's running too fast. *Cinder* is on the way. But Angelina can't stop running. She sees *Cinder*. She's closer and closer to *Cinder*, but she can't stop herself.

Cinder walks through Angelina. A heavy bundle of guilt, shame and worry falls into Angelina's heart, merging with *Victima's* bundle. Her heart sinks down into a well of neglect.

She can't breathe! Angelina falls to the ground right at the end of the hall.

She drags herself through the threshold into a large room. She tries to breathe again, but a new wave of ashy shadows drifts into her mouth, choking her.

Angelina coughs desperately.

"Get a life, lady!" barks *Badger Bully*, jumping into a suit of armors nearby and picking up a double-edge axe from the wall. "I'm going to teach you some manners."

"No! I did my best, please!" cries a thin voice from behind a toppled wooden table. It's *Uglyducky*.

Angelina's heart is weary. She is terrified. Yet, her shoulders feel as hard as the armor and her eyes have turned into small, cold and hateful circles of hatred.

"See what you did, you good-for nothing!" *Badger Bully* screams at *Uglyducky*.

"I'm sorry! It's all my fault!" *Uglyducky* cries. "I'm so sorry. I tried. I really tried. But it's no good."

"That's what I said, that you are good for nothing," *Badger Bully* growls. "Don't repeat my words, you imbecile. That infuriates me!"

Angelina looks at *Badger Bully*. She is disgusted with this bully, yet she can feel the bully's cold fury taking a hold of her.

Then she hears *Uglyducky's* cries, and she is thrown into an ocean of pain. *Uglyducky's* pain washes over her. Large waves of abandonment and despair engulf her. She tries to fight back, only to feel a compelling pull take hold of her.

As the pull gets stronger inside Angelina, *Badger Bully* advances. She raises the axe above *Uglyducky*, who cowers, backing towards the corner.

Angelina grabs the axe and yanks it out of *Badger Bully's* hands. *Uglyducky* and *Badger Bully* disappear.

"I know this war," Angelina thinks somewhere in the back of her mind. Painful memories gush out again.

"I won't go!" Angelina argues.

"But we'll have fun," Omar says, pulling her towards him by the arms.

He doesn't understand. It hurts too much. Now that she's not writing. Now that she's working in this boring job, it hurts too much to be among others, hear their poems, and feel empty handed.

Omar keeps trying to entice her, but she can no longer hear him. A harsh, cold voice inside is badgering her.

> *"You were not meant for greatness. Stop faking, lady. You've done well to get a normal job and settle. If this man wants to play with his crayons all his life, that's his problem. As for you, grow up."*

"But I want to create. I love to write. I love poetry. Please let me go. I'll sit quietly in a corner," a soft, tiny part of her implores.

"What for? To see those mediocre writers declaiming their entrails, vomiting their feelings onto anyone who'll listen. As if your presence would even be noticed in that sea of narcissists. Go to bed. You've got real work in the morning," the bully commands.

"But I'm miserable..." her heart laments.

"You are not going. Period!" the bully triumphs.

"Cut it out!" Angelina barks at Omar. "I won't go, and that's that. You can go, but don't drag me into it."

She watches Omar pick up his stuff and leave while a part of her crawls into a tiny ball inside.

Angelina wiggles in pain, trying to shake off the memory.

She had thought that she was going mad, hearing voices, having people fighting inside her.

And now madness has taken full possession of her. This is her ride to the madhouse!

A dense, dark fog penetrates the room. It carries heinous whispers, full of dread and mockery. Angelina escapes through a corridor and flies down narrow stairs. She swings open an old gate and enters, shutting it behind her.

The loud clank of the iron gate slams against the still darkness ahead.

She hears a whimper somewhere. Something stirs inside her.

Angelina blindly probes the darkness in front of her, still coughing and squirming. Her shoulders and her heart are heavy with the weight of the bundle.

She is so tired. She wants to drop down and give up. She yearns to stop running, fighting, struggling. But the cold stone floor below is as uninviting as the darkness.

The whimper faintly rises again. Angelina stretches her hand and feels the wall as she pricks her ears, focusing all her senses towards the direction of the whimper.

The stone wall is cold and humid. As she feels her way along the stone wall, her bones begin to ache. Her pelvis and lower back constrict. Her knees hurt.

"I got to..."

"I just got to..."

The whimper is now audible.

Angelina turns towards the voice and sees a sliver of light. She carefully walks towards it, feeling the way ahead with each foot before taking each step. The wall comes to an edge, then turns. The words become clear as she follows the wall in the direction of the light.

"I got to do it better. I got to... I got to do more," murmurs a young female voice.

Angelina recognizes the voice. It's *Ms. Slaveaway.*

"Oh, please, don't trap me here. Don't sink me into oblivion," Ms. Slaveaway pleads as she struggles with thick iron chains binding her to a desk.

A sniveling *Ms. Slaveaway,* bent over a keyboard, types away. The screen frantically repeats two words.

"DO MORE. DO MORE. DO MORE. DO MORE."

The prison is covered in paper. Curled, crushed, crinkled and old to-do lists lie around the floor. Calendars, outlines and more to-do lists plaster the walls. A thin rectangular opening up on the high ceiling lets a sliver of light in.

"Give me another chance. I'll do more. I'll do better!" *Ms. Slaveaway's* cries. Her cry is echoed by another cry as more memories wash over Angelina.

"It's good, really good," Jocelyn is saying. "You got to believe me."

"You are my friend, Jocelyn, you would love what I write even if it sucks," Angelina smiled.

"No, I would not!" Jocelyn says angrily. "Have I ever told you a lie?"

"No, but you can dress up Jack Nicholson to look like Jlo," Jackie laughs.

"The point is not whether Jocelyn likes it or approves it," Jackie tells her. "The question is if you do. And judging by your attitude, you don't like what you do."

"Frankly," Angelina says in a nasal, petulant voice. "I could do better. It's not bad, and audiences like it. But it's not..."

"Perfect?" Jocelyn ends.

"Not..."

"Better than Byron," Jackie ends.

"You've read Byron?" they both say in unison.

"No, but you guys are always raving about him, so I thought..." Jackie says. "Never mind. To tell you the truth, I don't like poetry that much."

"You see?" Angelina says.

"But I like yours," Jackie confesses, hitting her chest. "It's real, buddy. It gets me here!"

She still did not believe her friends. She never believes those who praise her. But she always believes those who put her down. Why?

Her throat is on fire. Angelina grabs her throat. She feels the cold, rusty prison bars in her hands.

She tries to talk, but her mouth is so dry, and she doesn't know what to say.

"Ooout!" she manages to moan.

The rusty prison bars open with a ringing groan.

But *Ms. Slaveaway* cowers into the darkness.

"Oh, please, give me another chance. I'll do more. I'll do better!"

The cold wind blows again, rushing into the dungeon, carrying a multitude of moaning voices.

Angelina runs, but the wind catches her in a whirlpool, dragging her into further darkness.

"Oh-my-god-what-am-I-going-to-do-with-you?" screams *Do-do.* She is pulling Angelina frenetically by the neck. Angelina struggles with the dog collar.

"It's your entire fault, for being so lazy. Wake up! Do something!" *Do-do* screams hysterically.

"I am ex-haus-ted," murmurs Angelina, trying to take off the dog collar. In her desperation, she is beginning to strangle herself.

She would give anything to fall, to faint, to fade away. But the wind picks up again, dragging her further into the dungeon.

A grating sound alerts her. She turns just in time to see the spinning wheels. They crisscross the darkness ahead, their razor-sharp edges shining against the darkness.

"Swash!"

The chain in her dog collar is broken by the first spinning wheel. Angelina pulls back. She is frantically unlocking the collar when she feels the air around her whooshing.

Her body responds instinctively, dodging under the second wheel. Angelina catches a glimmer of a face reflected in the shiny razor. It's the mother she saw in the wagon.

"You can do better than that," the *Measuring Mother* says with a smug smile as the razor crosses inches from Angelina's chest.

Angelina is thrown off balance and swaggers between this blade and the next; barely catching her balance to escape the third wheel. This one suddenly shots out from the left, almost cutting through her waist.

"Come on, Angelina, you can control this madness. I know you can," The *Measuring Mother* cajoles.

"But... but..." Angelina says. Her voice is muted by a girl's plea.

"But...I don't know how!" the *Disappointing Daughter* is saying.

Angelina bends down to hug the girl and a wheel crosses inches from her head, slicing a couple of hairs.

"You are so damn incompetent!" snarls *Ms. Perfecta* from the other side of the darkness. "Here, let me do it."

She marches in a straight line through the wheels.

"Use your head, you useless fool!" she screams. One wheel beheads her.

But *Ms. Perfecta* keeps marching and her head keeps talking from the floor.

The *Disappointing Daughter* is screaming, terrified.

"One: stay focused. Two: cut-off any distractions. Three: keep moving forward," *Ms. Perfecta* drills.

Another blade cuts her in half by the waist. The upper part lands perfectly on the floor and keeps swinging its arms while the lower part keeps marching. The head, now rolling, keeps yapping.

"Shut up!" Angelina screams at the top of her lungs.

There is a momentary silence. Only the swooshing of the blades is heard. Angelina exhales.

"There, that's how it's done, you nincompoop," says *Ms. Perfecta* as her head rolls, landing on her own feet; her torso having reached Angelina. "Show them who's the boss."

The *Disappointing Daughter* is screaming hysterically. Angelina hugs her.

Suddenly several things happen at once.

The oscillating wheels are substituted by a crude white light from a large lamp swinging from the ceiling.

They are at the center of a huge, bare room with high walls. The lamp swings away, leaving them in darkness again.

Rack-track-crack-track-rack.

Angelina's hair stands on end.

The lamp swings forth.

The blood splattered across the walls tells the other half of the story. The first half her instincts recognized immediately in the metallic sound: a battalion loading their rifles.

The lamp swings away.

Angelina hugs the *Disappointing Daughter* and covers her eyes. She wants to close her own eyes, but her curiosity is stronger than her fear. Last she knew she was in a train. What is this place? Are they really going to die? She both wants and dreads the answer.

But no answer is coming. Only the reckless pounding of her heart breaks the endless seconds of darkness.

The lamp swings forth again.

They are surrounded by firing squads in all flanks. The soldiers are in shadows. Or perhaps they **are** *Shadows*. But the weapons are visible. Angelina can see the barrel of dozens of rifles pointing at them.

The *Disappointing Daughter* buries her head in Angelina's chest.

"Ready?" Says *Perfecta's* head. "Fire!"

> *I'll show you who's the nincompoop, you frigid bi...I want my mami!... Shut up and grow up!... I want to get out of here.... Oh, why is this happening to me, when I am so giving...? Get the hell out of my face, you blood-sucking righteous vampire!... What's wrong with me? Why can't I do anything right?... After all I've done for you...There's nothing I wouldn't do for you...I'll do more. I'll keep trying...You are nobody, piss off!...*

The voices blast out all at once, piercing Angelina's body. Fragments of memories, beliefs, thoughts and judgments penetrate her heart, solar plexus and womb; her left thigh, her right leg, her right shoulder, her left arm.

Each voice carries a different feeling that bleeds through her being. Anger, terror and sadness collide inside her guts, swelling up, whirling inside her.

Angelina's insides explode in a mass of hot lava that binds with the smoke from the rifles creating chaos.

She is lost. Lost inside herself.

In the empty wagon, Angelina convulses.

"Feel the warmth at the center," a voice whispers.

A fresh breeze carries this gentle, firm voice through the upper windows into the firing room.

Angelina opens her eyes. With great effort, she seeks the voice.

Dragonfly Diva's piercing eyes are beaming at her from the upper windows. She seems gigantic!

Her wings flutter strongly, sweeping away the smoke. Angelina collapses.

She wakes up inside the fog. The voices are now all around her, a screaming jumble. Angelina cowers away, her body compressed into a tiny lump.

"Look at me," Dragonfly Diva whispers.

Angelina seeks the soothing voice, opening her teary eyes.

The fortress is down below. She is now in a forest. But there is such a dense fog she can barely see the shadows of trees.

"Look at me," Dragonfly Diva repeats, and two tiny dragonflies shimmer in the darkness, landing on Angelina's chest.

A warm light spreads through her chest and warms up her heart and her entire body.

"Move towards the center," Dragonfly Diva whispers.

Angelina feels that her arms are two invisible antennae tentatively probing in the fog, seeking the warmth.

She has barely given three steps when the ghosts assault her, each trying to claim her. Angelina runs, the voices following her, one screaming louder than the other. The fog gets denser and colder.

There's a rustling of leaves somewhere to her right. She hears a faint whisper.

"Who's out there?" Angelina asks.

"*Shadows*," Dragonfly Diva replies, her voice echoing around Angelina. "They are *Shadows*."

Angelina stays still and quiet. The dark gray blanket folds around her as the whisper trails away. A sense of utter abandonment and despair clutches her heart.

"*Shadows*?" Angelina whispers. "Are they ghosts?"

"You could say that," Dragonfly Diva says. "*Shadows* are the ghosts of fears and defenses from your past that have refused to die."

"Ghosts of that which has NOT died," Angelina repeats as she probes inside the fog.

She hears footsteps to her left. Several people are running. Angelina opens her pores and ears to sense what she cannot see.

"Who's out there?" Angelina asks again, feeling a sense of frightful urgency.

"What's going on?"

The steps rush away. She can hear the people panting as they run.

Should she follow the steps? They seem to know where they are going. At least they know what they are running away from. That thought is charged with unbearable fear. Angelina wants to run.

Just when Angelina starts on their direction, a ghostly shadow crosses her path, living a trail of cold, shivering fear.

"What am I doing here? Where am I?" Angelina asks herself as she stretches her hand into the dry, ashy fog. "How did I get here? Where am I going? Why am I following... what am I following?"

"*Shadows* are fear-based defenses that you have inherited during your *Domestication Trance,* Angelina," Dragonfly Diva says forcefully. She speaks as if Angelina was very far away. Her voice is both soothing and commanding. "Don't be scared of them. They are emotional memories. Just old balloons floating in your mind."

"I swallowed them," Angelina cries.

"They can't harm you," Dragonfly Diva whispers. "They are disembodied parts of you that live in the past."

"They want to take over," Angelina howls, as ghostly arms pierce the fog and grab her. "Get away from me!"

"Seek the warm center," Dragonfly Diva orders. "Release those memories."

"They won't release me!" Angelina screams as a violent earthquake shakes the darkness.

In the wagon, Angelina is climbing over the seats, running away from an invisible foe.

"Aaaancestraaaal Heaaaart!" Dragonfly Diva sings out in the note of FA.

A lake of soothing blue energy materializes around Angelina. It vibrates in peaceful harmonies. The blue melody cradles Angelina, like a hammock, bringing her down into the old woman's arms.

"You are real," Dragonfly Diva says, placing her hand on Angelina's heart.

"I am real," Angelina repeats, breathing into her heart.

"These beings are very small parts of you," Dragonfly Diva says.

"Small parts..." Angelina repeats, a bit calmer.

A soothing breeze is blowing in the forest. The dense clouds are moving away.

"Small parts, tiny ashes that the wind sweeps away," Dragonfly Diva says. "You are larger than all of them. You are the real one."

"Tiny ashes... sweeps away..." Angelina repeats as the breeze caresses her face. The darkness is lifting. She walks forward.

"*Detach*. That's it, Angelina. You are now *detached* from the *Shadows*." Dragonfly Diva says, "Keep walking towards the warmth."

"It's too heavy," Angelina complains as she stumbles and falls. "It's too heavy."

She tries to take off the bundle on her back, but it has grown heavier.

"That's your *Shadow Bundle,"* Dragonfly Diva whispers. "Release it."

"I can't!" Angelina cries as she tries to drop the bundle from her back. The women's pleas rise again. They are barely a whisper that could be confused with the rustling of the wind. But Angelina freezes, afraid to awaken *Victima* and the others.

"Remember who you love," Dragonfly Diva whispers.

Omar's face glistens in the dark. Angelina loves his big, warm smile.

The grass is shimmering!

Thousands of dragonflies shimmer among the thin blades of grass, humming a subtle song of joy and harmony in the cool breeze.

"Remember what you love," Dragonfly Diva whispers.

Angelina remembers the last poem she wrote.

Tree Perches on Earth.
Bird perches on tree.
My eyes perch on bird.
Poetry perches on my eyes.
Spirit perches on poetry.
Earth holds Spirit
through this poem.

The dragonflies surround Angelina, perching on her back. The bundle dissolves and the heaviness lifts away. Angelina's heart is flooded with healing light.

The fog is lifting away. Angelina sees that a fire glows in the distance. She moves towards the glow.

Dark silhouettes shuffle in the darkness. One bumps into her.

"Oh no!" the *Shadow* whispers anxiously, moving out of the way.

"Steady, girl!" Dragonfly Diva cautions. "Keep walking. *Detach* from the *Shadows*. They are the specters of learned behaviors left to trail inside your own psyche, wondering like ghosts, reproducing the past over and over, until you release them. They are an inheritance that you need to get rid of, Angelina, a *Shadow Inheritance*."

Angelina takes a trembling step ahead. There are murmurs around her, but no one attacks her. She takes another step.

Black blotches of vapor scratch her face as she walks into the trees.

"Go back! Go back!" tiny voices screech. They seem to be coming from inside the black billows flowing through her. The abrasive vapors run across her body, pushed by a strong wind that howls like a hungry wolf.

"What if... what if... what if?" the tiny voices in the haze cry in high echoes that recede as the black clouds move away.

Angelina is now walking steadily.

The howling wind whisks the fog away.

"Seek the clearance," Dragonfly Diva says, and two tiny dragonflies fly ahead, showing the way.

Angelina feels a strong clearance in her chest. She breathes deeply, enjoying the aromas of bark, leaves and humid soil.

"Seek the *Throne of the Ancestral Heart*, Angelina. A tree trunk. At the center. Seek the warmth. Feel the roots connecting you to Earth. Walk to it. Keep all your focus on it. *Detach* from the *Shadows*. Don't pay attention to anything they say."

As she walks towards the clearance in the forest, Angelina feels the woody, warm emanation and the presence of Tree.

The ghosts are howling now, but their voices are fading behind her.

Angelina walks into the clearance. A giant tree stands in the center. Its deep roots protrude around the trunk. Its massive trunk shoots up to the sky, bursting in a celebration of bird songs and shimmering leaves against the stars.

As Angelina steps into the clearance she feels a strong, silent center inside her heart.

Untouched by all the commotion around it, there stands the throne.

"Seat on the *Throne of you Ancestral Heart*," whispers Dragonfly Diva.

In the center of the trunk, a heart-shaped throne pulsates gently, beckoning.

Angelina seats on the throne. She feels safe and loved. She is home.

> *Silence breathes. Deeply. Slowly. Being. Now. The fragrance of Earth in her nostrils. Emptiness. Peace spreads like soft clouds. Light inside the darkness. The world breathes. Every creature breathes at once. She breathes with them. One long breath. She is still and she is dancing with the world. Alone. All one.*

In the wagon, Angelina opens her eyes and stares into the glowing eyes of Dragonfly Diva.

Part 2

The Rescue Zone

"'My heart is afraid that it will have to suffer,' the boy told the alchemist one night as they looked up at the moonless sky.

'Tell your heart that the fear of suffering is worse than the suffering itself. And that no heart has ever suffered when it goes in search of its dreams, because every second of the search is a second's encounter with God and with eternity.'"

—The Alchemist
Paulo Coelho

CHAPTER 8

Dreamboro Plaza

Trak-trak-trak.

Red. Orange. Yellow. Green. Blotches of color.

Trak-trak-trak.

"Are you well?" a voice asks.

Angelina lifts her heavy lids. Two glowing amber eyes examine hers.

She slowly looks around. The wagon is empty. The train speeds steadily forward. Color beams cross its flanks intermittently, like search lights. What are they searching?

Red. Orange. Yellow. Green.

A fleeting image. Another sign? Perhaps.

The Rescue Zone

Yes. That's what it said, though it was gone so fast. Angelina blacks out.

Trak-trak-trak.

"I saw it!" Angelina screams, eyes wide open. She grabs Dragonfly Diva's arm intensely.

"Saw what?" Dragonfly Diva asks soothingly, as she massages Angelina's back and shoulders. Angelina relaxes and releases the lady's arm.

"The trance, the inheritance, everything," Angelina reveals.

"Do you feel lighter?" Dragonfly Diva asks.

"Lighter? Are you mad?" Angelina snaps.

"I take the answer is no," Dragonfly Diva smiles.

"This *Shadow Inheritance* weighs a ton on my shoulders," Angelina says heavily. 'It's been like that ever since I was an adolescent. I just didn't remember it. But now I saw it. It's been like a dark cloud hanging over me."

"That's good!" Dragonfly Diva remarks.

"Good? What are you, a sadist?" Angelina barks.

"Good that you are seeing it," Dragonfly Diva laughs.

"I see it alright," Angelina says, frustration mounting on her voice. "I see that I don't see. This inheritance is a fog. It clouds my eyes. I can't see where I am heading. Sometimes I can't even see where I am standing. There's someone in me that knows there is more, who can intuit that there are better things, different ways of doing things; better ways of living. But this bundle of *Shadows* constantly screams their repetitive beliefs. I am carrying the ashes of thousands of dead aunts and uncles, dead illusions or dreams, layers of ghosts sticking to my pores, my dress, my breath. I never walk alone. Never! Yet, I feel utterly alone."

"Why?" Dragonfly Diva asks.

"The fog doesn't let me see those around me," Angelina surmises. "My friends say that I never ask for help. Some say that I clamp up when I have problems. I avoid them and become a hermit. But it's the fog. When it falls, then I am walking with all those *Shadows*. There's a war inside me, and there's no energy left in me for anyone else. It's raining ashes inside, and I can't see my way out."

"You could reach out," Dragonfly Diva whispers. "There's always a helping hand."

"I am terrified," Angelina says. She is just recognizing the feeling as she speaks.

"Of what?" Dragonfly Diva inquires.

"If...if I reach out... if I stretch out my hand... and hope," Angelina says in the thinnest thread of voice, "and there's no one. If no one comes. If no one takes my hand, then that's horrible. Horrible!"

"Why?" Dragonfly Diva asks.

"Because then I'll know... not just fear... not just suspect, but know with all certainty, that I am alone. That there's no one. No help."

"These voices have been within you for a long time," Dragonfly Diva observes. "Releasing them feels as if you were leaving your family, your kin. It is as scary as leaving behind your entire life, your home, all your possessions and belongings, everything that you've hold on to for years... and walking into a desert where you are all alone. You walk into that strange desert not knowing if there's anything out there."

"Yes, they've been with me a long time," Angelina echoes. "They're like family, but..."

"Not a real family," Dragonfly Diva finishes, hugging Angelina. "Not a nest to rest. Not a warm fire waiting. Not an embrace."

Tears are falling down Angelina's cheeks. Trying to hide them, she stands up and looks out of the window into the rolling darkness.

"No warmth. No life left in them," she echoes sadly. "They are just ghosts that haunt me."

A light suddenly illuminates Angelina's face. She is sad, but for the first time since she began the ride, for the first time perhaps in a long, long time, her voice sounds like her own voice. She is no longer pretending.

"They haunt me every moment of my life," Angelina admits. "And there are more. Dozens more. They shame me. Taunt me. Mock me. Make me feel inadequate. They make me a slave to their fears, and I keep doing more every day. But at the end of each day, I don't feel... I NEVER feel that I've done enough."

"They steal my time!" Angelina exclaims, turning to face Dragonfly Diva.

"You mean to tell me that they are not keeping your punctuality?" Dragonfly Diva asks, an ironic smile playing in her lips.

"That's what I thought!" Angelina yelps. "But today I saw their trick. They do not allow me to enjoy time. They do not allow me to be present, to fully feel the moment. They do not allow me to be touched by life and to touch life. I am never at rest. I am always forging ahead. I am so tired of running!"

Trak-trak-trak.

Trak-trak-trak.

Trak-trak-trak.

As the train forges ahead, a clear realization illuminates Angelina. This is the ride of her life. The crazy ride she's given herself. The non-stop, always-next, never-now, always-push-never-rest, don't-get-off-in-any-stop-because-you-may miss-the-next, don't-trust-any-open-door ride she's been living for years.

The train swiftly comes to a halt. Like a living beast, it gives a big huff and plops its large metal body upon the tracks, opening its doors as it hisses.

"It...it's dark out there," Angelina stutters. "I am afraid of..."

"Of the dark?" Dragonfly finishes for her. "I know."

"How did you know?" Angelina asks.

"You are afraid of yourself," Dragonfly Diva whispers as her beautiful wings stir, sending off sparkles into the darkness.

"Do I have to walk out there?" Angelina asks.

"No," Dragonfly Diva replies. "Now you have *Free-choice*."

And without further words, she flies into the darkness and disappears.

Angelina clutches her bag tightly as she cautiously dips one foot into the darkness and sees it disappear.

The only thought that crosses her mind as her body follows her foot into the darkness is the image of the woman in Omar's painting.

The minute Angelina's foot pierces the darkness and finds solid ground, the train releases a loud sigh of relief and dissolves.

The darkness swallows Angelina.

"Diva...Dragonfly Diva, where are you?" Angelina calls out in a tiny voice.

But the lady is gone, like the train. Angelina stands alone in utter blackness. A deafening silence climbs on her back. Angelina does not dare to break this perfect blackness. Has she stepped out of time and space? Out of reality? In the utter darkness there is no up or down. She is floating in a vast, empty cosmos. She is overwhelmed by a feeling of unbounded freedom, followed by a huge wave of terror.

"I am lost," she thinks. Even this thought intrudes in the seamless, silent darkness.

She stretches her hand in front of her face. At least she thinks she is doing this, but she cannot tell. If her hand is there, it has been swallowed by darkness. She begins to feel that she has no hands, no body.

“Help,” Angelina whimpers in a thread-bare whisper. “Dragonfly Diva, please help me.”

A tiny light emerges in the darkness ahead. Angelina follows it without a question. She orders herself to stop thinking. She commands any doubt to stay behind. There is no doubt in her steps now, though she takes each step slowly, consciously. All her senses are heightened.

“Where am I?” Angelina asks.

“Where do you want to be?” Dragonfly Diva speaks from within the silence.

“I... I don’t know,” Angelina whispers.

“Yes, you do,” Dragonfly Diva murmurs in the black velvety ripples that form around Angelina as she walks. “You just don’t remember.”

“Help me,” Angelina asks. “Help me remember.”

The tiny light grows slowly. Tiny sparkles fly out and dart towards Angelina, piercing her eyes, ears and mouth; then her heart. Angelina is falling.

Is she falling or flying?

She floats by a set of tall French windows, and is suspended below their arches. The pastel rays of dawn pierce the glass, bathing the large room inside in rainbow hues. The room has high ceilings and a fireplace embedded in the wall opposite the windows. There are hundreds of books behind the glass doors of bookshelves that rise to the ceiling. A mezzanine is also bordered by bookshelves. Beautiful paintings and sculptures add magnificence to the large room. To the left of the French windows, a huge antique wooden desk stands like a guardian, adorned by half a dozen red roses and a dozen books pressed between two wooden elephants.

As Angelina descends, she looks around.

She now stands on a green lawn, a glowing dawn behind her. Palm trees frame the arched windows of a mansion with pink stucco walls. A woman dances into the room.

The woman laughs as she opens the French windows and steps out. Angelina almost falls back as she sees herself in a beautiful magenta sarong, turquoise silk pants and a long scarf with big fuchsias printed along its soft length. She dances joyfully as she enters the garden.

Her hair is longer and wilder, as it gets when she's close to the ocean. Her eyes shine against the sunrise in hazel green hues that sparkle as she laughs. Her skin glows with the radiance of rest, pampering and happiness. This Angelina walks with a strong, graceful step towards a large, round water fountain in the middle of the garden.

The garden is designed as a beautiful mandala of flowers. Around the fountain roses of all colors blossom, along chrysanthemums and irises, tiger lilies and sunflowers. There is a hammock at one side of the water fountain, hung between two palm trees.

The other Angelina walks to the fountain and sits at its edge. A flock of birds swoons by and she laughs, closing her eyes. Angelina feels her body overwhelmed by the joy of dozens of birds singing from the surrounding trees.

The other Angelina walks to a desk under a majestic ancient willow. She gently moves aside the hanging branches that form a curtain, and enters the circle beneath the willow. She slowly caresses the bright ceramic tile top sitting on four cast iron legs.

Taking out a cloth from a basket, she cleans the dust from the tiles. She then fetches a binder, some folders, several stones and pens out of the whicker basket. She places the folders on the desk, a stone on top of each one.

Now she sits on a regal rattan chair. She places the binder on the ceramic top, opening it on a blank page. Taking a deep breath, she begins to write. The scribbling of the pen against the paper summons Angelina to this other self. Hiding, she comes closer to gaze upon her face.

There is such concentration in this Angelina's eyes, that they irradiate a fierce, precise arrow of energy. Angelina follows that arrow to its source.

Her heart is pierced and plied open. She is inside each scratch and tilt of the pen, flowing in a river of ink, drinking life as it falls into the white paper.

Dragonfly in the Night
An Invitation

You are a dragonfly flying through the vast night.
Your Soul illuminates your Presence as you cross the dark spaces.
Your tiny light shines as potently as the greatest star
in the deepest pools of darkness.

Your tiny light is capable of guiding the lost travelers.
Its delicate shimmer can lift the weight of despair from the crushed wings of fallen Souls.
There are wounds not even love can heal.

Yet, Soul can open a luminous, empty space where life can sprout out of the gravest cracks.

See the trail of light
in your words and in your silence.
Allow the shimmering fairies of your kindness to sprinkle their magic dust
over the loneliness of each Soul
that crosses your path.

Awaken the Angels in your luminescence.

There is no darkness you cannot cross
when your light glows from within you
and your Soul soars.

Some say that the Soul weights only 21 grams
and most agree that it is not measurable.
Yet it holds a potent lighthouse
that can bring the ships of the heart
safely into harbor.

Know this as you cross the darkness
—even your own unfathomable darkness: your Soul is the light
that brings you back home.

But do not look for that light out there.
You will search in vain for it
across the shroud of night
or beyond the fog
that clouds your vision.

Look inward.
Listen to the Ancestral Heart
that drums its steady rhythm
in your core.
The dreams of the Ancient Trees
run deep through the roots of your Soul.
Dive within.
Silently, make a place for Soul.
Its hidden light will emerge
from the murky corners of your forgetfulness.

Take off the Veil of Doubt, the Veil of Fear.
Rip apart the Veils of Guilt and Shame.
Let them drop away as your naked light rises and grows,
engulfing the darkness that seemed to swallow you.
Do not fear the darkness.
The darkness is there for you,
as the night is there for the star,
or the dark earth is there for the waters.
An invitation.

Angelina Semidey

As the other Angelina signs her name, Angelina feels a tremor. She hears a rustling of papers. The wind has caught the papers and they are spiraling out of the other Angelina's hands.

Off she goes, rising higher and higher, flying away in the spiraling wind.

Words and phrases sway and bump into each other as the papers flutter in the breeze. Angelina tumbles from one word to the other. She plummets from one feeling into the other as the poem flies away.

This is what she has always feared. It is healing to pour her feelings into paper. It is a catharsis. But if those papers were to escape her hands, to reach God knows who, God knows where...

She hears a roar. Is it the wind? No. It's a mechanical roar. She is being X-rayed.

Each of her feelings is being captured in its inner-most truth. Now she is being photographed. Now she is tumbling and falling into thousands of papers, all her feelings bleeding into the sheets. She feels about to faint from this massive hemorrhage.

Now she is embedded in these papers. Her temporary feelings forever carved in stone.

Unchanging.

Unerasable.

Fixed and unfixable.

Her wounds, her fears, her every weakness is being broadcasted into eternity.

Now she is distributed and sold to hundreds. Then thousands. Then millions. She feels all those eyes on her and wants to disappear, but she cannot. She is trapped in those congealed words.

And then it happens.

She looks up from every word into the eyes of the readers. Some of them sparkle with joy. Some of them deepen with truth. Some of them cry as their hearts open. She sees tiny dragonflies flying out of millions of eyes, illuminating their path.

Angelina truly sees herself for the first time. She sees that her words, though they gather pain and sculpt it into words, are not full of dreary, pointless pain.

This pain is transformed through her process; through her willingness to feel and surrender ~through her vulnerability~ into hope.

Through her verses her pain transcends its limitations and is transformed. She experiences her poetry as an alchemy that transforms limitations into possibilities, creating a balm that heals the soul ~not only the soul of the poet, but of those who are reached by the poem.

There is nothing to fear. She has lost nothing. She is freer than ever. She should be proud and grateful. Why was she afraid?

As her words lift up from the paper and pour into millions of pupils, Angelina is falling into the hearts of millions of people.

She hears new songs and poems rising from these hearts. New truths, new kind words, new hopes and dreams are pouring from millions of throats into the world.

At this instant Angelina realizes that this is what she wants more than anything else. The act of writing is only for her, for her own healing, growing and pleasure.

But the poems are not only for her. They are for the world. They came from the world into her to be painted, shaped and orchestrated into a unique composition. But now they must go back to the world.

Like children, they come through the parents, but do not belong to the parents. They belong to the world. They came from this beautiful world and must return to it. To keep her verses locked inside herself is to steal them from the world.

Angelina's body is split open. A locked iron door embedded in her solar plexus cracks open with a deafening clank. It is lifted like a feather up into the sky by a blazing hurricane of whirling light. All her hidden crooks and crevices are inundated with this spinning light. The locked and bolted places within her are broken open. The boundaries she has tightly kept between herself and others are shattered. She flows through a spiral of light, from her physical body to her emotions, from her emotions to her words, from her words to her acts, her books, from there to the environment, to others' minds and hearts. It does not end. She does not end. She continues.

Angelina is falling. She hears a crack and feels soft, humid soil on her back. Her back hurts, but not so much as her heart. Her heart is broke opened, ripped apart. Light pours out of her chest into the darkness. She raises her eyelids, but her eyes hurt. Before she closes them again, she sees a flash of white words floating in the dark.

"Welcome to Dreamboro Plaza"

"You have remembered your future. Hold on to this vision. It is your own, unique, *DreamLife Vision*," Dragonfly Diva whispers within the light.

Dark waves swallow Angelina into oblivion.

CHAPTER 9

Bleak Station

Chilling cold crawls up her spine. There is cold stone under her body. She wiggles her frozen fingers and forces them to crawl on the stone, seeking the edge. Just as she feared, a square stone edge imprisons her body.

"A tombstone!" Angelina cries, seating up in one piece. She half-expects to bump her head against the coffin's lid. But her head throbs only from the sudden motion.

"Perhaps I am in a mausoleum," Angela thinks. Not that her family has even a plot in the cemetery. But it's the first thing that comes to her mind as she sees herself sitting on a stone bench, in somber silence. A thin, cold mist permeates the gravelly vicinity, fusing with the odor of dust and decay.

The eerie tops of engraved tombstones line up some fifty feet away. Soft moonlight trickles through the mist, bouncing off the tombstones. It reveals instead the broken portions of a gray stone wall glistening in the night.

To her left, the mist tightens like a blindfold. Is she in a cemetery? Angelina forces herself up and takes a couple of clumsy steps. Is she dead? Did they leave her there for dead? No, that would not make sense. They embalm people these days. A chill goes through her body.

One more step brings her to the edge, her body instinctively stopping. She pulls back and looks closer. Right in front of her the stone floor drops one foot. Angelina notices an abandoned train track running parallel to the stone wall. It is covered by weeds, but the iron tracks are still visible.

There is a ticket office behind the bench where she was lying. Perhaps Dragonfly Diva is buying the tickets. This raises another question. Tickets for what? The headache doesn't invite much thought. Angelina drops the investigation in favor of action. She walks towards the ticket office, rubbing her arms vigorously, trying to shed away some of the cold mist that sticks to her.

The old door opens with a long, rusty squeak. There is only darkness inside.

"Dragonfly Diva," Angelina whispers. It feels irreverent to speak in this ruined station, as if she was screaming in an abandoned church. No one answers.

She calls again. And again. But only silence responds. Slowly, however, her eyes adjust to the darkness. There is no room. Stone rubble litters the place where walls once stood. One narrow stone wall still stands. Something shines against its stones. Angelina carefully walks towards it, her heels caught here and there in the debris. A sign is embedded in the wall.

Bleak Station

How appropriate.

"How long has this place been abandoned?" Angelina wonders. "Why am I here? Where is Dragonfly Diva?" Her head begins to hurt again. As she moves back towards the platform, she bumps into something.

Having nothing else to do, Angelina bends and picks up the object. It is an old, rusty advertisement. She blows on it and a cloud of dust erupts into the misty night, making her cough.

"Thank goodness I hold on to my bag," Angelina thinks as she rummages through her large leather bag. "And thank goodness I always carry napkins."

She takes out a large paper napkin and cleans the surface of the sign.

The Dream Express

An unforgettable adventure

Worldwide contest across all train stations.

You could win a ride!

There will be a lucky winner tonight.

A beam of light bounces off the letters. Angelina looks around, but there is no one there. No light from lamppost or other source is visible. Could that light have been the headlights of a passing car?

She runs in the direction from where the light beam shone, still holding on to the sign. Her heels dig into a pebbly road, but she ignores the hazard, hanging on to the hope.

She flies through the mist, acutely aware that there are no sounds, not even the sound of leaves rustling in the wind or night creatures scuttling; not even the sound of pebbles under her feet. Her steps slow down. Ten minutes later, she is forced to give up. There is nothing except mist, silence and darkness. The minute she accepts this, she stumbles and falls.

Angelina rises, but her heart has sunk. She is alone. Dragonfly Diva has abandoned her. She is lost in some ruined, faraway place, and to mock her beyond all irony, the stupid sign invites her to a ride in some Dream Express; a ride she has missed perhaps by decades, if not centuries, judging from these ruins.

Enraged, she flings the sign into the night and fumbles back towards the station. As she walks, Angelina has an odd sensation. This ruined, abandoned place is completely strange, but not entirely unfamiliar. She has never been here before, but she has always been here.

"I am going mad," Angelina mutters. "Why couldn't I just stay in the local N train? I'd be seating at my new desk by now, instead of meandering alone, hungry and lost in this forsaken place."

"That's exactly it," says a voice inside her. "Even if you had gone on to work, you'd still be waiting in this station."

"Who is this? Is this *The Architect?"* Angelina is in no humor for irony. This voice, however, does not seem to fit any of her familiar *Shadows*. It is almost as if it were the voice of silence. It does not make noise. It does not judge. It isn't trying to make her feel bad or insufficient. Quite the contrary; it is a voice in the heart, not the head.

"I am *The Poet,"* the voice identifies itself. "My name is SoulSong."

Yes, Angelina recognizes her. This voice used to speak to her in her adolescence, when she sat in her rocker ~her poetry journal in one hand, her pen in the other~ watching the world walk past her balcony.

"You've always been here," SoulSong says. "Well, not always, but for a long time. No matter who's with you or where you go, this desolation, this ruin, is your true station."

"Gee, thanks, that makes me feel great!" Angelina snaps.

But it's true. The dust beneath her shoes blends with the mist, sending a scent into her nostrils.

> *The hospital where she waited into the night before they mend her broken arm. The lonely nights walking on barren dirt roads, longing for company and dreading the idiots that went by, whistling drunkenly. The many lonely Fridays when Mercedes worked and she waited by the phone for someone to call, for someone to talk to. The gloomy weekend jobs in greasy joints, crammed kitchens, and in back offices with pinching-ass bosses, trying to get money for her books and clothing while her friends partied with their monthly allowances. The dry, ashen absence after her boyfriends left her. The remote clinic where she had her abortion, a secret she still carries with herself. An endless grief of which no friend, not even Omar has ever known. Two deaths: her child's and her trust, at the hands of date rape. The shame, always the shame. The shame of poverty. Cheap clothing. Second-hand books. Poor neighborhoods. Ignorant mother. Her own ignorance. Her sense of being damaged. Defective. A defective item. She had come defective from the factory, like some of the things they would get from her mother's jobs. The gradual numbing of her heart, heavier every year. The endless wait for something to happen, to get her out of her mediocre existence. Yes, she knows this scent. It is the scent of despair.*

"That's a start," says a nasal, raspy voice. Angelina jumps.

There's a child seating on a broken-down stone fence. No. It's not a child. It's a tiny person. A very, very tiny woman. No. It's not a woman. She has very long, pointy ears and as Angelina watches with her mouth ajar, the lower part of the tiny body takes shape from the stones.

"I'm Planetjianet," says the tiny being with a large, rasping voice. "You can call me PJ. I am a gnome."

"Ple-please to meet you," Angelina says, doing a curtsy. How does one salute a gnome?

"I've lost it," Angelina begins to cry. "I've gone completely mad. Loony. Gone."

"No, you haven't, dearie," PJ consoles, leaping out of the stone fence and landing in front of Angelina.

"You are getting warmer," PJ whispers, taking Angelina by the hand. "Oh, you're cold."

"Make up your mind," Angelina mutters.

"Your hands are cold, but you are getting warm," PJ declares, as if that had clarified everything.

"Maybe it's not me who's lost it," Angelina mumbles.

"I heard that, dearie," PJ says. "Stay on track, or you'll miss the Dream Express."

"That old train?" Angelina snickers. "That must have come and gone ages ago. You're not waiting for it, are you?"

"No," PJ says.

"Good," Angelina comments.

"You are," PJ adds and laughs in a high-pitched gurgle.

"You ARE going insane," Angelina observes. "I am not waiting for that train. In fact, I am..."

"Yes, what ARE you doing here?" PJ interrupts. She has stopped pulling Angelina's hand and is examining her curiously.

"I... I don't know!" Angelina admits. "I was somewhere else and then I woke up here."

"That's how it plays out," PJ explains. "They are somewhere else and they wake up here... and then they have a chance to win the ticket!"

"Who are 'they'? Where is 'somewhere else'? What ticket?" Angelina asks.

"Oh-oh! You are getting cold. Questions make you cold," PJ warns.

Angelina remembers the guessing game she loved as a child. Whenever you were closer to the right answer, your friends would tell you that you were warmer, but you would get colder if you moved away from the right answer. How did all of this start? When did the gnome show up? PJ had said that it was a start. Angelina had been following the scent of... misery.

"Misery wins me the ticket?" Angelina inquires, "If that's the case, you should call it the Nightmare Express. I don't think I want to go."

"Good! That's a great move!" PJ gurgles and jumps enthusiastically.

"Not wanting to go wins me the ticket?" Angelina inquires. "Are you a trickster? Is this a joke, a mischief?"

"I don't like your tone of voice, deary," PJ declares, moving away slowly. "I am an Earthwise Elder, keeper of the wisdom of Earth. I am here to help you, but if you get an attitude, I'll take my knowledge somewhere else."

Planetjianet is beginning to sink, fusing with the humid earth beneath her rather large feet.

"No, wait! I am sorry!" Angelina calls out. "Please excuse my ignorance. I am a little confused, but I appreciate your help. A lot."

"Then we must get to work!" PJ announces heartily as she springs back up. "It'll be here any minute and you will miss it if you are not ready."

"How can I miss it if it's here?" Angelina inquires, sure that another illogical explanation will follow.

"You will miss it because you won't see it. You won't see it because you won't believe it. You won't believe it because you have forgotten," PJ explains as she pulls Angelina back up the tiny platform of Bleak Station.

"Forgotten what?" Angelina asks.

"What you can't remember," PJ says matter-of-factly.

"Great!" Angelina mutters. "Here we go again in circles."

"That's it!" PJ claps happily. "We are going in circles."

"You seem to enjoy it," Angelina barks.

"Oh, I loooove spirals!" PJ coons.

> *"Spirals are the way down.*
> *Spirals are the way up.*
> *Spirals are the way to grow!"*

PJ sings as she pushes Angelina through the threshold of the non-existent office in Bleak Station.

> *She is whirling in the dark. There is a flame rising high, burning steadily at the center. Angelina spirals around the flame, but it does not burn her. It warms her cold body. There are rings moving clockwise all around her. She feels that she is in a giant clock. The scents of wood and earth saturate her nostrils.*

"Close your eyes," PJ instructs. Her voice seems far away. "Keep them shut. Do not open them under any circumstance. Bring your knees to your chin. Now!"

> *Angelina does what she is told. She is shrinking. She wants to open her eyes, but does not dare to do so. She is lighter. Smaller. She becomes as light as a feather. She is pure light. She has no weight. No dimension. Yet, she is. She knows. There are no words, just consciousness. She opens her eyes, but has no eyes. There is no fear. There is vision.*

An army of women dressed in gray uniforms walks through an industrial complex. Smoke comes out of great chimneys. A deafening metallic roar rumbles through space, following the women. The roar dies out and a clock is heard.

"One. Two. Three. Four. Five. Six. Keep it up. Eight. Nine. Ten. No distraction. Twelve. Thirteen. Pay per pieces. Pieces per hour. Seventeen. Eighteen. Don't miss a bit."

A young woman punches labels into cans. She is sobbing as she works. Angelina remembers the few times she worked in the factories where her mom used to work. She learned that if she wasn't careful, the machine could break her soul. She remembers Lakshmi.

"One for Billy. One for Sandi," Lakshmi would count, assigning each product she labeled to one of her nine kids and multiple relatives. When the rhythm increased, she barely had time to mention them. "Ernie. Mom. Grandpa. Rent. Books. Food."

On and on Lakshmi would count, every hour of every day. No one dared to shush Lakshmi. She was a six foot tall, 300 pound African-American matron. She had a heart of gold, but suffered no nonsense. And her punch was as strong as the iron pump in the factory.

"Doesn't it take more out of you, to be talking like that while you work?" Angelina once asked Lakshmi during their lunch break.

"Take out?" Lakshmi exclaimed, surprised. "Why, no, child. It keeps me strong. In every move, I hold the face of my little ones, my family. I know that I'm doing this for a reason, for them. I see my rent being paid, my kids getting their books and being able to socialize with their friends with dignity. I get stronger that way."

"If..." Lakshmi added in a whisper. "If I did not name every goddam-sonofabitch-can that passes through my hands, I'd lost my soul. I'd lost it as sure as if I was selling it to the devil. You watch yourself, Angelina, you hear? You get the hell out of here as soon as you can."

"Why?" she had foolishly asked. "I'm as strong as you. I can handle it!

"You's strong alright, sweetie," Lakshmi said. "But you were not born to feed this monster."

"If my mom can do it, then..." she began, feeling guilty, even though she knew that Lakshmi was saying the truth.

"NO!" Lakshmi screamed. She got up, the wrapper of her sandwich falling down as she faced Angelina, her two chubby hands on her hips, and spoke from the depth of her soul.

The whistle swallowed her words, but not her terrible goddess-of-death look, not the fierceness of her body as she scared Angelina away from the metal monsters.

"Faster. Faster. We need more people. You must work another shift," the voice says as the stamping and the metal screams increase.

An older woman is sweating, trying to catch up. But she can't keep up with the speed. Two giant pliers come out of nowhere and pick her up from the assembly line, discarding her.

"Next," calls out the voice. "One hundred. One hundred one."

A terrible moan makes the air tremble. Roots reach out, but find only metal. The seed wants to burst, but cannot break through cement. A piercing cry propels her consciousness.

A murmur whirls around Angelina like the buzz of a hundred bees. Slowly, she distinguishes voices. Women's voices. Words. Prayers.

Their heads are covered in head wraps, veils, mantillas, scarves and hats. They kneel in hard benches and beat their chests with their own fists. They suffer. They plead. Always plead. They cry as they pray. Their hunger floats above them, like a vulture. It attacks them. Takes out their eyes. Takes out their ears. They pray louder.

An earsplitting howl shakes the space.

"My daughters, can't you hear me?" Earth cries out. Angelina feels the Earth's pain in her own bones.

"Why are you not laughing? Why are you not dancing? Have you forgotten the rites of gratitude and joy? Have you forgotten the old ways of The Mother? Have I not birthed you to be happy?"

But the women keep working and praying, deaf to The Mother's cries.

"I am birthing your memory."

The Mother sings, taking great breathes and pushing forth a stream of beautiful notes that catch the light.

"I am birthing a road back to your Soul, the memory of its dreams, the wisdom of my ways. I am birthing the mirror where you can see my face and find your smile, where you can feel my roots and find your place."

The Mother is breathing fire and air into Angelina's consciousness. A warm, wet substance bathes Angelina. She is fed dancing circles of light. Memories of the ancient faith. Desires for another language. Indignation in the face of alienation. Hunger for freedom. Recognition of all forms of slavery. Persistence. Courage. Eyes that see the stories. Eyes that see the contradictions and the lies. Ears that hear the truth in the emotions when the words deny it. Memory of a goddess that laughs and loves. Of a father that breathes life onto his children. Memory of goodness without shame. Memories of harmony and beauty.

The warm womb opens and pushes her through the trunk, back through the Tree of Life and Death, back up and down, whirling around the spine of fire.

"The passage will be hard, remember daughter. All that you are you will forget, so that you can reclaim it again. Every one of your powers will attract a wound, so that you can find your way back to your strength."

"You will be born through the absence of what you are. You will be taught to be what you are not. You will need to walk backwards to find yourself. Each step a verse. Each memory a story. Your journey is the map that will return them to themselves."

"I birth you, SoulSong, I birth you to the children of the roaring metal and to the mothers of the praying vultures. I birth you to their daughters, who sacrifice desire and long for sovereignty.

Show them my faces, my many faces, the mirrors of their gifts. Open a patch of beauty and hope, so they can follow. Burst open the locked doors of their forgotten dreams. You will be born to their slavery so that you can birth them into freedom.

Angelina feels the coldness of metal vibrating against her skin. She unfolds. Her eyes open slowly, blinking against the light.

"Welcome to the Dream Express," PJ says, as she gives Angelina a ticket and disappears through the wagon's floor with a burst of gurgling laughter.

The whistle blows. The doors close and the train begins to move. It is swift and silent, like an eagle. Its aisle is spacious and its seats are roomy and well cushioned.

Angelina stretches her entire body and sits up. As the Dream Express rolls away, she sees the station behind. Bleak station is sparkling new. Light garlands crisscross the platform. The walls are new and the signs are shiny. There are people saying goodbye in the platform. Who are they? They seem so happy!

CHAPTER 10

The Dragon in the Wagon

Her breath steams up the glass, making her own image fuzzy. Propped against the large window, her head rocks gently with the steady cadence of the Dream Express.

"Dinner is ready!" a voice announces through the speakers.

Angelina wakes up with a tiny cry. For a second, she does not remember where she is. Perhaps she has imagined the call for dinner. She begins to drift back into sleep.

"I believe you'll get a large portion today."

Angelina jumps, eyes wide open. Dragonfly Diva sits in the seat in front of her.

"Where did you go? You left me all alone in that bleak place," Angelina starts.

"My, my, I thought that Mercedes was the drama queen," Dragonfly Diva smiles. "Are you trying to make me guilty?"

"A little," Angelina admits. "But I'm glad to see you again. You missed all the fun."

"I bet," Dragonfly Diva laughs. "At least I won't miss dinner."

"It's true then, they serve dinner in the Dream Express?" Angelina asks, her mouth already watery.

"In the Dream Express what you need is what you get," Dragonfly Diva answers, as she rises and invites Angelina to step into the next wagon.

She expected to see many seats with tables between them. Instead, there is only a large table. Covered with a red velvet mantel, it holds every imaginable delicacy, from caviar to chocolate mousse.

At least six of her favorite dishes are displayed at the center of the table: shrimps in salsa verde, salmon in mango sauce, vegetables in tamarind sauce, all the dishes she dreams with and can rarely afford. ALL of them, together, just for her.

Trays of fruits and pastries surround the main courses, all exquisitely presented among beautiful flower arrangements. The only neglected detail is an enormous antique candleholder whose candles have not been lighted.

"This is incredible!" Angelina exclaims.

"You don't believe it?" Dragonfly Diva asks.

"No, I mean that it is fantastic!" Angelina corrects under her breath.

"What is fantastic about food?" Dragonfly Diva inquires.

"So much! So..." Angelina tries to describe what is in front of her, but words do not suffice.

"much!" Dragonfly Diva finishes, nodding her on.

"It's hot in here," Angelina whispers as she takes two steps towards the feast. "Is the air conditioner not working?"

The metallic noise sends chills through her spine. Her bones recognize this sound. Iron chains. Her mind refuses to accept it.

"Shall we?" Dragonfly Diva asks, signaling the huge table.

Angelina takes one step towards the feast.

The roar is deafening. It rides in a flame that bursts above the table, lighting the candles.

Angelina is blown back. Dragonfly Diva catches her in midair.

"What? What is that?" Angelina stutters.

The heat is spreading throughout the wagon. Angelina runs for the exit.

Dragonfly Diva sticks her foot out, and Angelina falls. Dragonfly Diva flies up towards a protuberance close to the conductor's cabin, and peacefully sits there as Angelina scrambles to her feet.

No sooner has Angelina stood up, when the deafening roar rises again. Shaking, Angelina sees the flame that shoots out of... of...

"It cannot be," Angelina mutters, her terrified face right on the line of fire.

Dragonfly Diva flies across the aisle, pushing Angelina out of the way. A cloud of smoke covers her.

"Dragonfly Diva!" Angelina calls desperately from beneath a seat. "Oh, no! No!"

A zooming sound clears the cloud.

"I'm perfectly fine," Dragonfly Diva responds as she flickers her large wings rapidly. "You, on the other hand, look dreadful."

Angelina is covered head to toe on black soot. She has no time to react.

The dragon is sending another tongue of flame in her direction. Angelina ducts.

"Let's get out of here," Angelina screams. "I thought I was having dinner, not being dinner!"

"It's fairly common," Dragonfly Diva laughs as she holds Angelina by her blazer. "The hunter becoming prey."

"This is no time for jokes," Angelina screams. "Let's go!"

"You are not going anywhere," Dragonfly Diva declares.

Two invisible ropes tie Angelina's feet and hands. She falls, struggling, to the floor.

The iron chains tremble, and so does Angelina, who manages to wiggle under a seat.

"Do you want me roasted?" she asks.

"I'm afraid I'm vegetarian," Dragonfly Diva says as she hovers over Angelina.

"That's a...a...dra...dragon out there!" Angelina manages to say.

"Is it?" Dragonfly Diva asks innocently.

"You don't know what that monster is?" Angelina asks. "Have you never seen a dragon?"

"Have you?" Dragonfly Diva asks.

The chains rattle terribly. The floor of the wagon trembles with the impact of giant footsteps.

"It's coming!" Angelina cries, trying to hide beneath the seat.

"Is that the best you can do?" Dragonfly Diva inquires.

"Against a fire-spitting dragon? When I'm tied up? Yes!" Angelina cries. "Untie me, will you?" Angelina asks as she struggles to get rid of the invisible ropes.

"Not until you promise," Dragonfly Diva says.

"Promise? Can't you wait 'till we are out of danger for those platitudes?" Angelina screams through her tight lips.

"Promise me you will use the key," Dragonfly Diva says, "and I shall release your ties."

"Promise you what?" Angelina asks.

Another giant footstep shakes the wagon. The dragon's breath hisses with heat waves that simmer in the air.

"Fine! I promise! Now get me out of these ties!" Angelina hurries to say.

"You must keep your promise at all cost," Dragonfly Diva says. "Or I will die."

Fire bellows through the aisle. Dragonfly Diva takes cover. Her face is now inches from Angelina's. The old woman's golden eyes are fixed in Angelina's olive eyes.

"Promise that you will not leave. You will face the beast and use the key. Keep your promise, or I will die," she softly affirms.

Angelina silently assents. The ties are released. Strangely, Angelina is not as terrified as before.

"Why would you die?" Angelina wants to know.

"That is The Law," Dragonfly Diva says. "Stand up."

Angelina checks to see if the dragon is anywhere near, but it seems to have withdrawn. She stands up. Her whole body is trembling.

"What law? Why can't we leave? What key?" she whispers, shaking like a leaf.

"Attention!" Dragonfly Diva screams.

Angelina moves out of the way just as a flame shoots by.

"Thank you!" Angelina says.

"Attention is the key," Dragonfly Diva says.

"What key?" Angelina asks impatiently,

"The key to his chains," Dragonfly Diva replies as she floats in front of Angelina.

"You mean that you want me to let him free?" Angelina mutters. "Have you lost your wits?"

"It is the only solution," Dragonfly Diva calmly states.

"I have a better one. Let's leave," Angelina says, going for the door.

"You promised," Dragonfly Diva says.

"Will you really die?" Angelina asks, staring into the golden eyes.

"Yes," Dragonfly Diva responds.

Angelina knows that Dragonfly Diva is not lying. She also knows, though she does not know how, that freeing the dragon is the right thing to do. If there is a choice between facing the beast and allowing Dragonfly Diva to die, then there is no question in her heart. There is only one thing to do. A quiet, cool peace bathes her body, washing away all doubt and fright.

Angelina is breathing deeply, slowly. Her heart beats loudly, but rhythmically. Her body still trembles, but it no longer wants to flee or hide. It has become intensely attentive to everything around her. All her senses are heightened. She feels every twitch of the dragon even before it moves.

Angelina suddenly runs toward the dragon at full speed and throws herself under some seats just as the beast bellows another tongue of flame. It roars in frustration. Angelina hears a muffled cry under its burning roar.

She is now midway into the wagon. She can see the dragon's paws under the seat. The chains are tied to an iron beam buried into the train's underbelly. The connecting link is an inch-thick ring with a keyhole. Angelina focuses her entire attention in that keyhole. She must reach it in two moves. She must open it in one move. That is all the time she has before the dragon notices her presence.

Angelina positions herself under the seat, ready to crawl straight towards the keyhole, when her necklace breaks. She catches the broken cord just as a bead rolls through the floor. Angelina sits up in one quick move and throws a handful of beads against the opposite wall. The sound of the many beads masks the sound of the one bead rolling on the floor next to her. The dragon shoots his fire against the opposite wall.

Angelina signals Dragonfly Diva, who moves her hands swiftly, sending all the bouncing beads to fly in one direction. The dragon fires that way. Angelina crawls swiftly beneath the seat. Above her, beads are bursting against one wall and the next, against the ceiling and the windows, and the dragon fires one flame after the other. Angelina gets to the chain in two strolls, grabs the link, ready to open it, when she realizes that she has no key.

"Attention? What kind of key is that?" she thinks as the dragon turns its eyes towards her, lying inches from its deadly tail.

The dragon opens its large snout, raising its tail. Angelina closes her eyes and presses her face against the floor.

The laughter bursts out in cool, bubbly waves that release her tense body. She opens her eyes and slowly turns her face towards the laughter.

Dragonfly Diva stands where the dragon was. She holds something in her hand. She floats towards Angelina.

"Open your hand," she says.

"I must be mad to trust you," Angelina says, but she opens her hand.

Dragonfly Diva places a small salamander on her palm.

"What is this?" Angelina asks.

"The beast," Dragonfly Diva laughs.

"That's not possible," Angelina exclaims. "It was..."

"It was what you saw," Dragonfly Diva laughs as she tickles the salamander and it crawls up Angelina's arm. "You saw what you expected to see. You expected what you most feared."

"You mean..." Angelina begins.

Dragonfly Diva is flying all over the wagon, laughing in bursts of tiny blue, green and pink stars.

"It was always... this small?" Angelina concludes.

"Oh, no, my dear!" Dragonfly Diva says, stopping in mid-air. "It was real. Your fears are always real. Deadly real."

"Then, it could have killed me?" Angelina asks.

"It is fear that usually kills you," Dragonfly Diva warns. "Not the actual situation."

"But the key... I never got a key. How did it..." Angelina asks.

"My, my, you do play the fool 'till the last line!" Dragonfly Diva says, sitting at the table and beginning to feast on the delicious entrées.

"You said that I had to use the key. Then you said that Attention was the key. Then..." Angelina stops talking. She is trying to put all the pieces together. Dragonfly Diva stops her eating, a piece of tasty prawn inches from her mouth.

"I used the key!" Angelina screams. "I did it!"

"Eureka!" Dragonfly Diva shrieks comically, and swallows the prawn.

"Hey, leave me some," Angelina exclaims, and hurries to serve herself.

The Dream Express rolls smoothly through the darkness as a tiny salamander happily plays in and out of the rings linking the huge, empty shackles.

CHAPTER 11

The Hungry-angry Head

Her belly is so full that she feels pregnant. Angelina rubs it contently as she elbows Dragonfly Diva.

"Tell me the truth," she starts, "was that first train I caught really the N train?"

"Most certainly," Dragonfly Diva responds with a wink. "But perhaps you did not catch it. Perhaps it caught you!"

Funny. This eccentric woman always has a card up her sleeve. But Angelina is not going to let her get away with vagaries.

"N local? N express? N to Queens? What does that N stand for?" she asks with a mischievous smile in her face.

"For many the N stands for **Never**. Those riders stay in the train, riding with their *Shadows*, never getting off," Dragonfly Diva says sadly. "For you, and for many other brave riders who decide to get off before or at **Dreamboro Plaza**, it stands for **Now**!"

"You mean that was my last chance?" Angelina says —her tummy rumbling.

"Last chance? That's hard to say," Dragonfly Diva considers, raising an eyebrow. "There is always a chance as long as you live. But that was the last stop to transfer to the Dream Express."

Angelina's mind wants to speculate about what would have happened had she not gotten off, had she not met herself living her Dream and caught her *Dreamlife Vision*. She was definitely heading in the wrong direction! But her stomach is growling. She must attend matters that are more pressing. Literally.

Angelina belches.

"I think I overate a bit," Angelina mumbles as she grabs her belly.

"That is a gross understatement," laughs Dragonfly Diva, who ate twice what Angelina ate and is light as a feather.

"Is there a bathroom here?" Angelina asks.

"In the next wagon," Dragonfly Diva says as she arranges some apples, grapes, bananas and peaches in a huge basket that she took from the banquet table.

Angelina has the odd thought that Dragonfly Diva treats the basket as if it were alive.

Holding on to her tummy with one hand and her leather purse with the other, Angelina makes her way to the door connecting the two wagons.

"It's a good thing, it is," Dragonfly Diva says.

"What is?" Angelina asks, her hand on the door handle.

"The way you hold on to that bag," Dragonfly Diva says casually. "You never know."

"Never know what?" Angelina asks a bit annoyed. She needs to go!

"Where you are going to land," Dragonfly Diva mutters under her breath, a sly smile barely showing. Then, turning to Angelina, she says out loud, "never mind my blather, go take care of your bladder!"

Angelina is shaking her head as she opens the door to the next wagon. This Dragonfly Diva is a rare fusion between a magnificent fairy and a batty old woman.

"Sometimes she is simply divine, awesome, even scary. At others times, she seems as crazy as a bat," Angelina thinks, smiling to herself.

The smile freezes on her face.

A terrible being fills the wagon. No. Not a being. A head. Not a head. A face. An iron face. A mask. Angelina tries to go back to the wagon behind her, but the door has been bolted from the other side. She is trapped.

She stays very quiet, observing the giant mask. If she is lucky, it may not be alive. And so it seems.

The mask has a terrible expression. Its eyes are open wide in fear and its mouth seems to utter a silent scream. Something flies by Angelina's consciousness. A fleeting thought that she can't quiet grasp.

The mask seems to be just an object, with no life of its own.

"It may just be a... a what?" Angelina tells herself, smiling slyly. "A work of art... yes. That's it. A work of art being transported."

Suddenly, her whole body tenses. She presses her back hard against the cold door. The mask features are changing! Its expression is now foolish. Its eyes are unfocused and it has a silly grin in its face.

"It's alive!" Angelina trembles, trying desperately to understand. "What makes it change? Who...what is it?"

Angelina considers the immense mouth. It could easily swallow her in one gulp. Just as she is looking at it, the mouth opens into a terrible hungry maw. It has two rows of razor-sharp iron teeth.

All Angelina can do is try to hold the bulk that is now pressing against her belly, pushing to be released. She locks her legs, but her whole body is shaking, which doesn't help.

The mouth begins to bite into the air.

"Can it move?" Angelina quickly considers. "Can it reach me where I stand?"

"Well, what do you think?" Dragonfly Diva whispers, standing beside Angelina.

"How did you get in?" Angelina whispers, thinking that if there's a way in, then there's a way out.

"I teletransported," Dragonfly Diva whispers back.

"What? How?" Angelina whispers. "Never mind. I can't do it, right?"

"No," Dragonfly Diva whispers back. "Not yet. At least not consciously."

"Why are we whispering?" Dragonfly Diva asks.

Angelina hushes her, pointing to the mask.

"Oh, that!" Dragonfly Diva says.

"Does it..." Angelina starts.

"Bite?" Dragonfly Diva finishes. "I'm afraid so. It devours you whole. It can also chew you into tiny pieces."

"Stop! You are scaring me!" Angelina cries.

"You should be scared!" Dragonfly Diva says, staring seriously at Angelina. "Unless you feel that being eaten alive is a good way to live."

"This is just another one of your tricks," Angelina decides, seating on the nearest chair. "Please, stop it. I need to go to the bathroom, and it's behind that!"

"My tricks?" Dragonfly Diva laughs. "You are giving away your power, lady."

Dragonfly Diva begins to fade.

"Please, don't go!" Angelina pleads.

"You send me away when you give your power away," Dragonfly Diva explains, regaining her solidity.

"How am I doing that?" Angelina asks. She does not understand anything that is happening in this Dream Express.

"You should know by now that everything happening here is your creation," Dragonfly Diva says.

Angelina considers her adventures. She was rushing. The train was rushing. She was depressed. The station was bleak. She was scared, the salamander became a dragon. What is this mask then? What is she creating?

The fleeting thought comes back. She grabs it. The mask has been expressing her moods and thoughts all along. Angelina looks at the mask intently. She finds herself face to face with her own face. Although it is grotesquely magnified and distorted, it is still very much her face.

"You need to go, don't you?" Dragonfly Diva reminds her.

"Yes, but..." Angelina squeaks, pointing to the monstrous face, trying not to look. It hurts to see her feelings exposed and magnified. She feels that her weaknesses are being broadcast.

"You prefer to drop it here?" Dragonfly Diva asks.

Angelina finds the thought disgusting. What can she do? She forces herself to examine the mask. It has a revolted expression, its mouth wrinkled in antipathy, its eyes shrunk and scornful.

That expression is not just momentary. It is not, and Angelina knows this in the pit of her stomach, just about the physical urgency she experiences right now. No. She carries this old expression deep inside her, a mask behind her social, nice expression. It hurts to see it. She feels skinned alive, as if her nerves and bones were exposed. What is this mood about? Why is this terrible grimace so familiar to her muscles?

Angelina's urgent physical need to release becomes magnified with a need to free herself from that painful tension inside her. What is it? Why does she feel all twisted inside? Why does she constantly pull back? Why does she expect the worse?

"This is the *Mask of Self*, Angelina," Dragonfly Diva whispers. "Your genuine expression has been trapped inside this iron mask."

This mask exposes what she has tried to hide for a long time. That she is a stranger to herself. She now feels that her ignorance is victimizing her.

"How did I get myself inside this lie?" Angelina asks, tears streaming down her face.

"The *Mask of Self* was slowly, painfully cast by those who labeled you at the start of your life," Dragonfly Diva whispers tenderly. "It was forged in the ovens of limited, scared minds that passed on their fears and molded you to their image. It was made by hardened beliefs, examples and limitations, until it became a solid lie you wear."

The bulge in Angelina's stomach begins to feel like a fetus. She feels that she will abort it at any moment. She cannot help but feel that this is her own birth being thwarted. She is aborting herself at every minute. That is exactly what she does, and she does not want to do it anymore.

"I want to take it off," Angelina declares, as she pulls at the muscles of her own face.

"There is only one way out," Dragonfly Diva says. Extending her long arm, her hand inviting Angelina to move into the large, open mouth. "And that is in."

Angelina swallows hard. She is terrified.

"Will you go with me?" she asks in a tiny voice.

"I am honored," Dragonfly Diva says, taking her hand. "But you must lead the way."

Angelina moves slowly towards the mask. The terrible mask opens its mouth hungrily as the women approach.

A terrible shriek heaving with pain and horror rushes out of the giant mouth, crawling inside Angelina's ears and bones. She hesitates. Dragonfly Diva presses her hand. Angelina takes a deep breath and walks between the rows of razor-sharp teeth. The mouth snaps close right as she crosses. Angelina cries in terror, not only for herself, but for Dragonfly Diva. Her wings! Will they be cut by these daggers?

It all happens in a flash. A gust impels her down the dark tunnel of the massive throat. She disappears.

Part 3

The Dreamscape

"The future belongs to those who believe in the beauty of their dreams."

—Eleanor Roosevelt

CHAPTER 12

The Mask of Self

The *Mask of Self* is staring fiercely at Angelina. Its eyes emit an evil flame that seems to scorn her.

Didn't they just go inside? How can the mask still be outside? Just then, Angelina realizes that this mask has the same features as the mask she entered, but it is not at all the same mask. To begin with, this mask is a huge fortress. Secondly, it stands farther away than the mask in the wagon.

"Wait a minute; we're not in the train!" Angelina realizes. She uncurls from her fetal position and seats upright on a large, flat stone facing the entrance to the fortress.

Her eyes slowly capture the landscape. Surrounding the fortress that looks like the *Mask of Self*, there is a filthy moat. A bright blue sky flows above an expanse of land abruptly cut off by a high stone wall as far as she can see.

"Where are we?" she asks Dragonfly Diva in a whisper.

"We?" She repeats, her eyes nervously darting around. She is alone. Dragonfly Diva has disappeared. Angelina stands up and carefully inspects her immediate surroundings.

She is standing in a dust road surrounding a castle. The dusty corridor is itself surrounded by a seemingly endless wall about 20 paces away. Beneath her feet, the soil is caked and dry. Weeds grow at the edges of the wide pathway that surrounds the castle.

"Castle?" Angelina asks herself, taking a second look at the huge mask in front of her.

Angelina surmises that the dust road is the horse road to this castle. And yes, the mask is no longer just a large façade, but an immense dark castle rising like a shadow against the bright blue sky.

She looks again at the castle. It is a gray, ugly citadel about 200 paces from her. It towers 100 feet high. There is a moat around the castle, but it's so dirty that it has become a stinking swamp. Upon closer inspection, Angelina sees large alligators crawling in the swampy waters.

"Thank goodness that I do not have to go inside that castle," Angelina prays.

Suddenly she is not so sure. Didn't Dragonfly Diva say that she had to go inside the mask? Well, for all intended purposes, she's still outside.

"The assignment was to go into the mouth of the *Mask of Self* that was in the wagon, and I did," Angelina mutters, trying to convince herself as she carefully moves away from the lower ditch where the alligators gather.

"If there was another mask inside the first one, well, no one told me anything about that. Since Dragonfly Diva is not here to explain, I am in no obligation."

Comforted by that thought, Angelina relaxes for the first time since she met the head in the wagon.

"At least I don't have to go anymore!" She consoles herself.

Only then does she realize that she is no longer wearing her beige and peach suit, but black pants and sweater. She lets out a sigh of relieve. The dainty outfit was not only physically uncomfortable. It was a mask.

"It corseted my freedom," Angelina confesses to herself, kicking a stone with her right foot.

She's about to cry in pain when she realizes that there is no pain. She is not wearing her fragile high heels anymore. She has a pair of sturdy black boots on.

"Now I'm dressed to travel," Angelina thinks. "But how did I change? And where have I traveled to? And why has Dragonfly Diva disappeared again?

Not having answers to any of her questions, Angelina decides to trade her frustration for a detailed examination of the castle and its surroundings.

The massive wooden bridge that crosses the moat is withdrawn. Angelina inspects the bridge. Great iron chains and pulleys raise or lower the wide bridge.

The chains run through huge iron loops attached to two tall iron poles, one at each flank of the castle's massive entrance door.

From there, the chains run back over the moat to four large poles across the castle's entrance.

Each pair of poles wraps the chain tightly around a spool. Large iron staples protrude from this spool at intervals, locking the chains in place.

Angelina surmounts that in order for the chain to move and bring the bridge down, these staples would need to be released and the chains would need to slide. It is a primitive, but impenetrable security system.

Angelina approaches the entrance poles carefully, for a giant effigy guards them. She wouldn't put it past this crazy journey if the statue were alive.

She stares at the guardian effigy in frustration. The stone-bodied female is blindfolded. She carries a set of scales in its extended right hand and a sword in its raised left arm. It reminds Angelina of the statues of Themis, the Goddess of Justice. Except that in most statues of Themis, the sword is shown at rest. This statue wields the sword menacingly, which gives Angelina little hope of justice.

The chains run from the entrance poles around the castle through a series of huge poles. As Angelina carefully scouts the road around the castle, she learns that each pole has a segment of chain wrapped tightly around it. There seems to be some enchantment locking the chain in each pole in place.

"How does this work?" Angelina wonders as she carefully observes the flow of the chains from pole to pole, keeping a good distance from the stone guardians that protect each pole.

She notices that there is plenty of chain wrapped around each pole to slacken the bridge hold, so that if each chain segment were to give its full length, the bridge would probably lower.

There seems to be no question, however, that if she were to touch those chains, the menacing stone guardians would attack her immediately.

After a long expedition from pole to pole, Angelina reaches the front entrance of the castle tired and disheartened.

There is no other entrance to the castle but the front bridge. She sees no other way in or out.

"In or out of the castle, that's one thing," Angelina considers. "But there is no way in or out of this place, whatever this is. I'm trapped."

It took all her courage to walk into the maw of that ugly mask back in the train wagon. And what did she accomplish? Absolutely nothing.

Now she is alone god knows where and this other mask is impenetrable.

A tiny figure shimmers above the castle. It's Dragonfly Diva! Angelina squints and catches a glimpse of Dragonfly Diva flying in circles above a balcony in the castle.

Angelina looks carefully and distinguishes her *DreamSelf* dancing in the balcony. She recognizes her at a distance not only because she'd recognized herself from far away, but because she is wearing the same magenta sarong and turquoise pants and the same fuchsias flowered scarf.

Two masked guards enter the balcony. They grab her and force her to stop dancing. They take her inside the castle.

Angelina sits dejectedly on a large flat stone in the middle of the dirt road, right across the bridge, between the entrance poles.

The stone is raised several feet high, like a stage. At the center, there is a large round hole where the ground is covered in ashes, perhaps from old campfires.

Around the stone's border some half a dozen wooden spikes rise from holes about four inches in diameter. Each pole has several holes drilled into it.

Angelina tries to loosen the spikes to no avail. They seem to be buried deep into the ground. Her best guess is these spikes are used to tie the guests' horses; which begs the question, who are the guests and where are the horses?

Her thoughts come back to her *DreamSelf.* She is imprisoned in this impenetrable castle. Perhaps she is in danger. What can Angelina do?

"It's not fair," she whispers. "Now that I finally met her, now that I want to make my dream come true, they've gone and lock her away."

"They?" asks Dragonfly Diva curiously as she appears near Angelina. "They who?"

"You tell me!" Angelina says, sulking. "You are the one who brought me here."

Dragonfly Diva begins to fade.

"No, sorry, please don't go. I won't do it again," Angelina screams.

"Give away your power one more time and you're on your own," Dragonfly Diva warns, as she regains solidity.

"It's just that I'm depressed," Angelina whines.

"Why?" Dragonfly Diva asks.

"Because my *DreamSelf* is imprisoned, perhaps in danger," Angelina barks. "Isn't that obvious?"

"She's been in that prison for years," Dragonfly Diva says. "Why are you sad just now?"

Angelina feels guilty. She has left her *DreamSelf* suffering in that prison. But she did not know that her dream was imprisoned. Why should she feel guilty?

Because she was the one who put her in the prison to start with. That's why. But that's not fair! She didn't know better. She didn't know about the *Mask of Self.* She was trying to do her best. That's like blaming the victim, Angelina thinks. She, of course, is the victim. Who is the bad guy, then? Who did this to her?

"Finished the council?" Dragonfly Diva asks. "What's the verdict?"

Angelina blushes purple red. Having someone hear your thoughts is not that pleasant.

"Ejem... is this the *Mask of Self*?" she asks, trying to change the subject. "It looks like the head on the wagon, but it's..."

"It's what's inside the head... your head, if I may say so," Dragonfly Diva laughs, playfully messing up Angelina's already untidy hair. "This structure is known as the *Shadow Castle*. You may have seen the *Shadow Scouts* marching inside."

"The guards?" Angelina asks.

A woman's cry breaks her rumination. Angelina clutches her heart. It is as if the cry kicked her heart. They both look up towards the tall windows behind the balcony.

"You don't have time for self-recrimination," Dragonfly Diva says. "We need to move. Now!"

Saying this, Dragonfly Diva catches Angelina by the waist and sweeps into the sky. Her hold feels strong. How can an old woman possess so much strength? Angelina wonders. But then, this is no ordinary woman. That much is clear by now.

As they fly above the *Shadow Castle*, Angelina sees a large sign in the distance.

The Dreamscape

"Is this a stop along the route of the Dream Express?" Angelina wonders. This, of course, leads to another question. "How did I get here?

They are flying high above the fortress. The morning sky is bright and clear. Oddly, Angelina feels resentful, as if this happy sky was indifferent to her torment.

The *Shadow Castle* is old, dingy and impenetrable from any flank. It has been built like a maze, with layers of stone walls. The first stone wall raises some sixty feet above the ground and about three feet away from the edge of the moat. It is sculpted into the face of the mask at the frontal plane of the castle. This wall has cannon ditches and observation holes all around its periphery, and a five feet wide walkway inside, running along the wall. The walkway is connected through narrow stairs with a 12 feet wide platform about ten feet below.

There are doors connecting the platform to the levels below, and dozens of soldiers run in and out of it, like ants.

Protruding from that first stone wall, there are huge mirrors capturing everything that moves below and around, and reflecting it back to other mirrors that are observed by soldiers.

"That is the *Outer Ring of Self*," Dragonfly Diva explains, pointing to the walkway along the outer wall.

"And the soldiers?" Angelina wants to know.

"*Shadow Scouts*," Dragonfly Diva reveals. "They defend the place and carry messages along the *Outer Ring of Self*."

"What about the mirrors?" Angelina asks.

"Those are the *Great Mirrors*," Dragonfly Diva explains.

"I don't like them," Angelina says, squirming in Dragonfly Diva's arms.

"Why not?" Dragonfly Diva asks, raising an eyebrow.

"I feel violated by them," Angelina responded. "I don't know why. I just do."

"Fascinating!" Dragonfly Diva mutters as she flies higher and deeper into the concentric circles of the castle.

"That is the *Inner Ring of Self*," Dragonfly Diva points out.

They are looking at an inner circular corridor surrounding a central clearance in the shape of a star.

The *Inner Ring of Self* is illuminated by a warm glow that changes colors in what seems to Angelina like a melody of hues. Red, orange, yellow, green, blue, violet, gold, one fusing into the other, like notes in a composition.

The inner wall of this magical *Inner Ring of Self* sparkles with shiny white light bubbles, like the ornaments on a Christmas Tree.

These light bubbles spread beautiful rays of white light across the *Inner Ring of Self*, making it look like a whirling wheel of light.

The *Inner Ring of Self* is encased on its outer edge by a tall wall. Angelina calculates that the high wall is about 100 feet tall.

As they circle above the high wall, the perspective changes and Angelina recognizes that this high wall is the towering wall seen from the road below.

From below, Angelina had only seen the iron shell rising from the *Outer Ring of Self* and forming the mouth of the *Mask of Self*, which is the entrance to the *Shadow Castle*. She had thought the entire facade to be one solid wall.

As they skirt the *Shadow Castle*, however, Angelina realizes that it is the high wall, the outer wall of the *Inner Ring of Self*, rising above the external walls of the *Shadow Castle* and forming what appears to be the forehead of the *Mask of Self*.

"Those are the eyes in the mask!" Angelina whispers to Dragonfly Diva, pointing at two large arched windows at the frontal area of the high wall. There is light behind these windows.

Angelina realizes that these lights were the flames that seemed to come from the eyes of the *Mask of Self.*

"And there's one ear," Dragonfly Diva whispers back, pointing to the balcony where they saw the *DreamSelf* dancing a while ago.

At this precise moment, someone opens one of the arched front windows. It is her *DreamSelf!*

The *Shadows* must have taken her into that front room. The *DreamSelf* waves at Angelina. But two *Shadow Scouts* appear and quickly close the window.

Did they see Dragonfly Diva and Angelina? Dragonfly Diva does not take chances. She flies even higher, still working her way towards the center of the maze.

At the center of the *Inner Ring of Self,* the star-shaped clearance is aglow in white light. Bubbles of bright color flicker at the borders of the star. Suddenly one of its border lights flashes on and off. Angelina follows the movement of the light.

Two *Shadow Scouts* have opened one of the doors in the second level wall, entering the *Inner Ring of Self.* The darkness from the *Outer Ring of Self* spreads into the *Inner Ring of Self,* creating patches of shadow.

There's movement as a response to the *Shadow Scouts,* but Angelina cannot see who is moving in the *Inner Ring of Self.*

They are flying too high to see the dwellers, but Angelina notices the contrast between the dark *Shadow Scouts* and the bright colors of the dwellers in the *Inner Circle of Self.*

She follows the movement of the bright dots and realizes that each of the crisscrossing inner walls of the *Inner Circle of Self* contains an archway leading into the star-shaped clearance. The white light from the star-shaped clearance filters through the archways, drawing rays of white light in the rainbow dance of the *Inner Circle of Self.* Conversely, the dance of color filters through the archways, creating a kaleidoscope at the edge of the clearance.

As the bright dots enter the clearance, Angelina notices movement there.

As if Dragonfly Diva sensed her curiosity, they begin to descend as they circle the star-shaped clearance.

Angelina is surprised to see an entire community living in the central clearance. There are many children playing, running and laughing. She smiles at the women, who are dancing and singing. Some men are practicing swordsmanship while others build or paint furniture. An abundance of animals, gardens and luscious trees thrives in that small village.

"Are they trapped in the fortress?" Angelina wonders. "Or are they being protected by the *Shadow Scouts*? But why? We are not their enemies. We mean no harm."

As Dragonfly Diva descends several feet, Angelina can see a platform at the center of the clearance. At the center of the platform, a great Ancient Tree rises, almost as tall as the High Wall. As they skirt the periphery, Angelina sees a beautiful heart-shaped throne carved in the body of the massive tree.

"It's the *Throne of the Ancestral Heart*," she whispers, remembering her escape from the *Shadows* she had swallowed in the train wagon.

Angelina had thought that the *Throne of the Ancestral Heart* was a place inside her psyche, a sort of private landscape. How could it exist out there, in the castle?

Burning arrows cross the sky, and Dragonfly Diva quickly rises, catching the wind that takes them away. Angelina feels that they are spinning, and suddenly they are back on the flat stone.

"I don't like this," Dragonfly Diva mutters, pacing up and down the dirt road. "These are ominous signs."

"What? Why?" Angelina nervously inquires.

"They've taken her inside, but are hiding her from view," Dragonfly Diva explains. "And they won't let her dance."

"Is that bad?" Angelina demands to know.

"Deprived of light, without seeing the sky or the green hills, unable to walk among the trees and without dance, she won't survive long. You have about three days at the most to take her out of there."

"What do you mean three days?" Angelina barks. "You mean that she can die?"

"She will fade quickly under these circumstances. We must find a way to her!" Dragonfly Diva declares.

"That's easy!" Angelina laughs. "We can fly in! We can wait until they get distracted and..."

"I can fly in," Dragonfly Diva said. "I could even teletransport myself, if..."

"Great, then we can..."

"**You** can't," Dragonfly Diva says. "I flew as close as you can get to that castle in the air. You can't get closer than that from the air."

"Why not?" Angelina asks.

"If you break into the castle, she will fade quicker. You must follow The Laws," Dragonfly Diva explains.

But Angelina is not really listening. She is seeing an obvious loophole in the so-called Laws.

“I can’t break in, but **you** can,” Angelina says. “You can get her out!”

“No, I cannot,” Dragonfly Diva says.

“Why not? It would be easy for you,” Angelina complains. “You can teletransport, catch her and fly out. It would be so simple!”

“If I were to teletransport inside those walls,” Dragonfly Diva explains softly, “I would not land inside your *Mask of Self.*”

“What do you mean?” Angelina asks. “Where would you land?”

“Inside my own memories,” Dragonfly Diva simply says.

“It must be me,” Angelina declares. She’s known this all along, of course. But she didn’t want to face the grim truth.

“But how? It is simply impossible.”

“If you say so,” Dragonfly Divas whispers.

“I don’t just say so,” Angelina barks. “I’ve examined everything, and there is no way in or out.”

“How do the people living there get in and out?” Dragonfly Diva asks.

“Through the bridge,” Angelina responds. “But it is withdrawn, and the security system cannot be breached.”

“If you say so,” Dragonfly Diva whispers.

“Stop saying that!” Angelina protests. “That’s not just what I say. That’s just the way it is.”

“If you say so,” Dragonfly Diva roars. Her voice shakes the earth and every bone inside Angelina.

The shaking uproots Angelina from an old, gooey place. What is she doing? She can’t just give up, pack and go. This is her *DreamSelf* in that prison. This is her happiness, her very life that is at stake. She won’t let her Dream just fade away. She hates bullies. She will not stand to see some ghost bullies kill her *DreamSelf.*

“I must find a way!” Angelina mutters, her fiery pupils burning like the arrows had burned around them, flying towards the castle with the same burning tenacity.

Determined, Angelina takes Dragonfly Diva to the main entrance and shows her the pulleys that bring the bridge up and down. While Angelina carefully examines the chains and the ring connections, Dragonfly Diva goes straight to the effigy.

“I know her!” Dragonfly Diva exclaims after a while. “She is the Alignment Effigy. Quickly Angelina!”

Angelina is by Dragonfly Diva in a second.

"Place this basket in the left plate of the scale," Dragonfly Diva instructs, producing the large basket she had taken from the banquet table, now empty.

"But it's empty!" Angelina protests.

"Do as I told. There is no time to doubt," Dragonfly Diva says.

"But, the right plate is heavy, look!" Angelina insists, pointing to the plate. Resting on the right plate is a cannon ball. "How can an empty bas..."

A searing cry breaks the distance. Angelina bends over in pain.

"Are you ready to do whatever it takes?" Dragonfly Diva demands.

Angelina nods. She forces herself up the five feet base, climbing carefully up its narrow steps, and reaches up.

But of course, she can't reach the empty plate, floating high above the shoulders of the ten feet effigy and kept there by the massive weight of the cannon ball on the lower plate.

Her spine collapses and Angelina deflates like a balloon. Her left foot searches for a lower step of the pedestal.

"Don't even think about it!" Dragonfly Diva speaks into her heart. "You intention is magnified in each movement you make. If you take one tiny step down, you will be sent crashing to the ground, dead."

"But..." Angelina starts.

"Silence. Your intention must be impeccable," Dragonfly Diva warns.

Angelina's whole body becomes alert. Her bones let her know that one little wavering will cost her life.

Angelina listens deeply to every inch of her body. She feels every stretch in her extended muscles, the fast beating of her heart, every organ, system and bone. She has never been as present in her body as she is now.

She is crystallized in an awkward position. Her right hand, carrying the huge basket, is stretched up while her left side is sagging down. Her right foot is up on the highest rim of the base while her left foot is edging towards a lower step.

"I can't fall back," Angelina instructs her feet. "That is NOT an option."

The moment she decides this, her whole body begins to stretch.

"Your intention is magnified in each movement you make," she hears Dragonfly Diva's words and realizes their meaning.

Angelina thinks only of the empty plate above. Her whole attention lies already inside that plate. Her right arm stretches higher. Her entire right side stretches up. Her left side begins to align with the right side and her left foot finds a higher stronghold.

There is no doubt anywhere in her body. No fear. No wavering. Her left side stretches and she reaches up with her whole body.

She has moved unbelievably closer to the empty plate, but there are at least two feet between her basket and the plate.

"You are doing great!" Dragonfly Diva speaks into her heart. "Keep reaching..."

"But..."

"No doubts. You can make it!" Dragonfly Diva affirms.

"How on earth...?"

"Breathe into your vertebrae," Dragonfly Diva instructs.

Angelina begins to inhale slowly and deeply, allowing the air to travel down her spine and spiral around and into her vertebrae, starting with her coccyx.

She keeps reaching up with all her intention and every inch of her body as she exhales slowly and deeply.

"Crack!" She hears, and there's a deep release in the lower part of her spine.

The basket floats up an inch.

Surprised, Angelina keeps inhaling deeply and releasing the next vertebra in exhalation as she stretches with all her body and mind.

"Crack!"

The basket moves up another inch.

"Crack! Crack! Crack!"

As Angelina breathes into her spine, she feels a deeper release. She is unfolding, as if she had been a folded garment. Every time she releases a vertebra, the basket moves up an inch.

"Crack! Crack! Crack! Crack!"

She feels light and tall. She now reaches up with enthusiasm and joy. There is a new, boundless energy flowing through her. At the same time, a heavy weight seems to have been lifted off her. As she reaches up, now effortlessly, Angelina realizes that this weight had folded her power, creating pockets of doubt and countless hide-outs inside her being. She feels that as she reaches up, she is falling into her greatness.

The basket reaches its lofty goal and easily slips into the empty plate.

"I made it!" Angelina exclaims, relaxing her body —that now feels three feet taller.

The Alignment Effigy lazily opens its stone eyes, a blind blue light piercing the blindfold and showering Angelina.

"The *Dream Basket*!" The Alignment Effigy declares, coming to life with a crackling noise. "A powerful object. I accept."

Angelina is pleased with herself. She's about to step down when the Alignment Effigy asks:

"What are the keywords?"

"Wha..." Angelina is about to say, but an invisible gag muffles her voice.

"Don't say one word!" Dragonfly Diva speaks into her heart. "Anything you say will be considered an answer. Think carefully back. Remember your *Dreamlife Vision*. Speak seven keywords that embody that vision. Do not hesitate. Do not lie. She will know the truth. If you do not speak the truth, she will cut off your head with that sword in a flash."

"Fine mess I'm in," Angelina thinks.

But there's no time for doubts or antiques. She closes her eyes, takes a deep breath, remembers her *DreamSelf* and speaks.

"Exuberance," Angelina states unequivocally.

The plate with the *Dream Basket* drops six inches down.

"Magic," Angelina clearly pronounces.

The plate with the *Dream Basket* drops another six inches.

"Insight," Angelina softly says.

The plate with the *Dream Basket* drops six inches again.

Words. Stories. Writing. This is essential. But what word to use? What is the key in her writing?

"Naming," she exclaims, the word leaping out of her lips into the *Dream Basket,* which drops another six inches.

"Three more. I need three more," Angelina thinks, her sweaty hands trembling. "What is important? What?"

"Stay in the vision," Dragonfly Diva whispers inside her heart. "Move towards the warm center."

"Presence!" Angelina cries out joyfully.

The *Dream Basket* immediately descends.

"Words truly have substance," Angelina thinks as the plate drops a half foot down.

"Soul," Angelina whispers without a doubt.

The plate with the *Dream Basket* drops another half foot. The plate with the cannon ball is now only six inches below the plate with the basket.

Angelina's heart is pounding madly.

"That's it!" Angelina knows, but just as she is about to speak, she pulls back.

"This is two words," she thinks. "That must be wrong. They're supposed to be one word. A keyword."

"Release doubt," Dragonfly Diva speaks inside her mind. "Know from within."

"A...Ancestral Heart," Angelina says, concentrating on the warm trunk and the wisdom of the *Ancestral Heart.*"

The plate with the *Dream Basket* descends as the plate with the cannon ball ascends. The ball emits a metallic cry as the *Dream Basket* catches up with it.

The effigy seems to smile.

"Well done, Angelina Semidey," the Alignment Effigy says. "You have achieved balance. I can now answer your question."

Angelina is going to ask how to draw down the bridge, but the Alignment Effigy talks before she speaks.

"First, you must *Awaken the Rose*," the Alignment Effigy reveals.

Upon saying this, the Alignment Effigy goes back to her stony dream. Angelina is released from the base of the statue, falling on the dry earth. Dragonfly Diva picks her up.

"I am so tired," Angelina whines. "Ex-haus-ted. I need to sleep."

She feels drowsy, heavy, as if she wasn't fully there, as if she was dreaming somewhere else and a part of her had been teletransported here, but the rest had stayed behind.

You are feeling the rupture," Dragonfly Diva remarks. "That's good. Very good."

"Good?" Angelina babbles faintly as she tries to lie down on the dust road. "Good. Now I can sleep."

"Not so fast, lady," Dragonfly Diva says, trying to hold her up by the waist.

"I'm sooo sleepy," Angelina mumbles as she slips through Dragonfly Diva's arms, drops to the ground and curls up.

"Not now. You cannot sleep Angelina," Dragonfly Diva says, trying to wake her up.

But Angelina is already snoring.

Each time Dragonfly Diva picks her up, Angelina falls back to the ground again.

"Angelina, do not give in. You have entered the *Trance Zone,"* Dragonfly Diva admonishes, picking her up by the armpits. But Angelina won't stand on her feet.

"Listen carefully, woman!" Dragonfly Diva insists, pulling her up by the arms. But Angelina seems made of water and spills right back into the ground.

"You are feeling the effects of the evil spell that put your *DreamSelf* in a trance, Angelina. You need to stay awake or you will fade away with her!"

But Angelina is snoring again.

Dragonfly Diva lets out a piercing note.

"Aaaancestraaaaal Heaaaaart!" she sings in the note of FA.

Angelina wakes up and sits straight up, her eyes wide open and her whole body alert.

"What do we do now?" Angelina asks as she jumps up, ready to go.

"Didn't you hear?" Dragonfly Diva says with a smile. "We need to *Awaken the Rose*."

CHAPTER 13

Awakening the Rose

"What is the rose?"

"How can a rose be asleep?"

"Where is it sleeping?"

"How can we wake it up?"

These are the questions playing on Angelina's mind as she follows Dragonfly Diva from one pole to the other. The old woman has insisted in examining the chains that run through these hideous poles.

Angelina told her that she has done this already, but the woman would not hear of it. Angelina resents this. Dragonfly Diva joins the many elders who have not trusted her, like Mercedes has never trusted her to succeed. Angelina is still trying to prove her mother wrong.

Her teachers had not trusted her either, no matter how good her grades had been. What was wrong with her that no one believed in her dream? What had Mrs. Warner said?

"Writing is a nice hobby, Angie, but poor girls need a shovel, not a pen, to dig their way out of misery. How about a good solid training as a nurse? A secretary? You're good at taking notes."

And now this odd being, whoever she is.

Angelina also resents that Dragonfly Diva has demanded absolute silence, while she herself is engaged in the most rabid rumination. Is she even aware that she is muttering?

Finally, Angelina is not the least happy to gaze into those horrible statues that guard the poles. In fact, she is determined not to look at them again. To be immune to their grotesque, menacing features, Angelina is engrossed in the collection of pebbles along the path.

"Aja! There she is!" Dragonfly Diva exclaims.

Angelina looks up. There is nothing to look at. Then she realizes that Dragonfly Diva is looking at the ground. Curious, she hurries to the place where the lady kneels. To her amazement, Dragonfly Diva is holding a caterpillar in her open hand.

"She? Who is she? This is not a she, but an 'it,' and it's just a brainless caterpillar!" Angelina growls.

"Careful," Dragonfly Diva whispers. "Don't alienate it."

Angelina cannot believe her ears. Has this woman gone completely batty? Not that she was normal to start with, but maybe the pressure's been too much.

Dragonfly Diva takes out an apple from the bag, cuts it into two and places the caterpillar in one half, giving the other to Angelina, who eats it ravenously.

The caterpillar wiggles contently through the apple, until it carves a nest inside it. Then it bends into a J and begins to move its many legs very fast. Angelina is impressed by the speed at which the caterpillar is weaving a cocoon.

"Quickly, your hair," Dragonfly Diva asks.

"Excuse me?" Angelina protests.

"Give me a strand of your hair," Dragonfly Diva commands. Her piercing glance does not admit arguments. Angelina does as she is asked.

The caterpillar takes the strand of hair that Dragonfly Diva offers. The cocoon grows at an accelerated rate, until it is as large as Angelina's bag.

"Quickly, your saliva," Dragonfly Diva says. "Spit on it!"

Without a question, Angelina does as she is told.

The chrysalis becomes illuminated from the inside.

"Pick it up," Dragonfly Diva instructs.

As Angelina holds the incandescent chrysalis, soothing warmth pulsates from the creature into the palm of her hands.

Angelina begins to walk fast, and then to run. She reaches a giant beehive, almost ten feet high. The bees are busily working, oblivious to their presence.

The buzzing of the bees increases and the bees fly faster. Angelina's eyes are entranced in the rapid darting of bees in and out, around and around the beehive.

The buzzing grows louder and louder. The bees fly faster and faster, until they fly in frenzy, circling Angelina madly.

Busy, busy, busy, busy
Faster! Faster! Faster!
Rush, rush, rush, rush
Start! End! Initiate!
Late! Late! Late!
Complicate!
Busy, busy, busy, busy
Faster! Faster! Faster!
Rush, rush, rush, rush
Start! End! Initiate!
Late! Late! Late!
Complicate!

The bees drill into Angelina's head as they zoom around her.

Angelina is dizzy. She feels exhausted, confused and overwhelmed. Her heart is pounding madly. Her thoughts get muddled. Sweating profusely, her body wavers and she is about to drop the chrysalis.

"Ancestraaaal Heaaaaart!" sings Dragonfly Diva in the note of FA.

Angelina catches the incandescent chrysalis just as it slips out of her hands.

"Stay completely connected to the chrysalis," Dragonfly Diva instructs. "Release the frequency of the bees or they will drag you into the beehive."

Angelina concentrates on the beauty of the luminous chrysalis, feeling its soothing warmth. Her heartbeat slows down and synchronizes with the pulsations of the chrysalis.

"Quickly, your sweat," Dragonfly Diva asks.

Angelina dries her forehead and lets a few drops of sweat fall on the chrysalis. It bursts into a luminous flight of multicolor wings! Inside Angelina, Angie is happily shrieking and dancing.

"I got the butterfly! I got the butterfly!"

The butterfly that bursts out of the cocoon is about 8 inches wide. It flies among the bees and swiftly enters the hole of the beehive. In a second, it comes out carrying a large thorn in its legs.

The second that Butterfly flies out of the beehive, the structure begins to disintegrate. The shell crumbles and the beeswax cells inside melt down into an amorphous lump.

The lump begins to shapeshift. It becomes more solid as its edges become sharp and square. Soon Angelina is staring at a suitcase. The bees that remained flying around Angelina now dart into the suitcase and are instantly transformed into the tags around its border.

"A suitcase?" Angelina asks in disbelief. "A freaking suitcase!"

She kicks the suitcase and a gut wrenching scream escapes through its crevices, filling every living creature around with dread. Angelina clutches her stomach with both hands. Dragonfly Diva is covering her ears.

"Are you mad?" Dragonfly Diva asks.

"It's just a suitcase!" Angelina justifies, still clutching her stomach.

"This is no ordinary suitcase, dear," Dragonfly Diva reveals. But at that moment, Butterfly insistently flies around the wizard.

"Don't you say!" Dragonfly Diva remarks.

Butterfly flies, flutters and flickers.

"I wonder!" Dragonfly Diva responds.

"Say what?" Angelina asks. "Wonder what?

"It's too early to know," Dragonfly Diva replies distractedly as Butterfly alights in her finger. They get involved in an intense exchange of whispers and exclamations.

Angelina feels left out of her own game.

She dejectedly wonders off. But the suitcase beckons her. No longer able to hold her curiosity, Angelina inspects the suitcase. It has a sliding clasp with a key lock and two straps.

Angelina tries the straps first, but they won't budge. She tries to slide the clasp, but it won't yield. She then tries using a thin stick lying around to probe open the lock, but it won't open.

She shakes the suitcase softly and presses her ear against it. The saddest sigh she's ever heard filters through the crevices and fills her whole being with unbearable longing.

Thick, large tears copiously fall from her eyes. She hugs the suitcase and runs, hiding behind a large stone on the side of the dirt road.

"Thanks," Dragonfly Diva says as Butterfly drops the large thorn on her hands. But when she turns around, Angelina is nowhere to be found.

"Angelina, quick!" Dragonfly Diva urges. "We can't miss this moment or we'll have to wait another season!"

Dragonfly Diva looks around the open dirt road, but Angelina is not in sight.

"And I don't have to tell you that we don't have another season!" Dragonfly Diva sings into the wind.

A spectacular sob makes the magical lady jump. She follows the dramatic sobbing and finds Angelina in a sea of tears.

"Who am I?" Angelina cries while she furiously digs a hole in the dirt with a couple of stones.

"What am I doing here?"

"What is the meaning of my life?"

"Nothing makes sense anymore."

"I'm so lost, so utterly lost!" Angelina keeps going. "My soul is drying out and there is no water. No water! Not a drop! I'm living in an existential desert."

Angelina has dug a shallow hole. She takes the suitcase and begins to bury it.

"Angelina..."

"Never!" Angelina sobs dramatically. "I will never be Angelina again."

"Take the suitcase out of that hole," Dragonfly Diva softly says.

"Never! I'll bury it with my dreams!"

"At least open the suitcase, Angelina," Dragonfly Diva suggests.

"Never!" Angelina cries, seating on the suitcase.

Another unbearably painful cry shakes the ground. Angelina covers her head as she rocks, but refuses to get off the suitcase.

"Show me your hands," Dragonfly Diva requests.

"Never!" Angelina cries, hiding her hands.

"Just one!" Dragonfly Diva asks.

"Never!" Angelina cries, giving her back to the wizard.

"Oh-my-Goddess, OH MY GODDESS! Angelina!" Dragonfly Diva screams dramatically. "The rose is fading! This is a life or death moment! Think! For the love of God, think hard! Where did you first saw the suitcase?"

Angelina turns around and points to the place where the beehive transformed into the suitcase.

Dragonfly Diva grasps her finger and quickly pricks Angelina's middle finger with the thorn Butterfly fetched from the beehive.

"Ouch!" Angelina protests, as a bean-size dot of blood spurts on her fingertip.

"Drop it into the suitcase's keyhole, quickly!" Dragonfly Diva instructs.

Angelina, shaken from her drama trance, does as she is told. Inside, however, her *Drama Queen* is still muttering to herself.

"She tricked you! She is always tricking you, making you do all the hard work. Why can't it be something simple, like 'Oh, there's a garden and in the garden a rose!' No, it has to be some convoluted, twisted list of tasks. A grueling work. A long, dangerous quest, demanding our sweat and blood. Why does rescuing the *DreamSelf* have to be such hard work? Why can't life be easy?"

As the drop hits the keyhole, the clasp slides open and the straps come undone. The suitcase opens with a jolt.

The passionate notes of a violin escape the suitcase as a radiant golden egg slowly rises and expands. Once it reaches a height of about fifteen feet, the egg cracks open.

A gigantic Goddess blooms right in front of Angelina and the wizened lady.

Mouth ajar, Angelina faces a colossal Goddess. Her skin is suffused in amethyst and golden hues that glow as she expands. She has a third, closed eye in the forehead. Eight long arms protrude from her torso, dancing gracefully around her.

The Goddess brings two hands together, her lower arms forming an arch in front of her belly. A luminous being made of sheer golden light emerges. It is seating on the Goddess' hands, as if in a hammock. It has seven shimmering gems aligned along its vertical axis.

The Goddess brings her two upper arms up into an arch above her head. A glowing moon floats behind the Goddess, like a hallo.

An object emerges in each of the other four arms. But Angelina can barely see what they hold because a bright red rose is blossoming in the upper hands of the Goddess. The radiance of the moon and the rose almost blinds Angelina.

Below the luminous being, merging with the Goddess' legs, two intertwined trees blossom and quickly fill with red apples. Butterfly flies towards one of the trees, alighting on an apple. The tree unravels a multitude of branches, presenting them as a ladder.

"Quickly, climb up!" Dragonfly Diva instructs.

Angelina climbs eagerly. This Goddess is so beautiful! She wonders what will happen next.

Angelina climbs from one branch to the next easily, and as she does, she begins to glow. When she reaches the top branch, the lower arms of the Goddess close around her. Warm, golden light envelops Angelina. She is held, turned and then tugged into the Goddess embrace. Angelina is now the glowing figure seating on the throne of the Goddess' arms.

Immersed in the Goddess' light, soothed by her warmth and feeling the healing love of her presence, Angelina is in ecstasy.

"What brought you here?" the Goddess asks into Angelina's heart.

"The tree," Angelina says. Then, without hesitation, she adds. "The Tree of Life and Death, Birth and Rebirth."

"What are its gifts?" The Goddess asks.

"The experience of interdependence. Oneness. Transformation," Angelina says. The answer is not in her mind. It is in her body.

"Where do you seat?" The Goddess asks.

"In the *Throne of the Sacred Child*," Angelina responds. "In your loving arms."

"What are its gifts?" The Goddess asks.

"Love," Angelina says, feeling that her heart is bursting with love and light. "Innocence. Nurturance. Self-intimacy. Communion."

The buzzing of bees again grows around Angelina as Queen Bee approaches.

"What do you see in the lower right arm?" Queen Bee buzzes.

Angelina is about to reply that she cannot see anything. After all, she is sitting inside the statue, facing towards the outside. She had no chance to look at the arms well. But she finds that her body somehow knows all that is going on in the Goddess' body. She closes her eyes, feeling that she is a part of that divine body.

"I see a magnifying glass. Inside the glass there is a closed eye that sees," responds Angelina.

"What gifts does it hold?" Queen Bee demands to know.

"*Metaphoric Vision*. Revelation. The ability to see the invisible," Angelina says confidently. Queen Bee flies away.

"What to do you see in the lower left arm?" a sweet tiny voice inquires.

Butterfly has perched on Angelina's nose. She is tickling Angelina.

"Nothing," Angelina answers, recognizing Angie's voice in her.

Butterfly happily spirals around Angelina's face.

"Bravo, Angie! That is the right answer. Look!" Butterfly says, lending her eyes as a mirror. In the multiple lenses of Butterfly's dark pupils, Angelina clearly sees the Goddess' lower left arm. The Goddess holds a clay pot full with darkness. The pot is tiny, but the night inside it is endless.

"What gifts does it hold?" Butterfly whispers.

"*Receptive Power*, *WombPower*, connection with the *Great Mystery*," Angelina declares.

"You heard it, you felt it!" Butterfly celebrates, "Bravo, Angie!"

Angelina feels a warm joy in her heart and tiny drops of happiness fall from her eyes.

A flock of birds dashes through, with a quick question.

"What do you see in the upper left arm?"

"A bell," Angelina responds.

"What gifts does it hold?" the birds sing in harmony.

"Resonance," Angelina sings. "*Emotional Intelligence*, passion, empathy. *Grace*."

The birds dash out in brouhaha of happy songs and chirps.

A spider climbs down her invisible thread and hangs in front of Angelina's eyes.

"What do you see in the upper right arm?" she asks in a raspy voice.

"A rainbow," Angelina responds.

"What gifts does it hold?" Spider asks, directing a sharp stinger at her right eye.

"Art, imagination, creativity," Angelina blurbs out.

Apparently Spider has no complains, for she reels up her thread and disappears.

The moon grows. Angelina feels it swelling behind the Goddess' head. The moon illuminates the third eye on the Goddess' forehead and it opens. It spreads a beam of magenta light all around, like a lighthouse. Angelina feels that the waters inside her body are dancing intensely.

"What are my gifts?" The moon quietly asks within its luminescence.

"Psychic senses, intuition, and the *Female Way of Knowing*," Angelina responds. "Magnetic power. The force of germination."

A beautiful note rises and fills the space. The Goddess' body is warm and trembling.

"What is my most precious treasure?" The Goddess asks.

"The *Alchemical Rose*," Angelina responds without hesitation.

"What is its gift?" The Goddess inquires.

"*Essence*," Angelina responds, knowing with all certitude that this is the truth. Knowing it in her body and her heart. In her Soul. In a wordless, silent center within her.

The body of the Goddess breaks into fragments of light. Angelina falls to the ground. Something soft falls on her lap. The *Alchemical Rose*. It glows and sings in the purest note she has ever heard.

"Good work!" Dragonfly Diva pronounces, a mischievous smile dancing in her lips. "It must have been grueling. I bet you wrecked your brains looking for the answers."

"Funny," Angelina replies, smiling from ear to ear.

Angelina's hands hurt from carrying the delicate, glowing rose in her cupped hands, but she is blissfully oblivious to that pain.

"How can anything so beautiful exist?" Angelina wonders. Her heart is filled to the rim with The *Alchemical Rose's* delicate beauty, which makes each step she gives as they walk back to the Alignment Effigy a sacred act.

"You are every bit as perfect," a soft, velvety voice whispers in her heart.

Angelina does not dare to rebuff this soft voice. Yet, it is unthinkable that she, in her imperfection, in her doubt and confusion, could ever be this perfect.

"Who could have made such a perfect creature?" Angelina asks herself.

"I am made by the love in the heart of the Goddess Mother Creatress. Your mind calls her life," the *Alchemical Rose* whispers into Angelina's heart. The note wringing in her ears and body sings of spirals growing in the womb of a universal force.

The scent of the *Alchemical Rose* lingers in the air, impregnating all her senses. It fills Angelina with love, peace, harmony and a deep sense of wellness that heals her usual irritability. The scent is an embrace that heals the fear buried in her heart. Angelina has never experienced such a simple and miraculous act of love as the scent of this rose. It brings her into the essence of each moment as it unfolds. Here. Now.

"This scent is the elixir of life," Angelina considers.

"I am *Essence*," the *Alchemical Rose* responds. "You are *Essence*, too. Just like my *Essence* blesses your senses, so does your *Essence* bless those who enter in contact with your *Presence*."

Angelina tries to imagine how she could have a similar effect on others, but it's hard to visualize. The *Alchemical Rose* does not talk, at least not out loud. It does not move. It does nothing, except exist. Yet it gives all of its being in its beauty, its presence and its *Essence*. It heals, uplifts, loves and harmonizes. What an awesome power!

Until this moment, Angelina had never considered power as something one **is.** She thought that power was something she needed to have, get or build. She had tried hard to exert, to give or take power. The *Alchemical Rose* is showing her another way to hold power. But could she ever hold such a gentle and spellbinding power?

Swarms of bees buzz around the *Alchemical Rose*. Butterflies of all colors dance around it.

"She must taste so sweet," Angelina smiles. "Her sweetness attracts so much life!"

"You too are sweet, Angelina," the *Alchemical Rose* reveals, laughing in soft, velvety puffs. "But you have grown thick thorns to protect the sweetness in you. As you see, that is quite unnecessary. That sweetness that you see as fragile is your greatest magnetic power. You, too, can magnetize all that you desire. You too can expand your reach and multiply your riches just by sharing the sweetness of your *Essence*."

Two soft tears trickle down her cheeks. It is true. She has become prickly, defensive and even hostile. She has grown thick thorns trying to protect Angie, her creative, innocent child. But Angie does not want that type of protection. She's just told Angelina in no uncertain terms that she wants to be out there in the world, creating, living her stories, and making money from those stories.

Could the *Alchemical Rose* be right? Could she draw down her defenses? Could she give it a rest and stop trying so hard? How could she magnetize prosperity and attract the forces that could help her manifest her dreams, just by being? It sounds too iffy to her. Yet, the *Alchemical Rose* is clearly doing it. The *Alchemical Rose* is evidence that it can be done.

A hummingbird zooms by, licking the *Alchemical Rose*, perhaps for the last time, Angelina thinks. It then occurs to her that the *Alchemical Rose* is dying for her. A pang of guilt rushes into her heart, blowing away all the ecstasy she was feeling.

"Release that guilt, beautiful child," the *Alchemical Rose* whispers. "How can anyone die when they have given their *Essence* to so many? As we speak, I am carried to all parts of the world by those who drank my nectar. They carry my pollen and multiply me beyond my wildest dreams."

Thick tears slope down her cheeks now. Angelina has been zealously protecting her manuscript against being stolen, read or in any way seen by others. She has carried it in her leather bag, afraid that if she leaves it home it will be stolen. No wonder she feels that every day that passes she is dying and drying. She is a rose taken from her stem, from her creative power. She is wilting, but she has not shared her *Essence* with anyone. She will be forgotten.

"Not anymore, beautiful child," the *Alchemical Rose* whispers, as she sends a strong, goodbye tendril up Angelina's nostrils.

They have reached the Alignment Effigy and Angelina gently drops the *Alchemical Rose* in the Dream Basket.

"You have *Awaken the Rose*," the Alignment Effigy declares as she comes alive with a crack, her eyes glowing blue behind the blindfold. "I will answer your question."

Angelina opens her mouth to inquire about the bridge, but before she asks anything, the Alignment Effigy tersely responds.

"Find the *Alchemical Key* for each Bridge Guardian. Oh, yes! Make sure that you get the first Bridge Guardian right or your quest may be cut short."

Once she delivers this succinct message, her eyes grow cold again and she becomes a lifeless statue once more.

CHAPTER 14

The First Alchemical Key

The sun is straight above, a blinding spotlight hanging on the cloudless sky, illuminating the two figures that seem to be melting below.

They've gone up and down the dirt pathway too many times. Angelina is hungry and tired. There's nothing new to see. There are eight wooden polls, presumably the Bridge Guardians, each uglier than the previous one. There are no keys hidden anywhere because there is nowhere to hide a key. The dirt road is closed off by the stone wall that shoots up endlessly and spreads around the entire castle.

"There's nothing here," Angelina says, kicking a pebble. "I'm so hungry that I can't think straight."

"That may be useful," Dragonfly Diva says as she carefully scans the stone wall with her antennae, which have popped up from her head wrap, precisely where the two white circles used to be. "Perhaps if you bend your thinking we may get better results."

"I have no energy left to laugh," mumbles Angelina, with a gesture that looks more like a show of fangs than a smile.

Dragonfly Diva straightens up and looks at Angelina with great curiosity.

At that moment, the French windows behind the eyes of the *Shadow Castle* open wide with a crack.

"Help!" the *DreamSelf* manages to scream before two *Shadow Scouts* get a hold of her.

As the *DreamSelf* struggles with the guards, Angelina realizes that she is flickering, like a candle. Angelina rubs her eyes and fixes her gaze, but still the *DreamSelf* seems to fade in and out.

The guards subdue her, taking her back into the fortress. The tall windows close. A bolt echoes in space.

For a minute, they can still see the shadow of the *DreamSelf* struggling. Finally, even the shadow fades.

"We must hurry!" Dragonfly Diva mutters. The tremor in her voice, more than the words itself, convey to Angelina the urgency of the situation.

"This is a nightmare," Angelina mumbles. "There is no other explanation. I fell asleep in the N train and I am having a nightmare. If I can wake up, I can still catch my job before it's too late."

Angelina pinches herself on an arm. When this doesn't work, she slaps herself on the face. When this doesn't work, she jumps up and down.

"I can't wake up!" she screams, banging herself against the stone wall.

"No, but you may succeed at killing yourself if you keep it up," Dragonfly Diva responds.

"Why is this happening to me?" Angelina exhales. She is exhausted. Slowly, she slides against the stone wall, collapsing on the ground.

"This is not happening to you. You are happening to it," Dragonfly Diva reminds Angelina. "You built this fortress. You placed your *DreamSelf* in this prison. You went to sleep, Angelina, and now that you finally wake up, you are pinching yourself wanting to get out of the nightmare you've created. I'd say you are looking for a way out of your responsibility, a way to fall asleep again."

"That's not fair!" Angelina protests. "I didn't create this stupid mask alone. You said it yourself. It was built by my elders and their expectations and by the tricks I was taught in the *Domestication Trance*. It's not my fault, and I am the victim here, don't you forget!"

"You were once a victim," Dragonfly Diva. "Now you are the perpetrator."

"What do you mean?" a scared Angelina asks, her eyes wide open.

"As a child you had no choice," Dragonfly Diva whispers. "As an adult you do."

Angelina does not want to hear this. It doesn't sit well in her stomach. She is the victim. This was done to her. What is this about her being the perpetrator? But the ring of truth resonates in her heart, and she knows that Dragonfly Diva is leading her somewhere deep into herself.

"No, this is too much," Angelina says to herself, shaking as she leans against the wall. She hugs her legs, trying to steady herself.

"You keep complaining that everything is so hard," Dragonfly Diva says, suddenly raising her voice. It is now blunt and challenging. "Fine, have it the easy way. You don't have to find a way out of the *Shadow Castle*. Do what's easy. Go back to sleep. Your *DreamSelf* is almost faded by now. Let her fade away."

Angelina can't take it anymore. She cuddles into a ball and covers her eyes. She doesn't want to give Dragonfly Diva the satisfaction of seeing her cry.

A heavy silence surrounds Angelina. Perhaps the batty lady has left. Angelina allows herself to fall into the stupor that precedes sleep.

In the darkness behind her eyelids, Angelina feels a strong magnetism. The silence around her penetrates the cries inside her, like a balm. The exhaustion is melting away. She can almost touch what is behind. She hovers close to an edge in her darkness, but cannot continue pass the edge. An invisible barrier does not allow her to see beneath the mood that disheartens her.

"You have a terrible memory," Dragonfly Diva observes.

"That is not true," Angelina protests defensively. She slams dry her tears and looks up defensively. Anger rises in waves through her body. The anger surprises her. Wasn't she exhausted? The anger is old, dense and volatile.

"I have an excellent memory. I am very good with numbers, words and scripts and can even remember stuff I read in old newspapers, years ago," Angelina retorts defiantly.

"But you have forgotten what you most want in the world," Dragonfly Diva simply says. "You have forgotten your determination, though you set it only hours ago."

Angelina remembers. Just this morning she swore to free her *DreamSelf*. She had understood, without a shadow of a doubt, that what was at stake in this quest was her happiness, the very meaning of her life. Now, at the first difficulty, she is backing out.

"I am spineless," she mutters between her teeth.

"No, Angelina," Dragonfly Diva whispers. "You are simply trapped. You are literally, banging your head against the wall."

"I know," Angelina apologizes. "How stupid!"

"On the contrary," Dragonfly Diva clarifies. "It's very human. You bang your head against the wall because the wall is constricting your thoughts."

"What..." Angelina starts to ask, but Dragonfly Diva is already flying towards one of the Bridge Guardians.

"I got it! I know which one comes first!" Dragonfly Diva cries, Angelina closely following her.

They reach one of the ugliest Bridge Guardians. Angelina has to force herself to look at the terrifying figure.

A sinister executioner grins diabolically as he holds the lever of a guillotine.

"Didn't they cover their heads?" Angelina asks, wishing that Dragonfly Diva could produce a cover to hide his dreadful grin and his vicious stare.

"Do you trust me?" Dragonfly Diva asks.

Angelina does not like this. She feels goosebumps in her arms. A sudden chill glides over her neck and shoulders, as if death had just brushed her. She takes one step back.

"Ye...yes," Angelina says. "Why?"

"How much do you trust me?" Dragonfly Diva asks.

"Enough," Angelina says, taking another step back.

"I see," Dragonfly Diva whispers.

"What do you see?" Angelina demands to know.

"How much do you trust yourself?" Dragonfly Diva asks.

"I...I don't know," Angelina honestly replies.

"Let's find out," Dragonfly Diva says, taking Angelina by the hand and moving her behind the guillotine.

"This is the first Bridge Guardian," Dragonfly Diva presents. "What do you believe he guards?"

Angelina examines the sinister executioner. He is obviously there to cut off people's heads.

"I don't know," Angelina mutters as a mid-day ray bounces off the sharp edge of the blade. The executioner may be made of stone, but that blade is not only real. It is really sharp!

"There is only one way to find out," Dragonfly Diva whispers, indicating the guillotine's hole.

Angelina crouches and looks through the guillotine hole. The only thing she sees is the tall wall in front of them, the same endless wall that surrounds the dirt road.

"You will not see it unless you cross the threshold," Dragonfly Diva states.

Suddenly Angelina understands the chill and the goose bumps. She knows exactly what she must do.

"No!" she cries, falling on her butt and crawling away.

"As you wish," Dragonfly Diva responds. "I can't say I blame you."

Dragonfly Diva walks away.

Angelina is sitting on the dirt, watching the hole of the guillotine. The breeze sweeps some dirt into her eyes. She tries to brush it off with the tip of her blouse, when she sees the wall warping.

It is just a split second, but Angelina sees it clearly enough.

"Dragonfly Diva said that I was banging my head against the wall. The wall was constricting my thoughts," Angelina thinks. "Yes. That's it. Why would there be a wall all around the castle? Where would the people in the castle go to? Where would they come from? Where would food come from? What is the point of living inside a wall?"

Angelina hears herself calling Dragonfly Diva as her confused mind rushes through an opening, seeing the light. She has remembered something else.

"When we were flying high above the castle I glanced towards the road. I still saw the wall rising above my sight. I couldn't even see the top. How can a wall go endlessly up?"

"This wall is not real," Angelina triumphantly announces as Dragonfly Diva lands next to her.

"I know," Dragonfly Diva says, smiling.

"You know? Why didn't you tell me?" Angelina protests.

"Would you have believed it?" Dragonfly Diva asks.

"Probably not," Angelina accepts.

"This is what The Executioner guards, isn't it?" Angelina asks. "It guards the wall."

"Yes," Dragonfly Diva whispers.

Angelina does not think it twice. She knows that if she thinks too much, she won't have the courage to do what must be done.

"Then off with my head!" Angelina yells as she places her neck across the guillotine hole, her eyes fixed on the stone wall.

The blade falls with a sharp, metallic snap, but Angelina keeps her eyes open and fixed on the wall.

The wall disappears.

Tall Ancient Trees rise from the fertile ground, regaled with a kaleidoscope of singing, chirping, flying friends. Red cardinals and green parakeets jump from one branch to the other. Blue hummingbirds zoom close to the large, exotic flowers growing in a moss-covered trunk. Black iridescent swallows flash their wings ostentatiously. Cute chubby sparrows swarm down to feed on the ground, where a ring neck pheasant parades his polka dots.

Green shiny bushes stand where the wall was, displaying fresh red and yellow hibiscus flowers. Angelina's heart leaps with joy at the site of the flowers she loves.

She breathes in the strong wooden scent of the Ancient Trees. The majestic forest brings her back to life. She feels as strong as if she had just eaten a hearty meal.

The luscious leaves in the long tree branches dance in the wind. Angelina releases a long exhalation, glad that it is not her last. She feels passionately free! As she rises from the platform, she realizes that the guillotine has also disappeared.

Hanging over Angelina's neck is an old golden key.

"You did it!" Dragonfly Diva celebrates. "You are a true Warrior, Angelina Semidey!"

The key is strung on a leather string. There is something inscribed on it. Angelina reads:

First Alchemical Key:
Break the Wall of Expectations

They march towards the Alignment Effigy, Dragonfly Diva happily pirouetting around Angelina, painting the mid-day air with iridescent hues. Angelina feels like a true hero.

She drops the key in the Dream Basket. The loud noise of grating iron chains resonates all around them as the north side of the bridge gives in with a thud. Now the bridge is partially hanging on one side.

"Well done, Angelina," the Alignment Effigy declares, coming to life with a cracking sound. Her eyes are glowing blue once more. "You have found the First Key. You have broken the limits that constricted your perception."

The left plate on the scales slowly descends, and the Dream Basket is now lower than the iron ball by an inch.

Angelina is about to ask if she gets a question, when the Alignment Effigy speaks.

"The next Bridge Guardian is the Disk Thrower at the Southeast pole. You must fetch his disk," The Alignment Effigy reveals. The minute she says this she grows lifeless once more.

CHAPTER 15

The Champion's Key

"It's already late afternoon, and I don't have a clue," Angelina mutters as she goes around the Disk Thrower yet another time, placing a pebble in the pockets of her pants, which are now full of pebbles. There must be at least 12 pebbles there! She has examined his features so many times, in so much detail, that she could sculpt him with her eyes closed.

"Where is the damn disk?" Angelina asks for the millionth time. "No other statue comes remotely close to being the Disk Thrower but this one. The Alignment Statue indicated that the Bridge Guardian was located at the Southeast. This is the only Bridge Guardian here. Therefore, this must be the Disk Thrower. So where on earth is the freaking disk! Yet... he does seems to be throwing something. But what? His hand is empty!"

Angelina carefully scans each of the already familiar features. Two large, well-grounded feet hold the muscular legs. His stance reminds Angelina of the twined trees at the foot of the Goddess. He seems to have grown roots deep down on the earth.

The well-built torso, light weight and finely tuned, rises like a tree trunk seeking the light. There is a large, round medallion in his chest. Perhaps a medal earned by his feats. The chain holding the medallion must have broken. The medallion seems to be made of gold, but it is opaque and rusty now. Angelina must admit that of all the Bridge Guardians, this is the only good looking one.

She observes his muscular body leaping forward, his right arm raised and the hand opened as if...

"That's it! I've been saying it over and over, but I wasn't really hearing what I was saying," Angelina exclaims. "As if he had already thrown the disk. I am too late. The disk is gone."

If only Dragonfly Diva was here, the news would not be so devastating. She would think of something brilliant, as always. Angelina, on the other hand, can only think about how hungry she is, how tired she feels and how clueless she remains.

"I've been lucky so far," Angelina concludes. "But I've run out of luck, and I obviously do not have the wits. Now that the Alignment Effigy is expecting more from me, because I did so well before, boy will she be disappointed! What will happen when I go there empty-handed? Will she crush me?"

Where is Dragonfly Diva? It is obvious to Angelina that without the magical old woman she is incapable of achieving one single task in the quest.

"Maybe it's not the right time," Angelina considers.

She looks at the missing left eye of the Disk Thrower. A pity, for the rest of the statue is intact, and it's the only one she really cares to look at.

"Poor Champion," she mumbles. "So handsome, and yet there's something essential missing in you. I mean, an eye is essential for a thrower. You and I have that in common, Champion. Not the handsome part, of course, but the missing part. Right now, there is something missing in me that does not allow me to get to my *DreamSelf*, no matter how hard I try. By now, I should be finishing with the last key, but here I am unable to find the second one."

"Bad timing. That's it. One must recognize when the time is not right," Angelina adds.

"You know what? I am not ready," she concludes. "That's the honest truth, Champion. I am not ready. I need to think this carefully. Perhaps I could go home and give it a try next year."

A mounting terror is possessing Angelina.

Could it be that the woman in the castle is not really her *DreamSelf*? Angelina feels all wrong for that powerful, creative writer. How can a woman so dumb that she cannot find a stupid disk in a statue have the imagination to write anything worthy of being read by millions?

Angelina can see the scene. She finally manages to free the *DreamSelf*, and when the woman sees her up close, she begins to yell.

"This is not me!" The *DreamSelf* is screaming. "This cannot be me. This woman has never been, is not and will never be me. There has been a terrible mistake!"

"Feeding the Dragon again?" Dragonfly Diva asks, fluttering behind Angelina.

"My God, that's exactly what I've been doing!" Angelina shrieks. "How could I allow myself to slide into such despair after only two hours? You go away for a little while, and I lose all faith and strength. Say it. Just come on and say it out loud. I'm spineless!"

"How often do you say this to yourself?" Dragonfly Diva asks, looking at Angelina curiously. Angelina feels like a specimen under a microscope.

"I...I don't know...often enough, I guess," Angelina confesses.

"Have you already forgotten the Dragon's Key?" Dragonfly Diva asks.

"Are you kidding?" Angelina protests. "I will never forget that key. It was earned at great peril. The key is Attention."

"That's the key alright," Dragonfly Diva says as she takes out a sandwich from her bag and offers it to Angelina, who eats it ravenously. "But a key alone does not open anything, does it?"

"What do you mean?" Angelina asks, fearing that she is not only failing this task, but may be shown to have failed even the ones she thought she had won. What could she have missed in that ordeal? She must not let Dragonfly Diva know that she doesn't know.

"What can a key do by itself?" Dragonfly Diva asks.

"Of course," Angelina laughs. "That is so obvious. The key goes into the keyhole. It needs the keyhole to open the door. Jajaja!"

"Laugh all you want, Angelina. But attention is only as good as the place where you place it," Dragonfly Diva declares. "You spent most of the time in the Dragon Wagon placing it in your fear. That didn't help a lot, did it?"

"There she goes again, making me feel small and stupid," Angelina thinks.

She has to admit that the magical lady is right again. She made the Salamander into a Dragon by feeding her fear. And now, what is she feeding now?

Despair. Defeat. Visions of rejection. That's a biggie in her life, Angelina admits. Rejection. She remembers the numerous rejection slips she keeps in a tiny drawer in her desk. Rejection from publishers, from total strangers. Still, they hurt like old rusty lances stuck deep into her heart. Each rejection slip took away a piece of her confidence, until she had none left.

Just remembering the rejection slips has taken away her appetite and the little energy she had left. Hunched, a hung neck and heavy shoulders, Angelina sits at the base of the statue, brooding.

"See the blind spot," Dragonfly Diva whispers into her heart.

Angelina stands up, climbs the base of the statue and looks through the hole in the skull, right through the Champion's left eye ought to be.

"This is the blind spot, isn't it?" she asks, hoping not to be completely off.

"That is his blind spot, but what is yours?" Dragonfly Diva asks.

Angelina is looking through the hole at the *Great Mirrors* that reflect the landscape into the castle. She imagines the *Shadow Scouts* watching her through that reflection, knowing her every move. They must be laughing at her right now.

"I am blinded by fear," Angelina confesses.

"Fear of what?" Dragonfly Diva asks.

"Fear of rejection," Angelina admits. "I am fine as long as I am working alone. I can see the truth and the beauty of what I write. I appreciate it. But the moment I begin to imagine how others see me, how they will interpret what I write, how they will judge me, then it all crumbles."

"What happens then?" Dragonfly Diva inquires.

"I believe that they will judge me and find me defective. I won't be good enough. They will laugh at me. They will ask for their money back," Angelina admits, her eyes on the heels of the statue. It is so humiliating to admit this about herself!

"You are seeing yourself with others' eyes, Angelina," Dragonfly Diva reveals. "It is time you place your attention in your own self-vision and reclaim what you know to be true about yourself."

"That's easy to say," Angelina snorts. "Don't you think I know that I should do this? But I don't know how to do it."

"Fire the pebbles," Dragonfly Diva instructs.

Is she flying off the handle again? This magical lady can go off when Angelina most needs her.

"Grab a pebble," Dragonfly Diva instructs.

"The only person madder that this old woman is me," Angelina mutters to herself as she grabs a pebble from her pocket. "That's why I go along."

"Place your left hand on your heart. Touch your *Ancestral Heart*. That's it," Dragonfly Diva instructs as Angelina does what she says.

"Look through the hole in his left eye," Dragonfly Diva continues. "Look at yourself with your own eyes, and name your virtues. When you see a virtue, then throw a pebble through his eye."

"When I see a what?" Angelina asks. She heard everything the lady said, but the entire concept of her virtues confuses her.

"You do have some good points, don't you?" Dragonfly Diva asks.

"I...I suppose," Angelina stutters.

"Name them. Your virtues. Your basic goodness. Your accomplishments. Your strengths. Your qualities. One pebble for each," Dragonfly Diva explains.

Funny. She has spent so much of her energy and time defending herself against others' criticism. But she herself has never taken time to look at her good side. Right then and there, Angelina realizes that she has been her worst critic. She has badgered herself more viciously and consistently than anyone ever could. But she has never named her goodness. Not once.

Angelina takes a deep breath and releases a long exhalation. As she looks through the empty left eye of the Champion, she sees one of the *Great Mirrors* up on the fortress. As she focuses on it, she catches the reflection of the landscape. Beautiful bushes and red and yellow hibiscus dance gently in the breeze, just behind her. In spite the turmoil inside her, Angelina is moved by the beauty around her.

"I see the beauty of our world," Angelina declares, tiny tears wetting her lower eyelashes.

"Bravo!" Dragonfly Diva applauds, using her wings to clap, and elevating herself above the statue. Her enthusiasm is contagious. "Throw a pebble!"

Angelina throws a pebble through the Champion's eye. Her body suddenly merges with the Champion's body. She feels his strong muscles and stands in his strong bones. Her left hand is on his chest. Something pulsates under it. It's the medallion. It is getting warm.

Angelina picks up another pebble from her pocket and looks again through The Champion's missing eye.

A few feet from them, she sees a mother squirrel helping her baby with its first nut.

"I am kind. I like to help others. I do not like to harm or mistreat other people, but to uplift them," Angelina proudly says. As she names this, she feels her heart in the Champion's chest, warm and happy. She feels her own kindness rising from the depth of her soul. The medallion spins under her left hand. Angelina throws a second pebble through the missing eye.

"I see the hidden truths behind every day appearance," Angelina says. "I can feel people's true feelings and can respond to their invisible needs."

As another pebble flies through the Champion's missing eye, the medallion gets warmer and spins faster under her left hand. It's as if the medallion was the Champion's heart and was being brought back to life.

"I am a creative, unique, extraordinary human being," Angelina boldly declares. "I am my own person, and I am full of delightful surprises and passionate, exuberant energy. I am a poem unfolding."

She is truly enjoying this ritual. Her whole body feels alive and strong, and she feels that her smile begins deep inside her.

As she throws the pebble, the medallion detaches from the Champion's chest.

"The medallion is the disk!" Angelina realizes. She is infused with strength and courage.

"I am courageous," Angelina declares. "I dare to take risks and embrace change to accomplish my dreams."

Another pebble flies through the Champion's missing eye and the disk spins very fast. Angelina takes her hand off her chest. The disk floats towards the Champion's hand.

"I name truth and beauty to nurture them in the world, in my soul and in the souls of others," Angelina exclaims, throwing another pebble through the missing eye.

The disk reaches the raised hand of the Champion. Angelina is engulfed in vertiginous movement. Her now highly tuned muscles respond in fractions of a second. The disk barely rests on the hand. It flies into space. It knows its destiny.

Angelina realizes that the Champion's left eye is not missing or broken. It is resting miles ahead, on the target. Like a magnet, it guides the disk to its destination. The disk is gone. The target has been hit.

She falls back from the statue's base and lands on the dust road. There's something glowing in her hands. It's a golden key.

Second Alchemical Key: See yourself with your own eyes and feed your self-value

As she deposits the second alchemical key in the Dream Basket, Angelina feels that peace is spreading inside her, like a healing balm.

"I've been fighting the world," she realizes. "But it was not the world who failed to value me. It was me who refused to embrace my own true worth."

"You have retrieved the second Alchemical Key," The Alignment Effigy declares as she comes alive with a crack and fixes her blue glance in Angelina. She is actually smiling!

"You have launched the Disk of Dream Retrieval into the castle. A formidable feat," The Alignment Effigy announces.

The grating sound of chains lets Angelina know that the south side of the chains holding the bridge is giving way. The bridge is now evenly lowered about two feet into the air.

Another lock in the bridge's stronghold has been broken. Soon there will be nothing separating her from her *DreamSelf*.

Dragonfly Diva is clapping with her wings as she dances around the effigy.

The plate with the Dream Basket goes down two inches. Angelina looks in amazement as the light Dream Basket, almost empty, overpowers the iron ball.

She does not bother to post any question.

"The next Bridge Guardian is the Lord of Lucre," The Alignment Effigy reveals, becoming a lifeless statue immediately.

The name sends shivers down Angelina's spine.

CHAPTER 16

The Power-Holding Key

The ocher rays of the setting sun suffuse the giant gold coin in an irresistible aura. The round gold piece glistens like the sun itself. Yet, its pull is as magnetic as a full moon. It cloaks her eyes, so that Angelina can't see anything but its glow. It quickens her blood. Angelina is burning to leap towards the golden shield. It beacons her hands, making them itch.

Ah, but the Lord of Lucre watches, wrapping his grotesque body protectively around the huge gold piece. His malformed body twists among the shadows of dusk, seizing his trophy possessively. His eerie stone eyes are dead and cold. Yet they possess a hellish fire that sends ominous warnings. Those evil eyes slash Angelina's muscles every time she itches to grab the golden coin.

Each perverse fold in his deformed face repels Angelina as strongly as the golden coin attracts her. Desire and fear are at war in Angelina's heart.

But there is something else. Greed is the true name of this gargoyle. Each macabre crease in its monstrous face holds centuries of avarice. This monster has held on to this treasure with all its claws and hoofs, but also with its own soul, until the golden poison has filled its soul to the rim, leaving no space for humanity.

The Lord of Lucre is the terrifying embodiment of Angelina's fear of wealth. As she looks at the monstrous greed in front of her, Angelina begins to feel the brutal force of a war she has waged for years.

In her poverty, in spite her spiritual devotion, Mercedes has become prey to greed. This greed comes out of hunger for money, the one thing that her mother has been denied and which she sees as the key to everything she lacks.

Angelina reluctantly admits that her mother's hunger has been carved into her own marrow. She is repelled by this hunger, which makes her cringe away from the very thing she craves: money.

Angelina cannot withstand the mirror that the Lord of Lucre presents; a mirror of both, the hunger for money and the repulsion to money that she has inherited. The tension between these two forces creates frustration and anger, so that the war inside her is constantly tearing her apart.

The frustration increases as Angelina accepts that, in spite her hunger; Mercedes cannot accept that she or her daughter will ever have money. Money has become a grotesque resentment that she holds on to, without possibility of resolution. Angelina has inherited that belief. She recognizes it at the bottom of her own resentment. To Angelina the mirror is ten times scarier than the demonic creature itself.

The intensity of her desire surprises Angelina. She knows that she wants money. She is tired of being poor, of doing without. This is no surprise. But she had no idea that her hunger for money was so desperate.

The gold coin is seducing her, and she wants to be seduced. She wants to take it. Take all of it. Take the entire treasure, all for her, only for her. Why not? How many years has she done without while others thrived? She's accrued this much wealth. She's owed it, and she is going to get it. Angelina feels dumbstruck, as swept off her feet as she was when she first saw Omar. This scares her.

How could she feel this way for a thing, for some filthy gold coin that may have generated who knows how many wars? Is she like those greedy men who have gone to war over gold, leaving their blood and the blood of their children as the only map to the treasures they have coveted? She has despised men's history of war and greed. Yet, she cannot deny the intense desire she feels for this gold coin. The warring forces inside her paralyze Angelina.

A water basin surrounds the stone gargoyle. It is slowly filled by a trickle of water dripping from the Lord of Lucre's lips. This makes the monster even more repulsive, as he seems to be constantly drooling for the coin he already possesses.

Reflected in the rippling waters, Angelina's body quivers. She wraps her arms protectively around her torso. But she could more easily stop the waters from shivering than she can stop the trembling in her body.

"A lot of gold went into making that giant coin. How much?" Angelina wonders, her mind strangely dissociating from her body to do the math. "Perhaps 100 ingots or more. How much is that worth?"

"It's even more than that," Angelina calculates. "This is an antique piece. It may be worth much more. If it is a unique piece, then... then it could be worth... millions!"

She is salivating. Her hands itch. If she could only get her hands on that coin, if she could only....

The evil eyes of the Lord of Lucre glide slowly towards her, a sliver of light sparkling from the dead stone pupils. Dark shadows flow across the cold, misshapen body. Angelina sees his spiteful sneer become a threatening grimace. She pulls back.

"Don't look at him, Angelina," she tells herself. "Don't feed your fear. Remember the Dragon. Don't feed his power. Focus on the gold coin. Direct all your intent towards the gold coin."

The magenta hues of sunset whirl in the glistening gold surface, taking Angelina into a dizzying jumble of thoughts and visions.

"What I could do with that money... think of it. I would not have to beg for years, searching for the agent or publisher who appreciates my writings. I could just publish my own book, right now. I could hire a publicist, editors and marketing consultants, and I could become famous. I could spend all my time writing. I could live in the house of my *Dreamlife Vision*: in a sunny tropical beach, with a pink stucco mansion and a gorgeous garden. All of it can be real, just like that, like Dorothy when she clicked her heels. Yes, with a simple click. A step. Reach out."

Angelina is standing on the border of the basin. She is reaching out with both arms towards the gold coin.

A deafening scream pours out from the core of the silent gargoyle. Something knocks Angelina into the basin. Violent bursts of water gush out of the gargoyle's mouth and ears. The gushing water pounds Angelina's back, knocks her down, rolls her around, punches her breasts and hits her face. Angelina covers her body with her arms as the water roars over her.

"So this is what you want, filthy beggar?" growls the Lord of Lucre, as he comes down from his pedestal and encircles the basin, walking heavily around the rim.

Each step he takes makes the stone basin tremble. His hoofs scratch the smooth stone surface, as the pouring waters crash against the rim, agitating the now overflowing waters in the basin. Angelina struggles to get out, but she slips and rolls in the chilly waters, the pouring streams knocking her and pounding on her torso and head.

"You want **my** money. You want the easy way out. The quick way to riches. Someone else's money. Someone else's work. That's what you filthy humans do.

Steal. Plagiarize. Copy. Follow someone else's formula," growls the Lord of Lucre in a gush of stony burble.

"I despise the whole lot of you. I spit on your spineless hunger and witless self-indulgence," the Lord of Lucre roars as he shows his razor-sharp teeth and claws, flexes his stony knees and leaps into the basin.

"You will not have my coin!" The Lord of Lucre screams in a thundering voice that echoes through Angelina's bones as his opened fangs and deadly claws come closer and closer.

An avalanche of pain batters her body as Angelina struggles in the water. She feels her chest searing as the claws slash and tear. As the waters run red with her blood, Angelina feels her strength leaving her body.

"You fool, you stupid fool, you blew it, you idiotic greedy, spineless, useless, hungry needy brainless stupid wimp, you failed. You failed. You FAILED!"

She hears the desperate splashing. She is mad with terror, yet she can still hear that something is wrong. The voice she hears is not the Lord of Lucre's terrible roar. This is her voice. Only her screams slash out as she splashes the water frantically. Angelina stops screaming. She stays still. The chilling waters still tremble around her, but there is no cutting claw. No teeth on her skin. No pain. No bites. No monster attack. Dead silence. Angelina opens her eyes. There is no water pouring down. No Lord of Lucre falling over her. The hideous gargoyle stands silent and still in its stony base.

Angelina shivers. Her body trembles in great spastics movements. Her mind cannot separate where the cold stops and the fear begins. The fear that won't leave her. The fear that keeps the cold stuck to her bones.

Tiny stars float above the basin, winking at Angelina from the still dark waters. They plunge into the water, cleaning and warming it instantly. Angelina relaxes into the warm, clear waters.

"Thought I'd add some bubbles to your beauty bath," Dragonfly Diva purrs. "You didn't seem too relaxed with the water massage, though."

Angelina has never been so happy to see the eccentric lady.

Dragonfly Diva helps her out of the basin. She stirs her wings at great speed, drying Angelina instantly.

"It attacked me," Angelina whispers as Dragonfly Diva hand-dries her hair by blowing on it while she pats it lightly at great speed.

"Who?" Dragonfly Diva whispers back.

"Him," Angelina points to the lifeless gargoyle.

"Him?" Dragonfly Diva asks, examining the stone statue.

"He doesn't seem too... animated. How exactly did he attack you?" Dragonfly Diva asks.

"You don't believe me," Angelina complains.

"So what?" Dragonfly Diva asks, sitting on the rim of the basin.

"What do you mean so what?" Angelina barks. "So you don't believe me!"

"What if I didn't?" Dragonfly Diva says. "Would that mean that it did not happen?"

"Well, you know more than I do about these... these magical occurrences," Angelina stutters. "If you don't think that he could be animated, then perhaps I did imagine the whole thing. After all, I found myself splashing all over the water, alone... and he was as still as a statue."

"Which he is," Dragonfly Diva finishes.

"Exactly," Angelina agrees. "Then I imagined it?"

"You are giving away your power, Angelina," Dragonfly Diva states as she gets up and walks away.

"Please, don't leave. I didn't blame you. That's not fair!" Angelina starts protesting.

"Who says anything about leaving?" Dragonfly Diva retorts. "I can't help you with this task until you stop giving away your power. That's all. When you do, I'll return. And I bet you a nice, tasty morsel that you won't need me by then!"

And saying this, Dragonfly Diva disappeared.

"Just like that, she takes off and leaves me struggling with the problem," Angelina mutters. "That's not fair. She's the expert. She's the one who's supposed to guide me in this journey."

Angelina is angry. She is hungry. She is also tired. It's been centuries since she last rested. Her mind simply won't work. She sits on the rim of the basin, looking at the still waters. Is it possible that these quiet waters, no more than three feet deep, almost drown her a minute ago? She softly caresses the waters, still warm from Dragonfly Diva's magic.

In the silent stillness of the waters, Angelina feels her mind emptying and her heart filling.

"What have I done?" Angelina asks in a bare whisper. She feels as if she were awakening from a deep trance.

"I came here to fetch the *Alchemical Key*, not to get money," Angelina whispers. She doesn't understand why she became obsessed with having the gold coin. What on earth was she thinking? Was she willing to get the gold coin and leave her *DreamSelf* in prison? How would that make her happy? Is this her idea of success?"

Angelina shakes her head. No. Never. Money is good. She wants money. But not without her dream. Not without her happiness. She already saw what her self-betrayal was doing to Angie. She saw her *DreamBirth Vision*. She knows her purpose. There is no way that she is going to settle for less.

For the first time in her life, Angelina realizes that money is not a goal. It is simply a means —a vehicle. It was never intended as a goal. She has made it the goal —in spite her good intentions and high values— because she has been too hungry for it. Her hunger has made her overvalue it. She has been confused.

"More like a trance," Angelina thinks. "The *Domestication Trance*. Dragonfly Diva was right. I've been giving away my power."

"How can I fetch the key?" Angelina asks herself. She is so engrossed in re-focusing her attention to find the Alchemical Key that she does not realize that she is talking out loud.

"Is there a way to fetch the *Alchemical Key* without having to struggle with the Lord of Lucre for his bounty?"

A crack and a grinding of teeth send shivers through her spine. Angelina jumps away from the basin as the revolting mouth of the Lord of the Lucre's opens wide. A high-pitch chirp streams out of his lips. A snake slithers out of the mouth. No. It's not a snake. It's a tail. A long tail. Attached to the tail, a derriere, and attached to the derriere, a monkey. Before Angelina's mind can make the necessary adjustments, the monkey jumps from the Lord of the Lucre's mouth to the basin's rim.

"That's more like it!" the monkey chirps. "How is a *Psychic Key* that opens invisible doors."

"Who... who are you?" Angelina blusters.

"The Merry Money Monkey," the monkey responds, jumping and clapping enthusiastically.

Angelina finds it almost impossible to assimilate the monkey's full name.

"The Merry Monkey?" Angelina asks.

"No. The Merry Money Monkey," the monkey corrects, again jumping enthusiastically.

"Oh, the Money Monkey," Angelina hears.

"No. The Merry Money Monkey," the monkey again corrects chirping and clapping.

Angelina decides to forget about the name and go for the task.

"You said something about a *Psychic Key*," Angelina reminds the monkey.

"How," the Merry Money Monkey clarifies.

"How what?" Angelina asks.

"How is the key," the Merry Money Monkey clarifies.

"How would I know?" Angelina complains, mortified at the monkey's stupidity. "I thought you knew. And the question is not how, but where."

"How is the *Psychic Key*," the Merry Money Monkey insists. "You must answer how before asking where."

"Great!" Angelina mutters. "I'm stuck between a demented monster and an idiotic monkey, and Dragonfly Diva is nowhere to be found."

The Merry Money Monkey gets terribly upset and jumps on to Angelina's head, screeching hellishly.

"What do you want?" the Merry Money Monkey asks, jumping excitedly on Angelina's shoulders and batching her head. "What do you want?"

"Okay, okay, I want to know how!" Angelina blurts out. She's read somewhere that when you are facing a mad creature, it's best to go along with their madness.

"How what?" the Merry Money Monkey asks, leaping into the fountain, taking a bunch of Angelina's hair.

"Ouch! How can I get the *Alchemical Key* without wrestling with that monster?" Angelina screams.

"The key! The key!" the Merry Money Monkey screeches, jumping along the rim of the basin.

"Where? Where?" Angelina asks, looking wherever the monkey jumps.

The monkey jumps into Angelina's lap. She intuitively grabs it, but he disappears.

Still jumping on her palms, Angelina sees the *Alchemical Key,* a tiny tip of a wiggling tail still fading from its golden body. She reads:

Third Alchemical Key:
Power-holding
Own your Power and do not give it away

"Good work!" Dragonfly Diva cheers from above. She begins to jump and applaud like the monkey.

"No more monkey business!" Angelina warns.

They walk once again towards the Alignment Effigy.

"You have retrieved the third *Alchemical Key*," The Alignment Effigy declares, coming to life with a crack.

“You have retrieved your ownership of power,” The Alignment Effigy announces, as she fixes her blue glance in Angelina. The screeching sound of chains reminds Angelina of the Merry Money Monkey.

It is only then, when she no longer seeks the gold coin, that the full power of the Merry Money Monkey’s name strikes Angelina. She has been seeking money with resentment, as a chore that stresses her to the point of thinning out her joy and making her forget her true desires. She is angry about money. How can she attract money when the more she needs it, the more she hates it?

As Angelina drops the *Alchemical Key* into the Dream Basket, the plate with the Dream Basket goes down three more inches.

A loud crackling noise sears through space, rattling the chains and producing a deafening metallic echo. Angelina’s heart leaps. The north side of the bridge now hangs open about two more feet, like a mouth ajar with surprise.

She feels a secret pride. The *Shadow Castle* is yielding. If the *Shadow Scouts* thought that they had nothing to fear from her, they must be shaking in their boots now.

“Take that, you morons!” She celebrates, a glorious smile lighting up her tired, tear-stained face.

“Congratulations!” the Alignment Effigy declares. “In retrieving the key from the Lord of Lucre, you have demonstrated extraordinary faith and commitment, as well as integrity. As a boon, I will grant you help.”

Just when Angelina is about to ask what kind of help is she getting, the Alignment Effigy closes her stony eyes and goes back to sleep.

“Thank you,” Angelina mumbles into the deaf stone’s ears. “I could definitely use some help. Why don’t you get me a plane that flies me through that stuck bridge of yours?”

“Don’t push your luck,” Dragonfly Diva warns, sitting on the flat rock across the entrance.

“Luck?” Angelina protests. “Hard work is what I call it.”

“Did I miss all the fun?” Dragonfly Diva asks.

“No,” Angelina replies, with a guilty look.

“Thank you,” Angelina whispers, suddenly hugging Dragonfly Diva so tightly that she lifts up the lady from the rock and wrinkles her wings.

“You’re welcome,” Dragonfly Diva responds with a satisfied grin as she floats an instant above the rock, shakes up her wings, and then slowly seats down.

Angelina feels a little odd after that sudden burst of emotion. She seats on the rock beside Dragonfly Diva.

They wait.

After what appears a long, long time, Angelina gets restless.

"Excuse me, ma'am," Angelina coughs up, hoping against hope that the Alignment Effigy comes to life," Didn't you say help was coming?"

Dragonfly Diva struggles to keep a straight face.

"Patience is a virtue," Dragonfly Diva whispers.

"This comes from the same mouth that told me there was no time to waste," Angelina observes.

They wait for what feels like an eternity. Angelina's stomach is growling.

"Oh, I forgot!" Dragonfly Diva exclaims, producing a mouth-watering grilled chicken on a skew. Angelina eats it enthusiastically, looking in all directions every few minutes.

"What will this help be like?" Angelina wonders between bites. "Will it be a giant wrench that plies open the bridge?"

She discards that idea. It's too clumsy. Besides, how will she use such a large wrench?

"How about one of the Bridge Guardians?" she suddenly thinks. "I'm sure that one of those sturdy guardians could leap and bring down the bridge."

She contemplates this possibility for a while. It's not unreasonable. She tries to envision cutting through the chase and getting into the castle without having to face any more *Bridge Guardians*.

"Let's prepare camp for the night," Dragonfly Diva instructs, taking thick blankets out of a huge canvas bag she had placed close to the flat stone. "You look like you need a good night's sleep."

"Not to mention a change of clothing," the winged lady adds with a wink as she produces a pair of beautiful magenta silk pants and a turquoise jersey from the bag.

"Hey! That's the outfit that my *DreamSelf* was wearing in my *DreamLife* Vision!" Angelina exclaims. "How did you...?"

"It's a long story," Dragonfly Diva says with a dismissive gesture as she hands the outfit to Angelina. "I'll tell you all about it when we've finished this job. Now you need to take a quick bath before putting those on."

"There's a pond behind those trees," she adds, pointing towards a copse of trees.

"But the help!" Angelina argues, "I might miss it."

"Don't you worry," Dragonfly Diva replies as she lays down the blankets close to the flat stone and levitates some sticks from the surrounding forest, arranging them inside a large hole at the center of the stone and lighting the fire. "Help always shows up at the right time. I thought you'd know that by now."

Angelina nods.

As she floats on the clear waters, Angelina lets her troubles wash away with the dirt.

"Help has come," she agrees as the trees around the pond sway gently with the evening breeze.

"Help came with Dragonfly Diva," she whispers gratefully as a nightingale releases a long, beautiful song that echoes her gratitude.

"I had earned no boon then," she remembers. "I was struggling to find my own place, my own success, but I was way off. Yes, I was determined, but I felt unsupported. I thought the Universe had no interest in my puny self. Not in my wildest dreams could I've imagined that miracles like this were possible."

Her heart is brimming with gratitude. This feeling of gratitude is so potent that it washes away all her exhaustion, just as the water is washing away the filth.

Angelina wonders what mysterious force hides in the feeling of gratitude that it can so quickly and easily dissolve the worry and wariness she has carried for so long.

Her mind —however uncharacteristically— refuses to dwell on anything but a good night sleep.

Part 4

The Knights' Keys

"Only as high as I reach can I grow,
Only as far as I seek can I go,
Only as deep as I look can I see,
Only as much as I dream can I be."
—Karen Ravn

CHAPTER 17

The Power Song

The earth is trembling.

Angelina seats up, eyes wide open. Dragonfly Diva is standing a few feet away, looking towards the horizon.

"It's coming," the magical lady says as she serves Angelina tea from a kettle resting over a grill improvised with sticks over the newly fed fire. She points at an assortment of bread and cheese laid close to the campfire. "Serve yourself."

"What? Who?" Angelina asks, wiping her eyes clean and trying to remember where she is.

The songs of the birds flying excitedly around the Ancient Trees and the towering façade of the castle quickly settle her doubts.

"Help," is the laconic response.

Angelina jumps up and looks in the direction that Dragonfly Diva has been surveying. All she can see is a cloud of dust.

"Are you sure?" Angelina says.

"Certain," Dragonfly Diva responds.

"There's water on the basin," Dragonfly Diva says dully while eyeing Angelina slyly.

Angelina washes her face, eyeing the lady back as she dries herself with a tiny towel by the basin. The comfort of the terry cloth makes her wonder where on earth Dragonfly Diva gets all the things she has brought: food, blankets, kettle, basin, towels.

"Where does she go when she disappears?" Angelina wonders suspiciously.

She has just chewed the last piece of bread when the unmistakable sound of horses' hoofs drowns the song of the birds.

Coming out of a cloud of dust, 5 horses gallop towards them. One is red. One is black. One is white. One is spotted. And the last one is a pony.

Seating tall on each horse, a knight rides. A child rides on the pony. Angelina rubs her eyes on disbelief. She was waiting for help, and here is not one, but 4 knights in shining armors. Can this be real?

As The Knights approach, Angelina observes that they carry large lances and heavy swords. They are completely encased inside their armors. Only a thin slot for their eyes is free of the metallic shield.

"Being a knight is not an easy job," Angelina concludes.

"Let's go!" Dragonfly Diva says and before Angelina can reply, they're flying towards the back section of the castle using the nearby trees as cover.

Angelina does not want to go to that part of the grounds.

"They won't see us if we go back there," she pleads. "Let's wait for them here."

But it's too late. They are already sweeping down, circling a thick black tree. Angelina's feet have barely touched the ground when she's thinking of flying off again.

Across the black tree lays what seems like a pile of rubble. But Angelina saw what is under that rubble. She was surveying the castle's surrounding when a rabbit jumped into the tiny circle of stones in front of that Bridge Guardian. She stills remembers the creature's screeches of pain. They followed her as she flew, swearing never to step into this hellish place.

"This Bridge Guardian is too dangerous," Angelina tells Dragonfly Diva. "The place is evil. We must leave at once."

"Good! I see that you are acquainted with the enemy. It's always better to know what you are up against," the old lady says, pushing her towards the circle of stones.

"I won't go in!" Angelina screams. She crosses her arms in front of her chest and makes her stand. "No force in the world will make me face this horror."

"Not even the death of your Soul?" Dragonfly Diva softly inquires, fluttering around her. "Not even the disappearance of your dreams? Is this horror worse than the vanishing of all hope and joy?"

Angelina grinds her teeth. She nervously stirs the soil around with her feet. She is furious. Her fury is all she can summon to hold her fear in check.

The horses' wild neighs jumble incongruently with the metallic clanking of the armors as The Knights come to a halt in front of the women.

"We are at your service," The Knight in the red horse declares, his voice is a distant echo inside the armor. "Tell us what you want us to do."

Angelina goes berserk. What does he mean? What do they want from her? She does not know what she'll do next. How can she lead anyone else? Her head is pounding. Any moment now she'll burst into tiny fragments.

Angelina's eyes whirl crazily in circles and her head is light and airy. She feels that she is going to faint.

"A fainting lady, how fitting!" Dragonfly Diva murmurs as she catches her and sits her on a fallen trunk.

Angelina is humiliated and annoyed beyond words.

"Can he get in there for me?" she asks defiantly, pointing towards the circle of stones.

"None of us can take on what is yours to do," Dragonfly Diva replies admonishingly. "But he is at your service, if you can get over your ego and make it your amigo."

"I don't need their help!" Angelina defies the magic lady. She knows she's pushing the envelope. She knows this is the very worse time to do it, too. But she just can't help it. She's steaming. There's an intense heat crawling into her nerves, a flame that wants to burst and burn everything around her.

"How often do you do this?" Dragonfly Diva asks softly as she flies around Angelina.

The soft quiver of the lady's long wings has a cooling effect.

"Do what?" Angelina asks, disconcerted.

"Refuse help," Dragonfly Diva declares. "How often do you tell yourself that you do not need help? How often do you refuse to receive what you want, Angelina?"

Angelina feels embarrassed and looks down, at a loss for what to say. Is it the vibration of Dragonfly Diva's wings or her own confusion? She's usually not this meek. She hates being docile. She...

"Is it because you trust no one?" Dragonfly Diva asks in a whisper, as her wings cool the air around Angelina and create a field of tranquility that dissolves the fire inside her.

"Or is it because you believe that asking for help or even needing it makes you weak? Which is it Angelina?" Dragonfly Diva continues with her soft inquiry as she circles Angelina.

"I... I don't know. I trust... I trust..."

"Yes, who do I trust?" Angelina asks herself, an alarm rising in her mind.

"I trust... my friends!" She declares triumphantly.

"Do you? Is that why you never ask them for help?" Dragonfly Diva asks.

Angelina is so shaken that she cannot even ask the lady how she knows this. She stands up without even realizing it, her eyes fixed on something only she sees. She's staring at something... something in her... something she does not like a bit.

"Look around, Angelina," Dragonfly Diva instructs as she widens the circle around Angelina. "This is the boon you got from the Alignment Effigy. Will you use it?"

"But I wasn't thinking of this type of help," Angelina protests. "I was thinking more of a tool that..."

"That YOU could use by yourself to keep in control!" Dragonfly Diva challenges. "But you are NOT in control. Do you really think that you always know better? Better than *The Source* to which you pray? Better than the *Spirits of the Place*? Do you? Do you know better now, even when you really don't know *The Laws* of this place?"

Angelina shakes her head. She definitely does not know what works in this place. She's been winging it until now.

Angelina is embarrassed to admit her own ignorance and helplessness. But now she also sees that she has ignored her own faith. How is she ever going to defeat this evil when she cannot even trust the goodness in her life?

"If you want to succeed, Angelina Semidey, you need to get out of your *Control Ruse* and allow your *Creation Partners* to do their job," Dragonfly Diva instructs.

"What?" Angelina inquires, raising her head abruptly. She is bewildered. What is this about some partners? She has no partners. She works solo.

"You are not alone, Angelina," the magical lady whispers, tenderly holding Angelina by the shoulders. This has a grounding effect in her body.

"I want you to **see** what you are not seeing," Dragonfly Diva says. Her voice is emphatic, as if Angelina was far away.

Every time she utters the word "See" something knocks in Angelina's heart and causes tiny explosions in her head.

"I want you to **see** how easily you accepted the existence of the *Shadow Castle* and the *Shadow Scouts*," Dragonfly Diva pounds. "I want you to **see** how you had no trouble at all accepting that your *DreamSelf* is a prisoner."

"I know these things to be true," Angelina defends. "I know them in my heart."

"But you cannot **see** your allies. You cannot **see** that the *Dreamscape* wants you to succeed," Dragonfly Diva challenges. "Don't you feel the support all around you in your heart? Does your Soul not point to the allies who have shown up? Am I not your ally? Yet you have resisted me fiercely!"

"I do appreciate you!" Angelina screams. "Please don't leave me now."

"I'm not going anywhere, Angelina." Dragonfly Diva laughs. "But you need to wake up. Open your eyes. You've allowed yourself to be orphaned from the Earth that birthed you."

Angelina remembers her *DreamBirth.* Her heart is stirred by the potent love Earth Mother poured into her, making her perfect for her purpose.

She hangs her head in humility as she flexes her knees, feeling the earth with each inch of her feet. She feels like a tree, digging roots deep into Earth. A spiral of blue fire shoots up her vertebrae, warming her heart. She feels the presence of the Black Trees. They are listening intently. They are sending her strength. She feels safe and grateful again.

"You have allowed your hardship to make you a stranger to your *Creation Partners,"* Dragonfly Diva reveals. "You only see what proves what you already believe, that the world is hostile and you are alone."

"This *Blind Spot* does not allow you to honor the powers of the *Creation Partners* that have shown up to help you."

"It's true. They've shown up..." Angelina repeats to herself, "...to help me. They have helped me. They are helping me."

The words have a strange taste in her mouth, like one of those scrumptious delicacies that is an acquired taste.

"You needed help and you got it," Dragonfly Diva concludes. "The question now is simple. Can you receive it? Or are you so arrogant and attached to doing it alone and with struggle that you cannot accept support?"

This word stirs Angelina's whole being. If there is one thing she hates it is arrogance.

She's seen it so often in people who were brought up in wealth, whose privileged life has spoiled them and who take others for granted. She's observed how these people despise those under their authority, those humble servants who make them their money and create their comfort. She knows firsthand of bosses who take for granted their employees and teachers who condescend to their students.

"It takes one to know one," Angelina admits to herself. She hates arrogance; yet at this moment she realizes that she has been arrogant and that this arrogance is a cover up.

"What did Dragonfly Diva call it?" Angelina tries to remember. "A *Control Ruse.* That's it. A mask to cover up my terror."

"I need support," she says softly. "And I welcome it."

"Good. Go get them!" Dragonfly Diva cheers with a clap of her wings that sends purple and blue sparkles into the air.

Angelina walks decidedly towards the circle of stone. She feels stronger now. She feels the physical support of Earth Mother and the magical support of the wizened lady. She feels the emotional support of all those she loves. As she walks, she remembers Omar, Pop, Jackie and Jocelyn. She feels their presence and she no longer feels alone.

As she gets closer to the small circle of stones, however, a dreadful chill wraps around her, squeezing the warmth out of her. The sparks fizzle out. The presence of her loved ones fades away. Her heart freezes.

She backs away.

"Trust the *Spirits of the Place,* Angelina. There's good helping you here," Dragonfly Diva speaks into her heart.

Angelina moves forward. But a cold wind spirals around her just as she is about to enter the small stone circle. It pricks her skin, pierces her pores and sends a chill all the way down to her bones. She pulls back.

"Can I be of service to my lady?" The Knight asks. He approaches Angelina, the reigns of the red horse still in his hands.

"I'm no freaking lady," Angelina explodes. "I'm a modern, free, independent woman and I don't need a knight in shining armor to rescue me!"

Her anger fires her up and sends the chill away. But her words, charged with anger, have also created a disturbance in the field around the place. Angelina can feel that she has awakened something evil. Dark clouds swiftly cover the grounds.

She is not the only one feeling the disturbance. It is fortunate that The Knights had just dismounted and had tied the horses to nearby trees. The horses neigh nervously, their hoofs pounding the earth. The red horse rears up and The Knight struggles to calm him down.

"Shame on you," the boy snaps at Angelina. "He was just trying to help. He's devoted to helping those who seek to yield power wisely. But there must be a mistake. You don't seem wise at all!"

The boy takes the red horse away and Angelina is left to brew on her shame.

"What is happening to me?" Angelina asks, trying to get her act together. She moves away from the stone circle to clear her head. "I finally get the help I wanted, and I am all over the place. Just minutes ago I saw my fear and the arrogance I use to cover it up. I just told Dragonfly Diva that I do receive this help. What's wrong with me?"

Angelina's face is scarlet red with shame. Just last night she was filled with gratitude and now she's lashing out at those who are trying to help her. All because she won't admit how scared she is. But then, they don't know what's in store for her.

Everybody is working around her, but avoiding her. Even Dragonfly Diva seems preoccupied looking at the clouds and the chains that run to and from the pole of this apparently invisible Bridge Guardian.

"You saw what lies under this rubble, Angelina," Dragonfly Diva whispers in her heart. "Your heart is scared and I sense that you have great reason to be. There is evil beyond what we commonly see moving in the air. But if you dive into your fear, you will see that it is only your *Second-hand Heart* that is afraid. Underneath, your *Ancestral Heart* holds courage and wisdom beyond your conscious understanding. Trust that courage. Trust your truth. And I beg you; trust that the help granted is the right support for the horror you must face today."

Dragonfly Diva walks towards the circle of stones and stands on its left, extending a hand towards Angelina.

The first knight walks towards her, takes his sword out and makes an oath.

"I am Minstrel. My skills and my life are at your command."

Angelina wants to give them thanks, but she cannot speak. Her throat is on fire. Her mouth is dry. Fear is rising in her body like tongues of fire, for she knows that she must stand in the presence of true evil.

Without words, she points to the left of the circle of stones. The Knight stands there.

Trembling from head to toe, Angelina enters the tiny circle of stones.

The rubble begins to shake and roll, revealing a pile of carcasses. The half-mutilated skeletons of children tremble as the earth around cracks and opens.

Even Dragonfly Diva gasps. Minstrel's armor rattles as he's taken aback with the horror uncovered in front of them.

A massive metallic cage rises from the ground, encasing the miserable burial ground. It rises until it covers the pile, some five feet tall. A wooden plank covers the cage.

A loud fluttering of wings is heard as all birds escape the area. The Knights struggle with the horses who neigh in horror as the morning sky grows pitch dark.

A shimmering silhouette hovers above the cage. The black tunic flows ominously in the night, though there is no breeze. The Dark Sorcerer's countenance is hidden from sight.

Angelina's legs are giving in. The Knight kneels down, offering his sword to her service.

This simple gesture kindles an inexplicable courage and calm in her. She is still afraid. But in her *Ancestral Heart* she knows that all is well. She knows that even though she faces danger, the Universe has sent help to her. She accepts these allies as part of the *Sacred Design* of this moment, as messengers of the miracle.

"Who dares to disturb me?"

The voice comes from the hooded silhouette, though it reverberates in the air, slithering across Angelina's skin like a poisonous serpent.

A horrid rattling of chains is heard as a beast creeps on to stage. Angelina's eyes are fixed on a huge white shaggy dog about four feet tall. He has large bull-like horns and goat's hoofs. His eyes are burning red and he's foaming at the mouth. He advances towards Angelina, snarling viciously.

"It's the Evil Cadejo!" Dragonfly Diva says loudly. "Do not look into his eyes."

With her loud voice, the winged lady attracted the eyes of the Evil Cadejo towards herself, who is looking at Angelina. Angelina is grateful, because she had been looking at the dog just then.

A bark from the left side of the Dark Sorcerer calls her attention. Only then does Angelina see the other dog. It is identical to its white counterpart, with the exception that it as black as the unnatural night looming above them.

Right now the Black Cadejo is waging its tail inoffensively. But during her scouting expedition, Angelina had not stayed long enough to see what this dog could do, so she keeps alert and focuses on the Dark Sorcerer.

"What do you want from me?" The hooded Bridge Guardian thunders. "Why are you wasting my time?"

Angelina tries to speak, but her throat, her tongue; all her speaking parts are paralyzed. It's like one of those nightmares when a monster is attacking you and you want to scream but nothing comes out. Except it's not a nightmare. It's happening for real.

"What is your heart's desire, my lady?" The Knight asks with such devotion in his voice that it melts the terror away.

A malevolent laughter sears the air, polluting it with its malice.

"So you have gallant help," the Dark Sorcerer spits. "For all the good it will do you! Answer this gentleman. What is your heart's desire?"

In his tongue the question reeks with venom and concealed wickedness.

"It's now or never!" Dragonfly Diva whispers in her heart.

"I am here to free my *DreamSelf* and I want the *Alchemical Key* that you hold in your possession," Angelina blurts. She had meant to be strong and bold. Instead, her voice comes out hoarse and broken.

The air reeks with laughter so toxic that the few grass patches close by instantly wilt. The leaves of the nearby trees turn to ashes that fall like dry, dirty rain. The horses are digging into the dirt, seeking an escape.

"It's going to cost you!" the Dark Sorcerer sings in a childish sing-song that seems more terrifying that all his previous bullying.

Just then Angelina sees the child in the center of the stage.

"Angie! NOOO!"

This is what she feared. When she saw the rabbit jump into the circle of stones, a bunny had appeared on stage. At that moment, Angelina had seen the children's carcasses below and had understood what was at stake in the encounter with this Bridge Guardian.

"I'm scared," Angie says. "Take me out of here."

"Don't be scared, baby," Angelina tries to sooth her.

"Quite the contrary, little one. Be scared!" the Dark Sorcerer thunders. "You should be terrified. Your mommy knows what I do to children, yet she summoned me and asked me a favor. She knows that I don't give something for nothing. She knows that YOU are the price for her foolishness."

"I'm not giving you my *Inner Child*, you piece of shit!" Angelina screams.

The white dog moves towards Angie, opening his snout. Two sharp sets of fangs advance towards the child as the beast drivels hungrily. Luckily, Angie closes her eyes, so that the Evil Cadejo cannot harm her.

"Fury is just fear disguised," Dragonfly Diva says into her heart. "You've made a mistake. But you can undo it. Remember the true source of power."

"What do you mean?" Angelina asks. But the telepathy does not seem to work both ways.

Angelina needs to think fast. The Evil Cadejo is advancing toward the child.

Anger exacerbates the dog. Fears exacerbates the Dark Sorcerer. Bluffing does not get through. So what works? What is left? What is the true source of power?"

Angelina hears a noise behind her and sees the boy running towards Minstrel, giving him something. He takes off Minstrel's helmet and the entire armor falls to the ground. Under the armor, Minstrel is a young man, soft and refined, with long blond hair and blue eyes. He's wearing a long mail shirt on top of a red, long sleeves jersey.

"Is this the moment for a change of clothing?" Angelina madly thinks. "What kind of Knight is this?"

The tender notes of a harp fill the air just when the Evil Cadejo opens his mouth to bite Angie. The devil-dog backs away, whining.

Minstrel is sliding his rough fingers through the chords, releasing a heavenly music. As he plays, the young knight shines like an angel.

The music brings back the memory of the Goddess and with her memory, the *Alchemical Rose* opens in Angelina's *Ancestral Heart*. The fragrance of the *Alchemical Rose* sends out love from every part of Angelina's being. Tendrils of calming, healing, protective love flow towards Angie.

The Black Cadejo advances, waging his tail, and comes between the Evil Cadejo and Angie. The Evil Cadejo moves away with the tail behind its legs.

"I see that you recognize the source of true power," Dragonfly Diva whispers into her heart. "The black dog is the Good Cadejo. You activated his powers. He is a protector."

Angelina's heart is ignited in the tender essence of the *Alchemical Rose*. Her love wants to grow. It reaches out to the boy nearby in gratitude.

Every time she extends love to someone, she gets stronger and more serene. She extends love to Dragonfly Diva and Minstrel.

Then she extends love to the trees, the horses and the grasses. A sliver of light appears on the sky and Angelina sees that the leaves are growing back in the branches and flowers are sprouting nearby.

"I see that you have decent allies," the Dark Sorcerer concedes. "You may have been well schooled, but you've changed nothing. She is mine!"

He seizes Angie and begins to cast a spell upon her. The child floats up, struggling against invisible ropes. She seems to be hanging from something. Her throat is being constricted.

The Knight stops playing.

"What are you doing? Angelina says. The dog will get her!"

The boy takes Angelina's hand before she can realize what his intentions are. Angelina's terror mounts as this boy may now be the next victim of this horrendous Bridge Guardian.

"He's waiting," the boy whispers.

"For what?" Angelina asks.

"For your *Power Song,"* the boy reveals.

"My what?" Angelina squeals.

"Your *Power Song*," the boy insists, as if he had not expressed himself correctly. "Surely you know it."

"My *Power Song?*" Angelina asks, clueless.

The Minstrel starts again, but Angelina cannot find her voice.

"You **must** sing," the boy whispers. "If not, we will all perish."

Angelina sees that the boy is saying the truth. Minstrel is growing pale and his fingers are trembling in the harp.

Angie is starting to convulse. The Good Cadejo has retreated and the Evil Cadejo is waiting beneath, to get her when the Dark Sorcerer drops her.

"Any words of advice?" Angelina mutters to Dragonfly Diva.

"Open your mouth," the lady simply says.

Angelina closes her eyes and opens her heart. A wave of green gratitude rises from her heart into her throat and unlocks her lips. Her voice leaps into the music as Minstrel begins the musical phrase.

Only love
Only love has the key
To unlock
The pain that holds you at the mercy
Of fear and fury.

Only love
Only love has the key
To unlock
The part of your soul that was stolen
Leaving you broken.

In your heart
Hatred is the specter
Of the villain
who wounded your essence so cruelly
tainting your beauty.

Every time you run away
Scream, abuse, spoil or destroy!
All you do is make him strong
And you stand alone.
It's that child whom you despise
For her fragile innocence
She's the truest power source
For she holds The Rose.

Only love
Only love has the key
To set you free.

The harp falls silent.

"Oh no!" Angelina thinks. "I must have spoken the wrong words. Now we'll all die!"

There is a huge cracking sound. Things are breaking. The beasts are growling and whining. The sorcerer is howling.

Angelina wants to open her eyes, but she cannot bear to see Angie's destruction. The only hope she holds in her heart is that she is not hearing any of her loved ones screaming. But this hope seems so thin against the destruction surrounding them. She searches in her heart, but feels no harm coming to them. She holds them there, in a safe place, bathed in the love of the *Alchemical Rose*.

Absolute silence falls upon the land.

From that terrible silence, a tiny note springs. Then another. Angelina's heart leaps as she hears the song of birds and feels the warmth of the sun in her skin.

Angelina musters all her courage to open an eye.

The early morning sky is shining in full splendor. Only the poles stand whe re the ominous Bridge Guardian once stood. Where the carcasses had been piled there is now a flower garden. Angie stands in the garden, holding something in her hands.

She joyfully skips towards Angelina and deposits a golden key on her hands. Angelina reads the inscription in the large key:

Fourth Alchemical Key:
Authentic Power
Receive the help of your *Creation Partners*
Open your *Ancestral Heart*
and extend your love to life's challenges

Angelina hugs Angie, who laughs and disappears into her body.

"Well said," Dragonfly Diva exclaims as she claps enthusiastically. "And well done! Well done, all of you!"

"Great song!" the boy claps animatedly.

Minstrel grabs Angelina and whistles for his horse. Free of his armor, he gracefully leaps on to his horse, helping Angelina up. They gallop to the Alignment Effigy. This time, Angelina reaches the scales from her seat on the red horse.

The rattling chains on the south side of the bridge slide a few feet. The two sides are now even.

Suddenly, the two sides of the bridge drop half-way down.

Minstrel and Angelina are whooping as they gallop in circles.

"Victory! Victory!" Minstrel clamors.

"We will prevail!" Angelina roars, raising her fist against the *Shadow Scouts*, who hide their dark faces.

"Back so soon?" The Alignment Effigy says, beaming as she noisily comes to life.

"Few meet the Dark Sorcerer and fewer yet live to tell," the Alignment Effigy adds. "The South and North poles yield one round to your Mastery."

And with a clank, she goes back to sleep.

Angelina is dumbfounded. She knows that defeating the Dark Sorcerer was no small feat. But then, she had lots of help. Still, the respect in the voice of the laconic Alignment Effigy impresses her with the importance of this moment.

"The tide is changing," Angelina acknowledges. "And the change is in great part due to receiving the help I've been offered."

"Fly, South Bliss!" Minstrel bids the red horse, and a flash of red dashes towards the west, bearing the good news.

Angelina is laughing mirthfully. No horse or bird could fly faster or higher than her heart is soaring now.

CHAPTER 18

The Marriage of Power

Everybody is busy preparing camp. Two Knights are setting a large tent in the northeast, close to a tree copse that has become a makeshift stable.

The boy is whistling as he piles hay for the horses. Minstrel is searching for wood, as now there are two fires to feed.

One knight is setting up a shinny contraction very similar to the *Great Mirrors* to spy on the *Shadow Scouts*.

Dragonfly Diva is making a big pot of soup that smells delicious. She's pouring herbs and spices that she's picked from here and there. Others, she takes out of her huge canvas bag.

> *Add basil to the tomato sauce to spice it up and recharge the brain.*
> *Garlic, to improve the circulation, though I may need to add parsley for aromatization*
> *Or the team spirit may suffer traumatization.*
> *Cayenne, to stimulate the heart*
> *And soothe aches and pains.*
> *Turmeric, to heal the wounds,*

and prevent infections
and, why not? To make our skin glow
no matter how hard we work.
I bet the old evil witch will hate that most of all!
Where are the lentils?
Ah, yes! The poor man's gold.
And potatoes, to fill the bulk.

"Give me something to do!" Angelina requests, making Dragonfly Diva jump.

"Why? Haven't you done enough?" Dragonfly Diva teases.

"I'm all charged up!" Angelina confesses. "I need something to do."

"Go fetch water," Dragonfly Diva instructs, giving her two empty buckets.

Angelina's taking her time filling the buckets in the pond. This is her favorite place. She likes seeing the sky reflected in the tranquil waters and the trees slowly swaying with the breeze.

"Well done, Lady!" the boy exclaims behind her, startling Angelina out of her contemplation.

He has two empty buckets that he's now filling with water. "The bridge is down by half. We will soon have it fully lowered."

"My name is Angelina," Angelina says, admiring the courage of this young boy, who cannot be more than 10 years old. "What is your name?"

"I am Boy," the boy says proudly.

"I know, but what is your name?" Angelina insists.

"Boy **is** my name," the boy declares with a frown. He fills the buckets with water and walks back to the horses, shaking his head.

"Women! They're weird," Boy mumbles when he thinks Angelina can no longer hear him.

Angelina hears Boy's voice carried by the breeze and smiles. From her part she wonders who on his sound mind would call a boy just Boy.

She returns to the flat stone, now transformed into the camp's kitchen, and leaves the buckets close to the edge. Minstrel is now helping Dragonfly Diva with the food.

As Angelina watches The Knights working enthusiastically on her behalf, a strange sadness overpowers her.

"It's more like a sad strangeness," she observes, remembering her father. There is little to remember, except what her mother mentions here and there, nothing positive.

"What have I received from my father?" Angelina asks herself for the first time. As she does, she realizes that she has not given herself permission to think of her father because it seems as a betrayal to her mother.

Is there anything to think about? It is pathetically clear what she has received from her father: Absence.

Angelina is walking towards the south. There's a nearby stream calling her.

A dark heaviness sinks into her body as she finds the streaming ribbon flowing towards the west. She crouches on the rock-strewn bank, throwing pebbles into the current.

A bundle of gloom drops its tight weight on her heart and presses down, pushing all her life force down into her stomach, where it becomes heavier. It then presses down, sinking into her belly, drowning her enthusiasm.

"Edward Semidey. That's his name," Angelina says out loud, trying to break out of the bundle of gloom.

Her dad's name sounds strange in her lips. But then, he **is** a stranger.

"To be honest, this male support is all new to me," Angelina tells herself as she walks past where the Disk Thrower stood. But the Bridge Guardian is missing.

"Absent. They are all absent," she mumbles. I've never had a man support my dream. Not dad, not my brother, not..."

"Why don't men stay in my life?" Angelina asks herself. "What's wrong with me?"

This time she's not asking the question ostentatiously, as she does when she falls into her drama. There's a tiny voice inside her, like a little orphan who truly wants to know why there's no place for her in the world.

This tiny, anemic girl is opening a fairy tale book. There are beautiful ducks and a mother duck gathered together, quacking and pointing at an ugly, clumsy duck in their midst. To this day, she remembers the feeling of recognition she experienced when she met the Ugly Duckling.

Angelina smiles. But a few droplets tremble in her eyelashes.

"What's this all about?" she wants to know.

The streaming water runs downhill and her memories run with the waters. The gurgling song of the stream penetrates deep into hidden crevices in her psyche, bringing old memories to the surface.

Angelina does not want to see these memories. She runs blindly, stumbles and rolls down the hill.

She sees their feet first. One pair of feet is wearing huge boots. The other pair wears sandals. Her legs are as massive as his, but softer.

Angelina sweeps off the dirt from her pants as she carefully examines them. There was something in these two Bridge Guardians that had kept her at a distance during her expedition, but she can't see why. They are almost handsome, were not for a strange expression in their faces and his sword, raised against the sky.

"What is it?" Angelina inquires, not being able to capture what is so disquieting about these Titans.

Their short tunics are ironically similar, but her exposed breasts proclaim the difference proudly. She reminds Angelina of the statues of the Greek goddesses. She even carries a classical looking pitcher on one of her hands.

"Yes, she reminds me of the Goddess Temperantia," Angelina muses. "But her expression is not at all of temperance. It's more like...what... sorrow?"

"How tall is she?" Angelina tries to figure out. "Well, an adult could drown in that pitcher of hers. I wonder why she's clutching it against her breasts. Is there something valuable inside?"

Angelina calculates that she's about the size of a four-story building.

"He must be about one story taller," she figures.

The Warrior raises his sword against the sky. He seems angry.

"Is she angry too?" Angelina considers as she walks around the round plaza that contains the statues.

"I got it!" Angelina deduces. "They've been fighting. That's why their backs are turned on each other."

Made of clay, their bodies have the color of flesh. They each hold a piece of an iron chain in a hand. Angelina follows the chains towards the poles and realizes that there is something odd. The chain on his hand rolls towards the southeast, connecting to the pole of the Disk Thrower. The chain on her hand rolls towards the southwest, connecting to a distant pole. But the two pieces of chain do not connect. The system is broken!

A giant hand grabs Angelina. The pitcher in the Goddess' hands comes closer and closer. She is falling. She is whirling inside a dark space, dense and draining. Angelina tries to find a foothold to stop the spinning, but heaviness pours over her entire body. She is drowning.

Angie's taking a nap on the couch. A young Mercedes is holding her head on her lap. There are people dancing, drinking and laughing all around them. Her grandma is there, dancing with Billy, who's about 11 years old. Her grandpa is handing out drinks and smoking a large cigar that smells like an old cedar tree.

There's a guitar playing nearby. Angie is drowsy, but she wants to know who is playing the guitar. She opens her eyes to see.

Just then, the notes of the guitar grow loud and a voice begins to sing. The musician is tall and slender. He is dressed in an elegant blue suite. He has honey-colored hair and olive eyes. It's her daddy!

Just when Angie wants to see more, to remember more, she hears a scream. The laughter and the dance stop. The guitar stops.

"You woke her up!" Mercedes is screaming. "I spent an hour helping her to sleep and you woke her up. She's got school tomorrow, do you know? No, you wouldn't know. You don't take her to school. You don't do anything for them, except charm them."

Everyone is still and quiet, as if they had stopped a movie and the last image had frozen on the screen. Angie sees that the laughter is still trembling on her father's face, as if it didn't know where to go.

"Mercy, it's his birthday," her grandma mumbles, moving close to her mom and trying to hug her. But Mercedes shakes herself away and stands up. Angie's head falls on the cushions. She is wide awake now.

"No! Don't you make excuses for him," Mercedes screams, moving towards her husband. Angelina notices something now that she had not seen then: a woman taking her hand away from his dad's shoulders, slowly moving back.

"He may have charmed you," Mercedes accuses, pointing first at her mother and then at all the guests. "But he's done charming me. An irresponsible husband and a derelict father. That's what he is, and you all dance to his tune because he sings pretty, plays pretty, dances pretty and talks pretty. Well, pretty doesn't cut it anymore. Pretty doesn't feed my kids."

One by one, the guests leave, so silently that Angie wonders if they are tiptoeing. Her father leaves last.

The sound of his guitar case as it snaps close still echoes in her memory.

Angelina can't breathe. She's drowning in this painful river of reminiscence. Her body feels as dense as the liquid memories pouring over her.

She's flying. She's propelled through air and falls into a hard surface with a thud. She is still coughing up water when the blow strikes.

"So that's why my father left!" Angelina realizes, as a sharp blade pierces her back, penetrating all the way to her heart.

Why had she forgotten this? All this time she thought that he had simply abandoned them. Well, he did. But there had been a fight, a humiliation.

A string of comments falls into her ears as the image of the woman moving away from his father repeats itself over and over.

She feels the blade cutting through the air.

"Musicians are like sailors: They have a woman in every town."

"You can't trust artists. They're all *Don Juanes*."

The blade cuts through her stomach. There is no bleeding. Everything is dry, even the cut. Angelina feels as if someone was dissecting her.

"A man should not seduce a woman if he has nothing to offer."

"Men these days don't support their wives. Some even want women to support them."

The sound of metal swishing and cutting inundates her senses. Her thoughts are garbled.

"A faithful man is as rare as a Black Swan."

"Words are a dime a dozen."

The echo of the metallic cold blade falls again and again, slicing her into pieces.

"Do not trust them."
"Do not trust."
"Do not."

The sword hits one more time, but it does not cut. It burns. Angelina is flying. She is falling into darkness again.

Running in her blood is the same irresponsible, untamed creature that burnt in her father's erratic heart. She is a wild card, not to be trusted. Mercedes knew this. That's why she always expected the betrayal. She always waited for the day when she would run off, like her father.

That moment came when Angelina met Omar.

Mercedes' face is reflected in the dark surface of the pitcher. A younger Angelina is talking to her.

> *"Mom, I love psychology," Angelina is stating.*
>
> *"I've seen social workers in the welfare office," she says with dejection. "They look miserable, and are obviously not well paid. That's not a good investment of your hard-earned money."*
>
> *"Mom, I love psychology," Angelina reiterates.*
>
> *"Why don't you study accounting?" Mercedes suggests.*
>
> *Angelina laughs cynically.*
>
> *Apparently, counting other people's money is the only way Mercedes can imagine having money on her hands.*
>
> *They come to terms when Angelina agrees to take some business classes, so that she learns how to develop a private practice.*
>
> *Mercedes' doubtful expression is carved in her memory. Angelina is drowning in anguish.*
>
> *It feels as if she's been sucked into some giant drainage.*
>
> *Mercedes doubt drains Angelina's faith. The doubt is omnipresent. Nothing mitigates it. Anything Angelina does feeds that doubt, and the doubt devours her.*
>
> *But then she met Omar.*

The violent whirling stops. Angelina is swirling slowly in an ocean of sweet memories.

> *It's her second year in college and she is in her lunch period. Omar is playing his guitar in front of the campus cafeteria. Angelina sees his guitar case opened in front of him, collecting money between classes.*
>
> *She stops and listens to his song.*
>
> *No faces... no faces.*
> *Numbers and tags*
> *And welfare cases.*
> *Diagnosis and prognosis,*
> *Prescriptions and professions*
> *first-class or shoddy addresses,*
> *but no faces... no faces... no faces!*
>
> *It is love at first sight. Omar stops playing the minute she moves away. As she begins to move towards the cafeteria, he hastily places the guitar in its case and shoves the money into his pocket.*

"Show's over," he tells the audience. "Hey, beautiful, where are you going?" Wait for me!" he calls out, while everybody laughs and whistles.

She thinks him rather presumptuous, but she smiles. They walk together to the cafeteria, and they kept walking together for six years.

The sweet memories have washed away the wounds of the sword, weaving her back together. Angelina floats in the beautiful sea of memories, feeling as luminous as a star at night.

"Oh, my love, why did I leave you?" Angelina sighs.

It is as if she is growing wings. Her poems keep coming and she keeps writing. Encouraged by Omar, she begins to read them in public.

Encouraged by the response, she registers for acting and dance classes and drops her business courses. She begins to take her poems into her body, to move from the images and words dancing inside her, expressing them in space. She begins writing stories. A couple of them win literary prices. She is published on the college's newspaper.

Omar and she become inseparable and well known in campus. Omar and Angelina, the artist couple, living metaphors and eating images. They move into a dilapidated building, sweating as if they were in a sauna most days and freezing at night. Ah, but those sunsets are full of magic! Angelina feels that she has lived inside a 2' by 2' cell and the walls have crumbled. She is free under a vast sky.

Something is pulling her out of the memory. She does not want to let go, but she is yanked and propelled out of the pitcher. Now she is dashing through space once more. She falls on a hard surface.

"Mother's sick." Bill is saying accusingly as the blade comes down. Angelina barely has time to roll over.

"You are killing her," her brother pronounces.

"She's always dying, Bill," Angelina snorts. "She's been dying almost since she was born. It's her weapon of choice."

Angelina begins a macabre dance as the giant sword, like a pendulum swings back and forth.

Dance with death, mommy.
There's the migraines.
She is so sick she won't eat.
Dance, dance with death, mom.
But then she'll devour candies,
Which make her diabetes worse.
Dance, dance with death, mom.
The diseases come rolling
one after the other.
Heart problems.
Diabetes. Circulation.
Dance, dance with death, mom.
She wears them like medals.
They are her conversational pieces.
But she won't do anything to prevent them.
They are her sacrificial axe.
A double-edge axe
That cuts me as it cuts her.
Dance, dance with death, mom.

The sword cuts into her ovaries. Angelina falls to the ground.

But then big, R-E-S-P-O-N-S-I-B-L-E brother married a rich woman, moved far away and stopped visiting or calling.

"There's your righteous boy!" Angelina screams to the wind as the sword swoops inches from her head.

She is the more furious because Mercedes still idolizes Bill, especially since he now sends her a good chunk of money every month.

Now it's your turn, Angelina.
See you changing.
See you become responsible.
Serious.
Bitter.
Boring.
The good daughter you mom expects.

Angelina recites between her teeth as she avoids the sword.

"Stop your little stage and pen hobbies."

"Get a real job."

She did. She got a job in a community clinic.

The sword scrapes her left arm, taking off all her skin and muscles. She can see the bones in her arm.

That's when the problems started between her and Omar.

"Why are you doing this to yourself?" Omar wanted to know.

The sword cuts off the skin and muscles in her other arm. She has skeleton arms.

"Because I am an adult now," Angelina hears herself saying, but inside she is screaming, just like Omar.

"What does that have to do with your Soul? You are betraying your Soul!"

The sword scrapes her frontal torso, and the skin, muscles and ligaments disappear. She digs into her ribs. She feels the cavity of her heart. Where is it?

Omar did not leave. He hung on for two long years, refusing to give up on her or on her dream, long after she had all but bury it.

In two clean cuts, the sword cuts off the skin and muscles of her legs. First the front. Then the back. Still her bones move.

Now that she finally had the money to spend in new clothing and a decent apartment, they spent two years of hell together. Omar insisted on going to exhibitions and literary soirees, to theatre and performances, but she always declined. She could not bear to see what others were creating, when she had given up.

Still, Omar persisted, even though they had drifted apart. The same passion for poetry that brought them together now became an ocean of distance that grew between them as Angelina clung resolutely to her new, "responsible," artless life.

Until she could not take it anymore. She left Omar and searched for a "sensible" job, which brought her to New York.

The sword rips off the skin and muscles in her back. She is a dancing skeleton.

Dance, dance with death, Angelina.
Skeletons don't have hearts.
Why is my heart hurting?
Poetry does not bring home the bacon.
But I don't eat bacon!
No matter.
You sold your Soul,
Angelina Semidey.
Dance, dance with death, Angelina.
Turn a deaf ear, Angelina
To the last note of that guitar.
To the last smile dying on his face.
To the song of love ringing in your heart.

Why is my heart hurting?
Skeletons don't have hearts.

Omar tried so hard. He did everything right, except for being himself.

"It had nothing to do with him," Angelina screams. "How could I trust him? He is a man, like my father. An artist, like dad!"

"Irresponsible!" she shouts against the wind as the swords falls against her bones.

In the Remembrance, all is broken.
A hand is probing among her bones.

She hears disjointed sounds, like horses approaching.

"Are there ghost horses?" she thinks, and becomes aware that she is thinking.

She wants to touch her body, but she can't find her hands. She does not feel her body. All she feels is pain. Only pain is whole. The rest of her is fragmented.

"You have been *dismembered,*" a soft voice whispers inside her heart.

Then she must still have a heart.

"Hurry, before they get to her again," someone is saying far away.

She smells the fragrance of rose, lavender and cloves. She feels a sweet, warm balsam gliding over her carcass. Someone is singing over her bones.

Aaaaancestral Heaaaaart
You are one.
You Remember.
You are Remembered.
Aaaaancestral Heaaaaart
You heart beats as one
with the heart of the land.
The heart of the Earth
remembers you.
Aaaaancestral Heaaaaart
Your breath is the wind
blowing you back to life.
The Sky remembers you.
Your body is clay
shaped to your Essence.
The clay remembers you.
Your thoughts are fire.
The fire Remembers you.

Your feelings are water.
The water Remembers you.
Aaaaancestral Heaaaaart
You are one.
You Remember.
You are Remembered.
You are whole again.

Radiant filaments of light are sewing her together. She feels her arms and legs again. Her heart is warm. It pulsates steadily. Her body is one massive pain, but at least she feels it.

"Ay! It hurts...sooo...much!" someone is saying.

"It's broken," Dragonfly Diva is whispering.

"The system is broken," she mutters. "The chains..."

"Never mind that now, love," Dragonfly Diva says.

The wizened lady is really worried. Angelina can hear it in her voice. Is she dying?

Dragonfly Diva and Boy roll her over to the edge of the plaza. But something prevents her body from moving farther than that.

"We can't get her out of the plaza!" Boy is screaming.

"They are coming!" someone is saying.

Angelina hears loud clanging. Human steps move fast around her. The giants are also moving. Their footsteps make the earth tremble. She cringes.

She must have eyes because she is seeing two knights fighting the Titans.

"Stop!" she yells. "It's my fight!"

"No, Angelina, it's your war," Dragonfly Diva says. "But the only way you can end it is by refusing to fight anymore, love."

"Am I dying?" she asks, seeing that Dragonfly Diva is calling her love and fussing all over her.

"No, but you have gone through death," Dragonfly Diva replies.

"Gone through death, but not died?" Angelina mutters.

Dragonfly Diva flies around Angelina, creating a blue gelatin-like bubble. It seems to prevent The Titans from moving too close to Angelina.

"You've gone through the *Remembering*," Dragonfly Diva explains. "The *Remembrance* is an initiation in which you remember the forgotten memories that keep you from being whole. Then you can bring your members back together. Sometimes in this *Remembrance*, you get a *Shaman's Bone*."

Dragonfly Diva produces a ring-like bone.

"This is your *Shaman's Bone*," the magical lady whispers. "It is a great honor. It means that you have a spiritual path to guide, teach or lead others. Your *Shaman's Bone* is the broche that pins your mind, body, emotions, soul and spirit together, making you whole again."

"Was I really skinned?" Angelina wants to know. "Was I really a skeleton?"

"What do you feel?" Dragonfly Diva inquires.

Angelina nods.

"Then it really happened," Dragonfly Diva smiles, helping her to seat up.

"Now that you feel better, you need to stop this war."

They watch the two armored knights fighting what seems an impossible battle against The Titans. She can't make heads or tails of the situation.

"Why are they still fighting, if I got my *Shaman's Bone*?" Angelina asks.

"You have faced the hidden ruptures within you and healed the fragmentation," Dragonfly Diva reveals. "But the *Inner Wars* continue. You must find out why."

In a flash of recognition, it all falls together.

"The system is broken," Angelina mutters in a tremulous voice. "**I** am broken!"

"When I was in the Goddess' pitcher I was drowning in awful emotions, but then I was propelled into the Warrior's shield and I was cut into slices by endless thoughts, and the emotions and thoughts were connected, but they fought each other, just like the Titans do."

"How's that?" Boy wants to know. He's attention is divided between watching out for his knights and taking care of Angelina.

"The thoughts created more awful emotions and the emotions made the thoughts cut deeper, but they pulled in different directions. I was torn apart."

"Yes, Angelina. Excellent *Hunting*! You are facing your *Inner Divorce,*" Dragonfly Diva announces. "It is an unfortunately common wound, but a difficult one to heal. There is only one ceremony that will heal it."

"I'll do whatever it takes," Angelina declares.

"Better make it quick before my Knights get killed!" Boy exclaims.

Boy whistles and the third armored Knight shows up with the reigns of his black horse in his hands. Boy takes the reigns as the knight approaches.

"Oh, no, here we go again," Angelina mutters.

"I am *Husband,"* he says, "I care for and protect *The Feminine* and I serve the Soul as Queen. Will you marry me?"

"Is he mad?" Angelina whispers, elbowing Dragonfly Diva.

"He's in love, does that count?" Dragonfly Diva replies.

"He doesn't even know me. I've never even seen him," Angelina mutters madly. "How can we possibly marry?"

"This is what we must do," Dragonfly Diva says. "This is the ceremony."

"But... but..." Angelina stutters.

"Yes?" Dragonfly Diva exhorts. "Is there anything you have to tell me?"

"N-no," Angelina says, backing away.

"Is there anything that makes it impossible for you to marry this knight at your service?"

"N-no," Angelina repeats.

"Well, then, let's commence the ceremony," Dragonfly Diva announces.

The Knight stands up and holds her hand. Boy brings a garland of roses and ties their hands together.

At the sight of the roses, Angelina breaks down.

"I c-can't... I can't marry him," she cries.

"Why?" Dragonfly Diva asks surprised.

"I am... in...love....with...Omar!" Angelina manages to get out.

The fighting stops. The Titans are frozen in mid-fight. The Knights clap merrily.

Minstrel plays a happy melody in the harp. Boy jumps mirthfully around them. Husband takes the *Shaman's Bone* and places it on her finger. It becomes a wedding ring.

"What... what's going on?" Angelina asks, confounded.

"I now pronounce you a *Marriage of Power*," Dragonfly Diva declares.

Just as Angelina is going to protest that she does not want to marry this stranger, The Knight takes off his casket. The rest of the armor falls into the ground.

Angelina is facing Omar.

"How can this be?" she begins to ask, but Omar is embracing and kissing her.

When their bodies and lips meet, they fuse. Angelina surrenders to Omar's strong, loving presence, feeling his Soul nested inside her being.

Before, she had feared disappearing in his embrace, but now she feels the fullness of this fusion. It is as if two opposing, but complimentary forces had merged to ignite a powerful current. This electro-magnetic current has so much power and momentum that it is capable of any miracle.

Angelina feels at peace and complete. The deep war inside her has ceased. Accepting Omar has helped her to accept herself.

The chains rattle as the two Bridge Guardians turn around, embracing each other. The broken chains link to each other.

The ring on her finger becomes an Alchemical Key.

Fifth Alchemical Key: **Marriage of Power** Marry your Sacred Feminine and Sacred Masculine

Angelina deposits the key in the Dream Basket and watches the bridge lower until it is only five feet away from the ground.

"You've come far," the Alignment Effigy declares.

The plate with the iron ball floats high above her shoulders, as if it were carrying a feather.

The Alignment Effigy smiles, but before Angelina can say anything, it goes back into its stony sleep.

Dragonfly Diva carries Angelina back to camp, flying in spirals as she sends sparks into the amber sky.

Back in camp, there is a celebration. *Husband* is there, free of his armor, like Minstrel. He looks so much like Omar, but is he really Omar?

Angelina's heart leaps.

"Are they real?" she asks Dragonfly Diva as they land on the flat stone.

"As real as you are," Dragonfly Diva responds.

"Yes, but will they... Is he Omar? Are we really married?" she insists.

"Certainly," Dragonfly Diva responds, winking at Boy, who laughs uproariously as he runs toward The Knights.

Angelina decides that she no longer likes the word "Certainty." It is certain to bring unexpected surprises.

Still, she eagerly responds to Omar's invitation and they dance as Minstrel plays and sings. The two remaining Knights are banging on their armors, producing an interesting percussive effect.

Boy is dancing with Dragonfly Diva, who laughs and sings with abandonment. That batty old lady sure knows how to have fun!

Angelina suspects that this is a dream. She'll wake up tomorrow and she'll be eating dust and chasing Bridge Guardians.

"But right now I am in Omar's arms," she whispers. "I am exactly where I want to be."

CHAPTER 19

Broken Vessels

Waves of merry chirping and fluttering of wings penetrate the dense, silent blackness. Angelina feels the soft dance of the trees in the breeze. Their leaves rustle, like long dressing gowns on a ball room floor.

Coming out of deep sleep, Angelina smiles and stretches her body on the warm woolen blankets where she is sleeping. The smell of coffee invites her to join this day's merry dance.

She opens her eyes to the dazzling pastels of dawn. A mystic sky smiles back at her, showering her with soft streams of lavender, amber and turquoise.

The soft earth below her body feels good after all her labor. Angelina knows there are more keys to fetch, yet she cannot make herself get up. Not just yet.

Today every color is brighter. Each texture is richer. The world is a beautiful, magical place.

Omar is back in her life. They are together: perhaps even married, if this quest holds true in real life.

"And if not... life still feels great by having him so close," Angelina muses.

"Even if this is not the real Omar," she tells herself. "Even if this knight is just the incarnation of Omar's memory or something to that effect; it still feels fantastic having him back!"

"Everything is better when you are in love," Angelina sighs as she stretches her body again, feeling the early sun in her skin.

Even this dangerous quest with dust-eating labor seems imbued with a golden glow, just because her beloved is nearby.

"I wonder if I could keep this magical, wondrous feeling for all of my life," Angelina ponders. "I wonder if I can fall in love with life. Wouldn't it be grand, to live ecstatically?"

Tiny sparrows dart across the trees above, chirping excitedly. A group of about twenty is moving up and down the nearby hedges. They issue one by one in quick succession, and ramble to a distance of about eight yards, with frequent jerking of their tails. Angelina finds them funny.

Some sparrows are hopping right next to her bed, looking for seeds. She tries to distinguish their stripes. There are striking differences among them, once she observes carefully. Some have a conspicuous white throat, with a narrow white stripe on top of a black head. These ones show a bright orange stripe across their eyes. Others have a grayish throat. Others lack the contrasting throat color. They have rusty caps, a black line through the eyes, a gray rump and black bills.

She closes her eyes and lies back lazily. What she had first heard as general chirping becomes two distinctive songs. There is a repetitive dry trill, much like a little sewing machine. But there's also a clear whistle followed by three quavering notes in a different pitch.

Angelina realizes that there is no sound coming from the camp. If there's coffee already brewing, why are there no sounds? A part of her wants to go check out immediately, but the part that wins is the part that's too tired to do any more questing.

Angelina's eyes follow the vertical ascent of a majestic pine tree. She inhales the piercing fragrance, expanding her lungs. High in the elbow of a branch, she spots a sparrow mother building her nest.

She is weaving some dead grasses and weeds. Angelina spots some twigs, pine needles and what could be animal hair as the busy mom plasters all the materials together.

Just then, the sparrow mother darts down, lands on Angelina's lose mane, and begins to pull on her hair.

"Ouch!" Angelina screams. "That hair is still on my head, mother."

Sparrow mother chirps apologetically and flies away. Now fully awake, Angelina gets up. She brushes her hair, making sure that there are still enough strands left on it.

She puts on the new purple boots that Husband gave her last night as a wedding present, wondering if they will be living together after this ordeal is over.

Angelina feels excited, but scared... and a bit doubtful, too. She still wants to take a good look at him, to make sure that he's really Omar.

She walks down to camp, taking a little detour to wash in the nearby pond. Once at the center of the camp, she finds it deserted. There's only embers left of the fire. She grabs a rag to pick up the coffee pot, still hot —and pours coffee into a tin cup. As she adds a bit of sugar from a nearby tin can, she notices the growing display of tin cups and plates, wash basins and eating cutlery.

"The Knights probably carried it," Angelina concludes with a smile. "They seem to love the clanking of metal."

She places the coffee cup on the flat stone and serves some bread and sardines in one of the adjacent plates.

Taking the food back to bed with her she savors each morsel, throwing some crumbs to the happy sparrows.

Just as she is finishing the last piece of bread, a chubby sparrow lands on her bed. He is chirping urgently and insistently.

Angelina feels her body perking up in attention. She picks up her bag and stands up. The sparrow is now fluttering in front of her, looking back to make sure she follows.

"I must be crazy, taking instructions from a sparrow," Angelina thinks.

Just then, she remembers the first time she observed sparrows.

Angie is sitting on the porch at her grandparents' house. She's about five years old. They're visiting Ojai for the first time since they moved to Arizona.

Pop is nearby, swinging on a rocking chair and smoking his pipe. Angie smells the tendrils of tobacco smoke that drift towards her in the morning breeze.

"You smell like trees, Pop." Angie says as the woody fragrance descends the steps and dances around her.

"You like it, don't you?" Pop laughs. "That's 'cause John Middleton's Walnut Pipe Tobacco is the best tobacco in the whole country."

But, of course, he would say that. He owns the tobacco shop. Angie's heard him say that to all his costumers, though the name of the tobacco blend or brand may not always be this one, which is his favorite. She smiles.

"You see them perky birds?" Pop asks Angie, who is watching some sparrows hopping on the ground, eating seeds.

"They walk funny, don't they?" Angie says.

"They're funny all right," Pop says. "Funny, perky and smart, like you."

Angie laughs.

"You laugh all you want, Tweedy, but that's you alright. Sparrow-spirit, that's what you have. You watch those tiny tweeters and you'll see."

"You're crazy, Pop," Angie laughs.

"Good crazy or bad crazy?" Pop asks.

Angie is confused.

"You see, Tweedy, I hear your mom calling you crazy, and I know she means no harm, but I want you to know that there's bad crazy and then there's good crazy. You understand?"

Angie frowns. She looks at the birds with great concentration.

"Is bad crazy like when mom starts yelling and crying and smashing things all at once?" Angie asks.

"See? You're pretty smart, just like 'em sparrows," Pop says, with a satisfied smile.

Angie thinks harder.

"What's good crazy, then?" Angie asks after a while.

Pop points at a bird wash. There are two sparrows mirthfully bathing in the water. One teases the other by splashing in the water and then shaking its feathers, sprinkling its companion, who chases it playfully for a while until they land on the wash basin and repeat the operation.

Angie and Pop laugh.

"I like good crazy, Pop," Angie says.

"You are good crazy, Tweedy," Pop says, getting up from his rocker and sitting by her side on the balcony's stairs, tossing her hair playfully. "And don't you forget it. Good crazy is the best you can be."

"Why?" Angie wants to know.

"Because if you are not a bit crazy —good crazy, that is— then you are going to be bored and crushed by life. You got to fly, like 'em sparrows. You got to build a nest, too, so you have where to land. But if you spend all your time just eating and nesting, well, that's not enough to make a good life. I tell you this from experience. I worked too dam hard in my business, and that's been a big mistake, now that I look back. You got to dream. You got to dance. You got to laugh. And you got to fly."

"Like 'em sparrows," Angie concludes.

"Like sparrows, Tweedy," Pop confirms, hugging Angie.

Angelina is following the sparrow down the hill that leads to the north section of the castle.

"I'm a sparrow!" Angelina proclaims as she follows her tiny feathered friend. She opens her arms and lets her body fly downhill, laughing contentedly.

The sparrow perches on the bowed head of a tiny clay statue kneeling at the center of a basin and holding a clay bowl.

Angelina drops to the floor in gales of laughter, but her laughter freezes on her mouth. A rising anxiety takes hold of her chest. It's becoming hard to breathe. She has seen this Bridge Guardian several times. She knows this. But she can't remember it. She can't bear to look at it, either. Something makes Angelina avert her eyes. Something snatches the image of the Bridge Guardian away, stealing it from her eyes.

But the sparrow won't have it and starts jumping, singing and spiraling over the tiny kneeling figure. The bird's song and dance seems to rearrange the energy lines around the statue, as if it was pulling away an invisible curtain —until Angelina's eyes can stay fixed in the Bridge Guardian.

It is a tiny adolescent girl holding a clay bowl. Water falls from the bowl into a small stone basin below. It is overflowing and the entire soil around the basin has turned into quagmire.

The anxiety is subsiding and Angelina's breath slows down. The sparrow flies onto Angelina's lap, does a summersault and lands belly up on the ground besides Angelina.

Angelina laughs, thinking that the sparrow miscalculated its acrobatic prowess and slipped. She picks it up and places it on the basin's edge.

But the sparrow repeats the movement.

"What are you doing, you crazy sparrow?" Angelina asks, picking up the bird again and holding it her hand.

The sparrow repeats the movement, leaping from Angelina's hand to the ground as it twists in the air and lands on its back. Then it wriggles itself back to standing position, chirping urgently.

"Do you want me to follow you?" Angelina asks.

The sparrow jumps excitedly and chirps affirmatively. Angelina does not wait. She throws herself onto the ground and rolls, landing face up.

Looking at the Bridge Guardian from the ground, she sees that the water overflowing in the basin is not coming from the bowl, but from the girl's face, partially covered by her hair.

The Clay Girl is crying, her head bowed and her tears falling into the clay bowl. But the bowl is broken, and the water falls through the cracks into the basin, constantly overflowing.

Angelina's face contracts as a wave of pain washes over her.

"This is me," Angelina says, crossing her arms around her heart, trying to keep her pain from spreading into her whole body. She swings back and forth.

"This is me," she softly repeats, like a mantra. "This is me. This is me."

Then something else awakens in her. The senseless waste of this girl's pain stirs her to anger.

"Why should she cry so that others drink?" She asks in a coarse voice. She is not asking anyone in particular. Yet, she truly needs the answer.

Then another, equally overwhelming feeling comes up.

"What sense is there in crying into a bottomless bowl?" What a waste!" Angelina cries out in despair.

The anger and pain in her voice surprise her. Why is she so sad? So mad? It's just a statue!

But it isn't. It's her life. She is looking at the way she's been living since she has memory of herself. She's been pouring her entire life force into broken vessels.

"What broken vessels?" Angelina quietly asks.

The gurgling waters ripple softly, carrying a name.

Mercedes. Mercedes. Mercedes.

"That's only one broken vessel," Angelina whispers. "And yes, I can see how she is broken, how no matter how much I give her, she can't receive it. But that's the only..."

Michael. Jack. Susie. Rachel. Ali.
How many will there have to be before you see them?

The waters gurgle.

Angelina swallows. What powers does this apparently inoffensive Bridge Guardian holds that it can read into her past?

What does this creature know about her old abusive boyfriend, about the date who raped her or about the friends who betrayed her? What kind of horror may be hiding under this innocent façade?

"They were... messed up," Angelina admits defensively as she kneels in one leg, frantically cleansing the other leg of her pants. As the clumps of wet clay fall, she mutters incoherently. "But that... don't... they did not..."

They did not value your gifts.
They did not receive your love.
They did not support your dream.
They did not bear your joy.
They did not appreciate your friendship.
They did not give back to you.

The waters gurgle.

"Yes! Fine! I get it!" Angelina screams. She does not want to hear this. She has not looked at any of those wounds. She has just kept on walking, closing those chapters and starting new ones.

The waters become silent. Eerily silent. They are still streaming, growing and overflowing, but Angelina cannot hear the tiniest sound.

This silence reverberates inside her. Still kneeling in the muddy soil, Angelina looks at the kneeling Bridge Guardian.

Suddenly she is the Clay Girl.

She is exhausted from constantly hemorrhaging her life force into this broken vessel. She wants to rest, to free herself from this constant leak of energy. But she must stay in this expiatory position. What sin has she committed, other than being poor and unappreciated?

She feels the futility of her suffering as her bitter tears plunge into the clay bowl, slipping through the cracks into the stone basin rising only briefly to then feed the dreadful swamp around her.

Angelina is sinking slowly into the swamp. But in her trance, she feels the swamp floating inside her, blistering with the poison of all the tears that have gone unheard. She heard somewhere that tears are the pearls of the soul. If this is true, her soul has wasted it treasures.

As the silence engulfs her, Angelina feels hollow. Emptied. Useless. Invisible. Insufficient.

An *Emotional Undertow* at the bottom of the swamp pulls her down, but in her state Angelina does not realize that she has sunk into the swamp up to her shoulders.

Sunk into silent meaninglessness, she welcomes oblivion.

But the sparrow won't have it and starts jumping on Angelina's head. Its clear whistle wakes Angelina from the swampy stupor. Its quavering notes warn her before she goes under.

Angelina experiences a revelation.

"I am not empty," she declares out loud. And just in time, too —for her mouth is about to be swallowed by the swamp.

The swamp releases her face and neck.

There is a beautiful silence in her head now. Angelina notices that the voice that constantly judges her has stopped. The litany of reproaches and recriminations is gone.

In the absence of that constant noise, Angelina feels like a tree. Sparrow seems to like this, as it happily perches in her head.

"I am full of beauty," Angelina declares. The swamp releases her shoulders and arms. Angelina the tree extends her arms into the blue sky, towards the Northern Hills. Sparrow jumps into one of her human branches, tweeting joyfully.

Angelina the tree slowly raises from the jaws of the swamp, as a log floats in the ocean.

Angelina the tree is a clean channel of life. Life runs through her, flowing from the earth below and the sky above. Light flows through her into the world. There is no heaviness to sink her now.

The labels others have stuck to her fall off and for this brief moment Angelina feels that she is a channel streaming light into the universe.

Angelina steps out of the quagmire.

The tree is gone, but Angelina is awakened from the trance of despair.

"I am neither useless nor insufficient," she now knows.

"I am not and have never been irresponsible."

A high-pitch screech, like the shriek of an old, rusty door opening, sends chills through her spine.

The Clay Girl looks up from her broken bowl. The long clay neck screeches slowly and the shoulders seem to soften and melt, rolling back and exposing her youthful breasts. Her clay tunic slowly releases its wrinkles as the girl's spine straightens.

Angelina is overflowed with a feeling of expansiveness and relief.

"You are no longer a slave girl," she softly murmurs.

But her satisfaction is short lived. The Clay Girl's face shows no signs of liberation. Her hair has fallen back to reveal a shocked, aggrieved face.

The Clay Girl's tears still fall disconsolately, relentlessly into the broken vessel as she fixes her imploring glance on Angelina's eyes.

"Please, help me stop," the waters gurgle.

Angelina stomach stirs. What can she do? How can she make this girl stop crying?

"It's not the crying, but the waste that must be stopped first," says an unmistakable voice behind Angelina.

Angelina can't quiet hear the words. An achingly familiar aroma inundates her senses. This woody fragrance... it can't be.

> *John Middleton's Walnut Pipe Tobacco, the best tobacco that's been around for a long time, the taste for men who know their tobacco, love their family and cherish the trees on earth.*

She sees grandpa swinging in the rocking chair, taking in the taste and sharing the aroma of his favorite pipe tobacco as he utters his familiar praise as connoisseur.

Slowly, hoping and dreading at once, Angelina turns towards the voice.

A circle of sparrows flies around The Knight as he walks towards Angelina, his white horse following behind, held by Boy.

Husband and Minstrel follow silently, helping Boy hold the horses. Behind them walks The Knight still clad in his armor.

Angelina hears a fluttering of wings and looks up. Dragonfly Diva hovers above them.

"I am Elderwise," The Knight says, kneeling in front of Angelina. "I am at your service."

"What did you say a moment ago?" Angelina asks in a trembling voice.

"It's the waste that makes you cry, Tweedy," The Knight says.

Angelina's hands shake visibly as she reaches out and removes the Knight's casket. The rest of the armor falls, revealing the presence of her grandfather.

"But you are dead!" Angelina cries, pulling back. "You died two years after dad left. You've been dead for years!"

"That don't stop me from a good dance when I see one," Pop says, taking a puff from his pipe.

The cedar-like aroma envelops Angelina, who runs to Pop, hugging him, holding on to him, as he holds his pipe high above his head and laughs.

"Where have you been? How's grandma? What..." Angelina shoots.

"We have a job to do, Tweedy," Pop replies, "and that's the only thing I'm allowed to do today."

They both stand, holding hands, looking silently at the Clay Girl whose tears fall endlessly in spite of herself.

"How do I stop the waste?" Angelina asks softly.

"Remember the Tree House," Pop says, taking her head in his wrinkled, chubby hands.

The fragrance of cedar and walnut inundates Angelina's senses, transporting her back to her early years and her very first lessons on life.

CHAPTER 20

The Gift Bundle

Angelina is climbing up a wooden ladder attached to a tree house. She recognizes the old tree. It grew in her grandma's backyard, though the place is better kept than she remembered it. Angelina lands on a plank that serves as the foundation of the house and extends like a balcony.

It's a sizable tree house, fitting about four adults or half a dozen children. It has happy colors. The outside walls are painted turquoise blue, with bright yellow window frames. The inside is painted adobe pink.

Below, Pop is doing his tobacco ceremony. He's smoking a pipe, turning around from east to north, then west and finally south. Angie is turning with him. Too small to smoke the pipe, she simply inhales the holy smoke as it drifts on the air.

Angelina knows that as she closes her eyes, Angie is sending her prayers. Up on the tree house, Angelina closes her eyes and joins them in silence, listening to Spirit.

Strangely enough, Pop's tobacco rituals are one of the few things Angelina remembers about her grandpa. He taught her that tobacco was sacred. An old native wise man, Pop said, had taught him how to talk to the Earth, the Sky, the Mountains and the Ancestors through the smoke.

Everyone thought this was a tale to justify his smoking habit. But Angie took it seriously.

Billy's face peeks out of the window of the tree house. He's about 12 years old.

"Hurry up, someone may see us!" Billy whispers loudly.

"Throw that rope down!" Pop instructs. He's just placed his pipe in a pouch and carefully placed the pouch in his backpack.

A brief flash runs through Angelina's memory. This was a year after they moved with Mercedes to Arizona. The next time they would visit, it would be for Pop's funeral. Two years later, they would visit again for grandma's funeral. And then, they would never again visit Ojai, though it would stay in her childhood memories as the place where she's been the happiest.

Angelina steps aside as Billy jumps out of the tree house onto the plank and throws down a rope resting on the plank, like a sleeping snake. The end of the rope is tied to one of the beams holding the tree house up.

Pop ties the rope around Angie's torso and waist, creating sort of a harness. Then he tugs on it.

"Ready!" He signals.

Billy pulls his five-year old sister up slowly, as she climbs up the ladder, Pop right behind her.

Angelina observes Angie's innocent, excited and scared face as the girl comes up.

There's definitely a sparrow-spirit inside this little girl. She is effervescent, even right now, when she is walking through her fear of heights. She already has the furrow that Angelina's had between her brows ever since she can remember. Angelina can see how it was created: through a determined, intense, deep concentration on what she is doing, and as the result of endless curiosity.

Angie looks up, and her eyes turn amber against the morning light. Angelina's chameleon-like eyes have been a controversy in her family ever since she was born. Each family member believes that they are a different color. Some argue that they are olive. Others, that they are amber. Yet others, that they are gray. A few insist that they are green. It has taken Angelina a long time to know that all of them are right. Her eyes change with her moods just as the sky's colors change throughout the day. Right now, Angie's eyes are amber with excitement.

Angie's face is radiant. Her curiosity overflows from her pores, igniting everything with that passion for mystery, for adventure and learning that is her most powerful motivation. Angelina feels her life force rising and beaming in the presence of that tiny girl who holds her Essence.

"Hold her tight," Pop is saying to Billy as he supports Angie on her way up.

"You're gonna show her our secrets?" Billy says. He's angry.

"I never told you they were ours alone, Billy Boy," Pop says. "Your little sister has as much right to the *House of Prosperity* as you do."

"But she's a girl!" Billy argues, as if this made his argument obvious. "Plus she's too small. She won't understand!" Billy complains.

Angelina can see that he is considering dropping the rope.

"You hold her well or I'll throw you down!" Pop thunders, as if he had read Billy's mind.

Billy holds the rope tightly and keeps pulling until Angie makes it to the plank, Pop helping her into the tree house.

"Sit there, Billy Boy," Pop instructs, "in your favorite place."

"Where's she going to sit?" Billy says, still glowering.

"Right about here," Pop says as he helps Angie sit beside him. Angelina sits across her 5-year old self. Pop is seating across Billy. "Now let's place our *Gift Bundles* in front of us."

"She doesn't have one," Billy accuses.

"That's right, and today you are going to teach her how to do her own," Pop says.

"Me? No way!" Billy says.

Pop exhales heavily, like a dragon about to cough up fire. Angelina knows this sign as well as Billy. Pop puffs when he is losing his patience and when what he is saying is extremely important. He puffs when he is really worried about something. Everyone knows not to push their luck once Pop begins to puff. Billy keeps quiet.

"I want you to listen to me very well," Pop says, fixing his eyes on Billy. Angelina notices that his blue eyes are sad. "Your father has left the family, and it looks like it's for good."

The words have a finality to them that hit the boy square on the chest. Billy drops his head.

"No, do not drop your head in defeat, Billy Boy," Pop challenges. "You're the man now."

Billy's head goes up and his black eyes open wide. Angelina can't quite tell if he's scared or excited. Perhaps both.

"You're the man in the family, Billy Boy," Pop declares in a crisp, loud voice. "And it's your job as a man to protect your family and to teach your little sister the ways of the world. It's your duty. Am I making myself clear?"

"What about you?" Billy asks anxiously. Angelina realizes that Billy feels that his father's shoes are too big for him to fill.

"I am an old man, son. I may go soon and you must carry on for me," Pop simply says. "Besides, you are the man in the nuclear family, and I'm your backup, 'cause I am from the larger family. That's how it works."

"You're my back up?" Billy Boys asks, astonished.

"Yes. That's how it works," Pop says. "I am your assistant. I am here to give you a hand, teach you the ropes. Train you in your manly duties. But it's your game, Billy Boy."

Billy's going through so many changes that his face seems like a slide show. The realization that his grandpa may die soon is a heavy blow. The confirmation that his dad will not show up has depressed his spirit. And now he has been given this torch to carry, this weight to bear.

He's proud, Angelina can tell. He feels that he is a man. That this moment is his rites of passage into manhood. But he is also scared.

Meanwhile, Angie has followed everything with the uttermost attention. Now Pop turns to her.

"Now, let's unfold our *Gift Bundles*," Pop instructs.

Pop and Billy open their bundles. Each contains about a dozen objects. There are an assortment of toys, miniatures, wooden animals, photos and old memorabilia.

"Here's your blanket," Pop says. "Lay it open in front of you, like ours is."

Angie does as told. She is excited by the contents in Pop's and Billy's *Gift Bundles* and wants to touch.

"No touching," Pop warns. "Whatever is in these bundles is a secret and belongs only to the bearer. No one else can open or touch. Is that clear?"

Angie assents.

"Make her swear, Pop," Billy insists.

"Mom doesn't let us swear!" Angie screams.

"See? What did I tell you? She's gonna blab it all out the minute we get down," Billy says, puffing much like his grandpa.

"No, I won't!" Angie says in a commanding voice. "I promise not to tell. I promise not to touch. I cross my heart and hope to die! There!"

"That's good enough, Tweedy," Pop says, the end of his lips quivering. "But you don't have to die to keep this secret."

Pop places a box between Angie and him.

"Here's your box," he says. "Did you choose as I told you?"

Angie nods.

"Things that I like, but can give away to the bundle, because I can't take them out. Only to look at them," she repeats as if she had memorized the instructions.

"Let's start. Are you ready to teach your sister?" Pop says in a ceremonial tone.

Billy nods.

"This is our *Gift Bundle*," Pop begins. "It contains the gifts and talents that we were meant to give the world. This means our talents, the things we like to do, the things we are good at, and the actions we can do to make this world better."

"I want to make my *Gift Bundle*!" Angie immediately declares.

"Good, but you must not interrupt," Pop cautions. "That's the rule. Wait for your turn and speak your truth."

Angie nods.

"The *Gift Bundle* is kept inside this tree house. Billy will reveal to you the secret name of this tree house and what it stands for in the world. Are you ready and willing to receive these teachings?" Pop asks ceremoniously.

Angie nods.

"You must say yes," Billy instructs. His tone has changed. He is serious, but gentle, like his grandpa. Angelina can tell that he has assumed his role as a teacher.

Angelina thinks of his brother, all the advice he has tried to give her. She has perceived his seriousness as pomposity; his sense of duty, as superiority, and his attempts to protect them as attempts to control. Perhaps they were. Perhaps he didn't know how to do better. But she now realizes that he has been trying to fulfill the duty that Pop entrusted to him.

"Yes," Angie says.

"The true, secret name of this tree house is the *House of Prosperity*. It holds our *Gift Bundles*," Billy starts in a whisper. "The *House of Prosperity* is the treasure box where we keep these bundles, because they are our greatest treasures."

"What's prospertee?" Angie inquires.

"Remember, no interruptions," Pop reminds her.

Angie covers her mouth.

"Prosperity means abundance, having all that you need and want," Billy explains, enthusiastically. "Like when grandma gives a party, and there's lots of food and deserts and music and fun. And there is a lot, all that you need, and then more."

"Wow!" Angie whispers. She immediately covers her mouth, remembering that she cannot interrupt.

"The *House of Prosperity* gives our *Gift Bundles* a place to be, to grow and to organize," Billy says.

"As we grow, our *Gift Bundle* grows," Billy continues, talking slowly and emphatically. Angelina can tell that this is the part that he finds important and at the same time, difficult to grasp.

"When our *Gift Bundle* gets very strong and we have learned to build our own *House of Prosperity*, then we can make a place for our talents in the world, so that we can become successful leaders or businessmen... businesspeople, like grandpa."

Angelina can tell that he is remembering all he has learned with great concentration, invested on the responsibility to pass it on well. Her heart grows fond of her big brother all over again, and she feels ashamed that she has allowed so many petty things to come between them.

"Well done, Billy Boy, I am proud of you!" Pop exclaims, clapping enthusiastically. Angelina can see the pride in his eyes.

Angie claps, too. She loves to clap.

"Now we will tell you about each treasure in the *Gift Bundle*, and you will choose one of the objects in your box to represent that treasure," Pop says. "Just watch and you'll get the idea soon enough."

"The first treasure is *Uniqueness*," Pop explains, lifting a beautiful carved pipe from his blanket. "This Sacred Pipe represents my *Uniqueness*. I don't just sell tobacco. I am the bridge between the power of the sacred tobacco and the people. That's my *Uniqueness*. That's how I am different and special."

They all clap enthusiastically.

"My *Uniqueness*," Billy says as he picks up a Rubik's cube with all the squares aligned, "is my ability to make things work by organizing them. See how I solved the puzzle?"

"Wow!" Angie exclaims. "That's difficult!"

"Shh!" Pop and Billy both say in unison.

Angie covers her mouth with her hands.

"Yes, it's difficult," Billy says proudly. "But I did it because I am very...what's the word again?"

"Methodic," Pop responds.

"Right," Billy says seriously. "I am a good problem solver."

"It's your turn now," Pop says. "What is your *Uniqueness*? How are you special and different from other people?"

Angie thinks hard. She suddenly remembers something and rummages in her box. She finds a white handkerchief. She opens it to reveal a handful of sparrow feathers.

"I am like the sparrows," Angie says. "I am good crazy. That means that I dream, I laugh, I dance and I fly."

"Well done!" Pop exclaims and they all applaud. Angelina finds herself clapping and cheering along.

Angie carefully places her first treasure in her blanket.

"Now remember: this first object is **not** the treasure. It is just a symbol, like a clue to remind you of your **real** first treasure, your *Uniqueness*."

Angie nods.

"My second treasure is my own *Expert Position*. This means your specialty, the thing that you do well," Pop says, lifting an old telephone auricular. "My *Expert Position* is my capacity to communicate in ways that my clients understand. Like this teaching, in which I reveal to you great secrets of prosperity, but I do it in a simple way that you can learn. I can translate the importance of my hand-made pipes and tobacco to my clients in ways that my competitors can't."

"What's competeeors?" Angie asks.

"Shh!" Pop and Billy both say in unison.

Angie covers her mouth with her hands.

"My second treasure, my *Expert Position*, is figuring out patterns," Billy Boy declares, lifting a paper and unfolding it. It is a draw-by-numbers coloring picture. It is well done, the lines well-traced and the colors well applied. "I can take a look at these numbers and bang! —just like that I see the pattern. This helps me to draw and paint by numbers. It also helps me in math. It also helps me to see people."

This last observation seems to be new. Pop perks up his ears.

"How's that?" he asks.

"Shh!" Angie hisses.

"It's okay, Angie. Pop's allowed to ask because he's teaching us," Billy says, laughing.

He becomes pensive for a while, then he elaborates.

"I've been watching the guys in my class, Pop," Billy whispers. There is pain in his voice. "When dad was living with us and he was always making parties and playing the guitar, they all wanted to be friends with me. But now, they are whispering behind my back, saying nasty things, like my parents are divorced, and things like that. They are not real friends. I see that people act in certain ways, in patterns. Those egg-heads don't truly love anyone. They're in for the fun and out for the work, like you say."

"There are many people like that," Pop says. "And you ain't losing nothing if they walk away, son."

But Angelina could see that he was sad for the boy.

"Now you!" Pop says, turning to Angie. "What is your *Expert Position*? What is the one thing that you do extremely well?"

Angie is thinking as hard as she can. She's barely a baby. Angelina is surprised that she has understood every concept so well. But will she be able to grasp this one? The concepts are getting harder.

Angie's face lights up. She searches the box and picks up a woven rose that had belonged to grandma's winter hat, and she places it on her blanket.

"What does this stand for?" Pop asks. "What is your specialty?"

"I am love," Angie simply says.

Pop hugs her. He, like Angelina is crying.

"The third treasure in my *Gift Bundle* is the *Balance of Giving and Receiving*. This means what you want to give others and what you want to receive from them," Pop explains, picking up two objects from his bundle. In his right hand, he shows a cigar in its protective container and in his left hand a $50 bill. "I want to give my best service and cigars to the world, and I want to receive good money for it."

"Wow!" Billy says, looking at the $50 dollar bill. "Last year it was $20 and the year before it was $10. You're doubling...!"

"Shh!" Pop and Angie both say in unison.

Billy covers his mouth with his hands as Pop and Angie laugh.

"That's what happens when you work your *House of Prosperity*, Billy Boy," Pop announces. "Your profits grow!"

"My *Balance of Giving and Receiving*," says Billy Boy as he proudly picks up a candy wrapper in his right hand, "is that I want to give the kids at school candies when they want them, at school, where they can't have them!"

Angie gasps. They all shush her.

"And..." he finishes with a mischievous smile, showing a $1 in his left hand, "I want them to pay me EXTRA good money for it."

Angie claps, but Pop signals her to stop.

"I am proud of your ingenuity, son," Pop says slowly. Then, as if searching for the right words, he adds. "But you must consider if by doing this, you may not be throwing away the last and most important treasure in your *Gift Bundle*."

Billy Boy is shocked. He searches his bundle and picks up a photo of himself as a two-year old. He looks at it carefully.

"See his innocence," Pop says. "He is a pure, perfect gift from the Creator to this world. If you do something illegal, you will lose your innocence. Then, will you still be this pure gift? Will you destroy what God gave you on a whim, for a few extra dollars?"

"I was trying to do what you taught me," Billy says in a thin voice. "Listen to the demands of my market, and provide the goods."

"That's smart, and I am proud of you," Pop says. "But it's illegal. They don't allow those candies to circulate during class hours. You are breaking the law, and therefore, bringing shame to you and your family. Some laws may seem unfair, but most laws are there for a reason, and when you break them, you harm others. But firstly, you harm yourself because when you are caught, you can destroy your good reputation and trust, and then no one will buy from you anymore."

"But Pop, that's been my best business so far!" Billy protests.

"No doubt," Pops says. "Until you're caught and then placed in detention, and your mom is called."

"I prefer hell," Billy screams.

"What about right outside the gates, before and after class?" Pop winks, "is that against the rules?"

"No, it isn't!" Billy says grinning.

"There you go!" Pop says. "You got your *Balance of Giving and Receiving* corrected, and you are not ruining your last treasure."

"What is the last treasure?" Angie asks.

"Shh!" Pop and Billy both say in unison.

"That's not fair, you've talked a long time, both of you!" Angie protests.

"It's your turn, Tweedy," Pop says. "What's your *Balance of Giving and Receiving*?"

"That's too hard for her," Billy warns. "I couldn't do it until I was seven, remember?"

"You'd be surprise," Pop says. "Girls know more about these things than boys, and much earlier. If you can understand what it is, then you can choose your objects, Tweedy. Otherwise, we'll wait 'till next year."

"What was the third treasure again, Pop? Say it slowly," Angie pleads.

"The *Balance of Giving and Receiving*," Pop reminds her. "What you want to give the world and what you want to receive from others. This is not necessarily a thing. It is a blessing, a service or a talent."

"I would like to make mom smile," Angie says, picking up a broken angel top from last year's Christmas Tree and placing it on her blanket.

"That's doesn't count," Billy says. "That's just one person..."

"No. That's perfectly good," Pop says. "It may change later, Billy, and that's fine. The *Gift Bundle* is meant to grow. You make sure to do this with her every year, and consider what **she** is able to do, not what **you** are able to do. You are older, you see."

Billy's chest puffs out. He nods seriously.

"And what would you like to receive in return?" Pop asks.

"To be happy!" Angie responds, hugging a tiny teddy bear with half the stuffing spilling out of the tummy. She puts it on the blanket, beaming.

She suddenly disappears in Pop's embrace.

Billy is fighting back a tear.

The *House of Prosperity* is spinning down. For a second, Angelina thinks that the tree house is crashing. Then the spinning slows down and the tree house lands in front of the Clay Girl.

Angie and Billy are gone. Angelina can see the Clay Girl's disconsolate face from the tree house's window.

"I haven't been very good at my rose for a long time," Angelina whispers, looking at the Clay Girl's face as a traveler looks into a map.

"But my art does what the rose promises. It brings beauty and harmony. It touches people's soul and helps them see into their depths. I'd say that's love."

"Well said, Tweedy!" Pop applauds. "How about these two?"

He's pointing at the broken angel and the teddy bear.

"They stay," Angelina declares.

"But I'm done with trying to make mom smile. That's a choice she'll have to make for herself." For the first time in a long time Angelina feels no resentment towards Mercedes.

She's letting go, but instead of feeling distant as she imagined she would if she detached from her constant enmeshment with her mom, she is feeling compassionate, but free of expectations.

A movement stops abruptly.

Angelina looks around, but nothing except the waters had been moving.

She realizes that the movement had not been out there, but inside her. As she touches the new stillness inside herself, Angelina becomes aware that there has been a constant crying inside her, a habit of misery that goes against Angie's sparrow-spirit.

A window appears in Angelina's vision. Showers of blinding white light stream into her eyes. But instead of blinding her, the light opens her inner sight.

Angelina sees inside herself. She sees that this constant barrage of misery is inherited, like a family jewel. In spite her natural joy, she has been running an inherited rosary of complaints and misery through her psychic fingers.

For the first time in her life, Angelina is still and silent inside herself. In this tranquility, she sees that her inner crying has wasted energy constantly, like a leaking faucet that wastes the precious water of the planet.

"Happiness is a choice, Pop," Angelina exclaims. "I'm choosing to be happy myself, that's my *Receiving*."

"Well said, Tweedy," Pop replies. "Happiness is all around us. In my life I had thousands of clear blue skies, millions of bird songs and billions of reasons to smile. We all do, if we choose to receive them."

"I do. I truly do," Angelina declares with a wide smile. "And that's what I choose to share with others. My *Giving* is to inspire others to choose happiness, freedom and fulfillment in their lives."

The Clay Girl stops crying. The last drops of tears flow through the broken bowl into the basin. Silence follows.

Angelina looks into the clay countenance. The despair has been washed away. The face, still wet, is melting into an odd blank expression. The Clay Girl seems to draw a blank. Perhaps she has no memory of how to smile.

"We don't have much time. We must be done before night falls, for today you must finish this quest," Pop warns as he spills the objects in Angie's box on the floor. "There can be no doubt or resistance."

"There is none," Angelina replies.

"Then you are ready for the fourth treasure," Pop says. "What is your *Quality of Life*? This is the texture and substance that you desire for your life, what would bring happiness and fulfillment to you personally?"

"Poetry," Angelina responds, picking up a metal ring she had won in a raffle, with a tiny pink moon on top, and placing it on the blanket. "I want a life of creativity, delight, depth, imagination, magic and beauty."

A radiant smile appears on the face of the Clay Girl.

"Your fifth treasure is *Renewal*," Pop reveals. "How do you renew your energy every day?"

"Receiving my own gifts," Angelina answers. "I've learned that I am the first one who needs to feel my own value. I've learned that the *Alchemical Rose* lives within me, and if I open my heart, I can extend love to myself, first and foremost."

"When I do this," Angelina adds, extending her hands to include those around her, "I am able to surround myself with people who see, receive, support and name my gifts."

She picks up a cup-size silver bowl with beautiful engravings all around it. Angelina inspects its bottom, solid and whole. She places it on the blanket.

The bowl in the fountain falls down with a crack, shattering into pieces. The bowl on the blanket is now in the hands of the Clay Girl.

"Your sixth treasure is *Affluence*. How can you obtain affluence? Pop inquires. "How can you earn abundant income from these treasures in your *Gift Bundle*?

"That's tough, Pop," Angelina says. "I've been trained to believe that art doesn't bring home the bacon. I don't know how to change this way of seeing."

"What do you know in your heart?" Pop says. "What does your *Gift Bundle* say?"

Angelina goes through the treasures in her *Gift Bundle.*

Sparrow-spirit, love, a desire to help others choose to be happy, a desire to be happy herself, a magical quality of life lived in beauty and imagination, in truth and creativity. A renewal that comes from receiving and valuing her gifts and having others do the same. What does all of this spell out? Something is staring at her, but she can't quite touch it.

She rumbles as she picks each object, examines it and throws it back in desperation.

"I know it's here," she whispers. "It's right under my nose."

The roof of the tree house lifts up with a crack. The Knights are galloping around the house, and have brought the roof down with ropes.

Husband jumps in.

The sight of Omar catches Angelina by surprise. Her heart beats wildly. She wants to hug and kiss him, to ask forgiveness.

"Remember 'The Dream,'" Omar says, landing with a thud next to Angelina.

They are on stage, bowing to a standing ovation. Omar holds her hand.

"Thank you all for attending our last performance of 'The Dream'," Angelina is saying to a full house.

"Projections by Bobby Roig," Omar says, pointing to the back of the house.

"Art by Omar Archer," Angelina says.

"Poems and performance by Angelina Semidey," Omar says.

"Music and composition by Omar," she says, and they kiss.

The audience is cheering.

Backstage, the dean of the theatre department and her psychology professor approach them.

"You have a jewel here," the dean says. "I don't just mean a good touring piece. I mean a great material that can find its way to multiple media and events. The sky's the limit for you two."

"Listen, Angelina, I am proud of you," her psychology professor says. "Your work reminds me of the ancient shamans. You are taking the people in a ceremony of healing and transformation. It's very powerful."

"The sky's the limit for you two," Angelina repeats, savoring each word.

How come she gave so much importance to these same words coming from her corporate employer, but did not remember having heard them first in reference to her art?

How come she did not believe her psychology professor either? Why did she run away from this opportunity, when it is exactly what her *Gift Bundle* contains?

What kind of idiot wastes her talents and betrays her dreams to follow a stupid little formula just to make a buck?

Omar pulls her towards him and kisses her in the lips. Her self-recriminations dissolve.

These old rosary of judgment and recrimination belongs to her *Mask of Self*. The *Inner Wars* kept her running from dream to doubt, and that was just another way to waste her energy, like the constant crying inside.

"No more," Angelina whispers as she kisses Omar. "I'm whole. I live within my *Marriage of Power*."

"What is your sixth treasure?" Pop insists. "How would you generate income?"

"My *Affluence* comes from combining the alchemical power of my art, its beauty and my imagination with my desire to help people heal, fulfill their purpose and choose happiness," Angelina says.

"My *Affluence* is *Prosperous Creativity*," Angelina continues. "My art creates a magical experience where they are transformed, inspired and liberated. In return, they buy my books, products and events, gifting me prosperity."

"That's my girl!" Pop exclaims, hugging Angelina. "That's my Tweedy!"

"Affluence is flow, and this gift is deeply connected to your third treasure of the *Balance of Giving and Receiving*," Pop says. "Lots' of time what we don't have is simply what we can't receive."

"That's it, Pop!" Angelina admits. "My mind was like a broken puzzle and it's not until now that all these pieces are falling into place that I am beginning to see. There's been this big gap there, in the place of prosperity. I could not believe that I could make a living from my gifts, especially my art. I still don't know how it will happen, but now I know that abundance flows naturally from my gifts. I can feel it."

A loud murmur catches their attention. They look at the Clay Girl. Water gurgles joyfully down her hair. Water playfully springs out of her ears. Water sings a merry song in her lips.

CHAPTER 21

The Service Vision

The sound of the water is a song of affluence that flows through their hearts with a promise. It's a promise that fulfills itself as it is given. It is the promise of bounteousness.

"It's happy water!" Boy murmurs, transfixed.

Indeed, the sadness has gone from the Clay Girl and the old quagmire around the fountain is drying up.

The Clay Girl is looking directly at Angelina. The waters sing a question.

I am mostly gratified.
I am almost liberated.
For the deeds that you have done,
for the choices you have chosen,
now my vessel is not broken
and my curse almost undone.

True, my heart is fully mended.
But my bowl is hardly emptied.
True, because of your bravery

I'm no longer miserable.
But in spite this fine miracle
I still kneel in slavery.

True, no constant bitter tears
Add their sorrow to my years.
True, no longer I squander
My life in dreadful misery
But my pretty bowl is meagerly!
It can barely hold the water.

I kneel when I long to stand
And I struggle to understand
If my bowl is mended well
Why does my song still waste away?
What good is the toil of the bell?
If no one hears, no one prays.

Angelina feels like it's raining in her parade.

"Why, I've never seen someone so ungrateful," she begins.

But just then her eyes fall on the Clay Girl's knees. They are cracking so badly that they are about to crumble. If something is not done, the girl will fall.

But there is something else, something less tangible. There is still a quality in this girl that makes her presence almost indistinguishable in the Northern Hills. What it is, Angelina cannot tell, but it is plain to see that her joy —whence before it was her sorrow— is wasted.

"Sorry Clay Girl, for my callousness," Angelina quickly rectifies. "Your predicament is plain to see, and you are right to object. I don't know which is worse, the waste of tears or the waste of joy."

"It didn't work, Pop," Angelina concedes. "We stopped the crying, but not the wasting."

"How?" she begins to ask. "How do we...?"

"Who?" Pop replies.

"What?" Angelina asks. Then she remembers the Merry Money Monkey and its mischief with words.

"You mean that the key is not in the how but in the who, right?" Angelina asks Pop, tickling him playfully. "Right? Confess now!"

"That's my smart sparrow," Pop confirms, a twinkle in his eyes.

"The seventh treasure in the *Gift Bundle* is your *Circle of Service*." Pop explains. "Who are you here to serve?"

The breaking knees and wasteful joy of Clay Girl move Angelina beyond anything she has experienced before.

"Who are you?" She wants to know.

"I am a grieving woman," the Clay Girl says.

"You mean a girl, don't you?" Angelina asks.

"I was a girl once, and in my heart I am still a girl, but I've left my adolescence behind. My heart, however, could not find its way to the wisdom of woman," the Clay Girl responds. "I have been trapped in my sorrow."

The tree house disappears.

A pair of strong hands sweeps Angelina off her feet.

"Where are we going?" Angelina wants to know.

"To interview your clients," Dragonfly Diva replies as she flies towards the Dark Forest.

The flock of sparrows around Pop dives into the overflowing bowl, thoroughly dipping themselves in the joyful waters. They then dart after the wizened lady and her passenger.

They soon reach the Dark Forest.

"Don't call him, please!" Angelina begs.

But there is no need to invoke that malevolence. The trees in the Dark Forest are whispering.

> *The darkness that afflicted us was born from a festering wound. We know that a wound has the potential to heal. When that happens, the scarred place becomes stronger and the toxins extracted are transformed into Medicine.*
>
> *"Why, some of our strongest newborns shoot out from the roots of our fallen ones,"* a tree mother sighs.

They land on a boulder among the trees. The sparrows play among the black cherry trees, darting from one tree to the other. They peck the trunks and sprinkle the waters.

Angelina smiles remembering the bird wash at her grandpa's house. Suddenly traces of white emerge from the black bark of the trees.

"They are not black cherry trees, but Quacking Aspens!" Angelina realizes. "Their trunks were scorched by the Dark Sorcerer's evil and are now healed by the Clay Girl's waters."

The evil that haunted us for decades developed from a man who refused to feel the pain in his wound. Instead, he nurtured the poison in it through causing fear and feeling fury, until it corroded his Soul.

The Quacking Aspens whisper as they tremble, perhaps remembering the curse.

The Dark Sorcerer began to cherish the poison because it covered his ever-present pain and fear. We trembled as we saw him become addicted to inflicting that same pain in other innocent people. From their suffering he fed his poison.

"But why?" Angelina wants to know. "Why would someone pass on to others what caused them so much pain? Why feed the wound?"

"It made him feel strong. We witnessed how he used that false sensation of power that came from hurting innocents as a way to bury the terrible feeling of helplessness that haunted him; a helplessness that had never been healed." the Quacking Aspens reveal.

This pain became a scourge on our bodies and on the earth that nurtures us. It caused terrible pain and injury to others. Until you put an end to it, brave Angelina. For this we are deeply grateful.

Angelina waves goodbye as the sparrows wash away the last traces of poison. The white Quacking Aspens swing joyfully, bidding them farewell.

Dragonfly Diva flies her over The Titans, who are engaged in a most compromising position.

"Em. Err... Sorry to interrupt!" Angelina yelps.

"Oh, honey, for you we'll even stop our hug...but not for long!" laughs the Greek Goddess.

"Who are you?" Angelina asks as The Titans disentangle from each other.

"We were once in love," the Warrior says, "but we had lost the way to each other. We allowed our differences to make us enemies."

"I could not understand her need for beauty, for words of love, for tenderness and poetry," he continues. "Her emotions scared me, so I stopped paying attention to her emotional life, not knowing that she'd dried up and then I'll miss the very thing I love."

"I could not understand his constant need to help me," the Greek Goddess confesses. "I thought he wanted to control me. I felt that he undervalued me and that's why he tried to save me, as if I was that fragile. I got tired of his need to prove himself. I began to fight with him, until our relationship became a war. Instead of receiving his support, I created more strife in both our lives."

"Until you showed us that opposites not only attract," the Greek Goddess says, caressing the Warrior, "but actually must marry for the power of love to heal what is broken."

The sparrows land on the face and shoulder of the embracing couple, sprinkling them with a golden shower of water and seeds. When the couple kisses, the seeds blossom into a rainbow of multi-colored flowers.

They are flying along the southeast when they see The Disk Thrower picking up some flowers. He hides the flowers behind his back when he spots the two women.

"Who are you?" Angelina calls out as she flies above The Champion.

"I was a man who had forgotten his destiny. You showed me that what I had lost was not my destination, but the valor in my heart. In finding it, I have found my mark."

Three tiny sparrows land on The Champion's free hand. They each leave a feather. They merrily chirp on his ears.

"Thanks!" The Champion says and runs towards the entrance of the fortress, flowers in one hand and feathers in the other.

Angelina has no time to figure this riddle, as Dragonfly Diva has landed in front of the guillotine.

"Who are you?" Angelina asks The Executioner.

"I am the potential each human being has to cut away the limits of perception," The Executioner responds in a shockingly soft and tender voice.

The sparrows whirl wildly around the guillotine. The fallen blade slowly rises and begins to glow, stretching as it transforms into a large mirror.

As they look into the mirror, they see the image of the Clay Girl growing into a woman. The bowl in her hand is also growing. Dozens of sparrows play and dip themselves in the joyful waters, darting in all directions.

Clay Woman is laughing. Her laughter is more precious than gold to Angelina.

There is just one more Bridge Guardian to visit, but Angelina is not looking forward to this. Thankfully, Dragonfly Diva keeps her distance, hovering some five feet away from the Lord of Lucre.

"Who are you?" Angelina hollers at the Lord of Lucre.

"I am a creature who is afraid," the Lord of Lucre responds.

This surprises Angelina. A look at this guy would send a lion into a run, how can he be afraid?

"Do not be surprised, Dreamer," the Lord of Lucre laughs. His laughter is hoarse. Angelina thinks that this monster hasn't laughed in a long time.

"I am scared of life, so unpredictable. Of love, so uncontrollable. I clutch to the only thing I can control, my gold. Yet, this too could disappear any minute, so I am as vulnerable as a baby," the Lord of Lucre confesses with a sigh. Then he growls, adding. "And if you say this to anyone, I'll hunt you down and kill you."

A flock of sparrows darts against the Lord of Lucre, picking his eyes, ears and mouth.

"Fine, fine!" the gargoyle screams. "I'll leave the lady alone if you leave me alone."

"There's no helping some people," Angelina mutters as Dragonfly Diva flies to the northwest.

"Thank you for reminding me who I am," Clay Woman says with a smile. "I had been drowning in my sorrow for so long that I completely forgot that joy also streams from the same fountain within me. "

"How did you remember?" Boy wanted to know.

"I was drowning in my own sorrow. This sorrow was true once. But it had become a habit. I got used to seeing my water as tears and myself as the crier of sorrows," Clay Woman replied. "But I have now seen what my waters do for the world. I've seen that my water is the bearer of clarity and love. That it reveals the light and the essence hidden under layers of sorrow. That it makes life and joy blossom. I no longer see myself as the bearer of sorrow, but as the nurturer of life."

"Who we are and who we are here to serve are often close cousins," Pop adds, exhaling a garland of aromatic smoke that the sparrows around him use as a hoop.

The clay knees crack and Clay Woman wobbles.

"You are not free yet, are you?" Angelina asks.

"I don't know how to stand, and I've been kneeling for so long that my knees are breaking," Clay Woman confesses.

"Have you tried holding on to something while you straighten your knees?" Boy asks, suddenly interested. He produces a lance and offers it to Clay Woman. "When my knights are very stiff sometimes it's hard for them to get up, but if they hold on to the lance, they can usually get up."

"I cannot hold on to the lance, sweet boy," Clay Woman smiles, "for I must hold my bowl."

"Sorry," Boy mumbles, "I was just trying to help."

"You did well, Boy," Angelina says. "But that is not her way."

"Is this a good time to ask how?" Angelina asks Pop. "How on earth are we going to help her stand before she breaks?"

Another crack shakes Clay Woman. The bowl slides to the side.

"It's time to retrieve the eight and last treasure in your *Gift Bundle*," Pop says.

"Pop, she's breaking!" Angelina protests.

"Then help her by retrieving your *Core Essence* for the *Gift Bundle*, Angelina," Pop says.

"What does that mean?" Angelina asks. "I don't remember, Pop."

"You never got this lesson, Angelina. You've been running away for so long that your brother has never been able to finish the teachings of the *House of Prosperity* with you."

Boy has gone to the Knights, who are trying to cheer him up by teaching him how to use the lance in combat. But Boy is so distraught that he simply leans on the lance.

"Watch and learn," Pop whispers.

Minstrel holds on to the lance and begins to pull it. Boy slips and falls. He's furious.

"Hey! Cut it out!" he growls.

"Pop, this is no time for monkeying around," Angelina urges. "She's breaking!"

"She's breaking. He's falling. And you're failing," Pop answers. "Pay attention."

The image of the dragon flashes by Angelina's memory. She stands firm and alert. As she shifts her attention to the present moment, Angelina feels a powerful shift in her body. Her body feels rooted in the ground, like a tree.

Boy has picked the lance and is now swinging it in front of him, holding it with his two hands. By stretching his arms so far out, he's hunched his upper torso and crunched his spine.

Husband grabs the lance and pulls lance and Boy, who falls on his face.

'I got it!" Angelina cries out.

She goes to the boy.

"Give me the lance," she asks gently.

"No, they're going to throw me down again," Boy protests, thrusting the lance around haphazardly.

"No, they won't," Angelina promises. "Trust me."

She turns to Pop pleadingly. Pop smiles and nods.

"You are leaning on the lance, Boy," Angelina says. "That's why they can throw you off."

"No way I'm going to get knighting lessons from a girl!" Boy snarls.

"Of course not, Boy. You and I are going to help Clay Woman. Would you like that?"

Boy nods and hands the lance to Angelina.

"Then think of your core. Imagine that this lance stands at the core of your body. Feel it as your spine, standing tall and running vertically through the center of your body."

Boy stands stiff and straight.

"Bend your knees," Minstrel says, "or your back is carrying your weight. Alignment holds you. Stiffness breaks you."

Boy relaxes the knees, but he's standing chin up, challenging the Knights to approach.

"Lift your crown to heaven and allow your chin to float down," Husband instructs. "If your neck is misaligned, your body must compensate below, and you'll be thrown off center."

Boy does as told. Angelina is circling the boy, observing his stance, hunting for something that's so close she can almost taste it.

"How do you feel?" Angelina asks.

"Like a tree. The force is running through me!" Boy yells, excited.

"Yes! That's it! The force at the core!" Angelina yells excitedly. "What does the force want to do?"

Boy breathes deeply and walks tall.

"The force wants to help Clay Woman stand!"

"Of course!" Angelina yells, holding the lance in front of her with both hands. "That's totally you."

Pop snatches the lance from Angelina's hands, but she does not fall.

"And your force, what is your *Core Essence* all about?" Pop asks.

Angelina moves gracefully, walking tall like a tree and stepping as lightly as a bird. She snatches the lance from Pop and whirls it in the direction of Dragonfly Diva, who catches it in mid air.

Angelina leaps and hangs from the lance, which the magical lady now holds horizontally.

As in cue, Dragonfly Diva flies above Clay Woman while Angelina swings upside down, using the lance as a trapeze.

"Transformation," she cries out as she reaches towards the bowl and pulls it towards the sky. "The desire and power to uplift energies to a higher vibration. That's my *Core Essence*, Pop."

"That is your very nature," Pop agrees. "That is your journey, your magic and your message."

"My bowl!" Clay Woman cries.

"Reach up!" Angelina calls.

"Your bowl is your unique gift, isn't it?" Angelina asks Clay Woman, "It is your deepest desire to gather your waters and share them with the creatures in this land, to nurture them. This is the force of your *Core Essence*, is it not?"

"Yes!" Clay Woman cries out, reaching up for the bowl.

As she does, the weight of her body lifts off her legs. Clay Woman reaches higher up, her arms curling around the bowl. But Dragonfly Diva flies a bit higher.

"Hold on to the bowl," Angelina cries out, holding the bowl with all her might as Clay Woman is lifted from the ground. "Grasp my arms!"

Clay Woman's hands grip a hold of Angelina's upper arms. Her grip feels as if thick tree roots were squeezing her arms, but Angelina focuses on the task at hand and ignores the pain.

"You have strong arms," Angelina encourages, "You've been holding that bowl for a very long time. You can hold it longer. You have the strength."

"I do," Clay Woman agrees, though her voice is trembling. "It's just that I've never been uprooted before."

"Your muscles don't need to carry all that weight," Angelina says, remembering the instructions for alignment that Ms. Navarra, her movement teacher, would give her. "That's what bones are for."

"And Earth," adds Dragonfly Diva.

Clay Woman is hanging from the bowl in Angelina's hands —holding on to Angelina's arms— while her legs are stretching, her feet inches above the ground.

Unfortunately, lumps of clay are falling from Clay Woman's limbs.

"Have I made things worse?" Angelina wonders.

To her surprise, the Knights go to work instantly, massaging Clay Woman's legs. They pick lumps of mud and tightly cake it into her thighs, knees, calves and ankles; so that Clay Woman's legs grow strong. Boy splashes water from the basin on to her knees, which melt back into smoothness.

One of the knights lights up a torch and carefully applies heat to the renovated limbs, until they are baked into place.

Clay Woman's limbs now have a good size for her mature body.

"This feels great!" Clay Woman exclaims.

Dragonfly Diva carefully descends, until Clay Woman touches the ground and lets go of the bowl.

"I can stand strong now," Clay Woman declares.

Angelina gently deposits the bowl into her hands.

"The bowl... it does not weight anymore!" Clay Woman exclaims.

"Giving never should," adds Pop. "And when it comes from your *Core Essence*, it's as light as 'em sparrows!"

"Aaaay!" screams Angelina as she falls.

"Oops!" Dragonfly Diva exclaims.

Angelina falls in the mud.

"Congratulations, you've completed your *Gift Bundle*, Tweedy," Pop claps.

A whirling sound above Angelina makes them look up. The Knight's lance is twirling as it descends straight towards Angelina.

She instinctively reaches out with her hands as the lance suddenly shrinks and lands on her palms. It is a golden key. Angelina reads its inscription:

Sixth Alchemical Key:
Your Unique Service Vision
Gather your *Gift Bundle*
and develop your *Service Vision,*
giving to the worldfrom your Core Essence

"We did it!" Boy cries triumphantly.

"How will I ever thank you enough?" Clay Woman gurgles.

Clay Woman is standing tall at the center of the fountain. She smiles radiantly as rippling trickles of water come out of her ears, hair, mouth and hands.

As the Dream Basket reaches the bottom of the scales' range, the castle bridge hits the ground with a loud thud and a cloud of dust.

"Bravo!" the Knights and the boy applaud. "We've done it!"

"Now all we have to do is charge into the castle and rescue the *DreamSelf*," Boy screams.

“Not so fast,” the Alignment Effigy declares, coming to life with her usual clank.

“What do you mean?” Angelina demands.

“You have lowered the bridge, and you have free pass,” the Alignment Effigy declares.

“But?” Angelina asks suspiciously.

“There is one last task without which you will never free the *DreamSelf*,” the Alignment Effigy warns.

“What is it?” Angelina asks.

“You’re free!” a voice screams.

The Champion emerges from behind the statue, holding in his hands the link that tied the Alignment Effigy to the bridge.

“It’s yielded!” The Champion says.

“But… we got all the keys!” Angelina protests.

Oblivious to anyone else, The Champion climbs onto the pedestal and kisses the Alignment Effigy.

“This was OUR key!’ he exclaims as he shows the sparrow feathers.

The hand of the Alignment Effigy becomes human. The Champion takes off the sword and places the three sparrows feathers in the hand.

The huge carcass of the Alignment Effigy cracks open, revealing a beautiful woman inside.

The Champion leaps into the pedestal, grabs the woman, jumps down and runs away, carrying the happy lover.

“Thanks!” The Alignment Effigy hollers.

“You’re welcome,” Angelina responds. “But wait! What is the task…?”

But it’s too late. The couple is now a shadow receding towards the southeast.

The night falls in a silent burst of stars. The Knights, the boy, the Dreamer and the wizened lady stare at each other, one single question burning in all their faces.

Part 5

The Outer Ring of Self

"Many of us are frightened to look within ourselves, and fear has us put up walls so thick we no longer remember who we really are. By choosing not to allow parts of ourselves to exist, we are forced to expend huge amounts of psychic energy to keep them beneath the surface. Whatever we refuse to recognize about ourselves has a way of rearing its head and making itself known when we least expect it."

—Debbie Ford

CHAPTER 22

Crossing the Bridge

A strangeness in the night makes them instinctively stay closer to each other as they face the lowered bridge that leads into the castle of the *Shadow Castle*. The Spirits of the Night seem to wail in almost undetectable, grating whispers. The castle sometimes shimmers, as if it was a mirage.

"There is no time to waste. We have two hours at the most," Dragonfly Diva declares, breaking the trance.

The last clad knight steps forward.

"I am Foster," he says kneeling in front of Angelina. "I am at your orders."

Angelina wishes she'd knew what orders to give, but this time she is truly clueless. Should they charge into the castle without knowing what that last task is, or should they go chasing after the Alignment Effigy to find out what to do?

Angelina feels someone edging her on the shoulder.

"Stop elbowing me and give me some sound advice," she protests as she turns to face Dragonfly Diva.

The spotted horse is pushing Angelina's shoulders towards the castle.

"His guess is as good as mine," Dragonfly Diva says. "I suggest that you get going."

"Aren't you coming?" Angelina asks anxiously.

"I am foreign to your *Mask of Self*. All its alarms would rise instantly should I step into that bridge. I wait for you here," Dragonfly Diva says. "Good luck."

Without further words, Boy helps Foster and Angelina to mount the spotted horse.

Just as they are leaving, Dragonfly Diva hovers over the spotted horse.

"Trust Foster and your knights," she whispers into her heart. "Stay with Boy. And let your *Ancestral Heart* guide you."

Angelina looks up, but only a slight tremor remains on the spot where the wizened lady had flown.

They all begin their slow march across the bridge.

The horses are nervous. The old wooden bridge squeaks under the weight of the horses. That, however, is the least of their worries. There are moments when the bridge wavers, as if it was losing solidity. The alligators in the moat gather beneath the bridge, their large snouts snapping hungrily.

Angelina begins to doubt. What if the last task was another Alchemical Key needed to enter the castle, and that's why it's wavering? What if it disappears altogether? Perhaps she should have insisted, instead of taking her orders from a horse!

"Let's go back!" she whispers to Foster.

"No," Foster responds resolutely. "We move forward."

"But you don't understand," Angelina argues. "We don't know if what we are doing..."

"Spotty smells across the mysteries that we will never understand," Foster says. "I trust him."

Well, that is that. If it were up to her, they'd go back. But Foster won't budge and he has the horse by the reigns, literally.

"It's **your** quest," a cold, sharp voice begins inside Angelina. "Just tell him you're the boss and send the old idiot home."

"But Dragonfly Diva said..." Angelina protests.

"Oh, what does the batty old woman know about YOUR quest. It's your *DreamSelf*, right? Do you want to go back? Then get off the horse and **walk** back. You are in charge here. If they don't want to take orders, fire them!" the cold voice barks.

Angelina has been feeling so thwarted that she has not realized who is talking. Just picturing *Ms. Controller* talking to *Ms. Perfecta* brings her back to her senses.

"I trust Foster. I trust Spotty," she recites with her eyes closed, making a mental effort to empty her mind. "I trust my knights. I trust Boy. I trust my *Ancestral Heart.*"

"There you go again with that heart crap!" says another heavy, constricted, barking voice. "Don't trust. You always get into trouble when you trust. Stay alert. Raise your defenses. Don't be vulnerable."

Her skin is becoming as thick and hard as Foster's armor, while her *Ancestral Heart* is being squeezed into a tight ball. This is an old *Shadow*, Angelina tracks down as they advance. Oh, yes, she knows it. She is the *Armored Self.* This *Shadow* turned her into a hard, cold stone so that she could leave Omar.

Spotty neighs nervously. They are close to the entrance arch. Foster makes a hand signal to stop.

"You are making Spotty nervous," Foster says.

"Me? What did I do now?" Angelina says in a childish, plaintive tone.

"If you wear that armor as you cross this threshold, I am afraid that we will never find your *DreamSelf,*" Foster says.

Angelina, caught red-handed, squeals defensively in Foster's ear.

"How do you know?"

"Don't get defensive!" the *Armored Self* warns. "Don't admit to anything. The best defense is an offense."

Angelina taps with her finger knuckles into Foster's armor.

"Who are you to talk about wearing armors?" she says smugly.

The metallic resonance of the Knight's armor travels into the horse's body. Spotty rears up and leaps forward at full gallop, crossing the entrance arch in frenzy. The Knights get out their swords and charge forward. Boy kicks his pony into a fast trot and enters behind them.

Spotty comes to an abrupt halt as Foster reigns him in. Angelina falls from the horse. Luckily, she falls into a pile of hay. She emerges spitting hay and sneezing.

"Stay!" Boy whispers, sinking her back into the pile. He has hidden the horses in record time and is diving into the hay pile.

"Get off! You are tickling me!" Angelina says as Boy emerges by her side. They both bring their heads a few inches above the pile, peeking into the scene.

Horns are blowing. Running footsteps surround them. Screams and arrows shoot by them. The whole castle is in turmoil.

CHAPTER 23

The Shadow Scouts

"We are under attack!" voices are screaming.

The deafening pounding of boots marches towards them from several directions at once.

"So what's new? They always believe that they are under attack!" mutters Boy.

"You know them?" Angelina asks, eyeing the boy with suspicion.

"You don't?" Boy echoes, mirroring her expression.

More *Shadow Scouts* pour in. Their movements remind Angelina of something, but she's too scared to think. They move like ghosts, slowly and sneakily. But when they attack, they are heavy and ineffective. It is as if they are not really seeing what is in front of them; as if they are following instructions from a book.

"Thanks for small blessings," Angelina sighs. "If they were well trained, the Knights would be dead by now."

Foster is battling a huge armored *Shadow Scout*. The other knights are each fighting three *Shadow Scouts*.

"It's all my fault!" Angelina regrets guiltily. "I should have listened to Foster. But I always want to stay in control, and now look what I've done. If he... if he dies, I'll never forgive myself."

"No, don't!" Boy warns.

But it's too late. Two nearby *Shadow Scouts* spot her. They pick them up by the ears.

"Here they are!" one of the *Shadow Scouts* brags ostentatiously. "We will be rewarded!"

"We work for the honor and the righteousness of our acts," says a huge - *Shadow Scout*, hitting the other on the head, "not for rewards."

"Ehrm, that's right your highness, *Almighty Judge*," the smaller *Shadow Scout* mutters.

"Dam right I'm right, *Ingratietus*," *Almighty Judge* says, smirking. "Let's bring them to headquarters."

The *Shadow Scouts* hoist Angelina and Boy onto their shoulders and march towards the *Outer Ring of Self*.

Dozens of *Shadow Scouts* run down the ladders that lead to the towers in a flurry of swords, lances and arrows. Angelina worries. If all this power is discharged against the four knights, how can they possibly survive?

"No, don't!" Boy warns.

"What-did-I do-now?" Angelina stutters as *Almighty Judge* bounces up a pair of stairs.

"Your guilt is going to get us killed," Boy spits. "Just drop it!"

Just when Angelina is about to say something smart, they turn right towards the center of the *Outer Ring of Self*.

Angelina and Boy find themselves in the midst of a stream of tiny couriers skating up and down the wide hall, like blood cells streaming along an artery.

"Leave space for the *Shadow Heralds*." *Almighty Judge* commands pompously as they maneuver amidst the tiny messengers.

They are bleak and wrinkled, like old, faded dresses. Yet, they seem to be children.

"Do you see them?" Angelina whispers to Boy.

"Creepy!" Boy whispers back.

The *Shadow Heralds* skate along the corridor carrying long scrolls that they read over and over in a trembling, dramatic drone, like a recorded soap opera scene. Their voices quiver with fear and dread in the same spots, saying the words in the same exact tone each time. They speak in whispers, though each word is emphatic. Their messages travel through Angelina's bones and nerves.

"Don't listen to them!" Boy warns as he sticks both fingers inside his ears, "Don't pay them any attention."

He starts mumbling a song to himself.

But Angelina's attention is drawn towards the tiny mutterings.

"Beware of the Unknown. It's nothing but trouble. Stay safe. Stay with the old. An old, known problem is ten times better than a new, unknown solution. Beware of the Unknown. It's nothing but trouble,"

mutters one of the *Shadow Heralds* who wears blinders as he shakily skates down the hall.

"Who do you think you are? Just who do you think you are? Why would anybody trust you? Why would anybody help you? You are nobody! Stay low. Keep your head low. Don't ask for favors that you don't deserve. Who do you think you are? Just who do you think you are?"

mutters another *Shadow Herald* who crouches as he skates up the hall.

"She who lives by illusions dies by disenchantment! Do not get your hopes too high. Magical thinking is childish, do you hear? Grow up! Life is hard and then you die. Stop wearing those bright colors. Stop believing in fairy tales! There is no magic! She who lives by illusions dies by disenchantment!

mutters another *Shadow Herald,* who raises a shield in front of him as he skates.

Angelina's mind is clouded. She feels that she is a heavy burden to everyone and to herself. She feels hopeless, listless and useless.

"Wake up, silly girl," Boy barks in an attempt to whisper a scream. He is poking Angelina. "You idiot! I told you not to listen, you stupid, useless girl. Now you got yourself all mush up. Oh, I hate girls! All that soap opera. Aghrr!"

"Who are you to talk, you horse boy?" Angelina spits back. "You think you are the great knight? You are just a stupid boy who feeds the horses!"

"Yeah!" Boy says proudly with a grin, "But I am smart enough not to listen to the *Shadow Heralds*... and to wake you up from their spell!"

"How...you...what?" Angelina mutters. "You got me angry on purpose, you..."

"Anger raises the *Hara*, your *Female Power Center*," Boy says proudly. "The *Warrior Mother* teaches us that!"

"Mother?" Angelina says. "You are trained by a Mother, and she is a warrior? and there's a *Female Power Center*?"

"The *Queen of Hearts* is our Queen, and The Knights are sworn to her allegiance," Boy says proudly. "And yes, duh! There is *Female Power Center* and a *Male Power Center*... Gee, is there no school where you live?"

There is no time to answer. They have landed with a thud at the feet of a throne.

CHAPTER 24

The Evil Queen Witch

Angelina's body feels the coldness of the black and white tiles creeping into her skin. The room is cold and dry. A dry mist lingers on the air.

A heavy breathing echoes in the room, followed by a rustling of cloth. Their eyes follow the sound.

An old, baroque throne sits on a small stage at the far end of the room, in front of dark, tall windows covered by black curtains.

Cobwebs crisscross the old iron swords and axes motifs that decorate the throne. But there is a far more sinister embellishment. Live, rattling snakes wriggle their yellow, green and red stripes ominously, crisscrossing the cavities in the iron casing.

Sitting on the throne there is an old hag. Her hair is gray and whole patches of it have disappeared. Her teeth are falling, but she retains the two large, snake-like incisors. Her eyes are snakelike, green blinding pupils darting on red veined eyeballs.

"You made it," the old hag hisses on a raspy, sharp voice that cuts across Angelina's heart like a knife. "Good, the quicker you get in, the quicker you die!"

Angelina is terrified. The coldness in her bones and the terror in her mind are like a poisonous, infectious bite. Paralysis is quickly spreading through her body.

"You are the *Evil Queen Witch* and your words are filth!" Boy barks, spitting on the spotless tiles. "I'm not afraid of you!"

Boy's words shake Angelina out of the toxic sleep. She looks at him, then at the hag. She starts feeling hope, and her body becomes warmer.

"And you brought the boy with you," the *Evil Queen Witch* says with false happiness. "Great! We are now all a big happy family!"

"You are not happy!" Boy challenges. "You are a liar. Everything you teach and everything you say is a lie. You are not my family. You are the mother of fear, you filthy hag, and I am not scared of you!"

"Silence!" the *Evil Queen Wi*tch says, pointing her long, gnarled finger at Boy, her black claws shooting green rays.

Boy wriggles in pain.

"No!" Angelina screams, running towards Boy.

"Jajaja!" the *Evil Queen Witch* laughs mockingly. "Who's haughty now? Who's fearless now? You are nothing but the servant of the horses, you useless boy!"

Angelina shakes violently. That is what she called Boy. That is what she said to him. Is she as cruel as this evil queen?

"Horses are Medicine!" Boy barks triumphantly. "Horses are Power. Horses are Spiritpower, and I am their glad servant. You are the useless one, you ghost of a *Mother's Shadow*!"

The *Evil Queen Witch* lets out a wailing scream filled with fear and hatred as she sends rays of green toxicity to Boy.

Boy screams in rage and pain, wriggling on the floor. Angelina hugs him, crying.

"You are the true queen of this castle," Boy whispers, holding on to her right arm. He is transcending his pain to hold on to her, and Angelina can feel his courage and will power shooting through her arm. "You are the champion who conquered the Bridge Guardians. Remember! Remember!"

The *Evil Queen Witch* laughs madly as she approaches them, sending another green ray against the boy, who screams.

"You leave him out of this," Angelina roars, getting up to her feet. A hot stream of fire runs through her body. She is emanating waves of fire.

The *Evil Queen Witch* backs away, faltering for a second.

She then lets out a triumphant scream as four *Shadow Scouts* enter from a back door carrying a large cage.

"No!" Angelina screams as she sees her *DreamSelf* inside the cage.

The cage is made of shards of mirrors that float on the air around the *DreamSelf*, spinning dizzyingly in place. Around the mirror cage, a barbwire made of electric energy sparkles noisily.

At that moment, her tiny sparrow friend flies through an arched window and darts towards the *DreamSelf.*

When the tiny bird crosses the electric barbwire, it is instantly electrocuted, falling dead to the floor.

"No!" Angelina cries, running towards the sparrow that lies, burnt and dead, about five feet from the cage. But when she gets close to the bird, she is repelled by a strong electric field and thrown back fifteen feet.

"You hot headed, stupid girl," The *Evil Queen Witch* spits. "You thought you could defeat me, ME! And how? With you witless courage? With your moans? With you pathetic attempts to be free? Did you ever stop to think for a moment, to consider that SHE was in my power, that I could destroy her at will?"

"NO, you can't!" Boy screams.

"Silence!" The *Evil Queen Witch* thunders, sending another green ray at Boy.

Foster steps forward and takes the ray into his armor.

The *Evil Queen Witch* screams, pulling her hair in frenzy.

"That's how you've lost most of it, *Shadow Mother*," The Knight laughs.

"I'm not your mother, don't you call me mother!" The *Evil Queen Witch* screams, sending deadly rays with both of her arms as she advances towards Foster.

"What's the matter?" Foster laughs. Though the rays are clashing against his armor without harming him, they are throwing him back violently. "You don't want your family happy?"

"I'll give you happy, you metal mongrel," the *Evil Queen Witch* screams furiously. But she is backing away. She now gets out a wide, thick leather belt. She raises the belt on the air and brings it down against the cage where the *DreamSelf* is locked. The cage breaks into pieces, and the *DreamSelf* tumbles out of it into the floor. The mirror shards dart into her body and she is bleeding copiously through the wounds.

"No!" Angelina screams, running towards her *DreamSelf.* But before she has given three steps, the *DreamSelf* is floated up. The mirror shards are pulled out of her body violently.

Angelina cannot stand the screams and pain of her *DreamSelf.* She doubles-up in pain as the mirror shards rearrange themselves back into a cage and the electric barbwire reconfigures around it.

"I'll do whatever you want, but don't hurt her!" Angelina pleads.

"Don't!" Boy screams, grabbing Angelina. "That's what she wants. She's lying, don't you see? She can't destroy her!"

"No? Watch me!" The *Evil Queen Witch* screeches as she raises the belt again.

"There is only one person in the world who can destroy this creature," Foster roars, "and it is not you, *Shadow Mother*."

"Amarrus," the *Evil Queen Witch* curses, pointing her black long nails towards the Knight. The spell crosses the room suddenly, hitting Foster right on the chest. The rays bounce off his armor with a clank, but they hover around the body armor like tight robes.

"Call her, Angelina. She will come to you," Foster hollers.

"Mordaza," the *Evil Queen Witch* curses, pointing at the Knight. Bands of dark light wrap around his mouth, blocking it from sight or ear.

"Take her away, quickly!" the *Evil Queen Witch* commands.

Four *Shadow Scouts* spring into action and pull the cage by some invisible chords.

"*DreamSelf*! Come to me!" Angelina screams.

The *DreamSelf* stares at her with the saddest eyes Angelina has ever seen. But she does not move. She is taken away through the back door.

Everything is going deadly wrong. Angelina feels her heart squeezed dried. She falls on her knees, color draining out of her face.

"What have I done wrong?" Angelina mutters.

"How about being born?" the *Evil Queen Witch* responds, laughing mirthfully.

Boy has crawled towards Angelina, holding her.

"You are doing fine," he whispers.

"Oh, how sweet! Words of comfort from the horse's servant," the *Evil Queen Witch* sings.

"Words of deceit," the *Evil Queen Witch* hisses, pointing at Foster, who is struggling with the dark bands bounding him. "Do you know who he is?"

"Don't believe a word she says," Boy whispers.

"You are telling her not to believe **me**, you little cynical vermin?" the *Evil Queen Witch* screeches as she sends a ray flying at Boy, who is raised on the air and pinned to a wall.

"Let's see who is lying, shall we?" the *Evil Queen Witch* cries triumphantly, as she points towards the Knight and with a hand gesture, knocks his casket off. The armor falls to the floor.

Angelina knows this face. She has seen it before. Who is he?

"Don't you recognize him, Angie?" the *Evil Queen Witch* asks with false sweetness. Angelina's childhood name sounds obscene in this fowl mouth.

"Angelina," Foster says. Only a faint echo of his voice reaches her, as if someone was screaming miles away.

"Father!" Angelina mutters. Her face is blank.

She is struggling to comprehend quickly, but the truth is hard to swallow. Then her shock gives in to bitterness.

"You fooled me," Angelina whispers. "You tricked me!"

"No!" cries the faint echo of Foster's voice. "Angie, please!"

"Don't call me Angie," Angelina screams. "You have no right to my childhood. You abandoned me!"

"Please Listen!" Foster's faint echo pleads.

"No! **You** listen!" Angelina snarls. "You betrayed us. You betrayed my mother and you betrayed me. You are a liar and a cheat and you.... I don't trust you!"

"What a moving family reunion!" the *Evil Queen Witch* remarks as she moves towards Angelina.

"Don't let her get you!" Boy screams.

The *Evil Queen Witch* sends a ray that knocks Boy unconscious. She approaches Angelina slowly, dancing around her. She speaks directly into Angelina's mind in a sing-song manner, as you would talk to a child. But her words are poison. As she circles Angelina, her tongue hissing, her green eyes sparkling malignantly, Angelina wriggles in pain. She feels that she is being skinned alive, her innermost fears exposed and exacerbated. Angelina's energy diminishes with every word from the *Evil Queen Witch*, her face becoming pale as a paper.

> *You are alone, Angelina Semidey. Look at your pathetic father, a cheat and a loser who abandoned you. You are all alone, Angelina, surrounded by lies and deceit. No one believes in you. No one supports you. Who will help you, if your family doesn't? Who will ever care? Who has read your poems or stories? A bunch of losers! You haven't been published by the BIG publishers, have you? That's because you stink as a writer. Give it up! You are almost invisible. Don't swim against the tide. You were not made for greatness, but for hard work and anonymity. Find your comfort in me. I will protect you. I am powerful beyond believe. Look around! I have easily defeated your friends! But I will protect you if you declare your alliance to me! Give up the quest! Let go of that weak idiotic soul that only whines and longs. I am strong. I can protect you.*

"What have I done wrong?" Angelina moans. "Perhaps, she is right. Just to be born was a mistake. I **am** a mistake."

She has been defeated, in spite her best attempts. Her strength is running down her body, through her knees into the cold tile floor. She dared to dream, and she was defeated. Her muscles feel like thin scraps about to fall away.

"What did I do wrong?" Angelina silently asks Dragonfly Diva, as waves of despair overwhelm her. "I did everything you told me."

"I trusted Foster," Angelina considers, "and he had betrayed me even before we started off."

"I stayed with Boy, and what good has it done him or me?" Angelina asks as she sees the boy's unconscious body still hanging on the wall.

"I trusted the Knights, and they are obviously dead at the hands of the *Shadow Scouts*. There were hundreds of them! Didn't you know? Did you send the noble knights to their death? Have I lost Pop and Omar all over again?"

"What else did you tell me?" Angelina asks herself, getting angry at Dragonfly Diva. "What other useless piece of advice did you offer me, while you refused to enter the castle yourself?"

"Let your *Ancestral Heart* guide you," Dragonfly Diva's voice declares in her heart, just as the *Evil Queen Witch* commands...

"Pledge your alliance to me!"

CHAPTER 25

The Broken Heart of the Warrior

"Choose! You can die with those pathetic bleeding-heart fools who have lied to you. Or you can swear loyalty to me and live a sheltered life, without fear of uncertainty," the *Evil Queen Witch* entices with a falsely sweet voice.

> *"What is certainty?" Dragonfly Diva is asking. "Certainty is an attachment to the past. You have illusions about safety..."*

Angelina stands at a crossroad. Before her there are two roads, each leading in an opposite direction. She is painfully aware that this is no ordinary decision. The choice she makes now determines her fate.

"Choose!" the old hag orders, laughing obscenely. "As you see there is only one real choice."

> *"There is a war inside you" Dragonfly Diva is revealing, "and you have already chosen sides. You have sided with the army you believe to be more powerful. In fact, you have chosen the only side that has power in your eyes."*
>
> *"You, young lady, despise the gifts of the heart."*

These words keep churning in Angelina's solar plexus, mixed with the *Evil Queen Witch's* words, each pulling her in an opposite direction. Her anxiety is rising, overwhelming her.

> *"I don't want a normal life," Angie is screaming. "I want my stories. I want my butterfly... I am hungry. I am lonely! You are just like her. You are deaf!"*

At that moment, Angelina's path becomes crystal clear. Her senses acquire a pristine acuteness.

Angelina closes her ears to everything except her *Ancestral Heart*. Deep within herself she dives.

Her *Second-hand Heart* is full of poison and despair, full of others' words and choices. There is fear, overwhelming fear and helplessness, resentment and doubt. Blame and judgment and terrible expectations pull her into despair. She can hear the drone of old dramas. Like living creatures, they reach out to grab her.

"Open," she says, and this surface-heart breaks apart.

From the black abyss at the center of the heartbreak, waves of excruciating pain and memories emanate.

Usually Angelina would run away from this throbbing pain, instantly sealing her *Second-hand Heart* around the rupture and falling into her daily dramas to cover up this unbearable pain.

This time, however, Angelina walks towards the edge of the precipice. As she approaches, she feels the grounding, centering power of her *Ancestral Heart*. Rising from the far bottom of this abyss, she hears the steady, deep drum of its *Ancestral Tree Throne*.

"Welcome to the *Broken Heart of the Warrior*," the drum beats.

She knows that she should jump without thinking, but she cannot resist looking down into the emanations of pain.

A blast of agonizing ache hits her on the face and chest. Boiling streams of dark vapors race through the shadowy abyss, carrying her wails. She pulls back.

"Do not hesitate. This is your old, toxic *Emotional Undertow*," her *Ancestral Heart* says. "Do now allow it to drag you away from the center. Cross it. Dare to dive and you will find my power."

"I am afraid," Angelina whispers.

"Your fear is your strength," her *Ancestral Heart* says. "What do you fear the most, Angelina: betraying yourself or facing your pain?"

Angelina feels something in her hand. Angie is holding her hand.

"It's not that bad," she says reassuringly. "There's a treasure at the bottom."

Part of Angelina wants to run away, like always. Part of Angelina wants to send Angie away, to protect her. Angelina does neither. She grabs Angie's hand and jumps into the pitch-dark abyss of her broken heart.

"NOOOO!" screams the *Evil Queen Witch*, throwing a terrible tantrum, destroying everything in her sight. She points her terrible rage at Boy.

"Die, you idiot!"

The walls of the chamber dissolve and a great figure hovers above the space.

"Now, now, little ghost of my long-dead sister, you must learn to be graceful when defeated," sings a beautiful woman made of rainbow-like clouds. Her multi-colored clouds wrap Boy protectively.

"Great Mother, *Queen of Hearts*," Boy says adoringly as he regains consciousness for three seconds, falling back asleep.

"I'll get her back!" the *Evil Queen Witch* snarls, pulling Foster towards her by the lasso of her spell. "There's still time."

She disappears, taking Foster with her as she screams.

"My curse upon you all!"

Angelina and Angie are falling through darkness. Waves of energy gush through them like potent winds, twirling and pushing them. Angelina is terrified, but at the same time, she feels elated.

"Am I good?" Angie suddenly asks as she holds on to Angelina.

"Yes!" Angelina answers. "You are a good girl!"

"But if I find the treasure, will I still be good?" Angie asks.

"Of course!" Angelina says.

Angelina knows in a flash, not in her mind, but in her whole body, that this has been the fear raging war inside her.

Angelina stands in the center of a wide, black river surrounded by dying vegetation and enmeshed in grey fog.

A toxic stench rises from its waters. Strong dark streams pull Angelina back and under, dragging her away from the *Ancestral Heart*.

As Angelina struggles to keep Angie and herself above the waters, every heavy, polluted stream that runs through her ignites a strong emotion in her body. She feels that her body is full of stains. Blobs of shame stick to her skin, making her feel dirty.

Overwhelming guilt rises and pulls her towards the muddy bottom. There's anger, too; an old resentment that uncoils like a snake, ready to swallow her.

She holds Angie up above the waters and desperately searches for an exit, pushing herself onto the other bank.

They crawl out of the black waters onto a field of tall, dry weeds. There are rotten corn cubs and wilted flowers along the trail.

A sweet, sad voice reaches them. It is a child singing. The tune is playful, but the voice is so sad that the petals in the wilted flowers begin to fall to the ground.

I am good.
No! I'm not.
I am happy.
No! I'm not.
I am smart and please the mother.
No! I'm not.
I shine like the stars in heaven.
No! I'm not.

They follow the voice through the tall dry weeds and find the tiniest girl they've ever seen seating by the banks of the black river, playing with the tiniest doll.

Angelina drags herself close. Perhaps the girl knows a way out of here, back to the *Ancestral Heart*.

"If I am happy, then I am being bad," says the tiny girl. "I am being selfish."

"Who are you?" Angelina asks.

"I am Good," the tiny girl says, spanking her doll.

"No, I am not!" screams a tiny voice.

The body of Good flips, but where her back should be there's another tiny girl. She is dancing and singing.

"I am Grace," says the other girl. "I am happy. I am graceful. I am a shining star."

"No!" screams Good, pulling on her sister with a twirl.

– "I am smart and I will please my mother and my teachers," Good says. "I want to be loved."

“It hurts,” Angie cries, pulling the legs of Angelina’s pants.

Angelina feels dizzy. She closes her eyes and seeks her *Ancestral Heart.*

“You are summoned to stand in the *Place of Paradox,*” her *Ancestral Heart* beats. “Duality is an illusion. There is no war in a heart that loves.”

Angelina opens her heart and feels Angie’s longing. She concentrates on the beating of her *Ancestral Heart* and sends waves of love to the two girls.

When she opens her eyes, Angie is sitting in front of her, playing with a tiny doll. But it’s not really a doll. It’s the two-sided tiny girl! She has shrunk to the size of a small doll and is now kicking in Angie’s hands.

“Time to go bye-bye,” Angie says, and breaks the kicking doll into two.

“Am I good?” Angie asks.

“Yes,” Angelina declares from the very core of her *Ancestral Heart*, tears streaming down her face.

Angie presses the tiny Good into her heart. She disappears with a sigh of relieve.

“Am I happy and graceful?” Angie asks.

“Yes,” Angelina declares, wanting to hug Angie.

Angie presses the tiny Grace into her heart. She disappears with a note of joy.

Part 6

The Inner Ring of Self

"That which God said to the rose, and
caused it to laugh in full-blown beauty,
He said to my heart, and made it a
hundred times more beautiful."

—Rumi

CHAPTER 26

The Mother and the Jewel Eye of Love

The note of joy grows and swirls as Angelina falls. Its reverberation creates a soft organic cushion of vibrations that cradles Angelina and Angie as they descend through darkness once again.

Someone sings. Angelina and Angie are enveloped by warm waves of love as they hear the song. The vibrations settle around them, forming clay walls that breathe softly and pulsate slowly.

As Angelina hugs Angie, she feels embraced by these clay walls and her heartbeat calms down inside the slow pulse of this chamber.

“This is not a chamber,” Angelina realizes. “This is a body. This is skin.”

Angelina timidly touches the skin, and feels it reacting to her touch. Strangely, her own skin reacts. She is both, touching and being touched. Angelina follows the skin and sees the muscles that give it shape. It is an arm. She follows the curve of the arm and sees that it is cradling her, just as she is cradling Angie.

Angelina follows the arm upwards. Her eyes meet love. Rays of compassion and unconditional love shine from the largest olive eyes she has ever seen. They bathe Angelina in wave after wave of safety, peace, acceptance and a deep sea of goodness.

"You are soooo good," *The Mother* sings in a soft note that warms her heart. I love you sooo much."

"As big as the entire world," Angie whispers, cuddling into Angelina's arms.

Angelina remembers . There was a time when Mercedes hugged her like this. There was a time in which she said these same words, and Angie would answer like this. And they would keep coming up with metaphors to express their love, each one bigger.

Slowly, however, Mercedes stopped hugging her and lovingly accepting her. She began to criticize and pressure her instead. As Angelina grew up, her longing for this acceptance increased. But she had forgotten it was ever there. Angie remembers.

"More," *The Mother* answers with a soft laughter. "My love is as vast as the entire infinite universe."

"Wow!" says Angie delightedly. "That's a lot of love!"

"And you deserve every bit," *The Mother* affirms without a shade of doubt.

The Mother sings a lullaby. Angie closes her eyes and with a sigh of complete abandon, disappears into Angelina.

You are the brightest star
in the night of my heart.
You are the prettiest flower
in this yard.

Just as God made the rose
perfect spiral of beauty
so did God made you
so kind, so soft, so pretty.

As Goddess made the moon,
the stars, the constellations,
so did Goddess made you,
a fountain of creation.

You are the brightest star
in the calm and vast
night of my heart,
where there's no sorrow;
where you now sleep in peace
until tomorrow.

Angelina is rocking softly in the arms of *The Mother*. She feels full, perfect, loved and complete. This feels like heaven! Her breath deepens and her whole mind empties. She is embraced in absolute serenity. This serenity frees her heart from the fist that usually holds it tight. Angelina finally feels that she has arrived home.

"Welcome home, my beautiful child," *The Mother* whispers. "You have arrived at the *Inner Ring of Self*. This is the first chamber. I put the tiny one to sleep because the job ahead is not appropriate for her. It belongs to you, my adult daughter. Before you take on this last task in your quest, I want to nurture you and make you strong. Then you will be able to move into the next chamber."

"Why can't Angie come?" Angelina sits up, nervous. "Is it dangerous? What chamber? What's the job?"

"There is nothing to fear, beautiful child," *The Mother* softly intones, smiling. Her smile comes from so deep within her, that it beams waves of love, calming Angelina. "You have gone through the most difficult and dangerous chambers of the castle already."

"You mean the chamber where that horrible witch attacked us? Where the *Shadow Scouts* took us?" Angelina asks.

"Yes. Ejem. Witch. Yes," mumbles *The Mother*. "About that... Let's see. How do I say this?"

"Just say it. I can take it!" Angelina declares with a courage she is far from feeling.

"When you entered the castle, your fear and defensiveness and your struggle to regain control alerted the *Shadow Scouts*. But perhaps, this was inevitable."

"It wasn't my fault?" Angelina asks.

"There's no one to blame. There's no judgment!" *The Mother* exclaims. "Anyway, sooner or later, you had to meet the *Evil Queen Witch*. It is always good to know as many aspects of yourself as there are, don't you think?"

No, she wouldn't. She would have preferred to avoid that evil witch. But she decides not to share this.

"Wait a second!" Angelina considers. "Are you saying what I think you are saying?"

"You entered the castle through the *Outer Ring of Self,"* The Mother explains. "You met your *Shadows*, who are at the service of the *Shadow Mother* within you."

In her struggle, Angelina had forgotten once more what Dragonfly Diva had said, that all of this was happening inside her, that she made it happen and that the castle was a mask because it was her own *Mask of Self,* the false self she had become.

She had kept this knowledge in the background, never connecting the *Shadow Scouts* and *Shadow Heralds* with the *Shadows* she had met at the *Trail of Shadows*. But now the pieces fit together.

"The *Outer Ring of Self* in this castle is the part of me that holds my *Shadow Inheritance*. These *Shadow Scouts* are the fear-based defensive selves that I've created. That makes that horrendous *Evil Queen Witch...*"

"My counterpart," concludes *The Mother*. "I am your *Inner Mother*. She is your *Shadow Mother* running amuck within you, raising the armies of defenses you learned or created during your *Domestication Trance*."

"That horrific *Evil Queen Witch...* is part of me?" mutters Angelina.

"I knew you would understand!" *The Mother* proudly says.

"But I don't," Angelina thinks. "I may complain about mom, but she was a good mother. I mean, look at all the SACRIFICES she made..."

> *"You are alone, Angelina Semidey. Look at your pathetic father, a cheat and a loser who abandoned you..."*

The *Evil Queen Witch's* words slither into her memory like a poisonous snake. Angelina recognizes that this exact message was repeated ad nauseam by Mercedes throughout her life.

> *"Who has read your poems? A bunch of losers! You haven't been published by the BIG publishers, have you? That's because you stink as a writer. Give it up!"*

That poison, word by word, was emitted by the *Evil Queen Witch* in her chamber. But she remembers these words because they are familiar.

Angie is nine. She is searching for her poetry notebook.

"Are you looking for this?" Mercedes says innocently.

"This is private. What were you doing with it?" Angie demands, snatching the notebook from her mom's hands. Her face is red with anger.

"Oh, I just took it to the famous poet who was visiting town," Mercedes says causally.

Angie cannot believe it. It can't be true. Her mother cannot be this insensitive.

Angie's head is shaking automatically, trying to deny what she is hearing. Her mouth is open in disbelief. Mercedes triumphantly strikes her last blow.

"She said that your verses were... I don't remember the exact words. She was trying to be kind. Let's say that she wasn't impressed."

Angie feels devastated. Poetry is her life. Is she not good enough?

"I've told you, honey. Please listen to me. I know it hurts, but it's for your own good. You won't be published and you'll waste years of your life. No one reads poetry."

"My friends do!" Angie screams. "My teacher does."

"Oh, please grow up," Mercedes spits. "Who are your friends? A bunch of silly nine year olds! And your teacher? Another writer who was never published. They are a bunch of losers!"

Even at that age, Angelina knew that this wasn't right. A mother was supposed to encourage you, not to put you down. These words, these acts, were not the product of a mother. They were not love.

"My girl's a genius!" says *The Mother*.

Angelina looks up, thinking that, like Mercedes, this mother mocks her. But *The Mother* is looking at her with deep compassion and a bit of sadness.

"You have often asked yourself why Mercedes refuses to see your authority, talent and courage and why she consistently undermines your faith in your Dream," *The Mother* says softly.

The pink hues of the room become a bit darker, reflecting the sadness in their hearts.

"Do you remember a battered manuscript with children's stories that you found at the bottom of an old trunk?" *The Mother* reminds Angelina.

Yes!" Angelina exclaims, remembering the old, musty paper that held such beautiful stories. "Mom refused to read them to me, but I saw her name in the cover page."

"These stories were part of your mom's *Gift Bundle*. But she never sent this gift into the world."

Angelina fights back the tears. The pain she felt when she found those stories was only surpassed by the pain she felt when Mercedes, finding Angie reading her stories, took them out into the yard and burned them.

"Your persistence and self-loyalty confronts her with her meekness, cowardice and lack of faith. She gave up pretty soon. She betrayed her Soul's purpose in order to follow the accepted path, to fit the roles others expected of her. She gave in to peer pressure, to difficulties and to her own limitations. She did NOT fight for her Dream. For this, she has given herself endless excuses. She has made the obstacles she met insurmountable. If you succeed, however....

"It would mean that she could have succeeded too, if she had tried," Angelina concludes.

"That's why her *Shadow* pours emotional toxins onto your psyche, to protect the precarious state of her own psyche," *The Mother* explains. "It's sad, but as you could feel even as a child, it is NOT love."

"But it makes no sense *Mother*!" Angelina protests. A part of her is enjoying this moment, in spite the sadness. It is so good to be able to talk to a mother with transparency, without expecting attack or judgment.

"What do you mean, my child?" *The Mother* asks.

"The obstacles she met were different from mine. It was another time. I've had the strength to meet my obstacles **because** she has loved me and sacrificed herself to send me to college, which was something she didn't have. So my success would be hers, too."

"Oh, my child, if she could only see this!" *The Mother* asks. "But a woman who has betrayed her Dream and her Soul out of fear cannot see this. She is her worst judge. It is this judge, not her failure, which creates her *Shadow*."

"I am not only breaking through the obstacles I have created with my own *Shadows*," Angelina grasps. "I have to break through generations of obstacles that my mom and perhaps her mom created and passed on."

"The love and success of the elders is meant to be the *Ancestor's Gift* that helps the young ones evolve the bloodline," *The Mother* says with a trace of sorrow. "But when the elders fail to address their own obstacles and fulfill their own purpose, they carry this as a *Family Karma* that is passed to the next generation as the *Shadow Inheritance*.

Then it is the young ones who need to dispel this karma, not only for themselves and the next generations, but to heal the *Karmic Wound* passed on by the elders. What you are doing is not only an act of love for yourself, my beautiful child, but for those that come after and even for those who have come before you. All in all, you are a true champion."

Angelina laughs. It sounds silly, but it makes her feel great. These are the things she always wanted to hear from Mercedes. That she loved Angelina. That she was proud of her. That she trusted her. That she considered her beautiful, perfect, smart. It's so silly, but now that *The Mother* is saying these things, Angelina knows that these words are food, pure food for her Soul. She feels strong, whole and invincible.

"Good, so you are now ready!" *The Mother* says.

"Ready for what?" Angelina snaps, her smile disappearing quickly. "Don't tell me there's more!"

"Just a teeny weeny more, baby," *The Mother* says. "But you'll do great!"

"Are you sure?" Angelina asks.

"Quiet sure," *The Mother* declares. "Remember that you are now in the *Inner Ring of Self.* Do you know what this means?"

The term sounds familiar. Yes, Dragonfly Diva pointed it out to her when they flew above the castle. It was the circle behind the *Outer Ring of Self* and before the star-shaped inner circle.

"I see that you now remember," *The Mother* says. "The *Inner Ring of Self* holds your *Creative Selves* and your *Developmental Selves*. The *Creative Selves* are the many talents and gifts that are organic to you.

Some of these organics gifts you know and have developed. Others, however, were not fully accepted or acknowledged by those around you, so you..."

"Repressed them and jailed, them, together with my *DreamSelf*," finishes Angelina, feeling rotten to the core.

"Don't blame yourself, beautiful child," *The Mother* softly says. "You have done the best you could, better than most, I would say, for you have crossed into the *Victory Zone*."

"Really?" says Angelina, feeling a bit more cheerful.

"Of course. Once you entered the castle, you are in the *Victory Zone*," explains *The Mother*. "Very few people even take the Dream Express, much less collect all the *Alchemical Keys*. You are a true heroine!"

"I sure don't feel like one," Angelina mumbles. "Look at all the people I've kept prisoners! Creative beings, develop... what were the others?"

"*Developmental Selves*. That's you throughout time. *Inner children* and *Inner Adolescents*."

"How come Angie is not there?" Angelina asks.

She's your *Sacred Child*, your *Wonder Child*. Only extreme abuse would send her underground," explains *The Mother*. "Plus she is the most resilient little tweedy I've ever known." *The Mother* is positively beaming. It's a bit embarrassing, really.

"Well, if I've imprisoned my *Creative Selves*, how come I can write and perform?" Angelina challenges.

"The selves in the *Inner Ring of Self* are not prisoners in the sense that your *DreamSelf* is, at least not all of them. The *Inner Ring of Self* is like a permeable membrane. Some of these selves are hidden, even from you, at the moment. But many come in and out of your consciousness. They all communicate, and this makes it possible for you to awaken a hidden talent, for example, by communicating to that self via a talent you recognize."

That's what happened to *Goddess Grace,* your *Dancer* and *StoryShifter,* your *Actress.* You had disowned them, but when you began to write poetry, your *Poet* helped you connect with them again."

"If they are not prisoners, what are they doing here?" Angelina asks. These explanations are confusing her more.

"Helping."

"What do you mean?"

"The *Mask of Self* is sculpted around your *Core Self,* sweetie," *The Mother* explains. She reminds Angelina of a mother talking about the birds and the bees with her child.

"With time, it gets a bit... sticky, if you know what I mean," *The Mother* says, her voice trembling at the edges. "They kind of melt together because you can't recognize the false perceptions you learned about yourself from your organic, true aspects. That's why it's all here. The *Outer Ring of Self* is the mask. The *Inner Ring of Self* holds the aspects of your *True Self.* It also connects you to the *Core Self.*"

"That's where the *Throne of the Ancient Heart* is!" Angelina exclaims. "I saw it from above. That's where they've taken her, isn't it?"

"Yes," *The Mother* confirms.

"So that's where I'm heading, then," says Angelina doggedly.

"That's my girl!" says *The Mother.* "She won't settle until she makes her Dream come true. That's the spirit!"

"And you say I'm in the *Inner Ring of Self,* with all my *Creative Selves*?" Angelina asks. There's definitely something in her mind. "Can't they help me?

"What do you think I'm doing?" *The Mother* responds, a bit put off.

"Sorry. Right. So what do I do now?" Angelina stutters.

"Meet them, of course," says *The Mother.*

"Who, me?" Angelina says, standing up, fixing her dismantled, dirty outfit. "How do I look? Oh, I'm a mess!"

The Mother smiles and hugs Angelina.

"You are perfect, my beautiful child," The Mother says into Angelina's heart. "You are perfect for your purpose just as you are right now."

"I am so proud of you," *The Mother* whispers. "I knew that you would come through. I knew it because you have always sought the light. You have always chosen to find your truth. You are courageous and impeccably honest and that is why you have succeeded so far. Your success makes me proud. But your joy is even more important to me. Your joy is my joy."

Angelina feels an immense ocean of gratitude dancing within and around her as she looks into the loving face of *The Mother*. She intuitively cups her hands over her heart.

She remembers her *DreamBirth*. This feeling of love is similar to the love she felt coming from Earth Mother when she climbed the *Tree of Life and Death,* at Bleak Station. Perhaps *The Mother's* love is all love, present in Earth, in life and inside herself.

"Mother's love is pure Love," Angelina feels as her free heart pulsates peacefully with the vibrations of life. "It is Divine Love. It is the love of the Universe that births everything. Only our human fears distort it into possession and judgment, as we try to mold our children to our own lacks and longings. But this pure, unconditional love is inside me, inside all of us. It is the fabric of life."

"Congratulations!" *The Mother* says, hugging her even more tightly. Angelina considers that this big mama may crush her, but feels elated nonetheless.

"You have now pierced the first of the six veils that will move you along the *Inner Ring of Self.* You have awakened from the grasp of the *Veil of Orphanhood.*"

There is something shining inside Angelina's cupped hands. She opens them to find a radiant rose quartz in the form of a heart. It is almost as big as her cupped hands.

"This is the first of *Indra's Jewels,*" *The Mother* reveals. You will need the others to place them in *Indra's Net."*

"What...?" Angelina asks.

"Shush," *The Mother* gently says, placing her index fingers over her lips. "Listen carefully now. This is the *Jewel Eye of Love.* Swallow it."

"But... But it's too big!" Angelina protests.

"Do you trust me?" *The Mother* asks.

Angelina nods. This *Mother* she trusts completely. She opens her mouth to swallow the gem.

"Just touch your tongue to it, my love" *The Mother* instructs.

Angelina does as she is instructed, and the jewel shrinks, disappearing down her throat. It leaves a delicious, sweet aftertaste.

"To retrieve it, simply call out your love," *The Mother* instructs.

"Retrieve? When? Why?" Angelina wants to know.

But a distant howling makes *The Mother* giddy.

"Quick, our time is up. I got some last minute instructions," she adds in a hurry. "There's so much to know and so little time!"

"What's the hurry?" Angelina asks. She also heard the howling and is apprehensive.

"Never mind. Listen carefully," *The Mother* says. She is making an effort to remain focused.

"The *Inner Ring of Self* is vast. You don't necessarily meet the same selves every day. But there are six *Creative Selves*, me included, that you **must** meet today if you want to awaken *Indra's Net*."

"What's *Indra's Net*?" Angelina asks.

"Didn't I tell you?" *The Mother* asks. "*Indra's Net* opens the *Golden Rift*. Oh, my Goddess! I'm so excited that I'm all over the place."

"One step at a time," *The Mother* tells herself, breathing deeply. "One foot first, then the other. Let's see. There are six jewels from *Indra's Net* that open the *Golden Rift*. You will find one in each of the chambers of the *Inner Ring of Self*. Is that clear, sweetie?"

"I have to find six jewels?" I thought I was almost done!" protests Angelina.

"There's no time for complaints!" *The Mother* barks, sounding very much like Dragonfly Diva.

"In each chamber in the *Inner Ring of Self* you'll meet a *Creative Self* who will help you pierce a veil. If you succeed," *The Mother* now smiles reassuringly, "as I'm **sure** you will, the veil will transform into a jewel like the *Jewel Eye of Love*. You **must** have those six jewels to cross the *Golden Rift*."

"What's the Gold...." Angelina begins.

But the soft pink light that had enveloped them goes off and Angelina is again in total darkness.

"Oh, yes, I forgot!" *The Mother* says quiet casually in the darkness. "Don't be afraid of the presence in the dark."

CHAPTER 27

The Huntress and the Jewel Eye of Truth

Dense darkness wraps Angelina, as cold and silent as *The Mother's* chamber had been warm and harmonious. She stays very still. *The Mother* said there was a presence. What presence?

A low growl reverberates in the darkness, echoing all around her. She cannot determine where it's coming from, so she coils inwards.

"Not to be afraid? *The Mother* must have gone batty. This is a large cat or worse," Angelina thinks.

A pair of large golden eyes pierces the darkness. Terrified, Angelina jumps back. Her eyes are adapting to the dark and now she sees the outline of an animal. It's a wolf.

All her fear dissolves. Angelina feels a fear alliance, a wild belonging. Strange as it may seem, she recognizes this wolf as kin. There is no strangeness. The wolf has spoken into her heart. Something is awakening within.

Inside her, a fierce Huntress steps out to meet the wolf.

"*Night Wolf," The Huntress* salutes as she merges with the She-wolf.

Angelina feels the strong, vibrant body of *The Huntress* in her own body as she walks inside the She-wolf.

Night Wolf walks in the darkness, her footsteps so light that her paws make no noise against the stone floor.

Night Wolf's presence is silent and playful, yet fierce. It speaks without words, in energy, sensations and inner knowing. Her senses are heightened. Angelina enjoys the strong physicality of *Night Wolf.*

"Come back you idiotic girl, or you'll be responsible for your idiotic father's death!"

The terrifying scream, reeking with the *Evil Queen Witch's* malice, breaks through the darkness like lightning cuts through the night.

Angelina shivers inside the wolf. *Night Wolf,* however, lowers her body to the ground and sniffs.

Night Wolf does not understand words. Instead, she understands vibrations. Therefore, she is not fooled by lies. There is no substance to this sound. This creature is afraid and defeated. This is an idle threat.

Night Wolf leaps and runs. *The Huntress* runs through the night. She pierces the night, becoming the night.

Night Wolf is on the trail of a vague scent. As *The Huntress* runs, Angelina hears the *Evil Queen Witch* crackle.

"You'll never see him again!"

Flashes of memories speed through the darkness, but Angelina can't catch them. A black veil falls over the visions as soon as they rise.

"Release the lies," *The Huntress* says.

"What lies?" Angelina asks. She is trembling.

A long howl breaks the night. Angelina is pushed out of *Night Wolf's* body. She falls to the stone floor, curling into a fetal position.

"No, no!" Angelina pleads.

"Look up!" *The Huntress* says inside her.

Angelina uncoils and looks into the golden eyes of *Night Wolf.*

The screen door bangs loudly against the frame.

"I'm home," a nine-year old Angie calls out.

"Go to your room," barks Mercedes from the kitchen.

"But, mom..." Angie starts.

"Go to your room! NOW!" roars Mercedes. The cry crashes like a tidal wave against some hidden wall, breaking into sharp fragments of glass; mirrors cutting through Angie's soul. That pain, again that pain. Always that pain."

She hides and eavesdrops.

"You can't do this. It ain't right," says a stranger. It's a male voice.

"Never!"

"Mercy, I'm their father."

"You should have thought of that when you left them."

"I didn't leave them. I left you."

The voice says this almost quietly, as if it could soften the blow.

"Tell that to them!"

"I would, if you left me!"

"What's stopping you?"

"You've poisoned them against me."

"There you go. Blaming me. You never change. It's always someone else."

"I've done this and I recognize it. I've passed the buck around more often than I care to remember and I have refused to assume responsibility for my children. I admit it. But losing my family has been a harsh lesson. I've realized what really matters. I've changed. Give me a chance."

"Give YOU a chance. Who's given ME a chance?"

"This is not about you, Mercy. It's about the kids."

"Don't call me Mercy. Never again. NEEEEVEEER."

Angie knows that tone of voice. Crazy Woman is coming up. And this kind of crazy is bad crazy! Angie tiptoes into her room.

"Think about it. You are hurting them more than you are hurting me," says the voice loudly. "You know where to find me."

Angie hears the screen door slam against the frame. She runs out. But he's gone. She never even saw his face.

"He tried. He never left us. He left HER. She lied. He did TRY!" Angelina cries. "I'm so sorry. I'm sorry dad. You're not perfect, but it was wrong to keep you away. It was not fair."

"NOOOOO!"

The *Evil Queen Witch's* scream shatters the glasses of hundreds of windows. The walls tremble.

Foster's image glows in the dark.

"Thanks, my Angel!" he says as the image dissolves.

He is gone. The *Evil Queen Witch* no longer holds him. Of this Angelina is certain. He is free from the lies, and so is she.

Night Wolf joyfully barks and jumps.

"You have gone through the *Veil of Forgetfulness and Lies,*" *The Huntress* declares. "You have retrieved the *Jewel Eye of Truth.*"

Angelina feels a weight in her hands. There it is, the second *Jewel Eye*. It is a black obsidian sword about the size of a yard stick. The razor-sharp edges glistened like mirrors.

Angelina remembers that she must swallow the jewels. This sharp gem is really testing her trust in *The Mother*. Dare she taste it?

"It's better not to think too much about it," Angelina tells herself. "A woman's got to do what a woman's got to do!"

She takes a large gulp, opens her mouth and touches the sword with the tip of her tongue. It disappears leaving a strong aftertaste, like the taste of fresh basil.

CHAPTER 28

The Sassy Self and the Jewel Eye of Laughter

Angelina is spinning. When everything stops moving, she finds herself in a dance hall. It's one of those tacky, over the top dance places, designed for night use. The walls are dressed in orange satin with gold motifs. Party banners crisscross the space.

"Happy birthday! Happy anniversary! Happy holidays! Happy Thanksgiving! Happy life! Happy day! Happy hour!"

"They seem very happy here," Angelina mutters as she wipes the dust from her already grimy outfit.

"Salsa!" cries out a gorgeous red-haired woman, dressed in a golden rumba gown and dancing across the wall to a hot salsa rhythm.

"Hi, honey, you rule!" she says with a sassy step while she sings.

I am too blessed to be stressed.
Too pretty for self-pity.
Too delicious to stay suspicious.
Too fun to hide my tail and run."

"Like it? I composed it especially for you!" the red-hair says, slapping Angelina's buttocks. "I am *Sassy Suzette*. I am your spicy, sexual creative self. In short, your *Sassy Self*. I am here to put a little chutzpah into your life, honey."

"Let me take a good look at ya'," *Sassy Suzette* says, rolling some imaginary sleeves. With a wave of her hand, she makes Angelina rotate. Sassy lowers Angelina's decoupage, raises her pants' legs and pulls and pinches here and there as Angelina gyrates.

"Hands off!" Angelina snaps, slapping *Sassy Suzette's* hands away. "Do I look like a mannequin to you?"

"Ay, sweetie, take it easy, will ya'? Don't get irritated!" *Sassy Suzette* intones while she manifests a multitude of fabrics of various colors, scissors, needle, thread, hair rollers and a host of beauty products.

"It's bad for the blood pressure, the liver and the heart, you know?" *Sassy Suzette* says as she takes Angelina's measurements. "And what's bad for your heart, is bad for your love life! And we can't have that, can we?"

Before Angelina can respond, *Sassy Suzette* snaps her fingers.

"Rolling!" she says, and the scissors are cutting the fabric while the needles are sewing them together. A team of beauty experts in the most extravagant outfits materializes on the spot.

Angelina is stripped, washed, dried and dressed in a red silk Japanese robe; all the while she is fighting with the strangers who dare to touch her naked body.

When that ordeal is over, she is sat in a high revolving chair. Her hair is washed, cut, dyed and styled in moments. She is given a facial, her nails are polished and she gets a pedicure, all simultaneously.

Angelina feels that she has been captured by a giant octopus. As the *Beauty Team* works on her, she is stretched this way and that. Her head is in a pair of hands while each of her feet is being worked by another pair of hands. Her arms are wide open and each of her hands is being worked by a different beauty expert.

Her head rests on the chair's cushion while she is brushed. Her face is covered with a mask, washed and then covered with a warm towel. She is patted, rubbed, anointed and brushed by half a dozen hands.

All these people, here for her.

All this attention.

All this pampering.

Angelina feels that she is being stretched beyond her tolerance. She's stretched, like a rubber band, and she's breaking. No one asks her if she wanted this. She feels violated. Manhandled.

But why? They're not hurting her. Why does this feel more threatening than her struggle with the Lord of Lucre?

The first group of experts leaves and another group of experts show up. They have brushes, colors, pencils. They bend over Angelina and begin to paint her. She feels like a blank canvas.

"Ooh!" says a beauty expert. "These hairs got to go!"

"Leave my eyebrows alone!" Angelina squeals.

"Ah!" says another beauty expert. "This soft hues work wonders on you!"

"I'm on a quest, you moron!" Angelina yells. "Not in a beauty contest."

"Mon dieu!" says a French artist. "These eyes defy my palette! Ques'que se culeur?"

"Wouldn't you like to know?" Angelina grins, trying to take the brush away.

But her efforts to gain control of her body are useless. She is plastered with make-up, wrapped in some soft fabrics and whirled in front of a mirror.

"Voila!" *Sassy Suzette* says. Angelina stands before a mirror. She does not recognize herself. Her honey-colored hair, now glowing with auburn-red hair streaks, has been cut and fluff to look as wild as a lion's mane. She wears a beautiful silk dress in swirls of fuchsia and orange spattered with gold flowers here and there.

"It's so..." Angelina stutters, thinking that Mercedes would have no problems finding a word: 'loud, cheap and screaming' are some of the more subtle words she would use.

"Daring, isn't it?" *Sassy Suzette* says grinning. "Just like you!"

"I do like it," Angelina admits. "It's..."

"Exuberant," *Sassy Suzette* finishes. "Just like you!"

The skirt fits her hips and thighs perfectly and then opens at the legs, flowing softly. The cleavage is quiet daring. Her makeup looks great. She looks like a famous movie star!

"Oops!" *Sassy Suzette* exclaims, painting Angelina's lips fuchsia with one swipe of her fingers. "The devil is in the details."

"Shooooes!" *Sassy Suzette* whoops.

"I'm very grateful, but I really most go," Angelina insists. "I have an important thing to do, like save a life —mine actually— I can come back for a makeover another time, if you don't mind."

"You heard her," *Sassy Suzette* hollers. "She's got an important mission. Bring it on!"

The *Beauty Team* shows up with dozens of shoes, each of which is tried on Angelina's feet.

"Stilettos!" sings *Sassy Suzette* adoringly as Angelina's feet are clad in 4 inch high red stilettos. It's all she can do to avoid a fall, but Angelina worries that she will break an ankle is she gives a step.

As if she'd read her mind, *Sassy Suzette* shakes her head disapprovingly.

"No. Too flimsy. I hate when the protagonist falls in a chase, don't you?"

The *Beauty Team* agrees.

"Sandals!" She calls out.

One fourth inch heel sandals appear in Angelina's feet. They are quite comfortable and beautiful at the same time.

The top features thin silver stripes woven together. The silver net is adorned with a small gem in each intersection. The gems are orange, fuchsia and gold. Angelina wonders if this is how *Indra's Net* looks, with a *Jewel Eye* in each point of intersection.

"Heavenly!" *Sassy Suzette* sighs. "But No. Too fragile. Imagine one of them bursting and all those gems rolling, and she's slipping down a precipice, Oh, my god the drama!"

The *Beauty Team* is excited.

"This ain't a soup opera, people!" *Sassy Suzette* remarks. "She's got an important job to do. You heard her. This is no picnic. Though coming to think about it, these sandals would not do for a picnic!"

She laughs with such abandon that Angelina feels the end of her lips curling up into a smile, in spite or herself. The *Beauty Team* is whooping and laughing.

They produce a pair of golden ankle-high boots. They are as soft and flexible as slippers, but quite sturdy, with a non-slippery rubber sole and half-inch heels.

"Lady, I got to run!" Angelina presses.

"Why?" *Sassy Suzette* inquires.

"Because..."

"Why run when you can dance?"

The *Beauty Team* starts to dance as in a Bollywood movie.

"What are you all doing? Are you nuts?" Angelina screams. "All you've done is waste my time. I didn't come here to be err... adorned and painted. This is so frivolous. I can't even imagine why I'd have some useless bimbo like you inside my head."

"Oh, no, dear," says *Sassy Suzette*. "I don't live in your head."

And with a firm grip, she grabs Angelina's crutch. "I live in your VAGINA."

She pulls Angelina by the crutch as she dances a rumba and sings.

I am not a useless bimbo
Just because I dance the mambo.
But I do prefer hilarity
To a pompous ass....acidity!

Oh! I like this. One more time!

There's a great misunderstanding
Right about where you are standing
That confuses beauty with bauble,
And that idiocy is incurable!

Angelina is furious.

"How dare you, *Sassy Self,* or whoever, whatever you are, to grab my privates?"

"They are mine, too, you know."

"No, I don't know and I don't care. How do you dare..."

"That's your problem."

"What?"

"That you don't care."

"About what?"

"About your privates."

Angelina is shocked.

"That's the truth. You have rejected them," whispers *Sassy Suzette.*

Angelina looks at the red-haired diva and she is suddenly, blatantly aware of the stupidity of her anger and indignation. This is a monologue. She is talking to herself. Why is she so upset? Why does she feel so angry about her body, about sex, love? She didn't use to be this rigid. What has changed her into this pompous ass?

While Angelina is going on with her monologue, the *Beauty Team* divides into two teams: boys and girls. The boys begin to pursue the girls. At the beginning it's all quiet fun, but it soon degenerates into physical abuse, sexual harassment, physical manhandling and rape.

At the sight of these garish scenes, hot lava rises inside Angelina. The fire is burning her belly, her chest, ascending up her throat. A dark red flame is burning inside her, carrying the filth and humiliation of years. The need to expel this filth overwhelms her.

"Freeze!" *Sassy Suzette* exclaims.

Everyone freezes, including Angelina.

"Feel your rage, Angelina. Don't fight it. Don't suppress it," *Sassy Suzette* whispers. "But don't just let it boil over, out of control. Feel it as the pure energy of fire it is. Are you feeling that pure emotional fire?"

Angelina blinks. It's the only think she can move.

"Now comb it. *Comb Out* all the scenes from your past," *Sassy Suzette* instructs. "Use your breath as the comb and *Comb Out* all the experiences you've linked to this anger."

Scenes from her life swirl around the hot flames; her ass-pinching boss, the boyfriend who bullied, mocked and then hit her, her nightmarish date rape, the cat-calling, the sexual objectification, the pornographic mind-set that chops her body into pieces, the lascivious, aggressive glances, the omni-present double-standards. One by one she brings up these shameful, painful experiences.

"I can't release them!" she whines.

"Are you the victim?" *Sassy Suzette* asks.

"Yes!" Angelina howls. "And I don't want to be their victim anymore!"

"Then don't!" *Sassy Suzette* howls back.

"You were abused and oppressed by these men once," *Sassy Suzette* says. "But you've been repeating their violation by blaming yourself, then blaming them, then seeking more people to blame. Stop blaming! Stop holding on to this poison, sweetie-pie."

"I don't want to hold on!" Angelina cries. "But how can I let it go?"

"What would happen if you do?" *Sassy Suzette* asks.

"It will happen again! I got to remember, so I don't forget, or it will happen again!" Angelina hears herself saying.

"No, it won't," *Sassy Suzette* declares.

"Bring each memory into the flame of your anger," *Sassy Suzette* instructs.

Angelina picks the memory of Michael and lets it burn hot inside the flame of her anger.

She was so young then! Barely sixteen. He was much older. At the beginning he was Prince Charming.

Angelina remembers her anger at *The Knights* when they first arrived. She realizes that she attached her anger and distrust of Michael to any gallant man.

Slowly, but increasingly, Michael began to put her down. At the beginning it seemed reasonable and it was an isolated incident here and there, so she let it slide.

Then she began to criticize her constantly. Then he made her feel incompetent in any and every situation. He then scared away all her friends. And when she felt insecure and alone, he began to slap her around.

"How did you collaborate with this abuse?"

"You are blaming me? I'm the victim!" Angelina protests.

"If you say so!" *Sassy Suzette* replies in the exact same tone Dragonfly Diva use. For a split second, Angelina considers that the batty lady may have shapeshifted into *Sassy Suzette.*

But she remembers her quest with the *Bridge Guardians.* She remembers how her perception has shaped every twist and turn in this adventure. She also remembers that she is in this chamber to be helped, and that she needs the *Jewel Eye* that *Sassy Suzette* probably holds somewhere in order to get to her *DreamSelf.*

"I'm not seeing what you are showing me, but I'm willing to see if you help me," Angelina asks.

"Would you go out with Michael now?" *Sassy Suzette* questions.

"No way!" Angelina snorts.

"Why?" *Sassy Suzette* wants to know.

"I'm wiser now. I see beyond sweet words and charming promises. I look at a man's actions, not just his words. Plus I don't allow men to diminish me now. The second they start putting me down, I cut off the relationship and put them in their place, that's why!" Angelina snaps.

"How about the other memories?" *Sassy Suzette* insists.

Angelina is stroke by a revelation.

She has learned. She has grown. She has become wiser, stronger, more confident, more able to see a person's character from the way they talk, act and respond.

Was she stupid when she was young? Was it inexperience that led her to allow Michael's abuse?

Perhaps. But it was —more than anything— her low self-esteem and her orphanhood. Now she has given herself the love and attention to heal that terrible gap inside her. She would never allow a jerk like Michael into her life. And if she made a mistake and did, she would cut the relationship off at the first signs of disrespect. Plus, she would not allow his opinions to diminish her dignity. She doesn't give away her power like that anymore.

And that's the revelation. Angelina does not need to keep the memory in order to prevent the mistake from happening again. She is not in danger anymore.

Angelina is shocked that she could not see the evident nature of this truth before. It's so obvious. She's grown. She's not that naïve young, hungry woman. In fact, those types of men don't even show up in her life anymore!

"As long as you hold on to the past, you cannot see the present, sweetie-pie," *Sassy Suzette* clarifies. "Your attachment to your past keeps you playing the same role of victim and does not let you see your power."

"Is that why you want me to *Comb Out* these memories?" Angelina asks.

"Yes," *Sassy Suzette* confirms. "The anger is real. It is power. But the memories are not real. They are ghosts from the past. They attach the present emotion of anger to that toxic waste. That holds you a prisoner of the past. When you release the ghosts, you free your power."

"I welcome freedom," Angelina whispers, allowing her memories to float in all clarity in front of her and bringing each into the flame of her anger.

As Angelina breathes through the anger, releasing these memories, the hot flames begin to shine clear and bright. The flame is no longer an overwhelming, uncontrollable anger-fear infested with toxic emotions. The anger is no longer attached to a feeling of powerlessness. It is now pure hot energy, almost impersonal and completely manageable. Without the old memories torturing her, this energy feels good. Instead of feeling like a victim, she feels powerful, ready to fly.

"What do you want to do with this energy that you've liberated?" *Sassy Suzette* asks. "You can use it to heal, to propel yourself into action, to persist, transcend or manifest or you can store it for *Acts of Power*."

Angelina feels the bright red flame warming her body and clearing her mind.

"I am storing it now to use it for freeing my *DreamSelf*," she decides.

"Yipeeeeeh!"

The *Beauty Team* has become a cheerleader team. Pompons are flashing. People are cheering.

"You have pierced the *Veil of Toxic Anger and Sexual Shame*," *Sassy Suzette* declares. "You have released toxic waste and you have embraced the flow of passion that is life, right now, in the present."

There is a large carnelian in her hands. It has the shape of a conch shell. She touches it with the tip of her tongue, and it disappears.

Angelina feels and uncontrollable urge to laugh. She finds everything funny.

"You've retrieved the *Jewel Eye of Laughter*," *Sassy Suzette* reveals. "And you will soon discover that far from being frivolous, it is a key to freedom."

The *Beauty Team* raises Angelina and carries her on their shoulders as they cheer.

She is falling.

CHAPTER 29

Swan Woman and the Jewel Eye of your Unique Star Essence

She lands with a splash.

Angelina struggles to stay afloat. The waves she creates dance chaotically around her. Once she realizes that she is in a lake, she floats calmly, and the waves slowly disperse.

She is floating in a serene lake surrounded by a crown of tall pine trees. The trees and the sky are reflected in the still water.

There's a fluttering of wings.

A large swan lands on the water.

Angelina has never seen such a large swan. She contemplates its beauty, delighting on the grace that she has admired since she was a child. Swans are so graceful! She has often wished that she could be as graceful, beautiful and majestic as a swan.

A huge eye examines her. The swan twists her long neck in an "S," then in a "U" and then again in an "I" as she observes Angelina.

Again the swan twists her beautiful neck into an "S" an Angelina, curious, looks into the waters to see its reflection.

Instead of the swan's reflection, she sees a star shining at the bottom of the pond.

Angelina feels an irresistible pull and dives towards the shining star. When she tries to grab it, however, the yellow light coils around her.

"What is the nature of a star?" the Swan speaks into Angelina's heart.

"To shine?" Angelina guesses.

The lines of light whirl vertiginously around her, tightening as they swirl. Angelina fears that they will strangle her. Instead, they dissolve into her skin with delightful bursts of light. She feels a dazzling glow emanating from her body.

Angelina floats up just in time to see the swan twist her neck into a "U" again.

"She's communicating in codes," Angelina manages to think before an extraordinary scene enchants her.

There is a Unicorn drinking from the waters in the pond. His mane is pure white and soft. His hide is radiant. As his magical horn sweeps the waters, it creates a rainbow of sparkling streams. He looks up and Angelina feels that she is floating in a dark pool of mystery as his black eyes embrace her in a fluorescent violet light.

"What is the nature of a Unicorn?" the Swan speaks into Angelina's heart.

"Uniqueness," Angelina whispers without even thinking, entranced in the magical embrace of this extraordinary creature.

The fluorescent violet light begins to pulsate. It is pulsating with Angelina's heart. It beats louder and louder. Suddenly, with a swish and a zap, it pours its magic into Angelina's heart.

Angelina sees a beautiful naked, winged man drinking from the pond. His body is soft and glimmering, his hair white and long and his white wings large and luminous. In place of the Unicorn's horn this man has a jewel that shines, illuminating the true nature and the potential in all he sees.

Angelina knows in her heart that this is the Unicorn in one of his manifestations, invisible to the human eye. This naked man is not an Angel, but a demi-god from the ancient religions. He extends a mirror to Angelina.

She looks into the mirror and sees a mermaid. A beautiful mermaid swims in the pond, and that magical creature is Angelina. Her hair is made of water streams flowing happily into the pond. Her eyes are the color of algae. Her lips are corals.

Inside Angelina, Angie smiles a big grin. She loves mermaids.

The handsome demi-god bows to her and Angelina bows back. When she looks up, he has disappeared, as has the Unicorn.

Instead, the swan is floating while she twists her neck into an "I" once more.

Angelina is waiting for another magical scene to appear. Instead she is looking at herself in the waters.

"What is the nature of I?" the Swan speaks into Angelina's heart.

Angelina doubts. There's a strong force bubbling up from the depths of her being, but she does not dare to seize it. It can't be. She goes up to her head and begins to figure it out.

How about intelligence?

She remembers several intelligent people she can't stomach because they are cynics, bullies and lack a kind heart.

How about Illumination?

This sounds so holier-than-thou that Angelina is quite put out by it, especially when she remembers a couple of people who believe they are illuminated, but who are actually arrogant, callous and self-centered.

"Importance? That's too self-important," Angelina discards.

"Intuition? That's just too small, a part, not the whole," she considers.

"That's it. Integrity. The whole!" Angelina thinks.

But when she looks into the waters, her image is scrambled.

"The stream of your thoughts scrambles your image," the Swan speaks into her heart.

Angelina empties her mind. She goes back to her *First Thought*.

"Impeccability," she responds.

There is a powerful ripple in the waters where the swan was floating. Angelina looks up and gazes into the eyes of *Swan Woman*.

Her huge white wings, neck and eyes belong to a swan. But she has a woman's breasts and hips, thought they are covered in feathers. Angelina can see a pair of legs paddling under the water.

"Are you ready?" *Swan Woman* asks with a sweet, deep rippling voice that reminds Angelina of listening to music under water.

Startled, Angelina responds unthinkingly.

"Ready? For what?"

Swan Woman paddles gracefully away and remains serenely aloof.

Why is she here if *Swan Woman* will not help her?

Swan Woman takes off with a great fluttering of her large wings. She flies majestically through the sky. What a sight! Angelina remembers the *Alchemical*

Rose. She wonders how creatures, trees and flowers can simply be so magnificent, without struggling, without any feeling of shame or doubt.

The memory of the two swans killed in Central Park flashes through her mind. The news spread like fire through New York and reached all over the world. Who could possibly want to destroy such beautiful creatures?

"Watch your memories," a voice warns in her heart.

Angelina shakes her head. Yes, why this memory?

"Why this memory **now**?" *Swan Woman* is asking. She floats behind Angelina, her long neck oscillating close to Angelina's neck.

"I... I don't know," Angelina stutters. She compares her short neck with the long, graceful neck of *Swan Woman* and her neck contracts in shame.

"It just popped into my mind," Angelina answers.

Swan Woman swings her neck from left to right and back again. Angelina tries to watch, but as *Swan Woman* is behind her, her vision splits; one eye moves to the left and the other to the right. A strange stupor invades her.

"The blade that slices your *Essence* is wielded by your domesticated mind. It severs your integrity with a false sense of intelligence, stealing your intuition until you become a facsimile of yourself," *Swan Woman* warns, whispering into her right ear. "But if you embrace *First Thought,* you will become impeccable, which is your true nature."

Simultaneously, in her left ear, *Swan Woman* is saying:

The Shadow
wants to cut off
the Swan's neck.
It has been trained
to destroy beauty.
But the Shadow
does not know
that its fear
has been built
upon its power.
Its darkness
leaves traces
of luminescence
in all it touches.
Follow the Shadow
and you will find
a thread of darkness
that reveals the light.

"It's this negativity," Angelina apologizes. "It creeps up when I least expect, bringing negative memories or expectations when I am summoning my love or power, at the very moment when I need a positive boost."

"Oh, yes, negativity. It usually pops up in the same place," the voice says in her heart.

"Where?" Angelina asks.

"At the juncture," the voice replies.

"What juncture?" Angelina asks.

"At the threshold," the voice reveals.

"What threshold?" Angelina wants to know.

"The *Threshold to your Essence,"* the voice responds.

Angelina looks down into the waters and sees her beautiful olive eyes. They are the eyes of a swan. She lowers her neck to see her image better and realizes that her neck is very long and graceful. Just when she's about to see her wings in the water, a violent tremor of wings raises behind her. She's terrified. She wants to turn around to see what is happening, but she can't move. She's paralyzed with fear. The water in the lake is turning red. Blood! The blood is moving towards her.

"That's the moment," the voice whispers," that the *Shadow* brought to your consciousness. It is a present wrap around a wound. Yet, there is power in that wound."

What moment? What present? What wound? Angelina does not understand.

"The *Sacrifice of the Swan," Swan Woman* trumpets.

Angelina's heart is broken. A luminous tear falls into the sweet waters. It creates a tiny ripple, but as it grows, the ripple dispels the blood, cleaning the entire lake.

"I always knew," Angelina whispers. "Always."

"That you were one of us," *Swan Woman* reveals, looking into the waters, where Angelina's image is trembling.

Angelina nods.

"A majestic Swan. A creatress of beauty. A dancer of grace. A singer of truth. A unique voice. A visionary. A creature born to fly," *Swan Woman* whispers.

Angelina nods.

"But you don't believe it," *Swan Woman* reveals.

Angelina shakes her head.

"Why?" *Swan Woman* asks.

"Why me?" Angelina retorts.

"Why you and not others?" *Swan Woman* asks.

"What's so special about me?" Angelina asks in a trembling voice.

"Why you and not your mother?" *Swan Woman* asks.

Angelina looks up, shocked.

"If you unlock your neck and open your wings, then you betray her."

Angelina nods, tears rolling down her eyes.

"So you betray yourself. "

"No!" Angelina barks in a tiny voice.

"Then join us," *Swan Woman* says.

Reflected in the waters of the lake there is a circle of *Swan Women*. There are nine beautiful *Swan Women* looking at Angelina, who floats in the center of the circle.

There is gap in the circle.

An echoing voice resonates in the waters, as the *Swan Women* speak in one voice. Angelina's skin ripples. She feels the blossoming of feathers in her pores.

"Your place among the *Majestic Swans* awaits. Only you can occupy this place; no one else. And only you —no one else— can place you there."

Angelina sees her body fully reflected in the waters. It is covered in pure white feathers. She extends her arms and feels the huge wingspan, the rustling of feathers and the ecstatic grace of her perfect body.

She lets out a victory cry as she flies towards the gap, her neck in a straight line. She lands softly on the spot and turns gracefully around, facing her Swan Sisters.

"The circle is complete," the *Swan Women* speak in one voice. "You have pierced the *Veil of Self-sacrifice, Ordinariness and Insufficiency.*"

Angelina is holding a gem in her long yellow beak. It is a moonstone in the shape of a swan's eye.

"This is the *Jewel Eye of your Unique Star Essence,"* the *Swan Women* reveal.

The jewel disappears down her long, graceful neck.

The water ripples and Angelina is sucked into another dimension. As she ascends, her feathers dissolve and she is naked. Her large swan wings still remaining, she sees herself in the water below, and she sees an Angel.

She remembers Mercedes laughing when Angie remembered that she had been an angel. But her father did not laugh. He called her "My Angel."

Her entire being irradiates light and peace as she dissolves.

CHAPTER 30

The Architect & Associates and the Tiny Room of the Past

Angelina is in a wide, sumptuous hall. There is no one here to receive her.

She walks slowly through the hall, enjoying this moment of solitude. It's been even more hectic inside the castle than it was in the *Dreamscape*. She doesn't mind if her next *Creative Self* is late. She could do with the break.

There are vibrant works of art hanging on the walls of the hall. Exuberant Goddesses and magical creatures play in beautiful landscapes. The sun rises and sets over exotic places. Women's bodies merge with the body of the elements.

A subtle chime draws her attention up. Chandeliers made of real stars sparkle above, hanging from the ceiling, which is the open night sky. A sense of unbounded freedom overtakes Angelina. Her spirit feels an invitation to fly.

The hall leads into a huge round chamber. She cannot hear her steps here. The floor is made of soft, yielding clay that reminds her of *The Mother*. It welcomes her body.

A string of colorful tiles lines up the bottom of the walls, showing symbols that glisten as she looks at them. Angelina recognizes each symbol, though she doesn't remember ever seeing them before.

"Beautiful, isn't it?"

Angelina turns around, a ready defense in the tip of her tongue. But the being in front of her takes her breath away.

A handsome tall man stands before her with a warm, playful smile in his sensual lips. His smooth cinnamon skin contrasts with the elegant light blue of his attire. He's wearing a silk long three button jacket and pants. This man has flair.

"You can't be..." Angelina stutters.

"*The Architect*, live and in full color, at your service," the handsome man finishes in a suave tone, smiling mischievously while he bows.

"But I...I..." Angelina stammers.

"You thought that I'd look like your friend the Lord of Lucre. I know," jokes *The Architect*.

"Something like that," Angelina smirks.

"Enough about me," *The Architect* remarks. "This is about you. But there is one unhappy assumption that I'd like to clarify before we proceed."

"Please do," Angelina replies, on her best behavior. She obviously had a wrong impression about this *Inner Self.* She's called him the *Architecture of Failure* and fought him tooth and nail.

"My thoughts exactly," *The Architect* responds. "You have been under the impression that I'm bent on designing your failure. Far from that, Angelina. I am the head of the *Creative Design Team* that works **for** you. We live in your *Time and Place Palace* and we are here to design your success... if you'll only let us.

"I was under the impression..." Angelina starts, searching in vain for a good enough reason why she's been fighting this man.

"Your wires are crossed," *The Architect* whispers. But out loud, he cheerily asks, "Do you like the place?"

The monumental chamber is held by four palatial columns that sustain its circular structure. It is crowned by a high vaulted ceiling. Long arched windows descend from the high ceiling onto each wall, streaming the pink, lavender and soft golden rays of dawn.

Angelina has lost track of time. Is it really dawn? How long has she been here? She better pay attention and get this *Jewel Eye* as soon as possible. There's no time to waste!

She carefully examines the circular walls, dressed in tapestries where Goddesses and Gods dance with mortals and shamans shapeshift into beasts.

Angelina is concentrating in every inch of this place, intent in finding the *Jewel Eye*. Yet, instead of feeling her usual irritation, she begins to relax.

Something soft awakens in Angelina. She loves roundness. She feels whole and embraced in this place. At this moment she realizes that all her life she has been living in square spaces that feel prickly and aggressive. They cut into her being and make her movements jerky. But here, in this round chamber, her body lets go and relaxes.

"I've just realized how uncomfortable I am in my own skin," Angelina regards. "I've been straining every day, just to fit other people's spaces."

"It's a fairly common practice," *The Architect* comments.

"I'm sorry. I do not understand." Angelina asks, a bit put-off that *The Architect* is dismissing her problem as commonplace. "What exactly is a common practice?"

"To walk under someone else's shadow. To follow someone else's steps," *The Architect* replies. "To inhabit spaces created by others. In so doing, however, you pull the rug under your own feet."

"You are not making sense," Angelina says defensively. She's not a copy cat. What is he insinuating?

"I don't like his smug attitude," she thinks. "He's extraordinarily condescending."

Could it be that she was right from the beginning and this architect is nothing but an impostor? He doesn't have to look like the Lord of Lucre to be evil. As elegant and handsome as he looks, he could still be a jerk. Why, she knows a lot of handsome jerks!

Why is he criticizing her again? He's always criticizing her. Well, enough with that nonsense. She did not come this far to be judged. She's here for the jewel, not for platitudes.

"I'm not following anyone's steps and there's no rug under my feet. Just soft clay," she says huffily. "Which reminds me: I have a job to do, so I need to get moving."

The Architect takes out a gold pocket watch that softly pulsates.

Tick tock. Tick tock. Tick tock.

"So soon," *The Architect* says. "And without failing."

"What are you...?" Angelina begins to ask, but a huge crack makes the entire space tremble.

"Earthquake!" Angelina screams.

But there is no earthquake. The walls are shrinking!

The *South Wall* shoves Angelina several feet forward as the *North Wall* moves closer. She covers her face, thinking that she will be squeezed between the walls, but they stop at about ten feet from each other.

Angelina breathes a sigh of relief, but it came too soon.

The walls are shrinking vertically and Angelina covers her head and throws herself to the floor as the high ceiling drops vertiginously, stopping ten feet above them.

Tick tock. Tick tock. Tick tock.

"10 by 10 X 10," *The Architect* measures by sight. "That's exactly right. I thought it would be at least a bit larger by now."

"What..." Angelina starts.

"What you see is the *Tiny Room* of your existence," *The Architect* says.

"What *Tiny Room*?" Angelina barks. "My existence is not..."

"Actually, this is the *Tiny Room of the Past*, where you learned to hide in order to feel safe. This is the *Tiny Room* of your *Family Karma*, the time and space restrictions you learned, the habits and beliefs you hold on to. This is the *Architecture of your Psyche* that keeps you playing small."

"It's so tiny!" Angelina exclaims with a trembling voice. "But it does feel safe. How can that be, if I'm claustrophobic? And how about these tiny walls?"

"The floor, walls and ceiling of this *Psychic Architecture* are the dimensions of your limitation," *The Architect* reveals. "In each of these dimensions, you hold psychic patterns that keep this old architecture in place and keep it from expanding."

"How can I change this *Tiny Room* into an ample space?" Angelina asks resolutely while she stands up and brushes the dust off her dress.

She walks from one wall to the opposite, feeling the square constriction that the room creates in her personal space.

"I've always felt constricted," Angelina realizes. "It's like there is not enough room in my life for all of me."

"If the *Inner Ring of Self* is so vast, and it's the bridge to my *Core Self,* then I need space. And that's why I've been feeling that I don't have enough room. There's not enough space for all my gifts and dreams in my life right now."

"You must unfold," *The Architect* observes.

Angelina realizes that he's been following her rumination.

"I'm not folded," she snaps. "I'm not a blanket or a towel."

"Yet you feel constricted," *The Architect* observes. "You play small. You shrink when facing greatness."

"Well..." Angelina tries to find a way to deny it, just because she dislikes this smug man. But she cannot. It is true.

"You are saying that the constriction is not in the space around me, but inside me," she acknowledges.

"Outside mirrors inside," *The Architect* softly says, gracefully pointing to the dimensions of the *Tiny Room.*

"The *Tiny Room of the Past,*" Angelina considers. "What must I do with this cell to get my *Jewel Eye*?"

"Wise question," *The Architect* points out. "We are advancing at last."

Angelina wants to punch him in the nose for his smugness, but she can't allow her own ego to get on the way, no matter how much she hates this guy's huge ego.

"So self-possessed," she mumbles. "So self-assured."

"Where would you house your potential?" *The Architect* asks with a grin. "Where could your Dreams fit?...for they are not small, of that I am assured!"

"If this is the *Room of the Past*, then I need to build a...a *Room of the Future*!" Angelina guesses.

"That is the best you can come up with?" *The Architect* challenges. "Trading one tiny room for another?"

"Oh, yes, ja-ja!" Angelina interjects. "Instead of the *Tiny Room of the Pas*t, how about the BIG room of the future?"

"I thought you were a poet, a writer, an *artiste*!" *The Architect* barks contemptuously. "But your imagination is dwarfed."

That really stung.

But he is right. They were in a huge temple just now, and all she can think as an alternative to this dwarf space is another room.

Angelina finally admits to herself that she has secretly desired a mansion all her life.

"I want a house where all of my talents have a place," she finally says out loud. "Where I have a dance studio to dance and rehearse, a writing studio to write and... an art studio for... Omar."

She sighs.

"Keep focused, lover-girl," *The Architect* says teasingly. "You are doing well."

"I want the house of my dreams," Angelina dares to say. "I want a mansion."

"Is it truly about having a big house, a mansion, according to others' standards?" *The Architect* asks.

"No, it's not about that," Angelina responds. "It's about housing my dreams, my gifts, my totality."

"Now you are talking!" *The Architect* says enthusiastically. "You want your *House of Dreams*!"

"My *House of Dreams*!" Angelina savors.

"Let's do it!" she commands. "Let's build my *House of Dreams* and get that *Jewel Eye*!

"Now you're talking!" *The Architect* cheers.

CHAPTER 31

The Floor of Safe Grounding

There is a big crash followed by a crack-pat-rackata-pum.

The ground wobbles and Angelina falls flat on her fanny.

Night Wolf is giving her a nose kiss.

"Nigh Wolf! What are you doing here?" Angelina asks.

"I see you already know my first associate," says *The Architect*. "Night Wolf, your *Hunter Power Animal*.

"You must be kidding..." Angelina starts, but the ground is changing fast and *Night Wolf* is biting her."

"What are you doing?" Angelina asks as she tries to get Night Wolf's fangs out of her dress. But the she-wolf is dragging her towards the *South Wall*, where *The Architect* now stands.

"Shame on you," she reproaches Night Wolf. "You ripped off a sleeve from my beautiful new attire."

Just then a string of large black and white tiles spreads through the floor, like a violent game of dominoes won by an invisible hand. In seconds the tiles covered the entire ground of the shack.

Night Wolf barks and leaps. Angelina jumps just in time to allow the last tiles to fit under them. Angelina sees *The Architect* hanging from a white line of light that suddenly crosses the space above. With a gracious movement, his feet, clad on expensive leather shoes, land on one of the new tiles without as much as a tap.

"What's..." Angelina begins.

"This is your *Floor of Safe Grounding*," *The Architect* explains matter-of-factly.

Angelina looks at the huge tiles, each about four feet square. What she sees is a giant game board. Games are anything but safe in her book.

What about this....game board?" Angelina asks.

"The *Floor of Safe Grounding* is the measure that you use about what feels safe, real and grounded for you," he adds. "This is the floor of the shack."

Tick tock. Tick tock. Tick tock.

Night Wolf whines. She sniffs the floor and stops at the border of one of the huge black tiles in the center of the tiny room.

"What's wrong?" Angelina asks, as she follows the she-wolf.

Night Wolf jumps inside the tile and starts circling and growling. As the she-wolf circles, the tile gains three-dimensionality, becoming a black cube.

Nigh Wolf lets out a warning yelp and leaps out of the cube.

"What do you...?" Angelina starts, but she is interrupted by a crack and blinding lightning.

She is inside the dark cube.

"Get me out of here!" she yells, beginning to feel the immediate first panic symptoms of her claustrophobia.

"Isn't it ironic?" *The Architect* says. "In spite your claustrophobia, you constantly shrink your vital space. I welcome you to a palace, and look what you've done with it."

"I didn't..." Angelina begins.

The black cube shrinks.

"Ouch!" Angelina complains as she is compressed into a donut shape. "I don't fit here!"

"I agree." *The Architect* says. "Your vast potential and talent cannot possibly fit inside that tiny cube. But this is where you insist to be nonetheless."

Night Wolf is scratching the cube and whining.

"And you complain!" Angelina barks, rather pissed. "I'm the one who ended up inside!"

"Can you get me out of here?" Angelina asks her *Hunter Power Animal.*

Nigh Wolf follows a scent around the bottom of the cube.

> *Angelina is back in the Time and Place Palace talking leisurely with The Architect.*
>
> *"You are not making sense," Angelina says defensively. She's not a copy cat. What is he insinuating?*
>
> *"I don't like his smug attitude," she thinks. "He's extraordinarily condescending."*

"What? What do you want me to see?" Angelina asks Night Wolf.

Her left shoulder is tense and hard, as if an iron bulk had crept into her muscles.

"The *Armored One*!" Angelina spots. "She's the *Shadow* that creates a defensive armor in my body, especially in my back and shoulders. But why? What is she doing?"

Night Wolf barks and runs from *The Architect* to the black cube.

"She's defensive. She closes off. She tries to protect me. But what does...?" Angelina is tracking.

"I got a chip on my shoulder, don't I?" Angelina says begrudgingly.

"Bravo!" *The Architect* applauds.

"The cube is not dissolving. It is not going away. Please, get me out of here," Angelina says as panic rises within her. She is suffocating.

"Panic will not get you out of there, Angelina," *The Architect* answers. "Neither will waiting for rescue. Only you can get you out of where you put yourself."

"How?" Angelina moans.

"How! How!" Night Wolf barks.

"How? Asking how! How did I get myself in here? How did I transform the huge *Time and Place Palace* into this shack?" Angelina tracks.

She remembers that *The Architect* called this the Floor of... what was it? She struggles to breathe.

> *"The Floor of Safe Grounding."*
>
> *The Huntress says inside her. The cube may be small, but inside Angelina there is vast space. The Huntress follows Nigh Wolf in that vast space, tracking the recent conversations. She connects the dots in the design she has just created, pulling old threads together.*
>
> *"A chip on your shoulder."*
>
> *"Ms. Perry Mason. You never lose."*
>
> *"You got to say the last word."*
>
> *"You're a rebel. You fight everything."*
>
> *These were the criticisms of her elders.*
>
> *But even as a child she was fighting to keep her Spirit. She was fighting not to be crushed by the detrimental opinions and constant judgments of her family and society. She would never give in to those righteous elders who were always ready to shrink her imagination, tame her wildness and deny her psychic senses. She would not, could not shrink to fit in the cell of their mediocrity. She would not allow them to invalidate her own perception of what was going on in order to keep her from seeing their lies. If she's got any sense of truth and any dreams left, it's because she fought them tooth and nail.*
>
> *And now that she's grown up... why is she in a small cube? Why does she shrink her vast possibilities? Oh, no! She is doing to herself what they wanted to do to her! But why?*
>
> *She's still fighting, struggling.*
>
> *She cannot tolerate anything that she interprets as criticism or judgment.*
>
> *She only feels safe if people agree with her, follow her lead or support her without question.*
>
> *But if they question her, if they show her anything new about herself, anything that needs to change, that is not perfect, then...*
>
> *"But I'm not like that!" Angelina protests. "I like to learn new things!"*

*"You do," The Huntress says. "But **she** doesn't."*

There's a little anemic girl seating on a tiny bench. Across her, a dozen grownups seat behind a balustrade, pointing their index fingers at her. On the other side, a judge bangs her mallet against her desk.

"Guilty as charged. Guilty as charged. Guilty as charged," The Judge repeats.

The girl shrinks with each verdict.

"I'm creating this *Floor of Safe Grounding* by reacting defensively to any criticism, right?" Angelina ventures in a trembling voice.

"Yes, Angelina. As a matter of fact, the entire shrinking project that turns your vast potential into a 10X10x10 shack can be summarized by the term defensive reactions," *The Architect* confirms. "But the floor... well, let's say that it is a particular phenomenon."

The cube dissolves and Angelina tumbles, legs spread, onto the tiled floor. She swallows large gulps of air. Night Wolf licks her affectionately.

"You were not criticizing me, were you?" Angelina asks, still flustered.

"That was the farthest thing from my mind," *The Architect* responds. "I was simply doing my job, which is to help you build your *House of Dreams."*

"My *House of Dreams*? I want that! I want that house very much!" Angelina exclaims. "I don't want to live in this tiny shack all my life!"

"But this is the house you've created," *The Architect* declares. "Which means that this is the tiny life you are living. Your life now is way smaller than your potential. It is too small for your dream."

"No wonder my *DreamSelf* cannot fit here," Angelina mumbles.

"Exactly," *The Architect* confirms. "As long as you hold on to the dimensions of this *Tiny Room of the Past*, the *Architecture of your Psyche* keeps you playing small and your subconscious will not accept anything that goes beyond these wall."

Angelina is fed up with playing small. She doesn't like the life she's been living. And if this life has to do with these *Tiny Room*, she'll do whatever it takes to remodel this shag into her *House of Dreams.*

"What you are saying is that my subconscious does not believe my true nature!" Angelina remarks. "My *DreamSelf* is my true self, is she not?"

"Right again," *The Architect* replies. "But your subconscious mind has been trained to hold this shack as reality and rejects your dreams as unreal. That's why your *DreamSelf* is vanishing."

"Enough talk!" Angelina declares, remembering that she has very little time left. "How do I create a floor that sustains my dream?"

Angelina has stepped into a white tile. The tile floats up and spins, opening a portal.

"Well done, Angelina!" *The Architect* exclaims. Your question and intention have opened a new *Window of Perception*. Look into it with an open mind."

"I don't see how what you say is true," a young woman is saying. "It's certainly not true in my life. I don't think so."

Angelina is on a big stage. There is an audience of thousands listening to her presentation.

Angelina holds her breath. Her shoulders tense up. But the Angelina on stage smiles and breathes deeply. She opens her heart and her love embraces the young seeker.

She has been there. She remembers when she could not see what others pointed out because she was so defensive. She remembers her many blind spots and how she could not free herself from these, though something within her pushed her to seek.

"You are here for a reason," The Angelina on stage responds, and there is so much love in her voice that the young seeker relaxes.

"There is a part of you that sees beyond your limits. That part of you has brought you here tonight. It keeps seeking. But you may feel frustrated because no matter how hard you seek, you keep bumping into the same limitations."

The seeker is nodding; tears are swelling on her eyes.

"Our blind spots were created very early on. They are like blinders placed on our vision by our Domestication Trance. After a while, we cannot see these parts of life anymore. That's why we keep bumping into them. But if we do not see them, how can we change them? Just because I tell you they are there is not a good enough reason. But neither is the fact that you don't seem them, because that is just a learned limit of perception. You need to explore and experiment. You need to be willing to see and to follow the eyes of those who point possibilities out to you, until you can expand your Field of Perception. The blindfold will fall then."

The floor of the shack changes into a beautiful mosaic of flowers and leafs that blend with Angelina's dress, feeling as a part of herself.

That of course, has thrown Angelina and *The Architect* back on the floor, but they are glad to be there, enjoying the new beautiful tiles.

The floor begins to stretch, and the tiny walls are cracking as the floor pushes them outwards.

"Enough!" *The Architect* says. "That's about what you can stretch for now."

The pushing and cracking stops as the floor settles.

"It was beautiful," Angelina whispers as she caresses Night Wolf. The she-wolf disappears, leaving Angelina caressing the empty space.

"What was beautiful?" *The Architect* requests to know.

"The way I answered the seeker," Angelina clarifies. "Had I been defending myself because she questioned what I said, I could not have connected so deeply with her."

"That's why you needed to release your defensive reaction to criticism in order to renovate the floor of your existence," *The Architect* explains. "Otherwise you could not become the leader you were born to be. A leader cannot be defensive when her Tribe challenges her. Her job is to help them see what they cannot see yet."

"And she cannot do this if she starts defending herself," Angelina continues. "In fact, had I done that I would have alienated not only the seeker, but the entire audience. They would not have dared to ask any questions. I would have come off as...."

"Extraordinarily condescending?" *The Architect* finishes with a smile.

"It was all a projection!" Angelina barks. "How often do I project my fears and defenses onto others?"

The *North Wall* transforms into a big mirror.

"Yeah!" Angelina retorts dejectedly. "A mirror ten times your size would still be small for all my projections. I never change!"

"In this beautiful earth we exist and express ourselves in time and space," *The Architect* softly says, as he looks at his gold pocket watch.

Tick tock. Tick tock. Tick tock.

CHAPTER 32

The Wall of Beliefs

Angelina feels sleepy.

"In fact, our thoughts and words **create** that space and time," *The Architect* declares. "In other words, what you say is what you get."

The *North Wall* of the shack turns into a dark green mass that swirls in space. Angelina gets dizzy.

Inside the swirling mass something begins to grow.

"Meet my second associate," says *The Architect*. "Merlin *The Alchemist* or *The Wizard*, however you want to see him."

An old, tall wizard dressed in a night-black tunic bows gracefully. Angelina notices that the tunic is decked on stars, and they seem to twinkle as if they were alive.

"At your service," Merlin says as he directs his wand to the green mass, "I'm your guide to the *North Wall*. Behold your *Limiting Beliefs*."

An electric green presence detaches itself from the wall and snakes towards Angelina while lines of sizzling energy crisscross the space from the North to the *South Wall*. Angelina backs away.

A beautiful cobra head emerges from the green energy.

Angelina is at awe. The large diamond-shaped head of Cobra is like a portal to another dimension. Her green hues are electrifying and her beautiful scales hold ancient glyphs that want to reveal their secrets to Angelina.

But the beauty spell is broken when the old Cobra falls down with a thud into the floor. Her trunk is weighed down by old scales and layers of old skin still adhered to her body.

"What happened to you, Great Cobra?" Angelina mourns.

"A nasty weight keeps me from my sacred dance," Cobra painfully utters in a raspy, hissing voice. "Clumps of waste hide my beautiful designs. I look more like a leper than a snake."

"How did this happen?"Angelina wants to know.

Cobra twirls her powerful body around Angelina. As she curls and hisses, she speaks into Angelina's heart.

"You said you never change. And it seemed contrite. But you don't fool me for a second. This is your *North Wall*, and I'm its guardian. I know that you pay change lip service, but resist it. You are proud to NOT change."

"That's not true!" Angelina retorts. But she immediately realizes that this reaction is the old pattern in her *Floor of Safe Grounding*.

"Sorry. I am listening," Angelina rectifies. She could swear that the floor wobbled again. But if it did, it is now steady.

"Your *North Wall* is about your *False Beliefs*, those that keep you trapped in your *Tiny Room*. And look at me, what do you see?" Cobra speaks into her heart.

"You have not shed in ages, Queenly Cobra!" Angelina realizes.

"That says it all!" Cobra laughs, slashing the air with her tongue.

"You seek change, innovation, freedom; but installed in this *Wall of Limiting Beliefs* is the old, learned conviction that change is hard and that others want you to change in order to control you. So you resist change while you seek freedom. Look at what you've done to me!"

"I?" Angelina begins to protest and catches herself again. "I... I'm sorry. What can I do to help?"

Cobra's head falls with a thud in the floor. Angelina screams.

The head becomes a huge radiant diamond.

"Look into it," Merlin demands.

The diamond is shrieking in a deafening high note.

"What's wrong with it?" Angelina cries.

"It's weakening," Merlin replies.

"Why?"

"Look at the central girdle that crosses it's horizontal axis," Merlin instructs, touching the diamond with his wand.

Angelina sees that the central girdle is being pressed by a force emanating from a band around it. The pressure is stressing the girdle.

"The strength of this girdle determines the quality of a diamond," Merlin reveals.

"What happened to the head of the Cobra?" Angelina wants to know.

"She's lending it to you. You are seeing into it right now," Merlin replies, tapping the diamond. "Less talk and more action, please."

The diamond spins and they are both suck into its vortex.

"This is the *Gem of your Sacred Self*," Merlin is saying.

They are both standing on the central girdle of the diamond, a thin, but sturdy energy beam.

"Feel the tension," Merlyn indicates.

There's stress in the beam and it's difficult to stand steadily on it. It feels like a wavering high wire.

"What's causing it?" Angelina starts to ask.

The central girdle suddenly wobbles and Angelina slides to the edge, banging against the diamond's facet joint. Her head is stuck there. She kicks, trying to get up.

Merlin points his wand at her. Angelina feels like a nail pulled by a magnet as she slides back into the center of the girdle.

"Thanks" she says with a grimace. "How on earth do...?"

The entire axis jiggles. Merlin holds Angelina from falling down into the abyss at both sides of the beam.

The radiance is being interrupted, like an electrical short-circuit.

"What's going on?" Angelina wants to know.

"This girdle is your *Personal History Girdle,"* Merlin points out. "The task of your *Personal History Girdle* is *discernment*."

"I don't understand," Angelina honestly says.

A teeth-grinding, grating sound approaches.

"Watch it or you'll lose your head!" Merlin cries, bending her torso as a spinning wheel floats by.

"There goes my discernment," Angelina jokes.

"You got it!" Merlin replies. "Let's follow it."

Not waiting for a reply, Merlin points the wand at the wheel, then at Angelina and himself.

A sailboat materializes out of thin air and they are on it. The sailboat is attached to the axis of the wheel, so that wherever the wheel goes, the sailboat follows.

"That sound reminds me of the dentist," Angelina complains, locking her jaw as they sail through the beam.

"These wheels sand, shape and polish the *Gem of your Sacred Self,*" Merlin says." They are your personal growth. Other, larger wheels polish your gem from outside. They are your circumstances."

The axis jiggles again. The radiance of the diamond gets interrupted and there's a very brief black out.

"What was that?" Angelina demands to know.

"As you realized, your acts of *discernment* allow you to keep this *Personal History Girdle* strong, so that it holds the strength of this gem," Merlin reveals as he pulls the anchor of the sailboat off the wheel and throws it into an island floating in the *Personal History Girdle.*

Angelina has not realized anything. She was merely joking. But she's not about to interrupt Merlin, much less to let him know that she's not as smart as he thinks, so she goes along.

The island is really two tiny islands sliding through the energy beam and joined by a dot of land no more than five feet in diameter and by a bridge. One island is grey and polluted. The other is green and healthy. Merlin shoves Angelina into the dot.

"You are standing in the *Spot of Discernment,*" he announces in a nonchalant way. "Seat there."

Angelina seats on a large old chair that reminds her of her grandpa's wooden desk chair. Each arm in the chair has two levels. One is red and one is green. The red level in each arm says "Release." The green level says "Keep."

What Angelina thought was a bridge is a conveyor belt. It rattles and starts moving, emitting a mechanical hum. Angelina sees an assemblage of objects moving from the islands towards a huge basket in the middle of the dot, in front of the chair.

"Your *discernment* allows you to separate your *Shadow Inheritance* —the polluted island— from your *Ancestors' Gifts,* which would be the healthy island, of course" Merlin explains.

"Do you keep a habit, belief or interpretation? Is it useful, truthful and healthy? Or do you need to release it? Only you can tell," Merlin says, pointing towards the conveyor belt.

There's an object approaching from the west, the polluted *Shadow Inheritance Island***.** Angelina immediately recognizes it. It's a huge ruler.

"Always judging, measuring and punishing," she thinks, "not to mention the beatings."

She presses the red handle in the left arm. A large arm at the corner of the conveyor belt picks up the object. Immediately a large canister with flaming tongues of fire rises at the center of the conveyor belt, and the object is thrown into the fire.

The conveyor level starts again and another object shows up from the east, the green *Ancestors' Gift* Island. It's her first journal, a gift from her grandpa.

Angelina remembers her first squiggles in that journal book.

"It was the first space that was all mine, the place I met myself," Angelina reflects." Pop recognized my gift as a writer even before I knew myself."

"That's a keeper," Angelina whispers, pressing the green level in the right arm. The large mechanical arm picks up the object and throws it into the central basket.

The conveyor belt is moving again. An object from the *Shadow Inheritance Island* moves into view. It is a set of boxing gloves. Angelina goes for the red level on the left arm, but it gets stuck.

"It's not working properly," she protests.

"There's interference," Merlin remarks, pointing all around Angelina.

Surrounding the *Personal History Girdle* there's a band of energy, like the Milky Way. The interference is coming from there. Angelina sees one lightning ray dashing out of the swirling energy cloud; then another. As they dash about, each lightning beam clashes against another. With every clash, she hears a distant thunder, then a piercing buzz. The air vibrates violently as the lightning war intensifies.

"Is that what's causing the mechanism to jam?" she wants to know.

"That's your *Identity Band,"* explains Merlin.

"Why is it shaking?" Angelina wants to know. "What are the flashes?"

"The band is your perception of who you are. Something in your identity resists getting rid of the object," Merlin reveals.

"That does not make sense," Angelina counters. "I hate violence."

"Interesting mixture of words," Merlin whispers.

"What do you mean?" Angelina counters.

"Hating is already violence," Merlin responds.

"What I mean is..." Angelina counters.

"What you mean is what you said, and what you said is what is resisting your release, Angelina," Merlin declares.

Angelina opens her mouth to counter Merlin's words with some other argument, but she remembers the defensive response to criticism. As she is not interested in having the *Floor of Safe Grounding* shrink again, she closes her mouth, pressing her lips tight.

It is obvious that her defensiveness and resistance are at the bottom of the level's malfunction. Why? Angelina looks at the boxing gloves and breathes deeply into her heart.

Sure enough, she feels an attachment to this object; a fear of letting it go. Why?

Her *Second-hand heart*, full of dramas and fears responds.

> *It's true that you don't want to fight, Yet you are always fighting and resisting. Why shouldn't you? The world is hostile. You never know what's around the corner.*

And that's the stinking truth. Angelina lowers her head. There go all her great notions of peace.

"Do not be harsh on yourself, Angelina," Merlin whispers as he glides on the conveyor belt. "Most humans see themselves as being who they have learned to be in the past and who others say they are. They enmesh their identity with their past history and as a result, their *Identity Band* does not support their own free-choices. This generates interference and their *Personal History Girdle* lacks the strength needed to develop a unique, radiant *Gem of Self.*"

"What can I do?" Angelina wants to know.

"Before you take an effective *External Action* in the world, you must take a genuine *Internal Action*," Merlin advices.

"What do you mean?" Angelina inquires.

"If you hate fighting, what keeps you fighting?" Merlin inquires in turn.

"I don't know!" Angelina moans. "Defensiveness. Fear."

"Look around," Merlin recommends.

The *Identity Band* is shrinking, bending the central girdle and causing everything to shake.

"That's the pressure!" Angelina observes. "That's the stress!"

"This *Constricted Identity Band* keeps you stuck in your *Personal History* as it was written by others in your past," Merlin reveals. "But there's something else."

"More?" Angelina wonders when the tests in this quest will come to an end.

"Yes," Merlin adds. "When your *Identity Band* constricts too much or for too long, it solidifies. This whole place will either break or turn into stone, or both."

"What do you mean solidifies?" Angelina demands. "Isn't it solid now? I mean, we're standing on it!"

"No," Merlin clarifies. "We are gliding through the energy pathways. We are standing on the **vibrancy** of the girdle. If this energy would solidify, the pure energy of life would no longer flow through the girdle. The diamond would lose its radiance and become just another piece of coal."

"What is the *Internal Action* to prevent this?" Angelina wants to know immediately.

"*Discernment*, of course," Merlin responds. "You better do it fast, because the *Identity Band* is about to break the girdle."

In effect, the *Personal History Girdle* is bending so deeply that they are standing in a diagonal slant.

"Wha...what exactly is *Discernment*? Angelina asks.

She had not wanted to ask before for fear of appearing stupid. But she needs to know or they won't appear anything because they will entirely disappear!

"*Discernment* is the act that allows you to grow beyond learned beliefs and the habits they create," Merlin instructs. "Discern the value of your choices based on your true *Essence*, your purpose, your freely chosen values and your genuine joy. When you make a choice based on *discernment*, your *Personal Identity* expands to include the rich vastness of your unique potential.

Angelina contemplates the boxing gloves.

"I release fighting and resisting as my primary way of meeting life," she discerns. "I keep the spirit of *The Warrior* that allows me to persist and work hard for what I want. I release the attachment to struggle and effort. I keep my sense of justice to battle injustice and oppression."

The *Identity Band* expands, relaxing the girdle. The diamond glows with a beautiful white blue light.

Angelina and Merlin are back in the shack, looking at the diamond. Cobra glides towards the diamond and reclaims her head.

Angelina is silently crying. This ghost of a creature is truly a magnificent serpent. But she has kept it from growing and renewing its beauty with her secretly held beliefs.

The worst part is that Angelina truly loves change. She IS change. She feels this in her heart, her muscles, her blood. Even her friends tell her that she is always changing and that she is an innovator, a visionary, someone with creative genius.

"Sometimes it's hard to follow you through a conversation because you change as you reflect," she remembers Omar saying.

Change doesn't really scare her, not in her heart. It's just a silly hidey-hole, this resistance to change.

The minute she realizes this, the *North Wall* starts growing and glowing with a fresh electric green color.

A hissing sound calls her attention.

Layers upon layers of old skin fall away from Cobra's serpentine body. The new body is fresh and radiant.

"Thanks!" Cobra speaks into her heart and disappears swaying with new sizzle.

"It was a pleasure meeting you!" Merlin says and disappears.

CHAPTER 33

The Wall of Interpretations

"As I was saying," *The Architects* remarks as he materializes. "In this beautiful earth we exist and express ourselves in time and space. Look at your circumstances and you can see what you have created. Examine what you miss and you can see what you need to co-create."

"Yet, instead of assuming our role as creators, we are constantly walking into spaces and following schedules designed by others for others. These alien spaces have become so familiar that we do not realize they are a prison. Time, as well as space, holds our doing or undoing."

"Time?" Angelina snaps. "Time holds nothing! It's always slipping away!"

"I take it that you have a beef with time," *The Architect* finishes.

"Well, no, but..." Angelina stutters. "But it seems that I never have time," Angelina admits. "At least not for what really matters."

The *South Wall* is shrinking.

Now the room's measurements seem absurd. The floor has stretched beyond some walls. The *North Wall* has stretched beyond the others and the *South Wall* has shrunk.

"Time is a convention," *The Architect* states as he looks at his gold pocket watch.

Tick tock. Tick tock. Tick tock.

Angelina eyelids feel heavy.

As *The Architect* speaks, the soft morning rays give way to blinding mid-day beams.

"We create it and then become its slaves," *The Architect* declares, using his long pencil as a wand. He draws blue gauze curtains over the windows in the shack.

The place is now suffused in a cool blue light. Lines of soft white light crisscross the entire chamber, buzzing across the blue space.

"I'm always running," Angelina blurts out in a daze. "But rarely do I feel that I'm really going somewhere... or getting anywhere. It's as if I'm running after...."

"A thief?" *The Architect* finishes.

"Yes. That's it." Angelina accedes, her eyes closed, her voice fading. "Tell me about this thief."

"What do you want to know?" *The Architect* asks.

"Who is he?" Angelina mutters as her knees give out.

"Why worry about him or her?" a soft but firm voice whispers in her ear. Someone's caught her before she fell.

"Meet my third associate," *The Architect* says. "This is Brigit, *The Healer or The Witch*, as you prefer."

An athletic mature woman dressed in a turquoise tunic is holding Angelina by the elbow. Her hair is red and she wears a breastplate adorned with multicolored gems that emit soft harmonies. Reviving warmth emanates from Brigit. Angelina's strength and wakefulness are instantly restored.

Brigit salutes with a wink and a tip of her head. For a brief instant, her green eyes seem to illuminate the entire room.

"Let's not focus on the thief right now. Why not worry about what's missing? That's what truly matters, isn't it?" Brigit says, leading Angelina to the middle of the shack.

The lines of light wiggle around Angelina and then snap her entire body into their grid. They fizzle with electricity as they pull her up. She looks like a spider crawling at the center of her web.

"What are you doing?" Angelina asks nervously.

Brigit rises in the air, using a hanging line as a rope. Her hand is red and crackling with fire. The line catches fire. The fire spreads through the web around Angelina.

Angelina is swimming in a sea of longing. She's walking under ancient trees. She's dancing with abandonment. She's laughing with her friends. She's writing under a willow. She's running inside a wolf. She's swimming with dolphins. She's painting her own furniture, writing poems in the drawers. She's looking at a sunset in the arms of Omar.

The sun burns in the horizon, hotter and hotter as it comes closer. The fire spreads from the web to Angelina's body. The fire magnifies the longing, spreading it through her entire body. The ecstasy of these desires merges with the pain of the longing, creating an unbearable chaos of cold and heat, pain and pleasure. Angelina screams.

"I don't know when I stopped being who I am," she moans.

She is in another time; another place.

She is burning at the stake. She is being drowned. She is stoned by a crowd. She's judged in a tribunal. She is wearing a muzzle and paraded through town. She's trapped in an asylum.

She is a child. She is being screamed at. Spanked.

No. No. No. No.

You must not do that. You must not be that.

No. No. No. No.

Don't waste time.

Not on yourself.

Don't be a selfish girl.

She sees her brother playing outside. But she's to stay inside. Go wash the dishes. Help mommy. Be a good girl.

"No time," Angelina is mumbling as she fights to set herself free from the burning web. "I have no time..."

Tick-tock-tick-tock-tick-tock.

A huge clock floats above the web. The numbers fall off the clock and into Angelina's eyes.

"What time is it?" Angelina worries. "Am I late? How much time do I have left?"

The clock suddenly transforms into the face of a vampire. He's sucking the numbers off Angelina's eyes.

"Give me back my time! Thief! He's stolen my time!" Angelina howls.

Brigit shakes the fiery line violently and pulls it out. The vision disappears.

Angelina faints.

Brigit opens her mouth and lets out a pure harmony that pours like water, running through the energy lines. The lines sizzle and cool down, emitting soft waves of steam.

Brigit sings as she massages and heals the broken line and then fusses the energy line back into Angelina's body.

Angelina wakes up laughing.

"There are simple things that make me happy, and that joy is who I am," she whispers tenderly.

"Good, Angelina! That's the simple truth," Brigit applauds.

Then she pulls on another broken line of light. The web vibrates in cool hues of blue, emitting streams of water, until the entire shack is submerged under water.

"What is missing is not only what has been stolen," Brigit indicates. "It is also what has been averted. What should have been born and was aborted. You know where it should have been."

> *"Yes! My Soul longs for these simple joys!" Angelina cries out, trying to hold on to something.*
>
> *Then, with a voice eerily similar to the Evil Queen Witch, her eyes green and in fire, she shrieks,*

"But I avoid those simple pleasures.

I repel the things I love!

I resist every joy in me and around me as strongly as I desire it.

I hold on to my problems as if they were my medals, my bridge to heaven."

"Why do you resist what you desire?" Brigit asks. "Go beyond the mask of time. Dive deeper. The truth is in your body, in your *BodySoul*; the sacred zone where your body meets your soul."

A thick line of energy shakes violently, snapping out of the grid. The line devours a window pane and it gets stuck midway down its pipe, making it look like a giant blue shark. It goes on devouring other lines that sustained Angelina, who falls into the sea of blue light, floating.

"Because I fear it," Angelina responds. Her solar plexus is whirling with anxiety and fear.

Like an enraged shark, the loose energy line attacks everything in space. It seems to be searching frantically for something.

"Why do you fear it?" Brigit requires.

"I am a wild, fierce creature. I am free! And that scares me," Angelina bellows as her Psychic Hands dive into her solar plexus and touch a wilderness inside herself.

The blue shark turns towards Angelina and attacks.

Brigit takes hold of the line and pulls. Angelina lets out a long lament as her whole body squirms in space. Suddenly her spine stretches and her heart and solar plexus areas open up. But she still struggles.

"I am fearless. And this fierceness scares me because I've never seen it until now. Until I met Dragonfly Diva, Night Wolf, Sassy Suzette, Swan Woman and you all, this fierceness was hidden, and I fought it. I thought it was pushing me to my doom; to be penniless, weird, alone. I fought it with all my might; willing to be timid, ordinary, to shrink myself into the box of normalcy, to fit in. I pitted furious fear against fierce fearlessness. And I believed that fear was my tool, my ruler to measure up, to stay sensible. I wanted fear to win! And when I came to New York to this new

normal job, I thought I had won over that fierce wilderness in me. I thought that I was finally in control." Angelina confesses, her voice going up as she speaks.

Brigit shakes the line and sends healing purple light through it. Angelina's arms open to the sides. She stops struggling and her body relaxes into space.

"But now! Now this wild thing has come to life, and it wants to be free. It doesn't fit in the tiny life I forced myself to occupy. It's all a lie! A big tacky lie. And I don't know how to get out of it without... without..."

Angelina falls silent. Lifeless and still, she looks as if dead. Suddenly she opens her eyes and smiles.

"It's not real, none of it!"

"It's like my projections. It's all... Interpretations."

"That is your *South Wall,*" Brigit reveals as she massages the shark. "The *Wall of Interpretations* is about the way you interpret the present based on learned *Interpretations* that distort your perception, creating more of the past."

Brigit lets go of the shark.

A blue dolphin leaps into the sea emitting a joyful yelp. Angelina shrieks in delights as the dolphin swims around her.

Time is life. Time is my friend. Time is not the thief, but the present. There's nothing missing! Nothing to be afraid of. No thief. It's me! I'm free!"

The *South Wall* opens into a huge dancing studio and the water runs down, forming a pool at the edge of the room.

A beautiful sunset glows in the horizon. Flying across the sunset, Brigit waves goodbye and plunges into the horizon.

"Time is always designing our present with fresh lines," *The Architect* softly says as he reappears. "Take any one of these lines, and you could create a new universe right now."

The Architect grasps a group of entangled energy lines hanging in a knot.

"But we get entangled in hurtful moments. We insist on bending ourselves out of shape to conform to familiar shapes. And we wrap our wonder-filled present into our boring past."

"It's sunset already!" Angelina cries. "I only had one more day. I've failed!"

"If you say so," a voice declares.

Tic-tock. Tick-tock. Tick-tock.

CHAPTER 34

The Wall of Expectations

The *East Wall* shrinks with a deafening crack. The room is suffering beyond belief with the tension between its dimensions.

Angelina turns to the east, half-expecting to find Dragonfly Diva. Instead, she finds a huge fellow dressed in a white overall and painting the *East Wall* yellow.

“Meet my fourth associate,” *The Architect* says before disappearing again, “*The Painter.*”

“Okay, I know this one,” Angelina declares, thinking to save time.

“‘If you say so’ is what Dragonfly Diva tells me when I’m insisting something’s got to be one way; usually the old way in which I’m used to seeing it. Therefore the *East Wall* is about ... ***Expectations.”***

The Painter takes a big brush and paints a large cup. He then paints steaming coffee and stirs it with the brush.

Angelina’s last word floats out of her lips and towards the *East Wall,* getting embedded in the cup.

“Hey, you! Aren’t’ you going to help me?” she demands from the big fellow. She’s seriously worried about failing the quest. She feels trapped in this stupid shack, unable to get the jewel in this chamber. Every time she solves one problem another shows up.

The painter draws a happy face on top of the cup. Then he grabs it, dips it into the coffee and takes a bite. He then offers it to Angelina.

"No thanks," Angelina retorts. "I'm here to save my life, not to eat cookies with happy faces."

"Would you prefer one with a sad face?" *The Painter* asks, and immediately proceeds to draw a cookie with a sad face. This time he does not bite it himself, but offers it to Angelina.

"Very funny," Angelina says with a moue.

"Funny? It looks sad to me," *The Painter* says. "Would you prefer an angry one?"

And he goes on to repeat the operation, this time with an angry face.

"You got to be kidding!" Angelina mutters.

"Architect?" she hollers, knocking on every wall. "Are you there? Is this your idea of a joke?"

The Painter comes back with an angry face.

"Is this to your liking?" he asks candidly.

Angelina is red-faced with anger and frustration.

"This seems to be the right face," *The Painter* says as he compares the angry cookie face with Angelina's countenance.

He takes Angelina by one hand and swat! bangs her against the wall. As she flies towards the wall, Angelina feels that she is shrinking.

The Painter catches her by the feet just before she crashes against the wall and proceeds to paint using her hair as brush.

"Get me out of here!" Angelina spits while she pours dirty ocre reds and grey-orange swirls of color into the cup. The liquid in the cup changes color.

The Painter puts Angelina down on a rag, among his tools and proceeds to pick up the cup and drink from it.

"Hot chocolate? Ugh! Too bitter."

Angelina is beyond anger at this point. She's been dragged this way and that while hanging upside down and she is dizzy and confused beyond words, not to mention dripping color through ears, nose and mouth.

It's in that wordless silence that she catches a glimpse of what is happening.

Angelina begins to laugh.

The Painter picks her up and paints again. Swirls of fuchsia, magenta and golden hues pour into the wall and drip into the cup.

The Painter picks it up and drinks.

"Mmm! Fresh berries and pomegranate," he praises.

"Emotions!" Angelina guesses.

The Painter hugs her.

"What about emotions?" Angelina asks. "Give me another clue."

The Painter shares the cup with Angelina.

"No thanks, I..." Angelina begins. "The cup. The cup is the clue, right?"

The painter smiles.

"What is the cup? A container. No. Not exactly. A... a what?"

The Painter goes to the *East Wall* and keeps on painting with his big brush. He transforms the cup into a beautiful goblet and offers Angelina wine.

"Wine?" Angelina asks.

The Painter nods and goes back to painting, returning with a bowl.

"Soup?" Angelina asks.

The Painter nods and goes back to painting, returning with a cauldron.

"I know. There's rice there!" Angelina exclaims. "Rice in the cauldron, soup in the bowl, wine in the goblet, coffee in the cup... they are all... what?

The painter is drawing a sailboat.

"Vessels. They are all vessels!"

"Each liquid goes into a different vessel. Each liquid is a different emotion. The emotion goes into the vessel. Not an ordinary vessel. That wouldn't do. No. I got it! A *Psychic Vessel*! Of course, this is a *Psychic Architecture*!"

The painter hugs Angelina.

"You've been very helpful," Angelina says.

She seats on the floor and mulls over what she has discovered.

"Helpful, yes," she mumbles. "But I'm back where I started. You've shown me that my emotions create or fall into *Psychic Vessels*. But I don't know anything about my *Expectations*, which is what I need to transmute if I want to expand the *East Wall.*"

The painter sits in the floor with a sad face. He takes his brush and paints his own face blue.

"Oh, no! You've been helpful, don't get blue!" Angelina remarks.

Their eyes lock in understanding.

"The *Wall of Expectations* is about emotions," Angelina pieces together, each word a stitch that weaves the secret of the *East Wall.*

"The *Expectations* color our emotions," Angelina continues. "These emotions create a vessel."

No. That can't be. The wine does not create the goblet.

"No! It's the other way around," Angelina figures out. "The *Expectations* are the *Psychic Vessels.* They call upon our emotions and these then pour into the *Psychic Vessels."*

"Okay, so the expectations summon the emotions. But... once the emotions fall into the vessel...what happens?" Angelina asks herself. "Why, they take the shape of the vessel, of course."

"That's it! Our emotions take the shape of our expectations," Angelina squeals delightfully.

The Painter applauds enthusiastically.

"Then what?" Angelina continues. She's in a roll now.

"I know. The emotions charge the *Expectations* with their electro-magnetic power!" she concludes. "Which means... what?"

The Painter draws a magnet and Angelina suddenly slides towards it.

"That we attract what we expect!" Angelina cries out. "I got it! I fixed the wall!"

But nothing happens. The *East Wall* does not move.

The Painter paints a blue line in space, but it dissolves.

'I'm falling flat, I see" Angelina complaints. "It seems that thoughts alone do not change the shape of the *Psychic Vessel...* and I thought I was so smart!"

The Painter makes a sad moue and seats down, his body becoming a bulge on the floor.

Angelina looks at that sad bulk and feels a force pulling her down. Such a happy fellow he was, and look what she's done to him.

"Emotions!" Angelina intuits. "My *Expectations* may be the *Psychic Vessels,* and they may attract this or that emotion, and yes, the emotion takes that shape. But what if I change the emotion? Will this in turn change the shape of the vessel?"

"*The Painter* is back on his feet, the brush ready.

"Allow me," Angelina says, taking his brush. She begins to sing and paint the *East Wall.* She puts all her enthusiasm in what she's doing.

She evokes Dragonfly Diva and Omar, and swirls of violet and bright pink mix with gold.

She evokes *The Mother* and Pop, and bright green and swirls mix with turquoise and adobe pink.

Angelina sings a happy song.

I was blue but now I'm ginger.
Let the sorrow go, not linger.
I am fuchsia, gold and crimson
Like a mango ripe in season.
Yes! I'm going for vermillion!
Let joy be my chosen timber.
Let the bliss stay, grow and linger.
I was blue but now I'm ginger.

"Impressive!" says *The Architect,* as *The Painter* paints the *East Wall* on and on, stretching it to meet the *North* and *South Walls.*

"I figure it out by myself!" Angelina says proudly, "with the help of *The Painter,* of course."

"Not to mention *The Executioner," The Architect* laughs.

'Don't, please," Angelina begs.

The Painter paints an archway in the *Wall of Expectations* and leaves with a curtsy.

The Architect takes his pencil out and draws a pair of scissors.

"We stop time, in a way," he reflects, testing the scissors. "We keep living in that *Tiny Room of the Past,* and we recreate the present to fit it. No matter where we are, whether it's a palace or a vast landscape, we redesign it to resemble that *Tiny Room of the Past.*"

"I admit that I've been a grudge lately," *The Architect* confesses. "My job is to design your *House of Dreams.* You can understand my frustration when you keep holding on to this tiny, old shack you carry in your psyche. There's nothing I can do for you as long as you hold on to this."

"But I **want** my *House of Dreams!"* Angelina protests.

"Are you asking for help?" *The Architect* asks nonchalantly.

"Yes!" Angelina barks.

"Ask nicely," *The Architect* warns.

"Please help me out of this mess," Angelina asks as nicely as she can.

"What would happen if I don't?" *The Architect* asks.

"That's a trick question! That's not fair!" Angelina protests. "If I answer, you are going to say that's an expectation or interpretation or whatever. And if I don't answer, then you're going to say that I didn't ask nicely or that I resisted. I will lose no matter what."

Tic-tock. Tick-tock. Tick-tock.

CHAPTER 35

The Ceiling of Possibilities

“Oh, no! There’s that clock!” Angelina thinks. “I blew it... again!”

Then many things happen at once.

The ceiling drops down with such violence that both Angelina and *The Architect* fall to the floor.

A large lamp pops out of the low ceiling, like a balloon landing in the center of the room.

The Architect pops it with his pencil.

“‘Pop’ goes the lamp and a small black box seats where *The Architect* was.

“Meet my fifth associate,” the voice of *The Architect* announces, “*The Oracle.*”

Angelina is fascinated with the black box. Until now, the associates have been living beings. This is a strange situation. A box? An Oracle?

“What did I do wrong?” Angelina asks the box. “I must have done or said something that revealed another limiting dimension, because that’s when things happen. And many things just happened.”

No one answers.

Angelina repeats the question.

Nothing happens.

She raises the lead of the box.

"You are a looser," *The Oracle* says.

"Excuse me!" Angelina protests, closing the door with a bang.

"Ouch!" she hears.

"Why are you insulting me?" Angelina wants to know. "You are supposed to help me."

Nothing happens.

Angelina opens the lid.

"Don't abuse me or I won't help!" *The Oracle* snaps.

"Sorry, I did not mean to hurt you," Angelina apologizes.

The Oracle does not reply.

"It seems that the only way this box talks is if I open this stupid lid," Angelina mumbles.

"Why did you call me a looser?" Angelina asks as she opens the lid.

"You said so," *The Oracle* snaps.

"You got a point there," Angelina says.

But she does not open the lid to talk. Instead, she starts tapping on the box while she lucubrates.

"I **did** say that."

Tap. Tap. Tippy-tap. Rackety-rap.

"I said that either way I lost."

Tap. Tap. Tippy-tap. Rackety-rap.

"But is that something I believe?"

Tap. Tap. Tippy-tap. Rackety-rap.

"Then it would be a belief, wouldn't it?

Tap. Tap. Tippy-tap. Rackety-rap.

"But that was the field of the *Wall of Beliefs...*"

Tap. Tap. Tippy-tap. Rackety-rap.

"Maybe this ceiling shows me nothing new."

Tap. Tap. Tippy-tap. Rackety-rap.

"Wait! Losing, failing and succeeding. Wouldn't those be *Interpretations*?"

Tap. Tap. Tippy-tap. Rackety-rap.

Maybe the ceiling is just an echo; it just repeats what others have said."

Tap. Tap. Tippy-tap. Rackety-rap.

"No, I get it! I expected to lose. It's an *Expectation*."

Tap. Tap. Tippy-tap. Rackety-rap.

"Hum. I don't know. *The Ceiling* should have a different personality to other dimensions, not be a copy-cat."

Tap. Tap. Tippy-tap. Rackety...

"I'm not a copy-cat, you nincompoop," *The Oracle* screams. "And stop tapping. You're giving me a headache."

"Oh, so you **can** talk without me opening the lid," Angelina smirks.

"You tricked me!" *The Oracle* complaints.

"What kind of *Oracle* are you that I can trick you?" Angelina responds.

"The very best kind there is," *The Oracle* declares pompously. "A state-of-the-arts quantum physics *Oracle* that considers and honors all *Possibilities* and the intrinsic relation between subject, intention, energy and attention that leads to such an infinite, surprising array of *Possibilities*."

"So that's the ceiling's dimension: *Possibilities*," Angelina declares.

"You are good, Angelina, I take off my lid to you," *The Oracle* says, opening and closing its lid.

"This is the *Ceiling of Possibilities," The Oracle* declares in its official voice. It resonates in all the walls and vibrates in the floor, tickling Angelina.

"What a bad time to say that I lose no matter what," Angelina comments. "I have a terrible timing."

The ceiling drops a few inches more. Angelina throws herself on the floor.

"Oops! There I go again," Angelina realizes.

"Oracle, will the ceiling drop some more if I reflect out loud about this... ehrm... loser thing?" Angelina inquires.

"If you **reflect**, the chances are it will not. If you **declare**, the chances are that it will drop and may even collapse, as it has very little breathing space as it is," *The Oracle* replies in its official voice.

"This would look like an *Expectation*," reflects Angelina, "as if I had an *Expectation* that I'm going to come out losing. So why is this creating my dimension of the *Ceiling of Possibilities?"*

"The *Ceiling of Possibilities* mirrors the *Set Point* in your expectations, beliefs and habits about your *Possibilities*," *The Oracle* explains in its official voice.

"Could you give me an example?" Angelina asks, opening the lid.

"What do you mean an example?" *The Oracle* whines. "This is not a classroom. I'm an *Oracle*, not a teacher. Draw your own conclusions!"

And with that, it closes the lid itself.

"Geez, you don't have to take it personally!" Angelina comments.

"The *Set Point*," she repeats. "That's like a boundary. A point in which something stands still and will not progress."

"Smart girl," *The Oracle* responds. "I foresaw that you would get it."

"And my *Set Point* is expecting to lose," Angelina says.

The ceiling quivers.

"Erhm...I'm reflecting, not declaring!" Angelina hollers.

"Wow! That's a really low point," Angelina considers. "Do I really expect to lose at any turn, no matter what I do? I'm reflecting!"

"Perhaps you need to see it from another angle," *The Oracle* suggests.

"What do you mean?" Angelina asks.

"See it from the other's point of view," *The Oracle* suggests.

"What other?" Angelina asks, turning to search for a third party.

"No, girl, what I mean is that you need to shift your point of view," *The Oracle* insists. "Instead of asking how you see it, you can ask how you believe it sees you."

"Instead of asking if I expect to lose no matter what the situation is, I now ask myself if...the situation... wants... me to... lose?" Angelina manages to gather.

The Oracle opens and closes the lid.

"I take it you are nodding," Angelina whispers.

"Does this chamber want me to lose?" Angelina asks.

The ceiling quivers.

"Just reflecting!" Angelina hollers.

The ceiling stops quivering.

Silence.

Angelina listens carefully to that silence.

“What do you think?” *The Oracle* asks, curiosity getting the best of it.

“I was wondering the same,” Angelina replies.

“You were wondering what you were thinking?” *The Oracle* asks. “That’s kind of redundant.”

“No, I was wondering what YOU were thinking!” Angelina responds.

“That’s neither here nor there,” *The Oracle* says. “I can only see what will happen AFTER **you** choose what you will see.”

“So that’s the trick!” Angelina cries out in joy. “*Possibilities* materialize as a consequence of *Expectations* that attract what I anticipate.”

“You tricked me again!” *The Oracle* puffs. “You’re getting too smart for your own good!”

“I’m a bit pressed for time,” Angelina mutters with a triumphant grin.

“Okay, I’ll tell you, since you already guessed,” *The Oracle* puffs. “*Possibilities* are here, there, everywhere, endless, infinite. Ohh, I simply adore them! They make my work so fascinating!”

“Ehrm, can you stay on course?” Angelina requests. “Time, remember?”

“Oh, yes! So there they are, *Possibilities*. Then they get ...you know... entangled with *Expectations*,” *The Oracle* says in a suggestive tone.

“You mean they... mate?” Angelina asks.

“Or not,” *The Oracle* says. “Depending on whether...”

“They attract or repel each other!” Angelina finishes.

“Exactly,” *The Oracle* says, applauding with its lid.

“So when I ask if this chamber wants me to lose, what I’m really asking is which of many *Possibilities* will my *Expectations* attract and mate?” Angelina inquires.

“Approximately,” *The Oracle* says.

“Not exactly?”Angelina observes.

“It’s complicated...There’s a love triangle,” *The Oracle* whispers.

“Don’t you say? Who’s the third party?” Angelina wants to know.

“I’m not a gossiper! But guess!” *The Oracle* giggles.

“North? No. Doesn’t feel right. East? Nah, that’s *Expectations*. East? Yes! *Interpretations*!”

“Yeeess!” *The Oracle* squeaks, jumping enthusiastically. “Once the *Expectation* attracts the matching *Possibilities*, there’s always a chance that a nasty *Interpretation* will thwart the romance and steal that fresh *Possibility*.

"*Possibility* seems fickle," says Angelina, a bit put down.

"Well, what do you expect?" *The Oracle* says. "You called. It came, and now you start finding fault with it. Why should it stay? So it leaves."

What about *Beliefs*?" Angelina inquires.

"What about them?" *The Oracle* asks.

"What's their role in this love story?" Angelina wants to know.

"They are the parents of the bride," *The Oracle* says.

"The bride being..."

"You, who else?" *The Oracle* says.

"Me? Of course! I'm beginning to see the sordid affair. My *Beliefs* are the parents of my *Expectations*. Therefore, as parents, they can give permission to or oppose the marriage, is that it? Angelina pieces together.

"You got the whole picture now," *The Oracle* agrees. "Now, to work."

"Let's see. I know for a fact deep in my heart that in these chambers my *Creative Selves* are helping me to acquire *Indra's Jewels*. Therefore my *Expectation* is that I will achieve this."

The ceiling lifts about five feet.

"Now in the past, I'd allowed my negative *Interpretations* to create doubt about this, but now I'm not letting that flirt of *Interpretation* steal my darling *Possibility*," Angelina affirms.

"No matter what others tell you or what you believe you see," *The Oracle* warns. "You must trust that *Possibility*."

"Yes! No matter," Angelina affirms passionately. "I'm 100% committed to my Victory!"

The ceiling lifts seven more feet. The vertical expansion realigns the walls, that grow to match the height.

Angelina stretches her whole body and takes a deep breath.

"Quickly! Make sure that the parents of the bride don't interfere," *Oracle* reminds her. "They're sneaky that way."

"As to my *Beliefs*, know this: I'm marrying the *Possibility of Victory,* and nothing can stand between us, so you better give me your blessing!" Angelina finishes off.

The ceiling lifts ten more feet and the walls grow vertically. The room is now a high-ceiling loft. The tall windows let in the pastels colors of dawn.

Angelina whirls around delightedly. She looks like a Sufi dancer as she whirls contentedly, her head tilted up, her eyes looking ecstatically at the high ceiling.

Of course, the *West Wall* is still small, so there's lots of pulling and pushing and noisy readjustment.

All in all, Angelina loves the spaciousness of her new room.

"That's all it takes," says *The Architect* as he reappears. He is cutting an entangled knot of blue lines across the *West Wall* and the ceiling with his scissors.

"Disentangle your present from the perception that distorts it, and pop! there goes the old *Set Point*," *The Architect* declares. "Now the sky's the limit for you."

"If it only were that easy!" Angelina whispers. "Look, I don't want another wall coming down or up or sideways at me. But it's **not** easy. I've been riding and questing for several days now. I've faced monsters and slain dragons...so to speak... and I still can't see half of what you show me. I mean' hind-sight is great sight. But I can't see it coming!"

Tick-tock. Tick-tock. Tick-tock.

CHAPTER 36

The Wall of Blindness

"Not again!" Angelina mutters. "I can't utter a full sentence without limiting my space!"

"You're doing fine, Angelina," *The Architect* comforts her. "After all, you got only one more wall to go."

The room goes pitch black.

"Meet my sixth associate, *The Seer*," *The Architect* announces.

"Let's make this quick," *The Seer* whispers into her heart.

"Ayyyyy!" Angelina screams.

She's been pricked with something sharp. She grasps her arm and pulls out a sharp, smooth object.

"What hit you, girl?" asks *The Seer* without speaking out loud.

"How should I know?" Angelina asks. "I can't see in the dark!"

She's feeling blood running down her arm.

Angelina wants to run and hide. She's so tired and frustrated! But she cannot see where she is, much less where she could run to. This gives her a feeling of desolation and helplessness.

"Only you can know what hurts you," *The Seer* speaks without words. "Use your higher senses."

"What do you mean?" Angelina whispers, as she tries to match *The Seer's* telepathic conversation by whispering.

"Stop playing *The Fool*. Asking for meaning is meaningless," *The Seer* communicates. "The experience IS the meaning."

Angelina sees that *The Seer* won't be of much help. She runs her fingers over the object that pricked her. It's smooth and about nine inches long. It's tubular. Angelina notices that at one end it has a sharp edge but at the other it has a hole of some type.

"It's a quill! Porcupine!" Angelina cries out.

"You are learning to see, Angelina," *The Seer* smiles into her mind.

"Wikipitipiki kipiliti," chatters a tiny voice as it scuttles away.

"Thanks, Prickly Chatter!" *The Seer* laughs.

"Oh, so you were in on it," Angelina mutters. "It was your accomplice!"

"Don't bore me, Prickly Girl," *The Seer* snarls, and then spits "So predictable!"

"I'm not predictable!" Angelina snarls back.

A large, dangerous purr fills the darkness. It sends shivers up and down her spine.

"You've made yourself available to danger," *The Seer* whispers in her mind. "This one is **your** guest, not mine."

There is no time to waste asking for help. Angelina grows absolutely quiet. She tells her breath not to give out any sound. She masters her terrified body into stillness.

"Let it think me a stone," Angelina thinks. Tears of terror are rolling down her cheeks, but still she makes no noise.

A pair of eyes flashes across the blackness. The beast is no more than twenty feet away.

Angelina feels the chill of death. She closes her eyes and prepares to die.

Then something strange happens to Angelina, something unexpected and almost impossible to believe.

Her body grows. She is becoming massive, furry and sinuous. She is voluminous, but light and agile. She feels her massive paws stepping naked on to the cold tile floor; one, then the other ~silent and precise. She feels her claws preparing to attack. She opens her eyes and flashes a warning flame at her opponent.

Whose eyes are flashing into the night? There is no other creature here; only her. She spots *The Seer* in the darkness.

The Seer is a tall black woman. Dressed in layers of black gauze, she blends into the pitch black space. Now that Angelina's *Leopard Self* can see into the dark, *The Seer* is not fooling Angelina any more.

Angelina *The Leopard* silently walks towards *The Seer*.

"Let's see who scares who now," Angelina thinks inside her *Leopard Self.*

The moment she thinks in words, her human self begins to take over parts of the *Leopard Self.* Her head becomes human again.

Angelina lets go of thoughts and words, concentrating in the strong physical presence of the wild cat.

She stealthily advances, body, legs and paws still those of a cat, head and fangs still sharp and ready.

"Now you know something you did not know before," *The Seer* whispers into her heart.

"What's that?" Angelina asks, unable to resist the curiosity.

"You are a shapeshifter," *The Seer* says and laughs in a velvety laughter that blends with the silence.

Angelina is lying on the cold floor, shivering.

"Shapeshifting takes a lot of energy, even for trained shamans," *The Seer* reveals. "And you've been bleeding, girl. You've lost a lot of energy. I hope that the lesson was worth it."

"What lesson?" Angelina asks.

"You ARE dense," *The Seer* laughs.

She can no longer see in the dark. But she could. She did it before. That means she could do it again. She tries to call *The Leopard.* But she doesn't even know how it materialized in the first place. But she knows how to call the she-wolf, and she can see in the dark too.

Angelina concentrates in the sense of smell and brings all her energy into her nose and ears. She begins to listen with her pores and blend with the night. Nigh Wolf should show up immediately.

But the wolf does not come.

Angelina closes her eyes and sees the she-wolf in her mind. But she's too weak to summon anything.

"Help me," Angelina whispers. "What is the lesson? What must I do?"

"This is not about doing," *The Seer* communicates. "This is about being. About awakening."

"Am I sleeping? Am I dreaming?" Angelina wants to know.

"In a way," *The Seer* responds. "You go through life half-asleep. You walk carelessly into an environment, your five senses blunt, your instinct drugged and your higher senses gagged. "No wonder you run into danger. No wonder you cannot see what's coming, even if it waved a flag."

"What must I do?" Angelina begs to know.

"Awake," is all *The Seer* responds.

There are shadows moving in the darkness.

Angelina is scared. What horror has entered the shack now?

"Good, Angelina," *The Seer* whispers into her heart. "Use fear. Like anger and laughter, fear raises your *Hara*, your *Power Center*. It energizes you. Use it to awaken your powers of perception."

Angelina gathers her fear into herself, like a quilt. She tames it, shifting her attention from being afraid to being alert.

"These are *Shadow Scouts*," her body tells her.

"Scouts. Scouts," Angelina repeats. "Why Scouts? Can they lead me to the exit?"

"Excellent, Angelina," *The Seer* says. "Now you know how to *Recast a Shadow*. You are beginning to use your powers to break the limits of your perception."

Shadow, shadow in the night

Show the edges of the light.

The Seer incants.

A circle of huge *Shadow Scouts* surrounds them. Each is as tall as one of the columns of the *Time-Space Palace*.

"They broke in!" Angelina whispers.

"Shush," *The Seer* murmurs. "All is well."

The Seer chants:

> *Cast the fear away from home.*
> *Show the power from whence it comes.*

The *Shadow Scouts* whirl in place, becoming giant torches.

CHAPTER 37

The Last Associate & the Jewel Eye of Freedom

Tick-tock. Tick-tock. Tick-tock.

The Seer stands close to one torch. *The Architect* stands next to another. Night Wolf, Merlin, Brigit, *The Painter* and a strange tall, box-like creature Angelina knows to be *The Oracle* each stands next to a *Shadow Scout*-turned-torch.

The *West Wall* is stretching. It becomes a glass wall, letting through a beautiful mid-day sun.

“Sunrise, sunset, mid-day or midnight? I’ve lost track of time,” Angelina considers. “In this place, time seems to shift with the moods.”

“Very good, Angelina” *The Architect* says. “You’ve learned to awaken your perception beyond your limitations. Developing *Second Attention* is quite a feat. You are ready to meet my next associate.”

“I thought I only had one more wall to go,” Angelina protests. “After all there are only four walls, a floor and a ceiling. You can’t possibly make up another freaking test! I refuse!”

Immediately she knows that this type of response is the veil that keeps her playing *The Fool,* as *The Seer* so helped her see. She stays still and breathing. Her gut is whirling. Angelina listens to her gut.

“I see. There are no more walls,” she says, looking at *The Architect* with a glint in her eyes. “Ceiling and Floor have also been taken care of. Yet, there’s one dimension missing.”

“Excellent,” *The Architect* says. “Meet my seventh and last associate.”

No one enters the room. Angelina looks around, but only the *Shadow Scouts*-turned torches, *The Architect* and his six associates are present.

“Well?” Angelina asks. “Where is she or he or it?”

The Architect and Associates look at each other, then at her.

Well?” Angelina barks. “I don’t have all day. Is this associate invisible or a procrastinator? Because, frankly, my patience is at an end.”

The Architect and Associates burst into laughter.

Angelina is red faced. How dare they take her quest so lightly? Who do they think they are?

One thing is to respect them as teachers, but this has gone too far. She has restraint herself not to react defensively or hastily. But she is not willing to play *The Fool* anymore. She’s not willing to be a victim any longer. She must put her foot down once and for all or *The Architect* will keep playing games with her!

“This chamber is more of a trap than a passage and enough is enough,” Angelina barks. “Show the next associate or give me the freaking *Jewel Eye*. Now.”

A loud crash is heard. A mirror appears right in front of Angelina but before she can respond, it shatters in large shards that spin around Angelina. Angelina tries to escape, but every time she moves towards an empty place, a shard spins and blocks her way.

The shards dance violently around her, leaping, twisting and shifting. Angelina is caught in a deadly dance.

She suddenly wonders if her old suspicions about *The Architect* may not have been right. She just allowed his handsome appearance to confuse her into thinking that he was a *Creative Self*. But what if he was a *Shadow Scout* disguised as a *Creative Self?* What if now they have both, her *DreamSelf* and her entrapped? How can she rescue her *DreamSelf* now?

As she gives way to these thoughts, the *Shadow Scouts* grow in strength, the torches disappearing. The *Shadow Scouts* advance toward Angelina. Angelina looks towards her *Creative Selves*, but they are shimmering out of shape.

"I am doing this," Angelina remembers. "I am doing everything that is happening. I just fed the *Shadow Scouts*. But that's not my intention."

"I receive the help of my allies," Angelina says from the bottom of her heart. "I do! I do!"

The Architect and Associates return in full strength. The *Shadow Scouts*, however, do not go back to being torches.

The Architect and Associates encircle the *Shadow Scouts* in ropes of blue light, holding them in place.

"This is it," Angelina knows in her body as she averts the sharp edges of a shard. "No one can help me. This is where I get the *Jewel Eye* or blow the quest forever."

"Good guess, Angelina," *The Architect* remarks. "This is the *'I'* space, the center of the *Tiny Room of the Past...* or the *House of Dreams*, ~whichever you decide to create."

"The *'I'* Space?" Angelina blubbers, twisting just in time to avoid a cut from a large spinning shard. "You mean that..."

"Yes, that's exactly what I mean, Angelina," *The Architect* says with a grin. "You are the seventh associate."

"It was me!" Angelina mutters under her breath as she crutches to avoid a shard that's flying like an arrow to her head. "Of course, you were all looking at me. I should have known."

"So why didn't I?" Angelina asks as a shard scrapes her arm. "Ouch!"

"Because..." Angelina answers herself as she kicks a shard only to see it bouncing back towards her and she dodges. "Because I am not used to perceiving that I have a role in designing my own life? Lame, but true."

The shards freeze in space at about five feet from her. Angelina's fragmented image flashes in front of her eyes, runs through her body and dissolves.

"Who are you?" *The Architect and Associates* ask in one voice.

"Who am I?" Angelina asks herself.

The shards are slowly moving towards Angelina, slowing spinning in place.

"It's your game now, Angelina," *The Architect* whispers. "Each of us is allowed to give you only one additional bit of help."

"I created this trap when I saw this experience as a trap," Angelina considers.

She examines the shards of the mirror. As they spin, they reflect the *Shadow Scouts* around Angelina. She examines them as they struggle to free themselves from the blue light.

In their faces she sees fragments of herself: suspicion, separation, resistance, resentment, blaming and insufficiency are reflected back at her.

"This is the way I usually see the world," Angelina agrees as the shards drift closer. They are now four feet away.

Angelina refuses to fall into fear or helplessness. If she created this trap then she can also destroy it.

"What is a trap?" Angelina asks *The Oracle*.

"Good move, Angelina," *The Oracle* replies, "as I am the best one to inform you that a trap is a concession to the *Expectation* of defeat. Flirting with the *Interpretation* that there is no way out closes any possibility. Therefore you know which *Possibility* you abort and which you attract."

"The *Possibility of Victory*, that's the one I just repelled," Angelina recognizes, "the very one I swear to embrace and not to let anything take away. And I've just conceded it by expecting defeat... again."

This time Angelina does not whine or wait for someone to rescue her.

"How do I embrace my victory again and release this odious attachment to defeat?" Angelina asks Merlin.

"Questions are *Psychic Keys*, Angelina. And you are mastering the art of questioning," Merlin replies. "You have asked just the right question; for *Attachment* is an entangled line that keeps you tied up to the very thing you want to get rid of. Your *Identity Band* and *Personal History Girdle* answered you before you post this question."

"Of course!" Angelina cries out. "What a fool I've been. I have all the tools I need. I was given all the lessons I need to get out of this cage!"

She remembers the *Identity Band*. How did she manage to unlock that stuck level?

"*Discernment*!" Angelina replies to herself.

"Had I used *discernment*, I would have asked *The Architect* who was the last associate, instead of assuming hostility. Questions are the best tool to confirm or dispel assumptions," Angelina reasons.

The shards waver and slow down, but they keep gliding towards her. They are now three feet away.

"Night Wolf!" Angelina calls. "What are these shards made of?"

Night Wolf smells the air and follows a scent to one of the shards. She scratches it. One of *the Shadow Scouts* scratches its thigh.

Night Wolf crawls towards the *Shadow Scout,* growling.

"This trap is made of my fear-based defenses," Angelina concludes.

The shards waver and slow down again, but they relentlessly glide towards her. They are now two feet away.

"Seer," Angelina calls out. "You said that I had learned to *Recast the Shadows.* What did you mean?"

"A *Shadow* is cast by using your power from a place of fear," *The Seer* instructs. "To *Recast the Shadow,* reverse the process."

"If I am defending myself by using a power from a place of fear," Angelina tries to understand, "Then I liberate myself by... by using fear from a place of power? No. Certainly not."

"By using power instead of fear," Angelina tries. "What the hell am I saying? There's no reversing these words!"

The shards are one foot away. Angelina can feel the sharp edges cutting through space.

"It's not words I need now," Angelina mutters. "I need experience."

Brigit and *The Painter* step forward.

Angelina's body breathes deeply. She relaxes into an ocean of emotional vibrations.

The entire room becomes an empty, dark space crossed with lines of white line. This space is both around and inside her. She breathes into the emptiness.

Angelina realizes that the shards are not solid. The blinding mirrors and wounding edges are just a façade. Beneath this facade there are hungry black gaps, like black holes in space.

Shadow, shadow in the night
Show the edges of the light.

The Seer's words are dancing in her belly as the shards waver inches from her.

Angelina feels her hunger and fear, and she feels how they contract her body. Even her bones shrink and her force dwindles when she sees herself apart and the world as hostile.

She feels that these shards, these gaps that hold her prisoner are not out there, cutting from the outside, but inside her.

Her breath becomes a way of touching her inner body. She grows *Psychic Hands* in her breath. With these *Psychic Hands* she grabs a broken line of energy inside her that feels like a tight nerve and follows it. She breathes into it and slides her *Psychic Hands* along it, like she saw Brigit do.

A searing pain twists her body as her hand falls into a gap. This is the place where opposition nests inside her.

"What do I do now?" Angelina asks. But she's gotten all the help she can get from her allies.

In breath, she plunges her *Psychic Hands* deeper into the place of discord.

Waves of painful expectation creep through her psychic fingers. Hunger snakes up her arms into her heart. Lack envelops her, like a rope that wants to strangle her. A deep cutting orphanhood tears at the very fiber of her being.

The spell of *The Seer* comes back to her.

Cast the fear away from home.
Show the power from whence it comes.

Angelina finally understands.

She breathes deeply into the place of dissonance within while her *Psychic Hands* tenderly scrape the fear and the hunger, cleansing the wound.

Deeper and deeper she goes, feeling the pain and the separation, releasing them in brave, long exhalations.

As Angelina exhales she releases the old, constricting emotions. They leave her body through her lips, crossing the space in jarring, aching, guttural sounds that make the air shiver in despair.

Ah! But the place within her where the friction festered now feels light and clean. In that new space, something stirs; something fresh and good.

The sounds leaving her lips change. A song emerges.

From the edges of the night
I embrace the nascent light.

And with gratitude I bide

adieu to the fearful darkness.

To the abyss, to the absence,

to the far and greatest hunger.

To the careless, lonely slumber

to the far and alien plunder.

You return from whence you came

You're not I, not any longer.
At the core of my gem
Shines the light in all its splendor.
There is love, for love I am
brilliant love glows at my center.
Shadow, shadow in the night
Show the edges of the light.
From this brilliance I recast
the darkness to its source.
I rebuild my house of dreams
with my heart's loving force.

The shards dissolve. Angelina faints.

The faces of *The Architect & Associates* examine her eagerly. She tries to get up, but lands back on her butt.

The Architect & Associates move away and Angelina's face goes from blurry confusion to a glowing grin.

It is her *DreamSelf's* house. She is in the pink stucco Spanish hacienda she saw in her first vision.

"Congratulations," *The Architect* says.

"You have finally joined us," Brigit exclaims, embracing her.

"Yes, finally!" *The Oracle* adds. "Of course I knew that she would pass the test!"

"What test?" Angelina inquires, fearing yet another puzzle.

"The test that graduates you as our seventh associate," Merlin exclaims.

"You are finally working **with** us in the creation of your dream, Angelina!" *The Seer* says with a wide grin.

The Painter is applauding.

"Thanks," Angelina says. "Thanks for everything."

The Shadow *Scouts* vanish. In their stead, there stand four beautiful sculpted columns. One is a blue-haired Warrioress. One is an Angel. One is an Eagle and the last one is a Lion.

"Do I get the *Jewel Eye* now?" Angelina whispers.

"Victory is yours!" *The Architect* declares. "You've pierced the *Veil of Attachment to the Past.*"

Merlin is moving from column to column, mumbling something.

"Ah! This is the first one," he says, tapping the head of *The Warrioress*. She drops a blue strand of hair.

Merlin catches the hair and wraps it around Angelina's hand. The blue hair turns into a blue stone. Merlin then takes Angelina to the column of *The Angel*. She kisses *The Angel's* feet, and it drops a feather from its wing. The feather wraps around the blue stone, creating a whirl of white hues.

They move to *The Eagle* and Angelina taps its beak. *The Eagle's* eye illuminates the stone, bringing it to life. It's a lapis lazuli.

Finally, they take the gem to *The Lion*, tapping its maw. *The Lion's* roar is like a strong wind that blows the white swirl, shaping it in the form of a star.

"You hold the *Jewel Eye of Freedom*," Merlin says with a glowing smile.

"See you around," *The Architect* salutes with a wink.

"Call us when you need us," *Brigit* whispers.

They hold hands and disappear as the walls of Angelina's *House of Dreams* rotate.

CHAPTER 38

The Poet and the Jewel Eye of Beauty

The chamber is bathed in the crimson and purple hues of the sunset. The walls disappear and Angelina finds herself in the ocean shore.

The Golden Rift is drawing closer,
kissing the purple breasts of night.
This will be the instant.
If I hold the portal open,
Will you enter?

"SoulSong!" Angelina runs to *The Poet*.

SoulSong shakes her long, black curls and the cascade falls down her back, rippling against her dark purple gauze dress. Beneath the gauze, a radiant orange chemise reminds Angelina of the sunset falling over the ocean.

I cherish this embrace, beautiful self,
But now is time for readiness.

As the sun goes down, the portal opens
Between day and night.
This is the age-old rift
That allows you to enter hidden dimensions
Or move between the Uni-verses.
Are you ready?

"Yes I am. I have removed my veils," Angelina fiercely declares.

One remains.
Tell me.
When you look back,
What do you see?

"A journey."

When you look within,
What do you find?

"My home."

The waters have turned purple against the dusk. The sun descends into the horizon.

SoulSong asks:

When you look ahead,
What do you see?

"I, unfolding."

"You have pierced the *Veil of Despair*. You have retrieved the Eyes that once were stolen from you." *SoulSong* declares. "Now you can see your beauty."

Shimmering in Angelina's hands is the last *Jewel Eye*. It is a large amethyst in the form of a rose.

"This is the *Jewel Eye of Beauty*," *SoulSong* reveals. "The gift of a poet."

"Don't swallow this one," *SoulSong* warns just when Angelina is sticking out her tongue.

The warm, crimson radiance of the sun gathers its rays vertically, painting a shimmering golden doorway against the purple night. The frame of the doorway is adorned in multicolored jewels. There are several pieces missing.

"What is the Eye that recasts Orphanhood?" *SoulSong* asks, extending her hands.

"Unconditional love," Angelina replies.

The Rose Quartz Heart leaps from her mouth into *The Poet's* hands. *SoulSong* embeds it into the frame of the Golden Rift.

"What is the Eye that recasts Forgetfulness and Lies? *SoulSong* asks, her hands extended.

"Compassionate Truth," Angelina replies.

The Obsidian Sword dashes out of her mouth into *The Poet's* hands. *SoulSong* embeds it into the frame of the doorway.

"What is the Eye that recasts Toxic Anger and Shame?" *SoulSong* now asks.

"The Laughter of those who *Comb their Emotions*," Angelina replies.

The Cornelian Conch flies from her mouth into *The Poet's* hands. *SoulSong* casts it into the *Golden Rift.*

"What is the Eye that recasts Self-sacrifice and Insufficiency?" *SoulSong* now asks.

"The flight of my *Uniqueness Essence*," Angelina replies.

The Moonstone emerges from her lips and *SoulSong* embeds the Swan's Eye into the threshold.

"What is the Eye that recasts Attachment to the Past? *SoulSong* asks.

"The freedom that comes from assuming my power to design my life through my *Free-choices,* Angelina replies.

The lapis lazuli sphere is casted into the threshold.

"What is the Eye that recasts the *Blindness of Despair*?" *SoulSong* asks —a bright smile in her tender face.

"The connection to the wisdom and beauty of my Soul," Angelina responds, remembering the first time she encountered *The Poet*, way back in Bleak Station, which now seems ages ago.

When *The Poet* places the *Jewel Eye of Beauty* into the threshold, a web of light sizzles around the frame, bringing each jewel to life.

Each jewel in the threshold glistens with the reflection of the immeasurable jewels in *Indra's infinite Net.* Each single jewel reflects all the stars in all the firmaments.

The infinite brilliance of *Indra's Net* awakens the doorway. It explodes in the brilliance of trillions of stars.

Angelina and *SoulSong* are showered in that radiance. Their eyes meet, bathed in the light of the infinite *Jewel Eyes*.

Angelina moves towards the *Golden Rift* and becomes light.

CHAPTER 39

The Hidden Key

Angelina stands at the edge of the inner star-structure of the castle. Just as Angelina saw when she flew above the castle, the center of the *Inner Ring of Self* is a clearance in the form of a star.

"There!" Angelina whispers.

Just as she saw in her vision at the beginning of the journey, when she was seeking refuge from her *Shadows*, a huge ancient tree stands strong and tall at the center of the clearance.

The warmth emanating from the *Ancestral Tree* bathes all the space, which pulsates with a golden light.

Her heart is instantly healed with fresh hope. She looks up the tree's massive trunk. But her hope dies a little.

The branches of this tree do not burst in a celebration of bird songs. Its leaves do not shimmer against the stars. They are bare and the branches seem to reach up imploringly.

At the heart of the trunk, Angelina sees the *Throne of the Ancestral Heart*. It feels empty and cold.

Angelina looks around, hoping to find another *Creative Self* that can explain what is happening and help her.

The tiny lights Angelina had seen from above are threads of light streaming from archways surrounding the star at each of its angles.

There she is!

To the left of the *Throne of the Ancestral Heart*, there is a shimmering presence.

The *DreamSelf* is still inside the mirror cage. There are no *Shadow Scouts* here, but the cage is still protected by the electric shield.

Angelina has to try. She runs towards the cage, but when she is about five feet away, she is instantly repelled by the electric shield.

An old silver haired woman dressed in a white tunic gracefully crosses one of the arches. Her luminous presence sends streams of serenity into all corners of the *Center Core.*

Angelina recognizes her at once, even before she hears the peaceful voice. She is Luna, her *Wise Woman.*

"Nothing you do will break the cage," Luna gently says.

If it were not for the serenity of her words, Angelina would be in turmoil.

"Then I'm still defeated," Angelina howls. "This entire struggle, the dead knights, Boy hurt... everything... for nothing!"

"That is not what I said," Luna replies in the same gentle tone.

"You said that nothing I do will..."

Angelina stops talking. Luna is smiling. She knows, without thoughts or words, why the *Wise One* is smiling.

"I need the *Alchemical Key*, don't I?" Angelina asks, knowing full well the answer.

"The question is really whether you have it or not," Luna says, still smiling.

"Well, the answer is no," Angelina barks.

"If you say so," Luna smiles.

"Oh, no, not that again!" Angelina protests.

This time, however, Angelina listens.

"Dragonfly Diva always says this phrase to show me that I am creating a limit with a negative expectation," Angelina reflects. "What am I expecting right now?"

"Struggle," Angelina answers immediately. "Effort. To do something more difficult and harder than I did for all of the *Bridge Guardians* or the *Jewel Eyes* combined. After all, it is the last key; the key key, in a way."

"Very well then," Angelina declares. "No struggle. No effort. No..."

In a flash of recognition, Luna's simple, precise words reveal their meaning.

"Nothing I do will break the cage!"

"I see that you are on its trail," Luna smiles.

Angelina walks to the *Throne of the Ancestral Heart* slowly. Will it accept her, even without her *DreamSelf*? She climbs the stage and sits on the throne.

She is home. She is at peace. The struggle has ended. Angelina smiles as she realizes that she has been a fool. This castle, the entire adventure, it is all her own Self. Why is she fighting dragons again?

"It an easy thing, to listen," Luna smiles. "Yet, it is so hard to trust its power."

Angelina breathes deeply, slowly, allowing herself to surrender to the strong, tree presence within herself. She hears and feels her heartbeat. Its drum dances steadily and slowly.

A high vibrating note rises from the *DreamSelf*. Angelina turns towards her.

She gazes into her golden eyes, her beautiful face.

"Who are you?" Angelina asks, opening her heart to receive her *DreamSelf*.

A silent song flows from the *DreamSelf* towards Angelina. She can hear it in her heart, though all around her there is silence.

A vision rises from my radiant heart

that pierces the darkness in fear.

The dread of mystery walks on the shards

of orphanhood and separation.

But once you see the threads that bind all life,

Fear gives way to emancipation.

Oh, Sacred One

Receive my invitation.

Walk through this night into this brilliant day.

Across the threshold of this pain

A sun more bright that Indra's net awaits.

Pain is now distilled into elation.

Grace is not barred by a hundred gates.
Cages cannot confine illumination.
Oh, Sacred One
Enjoy the transmutation.

For every poison poured into my being
There is a healing melody.
For every broken part I bravely mend
I heal kindred by the legion.
Fear not, for freedom is my way and end.
My alchemy of dedication.
Oh, Sacred One
Join this liberation.

My soul speaks the mother tongues of life,
The flash of image that endures,
The thread of story that turns magic on
by showing our limitations
and gathering our strength to overcome
our cowardly inclinations.
Oh, Sacred One
Hear this iteration.

If pain is only the churning of delight
And bars hold not my Essence,
What could you flee or fear, face or fight
that could ever halt my vocation?
The thieves out there could never steal my light.
But only you can free my vibration.
Oh Sacred One,
Complete my activation.

Angelina receives this song into her *Sacred Heart,* feeling the beauty of her *DreamSelf.*

As she opens her heart to receive the song, the melody floats into her being and inundates every space inside her.

A golden key falls on her lap.

Seventh Alchemical Key: Receive the Dream you already are

The cage shatters into tiny shards of mirrors that fly into the night sky above, becoming stars.

"NOOOO!" a terrible scream gushes through space as the *Evil Queen Witch* is hauled across the night, disappearing into the darkness above.

Dancing in waves of rainbows and tiny lines of light, her *DreamSelf* approaches. They look into each other's eyes, and then the *DreamSelf* leaps into Angelina.

She catches one last look at the **Dreamscape** as the *Shadow Castle* dissolves.

"Bravo!" The knights cheer, waving goodbye atop their gallant horses.

Minstrel plays a glorious melody in his lyre.

"I love you" Husband is saying, showing the wedding ring.

"That's my Angel, and she's flying!" Forest is proudly saying, now free of his armor.

"I'm always with you, Tweedy," Pop says in his horse and then horse and knight dissolve into the night.

"We did it!" Boy laughs, doing summersaults.

"Congratulations!" exclaims the Alignment Effigy, now an exuberant woman embraced to *The Champion.* "Thanks for freeing me from the curse of the *Evil Queen Witch.*"

"Bless you, ladie, for returning my one true love to me," *The Champion* says.

Angelina does not have time to answer. She's sucked by a giant tornado.

"Dragonfly Diva?" Angelina asks as she whirls through space.

She had believed that she was too small to make a difference, too insignificant for the Universe to care about her Dream.

But now, as she spins through endless mystery, Angelina experiences quite the opposite.

She is a star illuminating the vast night. Her light, unbound and bright, irradiates from the center of her being, illuminating the darkness around her.

She is *Indra's Net*. Each cell in her body is a *Jewel Eye* in the infinite Universe, reflecting endless possibilities. She dances inside this Universe. But the Universe also dances inside her.

Angelina no longer sees herself through the labels, limitations and expectations that painted her measureless beauty into a tiny mask. She's looking from the inside, from the core of her *Star Essence*. From this point of view, Angelina and the Universe are one.

In this Oneness, she is the seed of her vast potential flourishing every second; infused by life and blossoming on Earth and in endless other dimensions, where her *Jewel Eyes* reflect her beauty now and forever.

Part 7

Epilogue

"Your vision will become clear only when you can look into your own heart. Who looks outside, dreams; who looks inside, awakes."

—Carl Jung

CHAPTER 40

The Arrival

"Did you call?" a familiar voice is saying. Someone is shaking her.

Angelina wakes up with a jolt. The train is speeding smoothly, silently.

"Am I back on the train?" Angelina asks. "What train? The N train? the Dream Express? Did I make it? Did I save her?"

"First, your ticket, please," says a deep man's voice.

Angelina turns around to face the Dream Express conductor.

"Are you Santa Claus?" she says in a little voice before she can help herself. She feels Angie jumping and laughing inside her.

The conductor is a tall, full-bellied man dressed in red shirt and pants with white fur around the wrists and ankles. He even has the wide black leather belt. He's only missing Santa's cap.

"Perky, the new rider," the conductor comments, elbowing Dragonfly Diva.

"Oh, yes Nicolas, she is that and much more," Dragonfly Diva laughs, flirting a bit with the conductor.

"Your ticket, please," he says as he extends his hand, palm up.

"Ticket? I don't..." Angelina begins.

"Before you assume anything foolish, my dear, why don't you look in your bag?" Dragonfly Diva asks.

"My bag!" Angelina screams, hugging the bag on her lap. She had lost track of it during her quest, and thought she had lost it.

Angelina opens the now battered leather bag. Her manuscript is not there. She rummages nervously, ready to cry that she's lost it, when she finds a book. Her heart is doing summersaults as she takes the book out and drinks each color and word with her gleaming green eyes.

Angelina & the Law of Attraction

Angelina is about to frown, just out of cheer habit. She suddenly realizes that her anger is no longer there. The red lava is not rising. Instead, she breaks into laughter.

"Who..." she's about to ask, but she sees the author's name on the cover.

Angelina Semidey

"How...?" she begins to ask, but the question dies on her lips as she flips the book. There is photo of the author in the back cover. Staring back at her is the photo of a powerful, joyful Angelina smiling as she holds a copy of the novel. Angelina reads the biographical excerpt.

> *Angelina Semidey invites you to ride in the Dream Express. It is a ride that changed her life, and she promises that yours will never be the same. When she started this ride, Angelina was a talented woman, but she was playing small. Trapped in a war between her creativity and her material needs and ambitions, Angelina was ready to give up on her talents and dreams. But then she had the good fortune to Catch the Dream Express. This ride became her DreamQuest and she has come out triumphant. Angelina has transformed her vision into a unique creative service and she has embodied her life purpose in a book that opens beyond the page to take you, the reader into your own DreamQuest. Don't give up on your dreams! Read this book and see them come alive.*

"Good, I see you got your ticket," says the conductor. "Can you autograph it for me?"

"Gladly," Angelina says. Her hand is shaking as she signs the copy.

How often did she imagine herself doing exactly this! Can this be true? Who published the book? How much time has it elapsed since she embraced her *DreamSelf*?

"At this point in the journey, it's better not to ask questions," Dragonfly Diva whispers as she tenderly pokes her.

"Sit back and enjoy the ride," the Dream Express conductor says as he takes the book. "You've earned it".

The conductor leaves through a door at the front of the wagon. In that same instant, and before Angelina can ask anything, the train bellows and a voice announces.

"Your Dream Station is coming up. Make sure to take all your belongings as you leave the train. Watch your step as you exit. People are known to faint."

A band is playing. Flags and banners are waving. A multitude is waiting on the platform.

"Who's the big shot riding with us?" Angelina asks Dragonfly Diva, who lets out a bark-like laughter of delight.

As the Dream Express slows down, Angelina is able to see the faces of the welcome committee.

"Jackie! Jocelyn!" she screams, trying to lower the window glass to talk to her friends.

Jackie is holding a poster that reads:

Thanks for...

Jocelyn holds a poster that reads:

... the ride!

"I'm here! Hey!" Angelina calls out, finally able to slide the window open. "What are you doing here? Who are you cheering..."

The question trails in her lips as she sees Bill hugging Mercedes. Mercedes is crying, but it's out of happiness. She is turning around and telling everyone.

"That's my daughter. She is a famous author now."

The smile on Mercedes' face makes Angelina's heart jump. Inside Angie is leaping with joy.

Bill sees her and hurriedly raises a white poster with red letters that reads:

"You've delivered your Gift Bundle.

Pop is proud of you... and so am I."

Angelina feels dizzy. She looks at Dragonfly Diva, who returns a quizzical look.

"Go! Girl! Go!" We knew you would make it!"

reads a large red sign carried by a group of friends.

Angelina can't stop Angie, who's jumping excitedly and sending kisses to all her family and friends.

The group begins to roar. Angelina's heart is jumping wildly inside her chest. This is better, much better than she could have ever dreamt.

A second later, she sees her dad, waving enthusiastically. He holds a poster:

I am proud of you.

Angelina catches herself just as a bitter moue begins at the corner of her lips. She releases it, along with all bitterness.

What's the point of reaching her dream, if she's going to hold on to old garbage that's going to spoil her victory? She's gotten smarter than that! She would be ungrateful not to acknowledge that she owes part of her journey to her dad.

"You know what?" she whispers, pointing at her heart, and then at him, "I'm also proud of you, dad. You came through for me."

Omar's radiant face comes into focus as the Dream Express bellows and stops. Angelina is running like Night Wolf, light and silent. She is by the door before it opens.

The door opens with a hiss.

"Hurrah! Bravo!" the screams are deafening. Friends and strangers wave flags and banners, throw confetti and show their copies of the book.

Angelina's legs give in.

"I got you," says Dragonfly Diva, laughing. "It's almost a tradition. One falls before one flies."

As the wizened lady helps her back to center, Angelina looks deeply into her golden eyes.

"How can I say goodbye?" she says. "You've been my Fairy Godmother."

"Who said anything about goodbye?" Dragonfly Diva says as she embraces Angelina.

Angelina briefly closes her eyes. A warm wave of golden light is glowing inside her heart. When she opens her eyes, Dragonfly Diva is gone. Angelina catches a tiny dragonfly flying out of the wagon.

She steps out of the train and falls into the arms of Omar.

"How was your tour, honey?" Omar says. "I've missed you terribly, but now we can have a proper honeymoon."

Angelina sees the shiny wedding band in his hand. She looks at her hand, finding the match.

"It was real!" Angelina screams, hugging Omar as she jumps. They both start jumping, Omar joining her in the chorus.

"It is real. It is real! It is real!"

Just then Angelina sees the date on a schedule board in the wall of the station.

"Nine months!" Angelina whispers. "It's been nine months since I took the N train in New York. How is that possible?"

"What do you mean?" Omar asks.

"I don't know," Angelina stutters. "First, it seemed to take forever. All the quests and tests, the guardians and the keys, not to mention the *Jewel Eyes*! But then I hugged her, and everything seemed to spin. Time seemed to stop and flow at the same time... and I don't know...it just seems like yesterday."

"It's like I say," a familiar voice inside her speaks. She can feel *The Architect* smiling. "Time is a convention."

"I'd say it's more like a rubber band," Angelina grins. "The way it can stretch..."

"And how it can hurl you into your dream!" Merlin is saying, "If you only let it!"

"You know what Einstein says about relativity," Omar jokes.

"What's that?"

"'Put your hand on a hot stove for a minute, and it seems like an hour. Sit with a pretty girl for an hour, and it seems like a minute. THAT'S relativity,' Omar quotes. "And I am with the prettiest girl of them all, so time does fly!"

Angelina hugs him and the station with all its hustle and bustle dissolves in their kiss.

"Hey, lady!" a child's voice says behind her.

Angelina turns around to see Boy in a train staff uniform.

"You must have dropped your wallet," Boy says with a grin. He handles Angelina her wallet. It's bulky. Angelina opens it to see a pack of greens thicker than her book. As she shuffles the bills, she sees that they are all $1,000 bills.

"Hey, lady! Don't you have baggage?" Boy says, laughing.

"Oh, no, I left it all behind," Angelina says, as she takes out a $1,000 bill and tips Boy, who tips his hat enthusiastically.

"Thanks," Boy says. "It was pretty hard work, wasn't it?"

"That's what makes it such a good story!" Angelina laughs as she seeks the arms of her beloved.

The cheers and bravos, the smiles, hugs and kudos uplift her heart.

Angelina has been a loner all her life. But in this celebration everyone is sending her so much love and joy that she feels a profound sense of belonging.

As wonderful as the cheering is, it falls second to the loving arms of Omar around her.

Inside those arms she is no longer afraid of losing herself. She is fulfilled, wholesome and enduring. She holds a heart that is no longer foreign and a dream that is no longer a painful craving, but ecstatic reality.

The End

Get your Bonuses!

Enjoy a **Book Bonus Package** that includes:

- One month free trial of the **Catch the Dream Express Membership.** Become the protagonist and ride with Maria Mar as your Dragonfly Diva.
- A seat in an online book signing ceremony and conversation with the author. Get your book personally dedicated to you or a friend (digitally) and talk with Maria over chocolate and red wine (or whatever you want to enjoy at your side).
- Two additional chapters that were edited out of the novel. Available only through this bonus package.
- A slideshow to find out what is your *Dream Archetype*. Join any of the three channels in Maria Mar's Tribe and you will get this slideshow with additional bonuses.

Get the bonuses at:

http://catchthedreamexpress.com/bonus

About Section

Find out about us

"When I began this book I had lost everything in a home disaster. I was homeless but for a friend's hospitality, a room where I took refuge. At this book's publication, I am the CEO of my own corporation. I created **ShamansDance**, my business, as the structure and vehicle that allows me to deliver my life purpose while I generate income. My journey is the journey of a spiritual, creative woman who learns her place as a creator in her own life masterpiece and transmutes her obstacles and limitations into steps towards her dream. It is the journey I offer you in this book."

—Maria Mar

About the Author

" I am a sacred storyteller that tells stories to help you change YOUR story from one of learned limitations that hold you back to the new story of your brilliance illuminating the world. "

Maria Mar

Maria is an author, spiritual teacher, inspirational poet and storyteller, an internationally known shaman and a PBS-TV featured dance-theater performer, as well as a visual artist. She is a new renaissance woman who has freed her creative potential and self-expression and has helped women in three continents to do the same.

She is the author of dozens of books in fiction, poetry and non-fiction, including a treasure chest of products sharing her wisdom as a Transformation Artist and her tools and practices for personal growth, spirituality, women's empowerment, creativity, life-purpose and self-expression.

As a storyteller, Maria creates inspirational fantasy and shamanic stories that leap out of the page to guide you in your life journey. Her stories become ceremonies of transformation that help you shapeshift into your dream and embody your purpose. She also enacts her inspiring stories on stage using her veteran skills as an actress.

Known as the Dream Alchemist, she takes you in LIVE shamanic journeys for on-the-spot transformation that taps into your brightest potential, transmute your problems into possibilities, brings up your greatness and helps you express your unique gifts to make a BIG difference in the world.

As an artist, Maria creates magical, participatory installations that transport audiences into a place where transformation happens instantly. She creates stage events where spectators become *SpectActors*, active agents and members of a community ceremony of healing, transformation and empowerment.

Maria helps you step into your greatness through her writings and stage events and through a rainbow of experiences, including digital products, online events, books and ebooks.

Her ARTchemy™ uses arts and crafts as alchemy of manifestation, transformation and liberation.

She also offers live shamanic journeys and membership programs that transform her stories into blueprints for your real life manifestation.

Maria Mar helps you remember the *Female Wisdom* traditions and to awaken the *Sacred Feminine* within you, so that you can use your creative and heart-based gifts to quicken the manifestation of your dreams and achieve success with soul.

WHERE IS MARIA MAR?

Friend me, Follow me, Link to me, Enjoy my pins:

SITES

My sites

http://dreamalchemist.com

http://catchthedreamexpress.com

My Blog

http://mariamar.com

Dream Alchemist Store:

http://dreamalchemist.com/store

SOCIAL MEDIA

Facebook profile:

http://www.facebook.com/DreamAlchemist

Twitter:

https://twitter.com/DreamAlchemist

Pinterest

http://pinterest.com/dreamalchemist

LinkedIn

http://www.linkedin.com/in/catchthedreamexpress

About ShamansDance

ShamansDance Publishing & Productions is a magical enterprise that brings you the ancestral dance and stories of the shaman as ceremony of transformation for the entire village in its new, modern and urban expression.

The creation of Maria Mar and Corazón Tierra, this company follows the wisdom of the *Sacred Feminine*, fusing the arts with personal growth and non-denominational spirituality to create life-changing, inspiring and empowering books, events, products, experiences and services for women.

Art has long been the tool of shamans and alchemists for its power to make the invisible visible, give body to the intangible and localize abstract ideas and possibilities to give them form. Maria Mar and Corazón Tierra are two contemporary urban shamans who use art, poetry, performance, storytelling, fiction and non-fiction writing, dance, movement and energy modalities as well as conscious living practices to help women transmute their limitations into life mastery.

ShamansDance is the house of **ShamansDance Books**, our bilingual publishing branch and **The Poetry Botánica™**, our art events production branch. It also houses dozens of sites, blogs and membership sites as well as an online store where you can find the systems and experiences offered by Maria and Corazón. All our services, memberships and products are housed in our mother site at:

http://shamansdance.com

Appendixes Section

APPENDIX A

Book Beyond the Page™

This novel is one of our *Books Beyond the Page™*.

A *Book Beyond the Page™* allows you to go beyond **reading** a story. You can **ride** it. You become the protagonist and enjoy the same quest or journey that the protagonist is experiencing to achieve a similar transformation. In non-fiction books, there are activities connected to the book that expand the reading experience.

The way that this novel helps you to go beyond the page is through a series of tools, events, experiences and services that use the story as a map or blueprint. Each different tool or experience helps you in different ways.

To ride in the Dream Express with Angelina, you can choose any of the options below, depending on the level of your commitment and what you want or need to do.

The tools and events that help you ride the Dream Express include:

- **Book Bonus Package** (Go to the bonus page and subscribe to enjoy this bonus package.)

- **Catch the Dream Express** (Membership to travel with me through each chapter).
- **Chapter Resources** (Tools that you can use to explore the shamanic secrets in a specific chapter and apply them to your life.)
- **Institutional Resources** (Bring Maria Mar to your site, program, book club or group for a storytelling and collective transformation experience). You can also find resources for corporations.

For more information, keep reading.

APPENDIX B

Catch the Dream Express

Do you want to RIDE the story? Do you want to enter its magic and learn how to use the shamanic secrets embedded in each chapter in your real life? Then **Catch the Dream Express**!

Seat besides Angelina in her (and your) *DreamQuest* and I will become your Dragonfly Diva! I will guide you through each station in the journey to reclaim your *DreamSelf*.

Catch the Dream Express is what I call a *Story Quest;* a life quest you do in your real life journeying though a story as a map or blueprint for the transformation you need to achieve the goal, dream or purpose you seek.

Join the **Catch the Dream Express Membership** to enjoy:

- **One year journey to your Dream** with my guidance and support. I become your Dragonfly Diva! Each chapter becomes a station in your *DreamQuest* and each week you receive the shamanic secrets for that chapter. Each month you meet life with me to discuss how to apply these tools to your life. There are 40 chapters, and you'll enjoy 40 weeks of magical adventures (plus two free weeks and two bonus chapters).

- **Shamanic Secrets Templates and Playsheets** to discover and apply the shamanic secrets and the secrets of the *Sacred Feminine School of Wisdom* embedded in each chapter. The *Templates* reveal and explain the secrets. The *Playsheets* guide you to apply them to your life. If you like journal writing, this is for you!
- **Arts & Crafts Alchemical Projects (ARTchemy™)** in which you achieve the transformation Angelina achieved in the chapter through a fun, creative project. If you love arts & crafts, you will love this!
- **Seasonal online events**, including shamanic journeys, webinars, ceremonies and multi-media experiences to bring the magic in the novel into your life.
- **Resources for each chapter**. The membership offers you additional resources for each chapter at a discount. This helps you to become the protagonist of your own life, manifesting your dreams in your real life, just as Angelina does in the story.
- **Plus the DreamQuest Live Calls,** a monthly conversation with me to get your questions answered, share your experiences and explore how to transform your problems into possibilities.
- **A 30-day free trial:** Give it a try at no cost for the first 4 chapters and journeys. If you like it, keep going. No Risk!
- **The digital novel** in (tablet) format of the novel delivered in 4 seasons and 40 episodes (chapters), included in the membership fee once you become a paid member.

Are you ready to Ride the Dream Express?

The **Catch the Dream Express membership** is for those who take the Law of Attraction and other *Dream Laws* seriously and want to activate them in their lives.

If you have a heart-felt commitment to transform your life into your dream, embody your purpose and live your potential, this journey will allow you to transform your reality into your *DreamLife.*

This journey is also a banquet for lovers of shamanic secrets and the *Sacred Feminine.*

However, this is not for people who are just curious about this as a conversational topic.

It's for those imaginative, self-committed out-of-the-box individuals who want to **live** the magic of their soul and inhabit their personal power, abolishing the illusion of routine and embracing a life of grace, enchantment, freedom and conscious living.

If you love magic, like journal writing and arts and crafts and if the chapters in this story have moved you and you want to enter the wisdom in them more in-depth, then I created the **Dream Express** for you!

To RIDE the story, go to the **Catch the Dream Express** site at:

http://catchthedreamexpress.com/bonus

When you subscribe, you will get your **30-day free no-risk test ride** to see if this is for you. If you don't like it, you can unsubscribe.

APPENDIX C

Resources

Chapter Resources

Sometimes a particular chapter, part or season in Angelina's journey will resonate deeply with you and what you are going through in your life right now. In this case, I've created resources for some (not all) chapters.

These resources can be books, audios, home study courses, ARTchemy™ projects or they can be entire programs and memberships dedicated to setting you free from a particular set of limitations or challenges.

To find chapter resources go to:

http://catchthedreamexpress.com/chapter-resources/

Dream Express Events

Find out about any event related to the novel or its programs, such as:

- Online global events (shamanic journeys, story quests, conversations and ceremonies with me)

- USA local events (usually shamanic storytelling performances and ceremonies)

To find out ongoing live and online events, go to:

http://catchthedreamexpress.com/events/

Institutional Resources

If you work for an institution or corporation and you'd like to bring the magic of the *Dream Express* to your organization, explore our **Institutional Resources.**

These resources include:

- **The Catch the Dream Express Storytelling Journeys**, a series of 7 shamanic storytelling performances with collective journey.

  See Angelina come alive as I embody her (and Dragonfly Diva) in a storytelling event that fuses dance, storytelling, acting and shamanic journey.

  Each storytelling performance takes a chapter from the book and brings it to live. Then I become Dragonfly Diva and walk your audience through the shamanic secrets in the chapter, helping them apply the shamanic tools to their real life, projects, professional practices or businesses through self-assessment, self-reflection and hands-on experiences.

  You can request:

  - **One story** with a shamanic journey (interactive group exploration of the topic) for a 60-90 minute event.
  - **Three stories** with three journeys for a one-day event.
  - **The seven stories** with their respective journeys as a week-end retreat.

- **The Book Club Talks,** where your audience can explore their favorite chapter in a magical online conversation with me. Wherever your Book Club is located, I can interact with your members without you incurring in travel expenses! I can also do a digital book signing party to get personalized signatures to your audiences. (*Bulk rate book purchase is required.)*

- **Corporate Premium. As a corporation you have several options:**

- We can customize an edition of the book with your company's message as a premium for your promotion.
- We can provide a promotional event to help your clients or staff ride express into their Dreams.
- We welcome sponsorship for the book or our events from corporations that share our market and values.
- Let's get creative. Fill out the quick contact form and we'll call you back to find out how we can work together.

See the **Institutional Resources** here:

http://catchthedreamexpress.com/institutional-resources/

APPENDIX D

Books by Maria Mar

Fiction

- **A Place for Roses** *(Inspirational novella)*
- **The Alchemical Rose** *(Transformational novella)*
- **You've come a Long Way, Sister** *(Women's Empowerment Ceremonial Storytelling Multi-media experience including book, workbook, ceremonial guide and multi-media performance-journey)*
- **Song of the Ocean** *(Ecological Fantasy)*
- **The Healer Who Forgot to Dance** *(Transformational novella with Story Quest)*

Find out about my storybooks here:

http://dreamalchemist.com/genre/stories-by-maria-mar/

Personal growth/Spirituality/Women' s Empowerment

- **Rewrite your Fairy Tales for Success: Unleash your greatness**
- **Do you Deserve Success? The Answer is yes!** (Book 1 of the **Bless your Success Series**)
- **Give yourself Permission to Do What you Want!** (Book 2 of the **Bless your Success Series**)
- **Give Yourself Permission to Achieve what you Want** (Book 3 of the **Bless your Success Series)**
- **Unleash your Greatness!** (Book 4 of the **Bless your Success Series)**
- **You Deserve Love!** (Book 5 of the **Bless your Success Series**)
- **Give yourself Permission to Be Happy**! (Book 6 of the **Bless your Success Series)**
- **Broken Places, Power Places** (workbook for **A Place for Roses**)

Find more about any of my books at:

http://dreamalchemist.com/genre/personal-growth-2/

Poetry

- **Transformation** (Poetry experience in flip-book format)
- **Tao of Trees: Poems whispered by the Poet Trees for healing, relaxation, inspiration and meditation.** (Coming soon.)

Find my inspiring poems and prayers here:

http://mariamar.com/category/sacred-poetry/sacred-poetry-transmissions/

Stories

- The MagicMark your Life Story Series
- The Eye to the Heart Story Series
- The LifeBites Story Series
- Joy, Love and Dreams Story Bundle
- The Bewomaning Tales Series

Find my stories here:

http://dreamalchemist.com/genre/stories-by-maria-mar/

Subscribe to my **Story Lovers Club** here:

http://dreamalchemist.com/storetag/story-lovers-club-premium/

Publications

Butterfly You! Magazine (digital magazine for women who want to express their gifts to make a BIG difference in the world)

http://mariamar.com/butterflyu/

To find out more about products, programs and services, visit my store at:

http://dreamalchemist.com/store/

www.ingramcontent.com/pod-product-compliance
Lightning Source LLC
Chambersburg PA
CBHW080722020726
47503CB00010B/2758
9780984367009